U0033626

金選
新多益
單字

1200 KEY WORDS
FOR THE
NEW TOEIC

MP3 ｜四國口音
英澳美加

1200

作者 ■ Curtis M. Revis-Seubert / Michelle Witte / Jennifer Chen
譯者 ■ 陳怡靜／王婷葦

前言

出版本書的目的，在於專為意圖在新多益測驗中奪下高分的讀者，進行最有效集中的強力單字訓練！多益測驗最重要的基礎就在於單字，所以我們精心打造了一本精選高頻率必考的核心單字書，並提供全面且強效學習多益字彙的方法，透過全面完備紮實的訓練課程，多益金色證書必能手到擒來！

本書依照多益測驗經常出現的 30 個不同情境，提供每情境 40 個絕對要會的核心字彙，情境又下分不同的子單元，不但可以依情境將經常出現的關鍵單字一網打盡，也有助於自然記憶起相關的單字，使讀者一口氣融會貫通 1200 個常考的絕對字彙。

學習單字的重點在於集中學習精益求精，是以所收錄的精選單字，除目標單字之外，還包含了大量的字根字首拆解，幫助讀者加強背誦單字，快速累積字彙量；並提供各種單字應用、同義字／反義字／相似字的補充，在同一單字的脈絡之下打鐵趁熱，進行強效、倍數增多的字彙學習。

在每個單元前，提出五個最重要單字與定義的配對，先測驗自己的程度，作為正式學習的學前暖身。

每單元後則提供精選單字的練習題，幫助讀者檢測自己的學習成效。包含單字選擇、單字選填及聽力填空三部分，分別測驗對單字字義的熟悉程度、應用程度和聽力理解，讓讀者可以透過反覆練習提升實戰的能力。

為了不使讀者陷入「只會讀不會念」，或是「看得懂聽不懂」的窘境，本書提供四國口音的 MP3 音檔，收錄所有精選字的發音與英語例句，訓練英澳美加多國口音的聽力，提升對單字的敏感度與應用能力。

附錄另提供 60 組易混淆字的比較，說明多益測驗中經常出現、看似相似實則意思可能大相逕庭的 60 組字彙，並提供解析、例句與練習題，使讀者更能掌握這些易混淆字的應用，作答時不再輕易被相似字詞誤導而答錯失分。

有鑑於多益測驗的重點，在於測驗考生在國際的日常生活與商務環境中的英語溝通能力，所以應試多益更是刻不容緩，與其等到畢業在即、或是就業上有所需要才開始準備多益，不如就從今天開始跟著本書各種強效學習法記誦多益單字，一步一腳印打好基礎，提升英語語感與應用能力，最終稱霸新多益測驗。

目錄

Appendix

簡介新制多益

多益測驗的緣起

　　TOEIC 多益測驗的全名是 Test Of English for International Communication，是針對非英語人士所設計的英語能力測驗，測驗分數反映一個人在國際職業環境中的英語溝通能力，故相較於以學術英語為主的托福，多益測驗是專門為職場英語所設計的認證測驗，又有「商業托福」之稱。

　　1979 年美國的教育測驗服務社（Educational Testing Service），簡稱 ETS，為因應企業要求，而制定出一套可以用來評估員工英語能力的測驗，此即多益測驗。ETS 是目前全球規模最大的一所非營利教育測驗及評量單位，除了多益測驗之外，也提供 TOFEL、GRE、GMAT 等標準化的考試與評測服務。

　　多益測驗已在全世界 165 個國家施測，是為全球最通行、也最具權威性的職場英語能力測驗，每年在全球都有超過七百萬人報考；國內外各大企業中的人資部門也廣泛使用多益測驗的成績，作為企業員工英語能力的檢測標準，如今在各校園中也常被用作英語的入學或是畢業門檻等用途。

　　2015 年 5 月，ETS 發表聲明，為因應英語使用與發展上的變化，也為確保多益測驗真實反映個人的英語能力，新多益測驗的內容將自 2006 年改版以來，再一次為符合現實英語使用狀況做調整；然而 ETS 也宣布，此次改版僅止於測驗內容的更新，不會影響多益測驗的難易度、也不會有測驗結構、題數以及測驗時間的變更。**ETS 首先於 2016 年 5 月，在日本、韓國兩國進行新多益測驗的改版，臺灣也在 2018 年 3 月進行改版。**

多益測驗的內容

　　多益測驗側重於非英語人士對母語人士的英語溝通能力，故測驗內容不會涉及過於專業的知識與字彙，而是測試日常生活中英語使用的熟練程度。自從 2006 年改制為新多益測驗之後，多益測驗特別融入了四種不同的英語口音，即：「美式英語」、「英式英語」、「澳洲及紐西蘭英語」和「加拿大英語」，使測驗更符合國際英語的研發目的。

多益測驗的設計是以測驗職場英語能力為目的，測驗內容從全世界各地職場的英文資料中蒐集而來，題材不僅多元，囊括的範圍也非常廣。

多益測驗的主題分類		
01	一般商務	契約、談判、行銷、銷售、商業企劃、會議
02	製造業	工廠管理、生產線、品管
03	金融／預算	銀行業務、投資、稅務、會計、帳單
04	企業發展	研究、產品研發
05	辦公室	董事會、委員會、信件、備忘錄、電話、傳真、電子郵件、辦公室器材與傢俱、辦公室流程
06	人事	招考、雇用、退休、薪資、升遷、應徵與廣告
07	採購	比價、訂貨、送貨、發票
08	技術層面	電子、科技、電腦、實驗室與相關器材、技術規格
09	房屋／公司地產	建築、規格、購買租賃、電力瓦斯服務
10	旅遊	火車、飛機、計程車、巴士、船隻、渡輪、票務、時刻表、車站、機場廣播、租車、飯店、預訂、脫班與取消
11	外食	商務／非正式午餐、宴會、招待會、餐廳訂位
12	娛樂	電影、劇場、音樂、藝術、媒體
13	保健	醫藥保險、看醫生、牙醫、診所、醫院

新制多益測驗的結構

　　多益測驗沒有「通過」與「不通過」之區別——考生用鉛筆在電腦答案卷上作答，考試分數由答對題數決定，將聽力測驗與閱讀測驗答對之題數換算成分數，聽力與閱讀得分相加即為總分；答錯並不倒扣。

Part	題型	舊制題數	新制題數	題型變更
聽力測驗 Listening Comprehension 45 分鐘 100 題 495 分 測驗總題數、整體難易程度及測驗時間不變				
1	**Photographs** 照片描述	10 題 （四選一）	6 題 （題數減少）	
2	**Question-Response** 應答問題	30 題 （三選一）	25 題 （題數減少）	
3	**Conversations** 簡短對話	30 題 （四選一）	39 題 （題數增加）	加入三人對話、加入圖表
4	**Talks** 獨白	30 題 （四選一）	30 題	加入圖表
閱讀測驗 Reading Comprehension 75 分鐘 100 題 495 分 測驗總題數、整體難易程度及測驗時間不變				
5	**Incomplete Sentences** 句子填空	40 題 （四選一）	30 題 （題數減少）	
6	**Text Completion** 段落填空	12 題 （四選一）	16 題 （題數增加）	加入將適當句子填入空格的題型
7	**Reading Comprehension–Single Passage** 單篇文章理解	28 題 （四選一）	單篇閱讀 29 題 （題數增加）	
	Reading Comprehension–Multiple Passage 多篇文章理解	20 題 （四選一）	多篇閱讀 25 題 （題數增加）	雙篇閱讀 4 篇 三篇閱讀 3 篇

應試說明

Part 1	**Photographs** 照片描述	● 從四個選項當中，選出一個和照片最相近的描述，問題與選項均不會印在試卷上。
Part 2	**Question-Response** 應答問題	● 從三個選項當中，選出與問題最為符合的回答，問題與選項均不會印在試卷上。
Part 3	**Conversations** 簡短對話	● 從四個選項中，選出與問題最為符合的回答，對話內容不會印在試卷上。 ★對話中將會有較少轉折，但來回交談較為頻繁。 ★部分對話題型將出現兩名以上的對談者。
Part 4	**Talks** 簡短獨白	● 從四個選項中，選出與問題最為符合的回答，獨白內容不會印在試卷上。

★ 聽力測驗將包含母音省略（elision，如：going to → gonna）和不完整的句子（fragment，如：Yes, in a minute. / Down the hall. / Could you? 等省去主詞或動詞的句子）。

★ 配合圖表，測驗考生是否聽懂對話，並測驗考生能否理解談話背景與對話中隱含的意思。

Part 5	**Incomplete Sentences** 句子填空	● 從四個選項中，選出最為恰當的答案，以完成不完整的句子。
Part 6	**Text Completion** 段落填空	● 從四個選項中，選出最為恰當的答案，以完成文章中不完整的句子。 ★選項類別除原有之片語、單字、子句之外，另新增完整句子的選項。
Part 7	**Reading Comprehension** 文章理解	● 閱讀單篇或兩篇或三篇內容相關的文章，從四個選項中，選出最為恰當的答案以回答問題。 ★加入篇章結構題型，測驗考生能否理解整體文章結構，並將一個句子歸置於正確的段落。

★ 閱讀測驗將包含文字簡訊、即時通訊，或多人互動的線上聊天訊息內容。

★ 新增引述文章部分內容，測驗考生是否理解作者希望表達之意思。

★為新制題型說明

如何使用本書

學前暖身

正式進入情境單字之前，先利用學前暖身來測驗自己的英文能力，確認自己是否能夠配對英文單字與其正確的英文解釋。

學習字彙

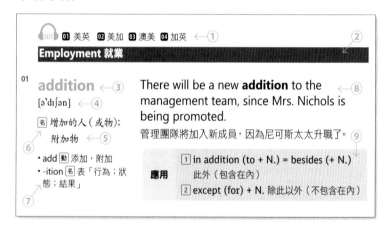

① 001 **01** 美英 **02** 美加 **03** 澳美 **04** 加英

②

Employment 就業

③ 01 **addition**
④ [əˋdɪʃən]
⑤ 名 增加的人（或物）；附加物
⑥
⑦ · add 動 添加，附加
· -ition 名 表「行為；狀態；結果」

⑧ There will be a new **addition** to the management team, since Mrs. Nichols is being promoted.
⑨ 管理團隊將加入新成員，因為尼可斯太太升職了。

應用
1 in addition (to + N.) = besides (+ N.) 此外（包含在內）
2 except (for) + N. 除此以外（不包含在內）

1. MP3 與口音：本書完整收錄所有英文單字與例句，由四國（美、英、加、澳）專業播音員以自然道地的語速錄音而成，每個單字例句皆由兩種不同的口音作搭配，讓讀者熟悉各國發音。

2. 子單元：藉由子單元的分類，加強字彙與情境的連結，更加深對字彙的印象，也更容易將單字背起來而不會忘。

3. 多益核心單字：精選應試多益測驗時，一定要會的字彙。

4. KK 音標：作為發音參考，要先學會如何念，記憶效果才會好。

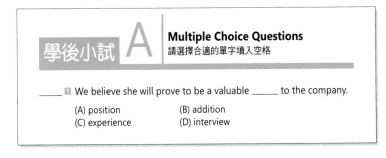

5. **字義**：在此情境之下的單字字義。

6. **詞性**：為了簡短說明字彙的詞性，本書使用中文的第一個字代表詞性，如：

| 名 →名詞 | 動 →動詞 | 形 →形容詞 | 副 →副詞 | 名 片 →名詞片語 |
| 介 →介係詞 | 連 →連接詞 | 片 →片語 | 動 片 →動詞片語 | 形 片 →形容詞片語 |

7. **字根字首解析**：藉由字根、字首、字尾的原則做單字拆解，並列點以說明其意義，加強考生對字彙的了解與認識。

8. **英文例句與中文翻譯**：為避免死記單字，提供靈活且符合情境的實用例句，以及此例句的中文翻譯。

9. **應用／同義字／反義字／相似詞／補充／比較**：列出與核心字彙相關的補充與應用，在學習單字的同時，也把握住如片語的用法與衍生字詞延伸學習，以增加字彙量，供考生作記憶聯想。

請見以下字詞的簡稱：

N. 名詞	V. 動詞	Adj. 形容詞	S. 主詞
O. 受詞	Sb. 某人 (somebody)	Sth. 某物 (something)	

學後小試

正式學習完每單元的核心單字與補充之後，都會再收錄學後小試，藉由三個部分的測驗以檢視自己的學習成果。

> **學後小試** A **Multiple Choice Questions**
> 請選擇合適的單字填入空格
>
> _____ 1 We believe she will prove to be a valuable _____ to the company.
>
> (A) position　　　　(B) addition
> (C) experience　　　(D) interview

易混淆字

1. **MP3 與口音**：易混淆字部分所有英文單字與例句，由四國（美、英、加、澳）專業播音員以自然道地的語速錄音而成，每個單字例句皆由兩種不同的口音作搭配，讓讀者熟悉各國發音。

2. **易混淆字**：不容易釐清的兩個相似詞之比較，另提供 KK 音標與詞性。

3. **英文例句與中文翻譯**：為避免讀者一頭霧水，提供靈活且符合情境的實用例句，以及此例句的中文翻譯，深刻兩者的差異性。

4. **解析**：每一組單字的異同比較及用法。

5. **練習**：藉由習題以重新檢視自己，是否真的了解此組易混淆字的差異。

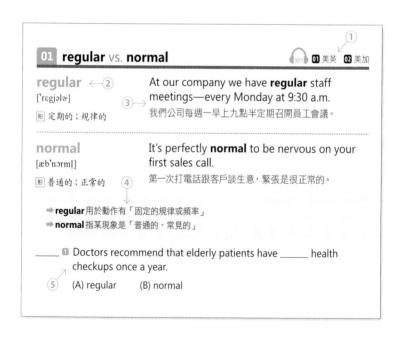

01 regular VS. normal

301 ▶ 01 美英 02 美加

regular ←②
[ˈrɛgjələ]
形 定期的；規律的

At our company we have **regular** staff meetings—every Monday at 9:30 a.m.
我們公司每週一早上九點半定期召開員工會議。

normal
[æbˈnɔrml]
形 普通的；正常的

It's perfectly **normal** to be nervous on your first sales call.
第一次打電話跟客戶談生意，緊張是很正常的。

➡ **regular** 用於動作有「固定的規律或頻率」
➡ **normal** 指某現象是「普通的、常見的」

_____ ❶ Doctors recommend that elderly patients have _____ health checkups once a year.
(A) regular　　(B) normal

讀書計畫

穩重型：六週學習計畫

此學習計畫適合喜歡穩扎穩打的讀者，以基本上一天一單元的進度，一步一腳印扎實的學習。每天花費 2–3 小時的時間記憶、背誦本書的核心單字，直至融會貫通，除了知新，讀者每週也可自行挑選一天，除了學習 10 組的易混淆字彙，也溫故前面六天所學習的單字，反覆的閱讀與學習將有助於讀者，漸進且有效的提升英語程度。

Week One					Review Days
Unit 01	Unit 02	Unit0 3	Unit 04	Unit 05	Unit **01–05**+Confusing words 1–10

Week Two					Review Days
Unit 06	Unit 07	Unit 08	Unit 09	Unit 10	Unit **06–10**+Confusing words 11–20

Week Three					Review Days
Unit 11	Unit 12	Unit 13	Unit 14	Unit 15	Unit **11–15**+Confusing words 21–30

Week Four					Review Days
Unit 16	Unit 17	Unit 18	Unit 19	Unit 20	Unit **16–20**+Confusing words 31–40

Week Five					Review Days
Unit 21	Unit 22	Unit 23	Unit 24	Unit 25	Unit **21–25**+Confusing words 41–50

Week Six					Review Days
Unit 26	Unit 27	Unit 28	Unit 29	Unit 30	Unit **26–30**+Confusing words 51–60

中庸型：28 天學習計畫

此學習計畫適合擅長於時間管理與規劃的讀者，能夠平心靜氣並且專注於單字學習，一天兩個單元，然而每天花費的時間則為 4–5 小時，背熟單字字義、應用與補充，集中背誦並反覆學習每個單元的核心單字。並且每週也抽出時間經常性複習學習過的單元，也自行學習易混淆字彙，規律並且密集的研讀字彙、例句和搭配用法，將會有助於提升讀者的英語語感。

Day 1	Day 2	Day 3	Day 4	Day 5	Day 6	Day 7
Unit 01–02	Unit 03–04	**Review Unit 01–04+ Confusing words 01–15**	Unit 05–06	Unit 07–08	**Review Unit 05–08**	**Review Unit 01–08**

Day 8	Day 9	Day 10	Day 11	Day 12	Day 13	Day 14
Unit 09–10	Unit 11–12	**Review Unit 09–12+ Confusing words 16–30**	Unit 13–14	Unit 15–16	**Review Unit 13–16**	**Review Unit 09–16**

Day 15	Day 16	Day 17	Day 18	Day 19	Day 20	Day 21
Unit 17–18	Unit 19–20	**Review Unit 17–20+ Confusing words 31–45**	Unit 21–22	Unit 23–24	**Review Unit 21–24**	**Review Unit 17–24**

Day 22	Day 23	Day 24	Day 25	Day 26	Day 27	Day 28
Unit 25–26	Unit 27–28	**Review Unit 25–28+ Confusing words 46–60**	Unit 29–30	**Review Unit 29–30**	**Review Unit 25–30**	**Review Confusing words Unit 01–60**

效率型：15 天學習計畫

此學習計畫適合講究效率與成效、對於多益測驗志在必得的讀者，每天花費 8 小時以上的時間，學習三個單元的內容，並且扎實的學習單字、應用與補充，高強度的加深對多益字彙的認識，並且也對學習過的內容進行複習；由於每日的學習量龐大，使用此學習計畫的讀者必須非常小心謹慎，切勿囫圇吞棗的不求甚解，應當把握所有內容並且再三確認，自己真的掌握了所有的重點。

Day 1	Day 2	Day 3	Day 4	Day 5
Unit 01–03	Unit 03–06	**Review Unit 01–06+ Confusing words 01–12**	Unit 07–09	Unit 10–12

Day 6	Day 7	Day 8	Day 9	Day 10
Review Unit 07–12+ Confusing words 13–24	Unit 13–15	Unit 16–18	**Review Unit 13–18+ Confusing words 25–36**	Unit 19–21

Day 11	Day 12	Day 13	Day 14	Day 15
Unit 22–24	**Review Unit 19–24+ Confusing words 37–48**	Unit 25–27	Unit 28–30	**Review Unit 25-30+ Confusing words 49–60**

Unit 01

Recruitment & Interview

徵才與面試

求職（job hunting）在多益測驗屬於必考的情境，重點在於：

1 靈活的使用形容詞以包裝經歷（experience），讓不論履歷（résumé）或是面試（interview）都引人入勝。

2 使用動詞時也應該謹慎，例如不可搞錯應徵（apply for）、僱用（hire）、招募（recruit）的使用時機與主詞；談論到興趣時，也應以偏好（prefer）取代討厭（dislike）。

學前暖身 請閱讀英文定義，並將正確單字與之配對

recruit	applicant	interview	fire	position

1 _____ : a meeting in which questions are asked to determine someone's fitness for a job

2 _____ : a job or group of duties

3 _____ : to get someone to work for you

4 _____ : to end employment, usually against employee's will

5 _____ : someone who has submitted a request for a job

Employment 就業

01 **addition**
[ə'dɪʃən]

图 增加的人（或物）；
　　附加物

• add 動 添加，附加
• -ition 表「行為；狀態；
　結果」

There will be a new **addition** to the management team, since Mrs. Nichols is being promoted.

管理團隊將加入新成員，因為尼可斯太太升職了。

應用	① in addition (to + N.) = besides (+ N.)　此外（包含在內） ② except (for) + N. 除此以外（不包含在內）

---

02 **admission**
[əd'mɪʃən]

图 獲准；許可；准許進入

• ad- 向
• miss 送
• -ion 图 表「動作、狀態」

Candidates must pass the entrance exam before being given **admission** to an interview.

求職者必須通過門檻測驗，才可以面試。

應用	片 admission fee 入場費 人 + apply for admission to a school 申請入學

---

03 **advance**
[əd'væns]

動 向前進；進步

Our company is seeking individuals to help us **advance** our goal of helping the community.

我們正在尋找有助我們邁向福利社會的目標的人才。

應用	in advance = beforehand = prior to + N. 事先

---

04 **be subject to**
['sʌbdʒɛkt]

形 片 受……約束；
　　遭受……

Regardless of their position or status, employees will **be subject to** annual evaluations.

不管什麼職務或職位，所有員工都將接受年度考核。

應用	① S. + be subject to + N.　受限於……；易受……影響 ② S. + V., + subject to + N.　在……條件下／依照……做事

05 committed
[kə`mɪtɪd]

形 盡心盡責的

We are seeking **committed** professionals in the fields of medicine and health administration.

我們正在尋找願意投身醫藥健康管理事業的專業人士。

> 應用 S. be committed/dedicated/devoted to + N. / V-ing 致力於……；投身於……

06 employment
[ɪm`plɔɪmənt]

名 僱用；工作

• employ 動 僱用
• -ment 名 表「行為，狀態」

Employment at our company is not determined by age, race, or gender.

我們公司僱用員工不會考慮年齡、種族或性別。

> 應用 employment opportunities/prospects
> 工作機會／前景
> 反 unemployment rate 失業率

07 fire
[faɪr]

動 解僱；開除

Employees who commit serious breaches of company policy may be **fired** with two-week's notice.

嚴重違反公司規定的員工，可能會收到兩週後被開除的通知。

08 position
[pə`zɪʃən]

名 職位

• posit 安置
• -ion 名 表「行為；結果；狀態」

Please inform candidates that applying for multiple **positions** is against company policy.

請告知求職者，同時應徵不同職缺違反公司規定。

> 應用
> 1 take up a position + as + 職稱 承接某職務
> 2 a position/vacancy + has been filled 該職缺已被填補
> 3 hold / apply for + the position of + 職稱 擔任／應徵……職務

09 accordingly

[əˈkɔrdɪŋlɪ]

副 照著；因此

· accord 動 一致，符合
· -ing 形 表「行為；狀態」
· -ly 副

Given the limited timeframe, selection procedures should be shortened **accordingly**.

因為作業時間有限，選拔程序應該跟著縮短。

應用 accordingly 依位子不同，意思也不同。
① 放句尾：相應地；照著
② 放兩句之間：因此 = therefore / as a result / consequently / hence / thus

---

10 hire

[haɪr]

動 僱用；聘請

This month, we will need to **hire** four people to fill vacancies in the human resources department.

這個月我們需要聘請四個人，來填補人力資源部的空缺。

---

11 ideal

[aɪˈdiəl]

形 理想的；完美的

· idea 名 主意
· -al 形 表「關於……的」

The **ideal** candidate will have at least five years of experience in C++, Java, and HTML.

理想的求職者會需要有五年C++、Java和HTML程式語言的資歷。

---

12 match

[mætʃ]

動 相配；符合

Hiring managers should **match** a candidate's experience to the most appropriate department in the company.

聘請經理時，求職者的資歷必須符合公司相關部門的要求。

相似詞 動 match 適合 = suit 使較量；比得上
名 matchmaker 媒人
名 形 matchmaking 交友媒合

---

13 responsibility
[rɪˌspɑnsəˋbɪlətɪ]

名 責任；職責

· response 動 回應
· -ible 形 表「可……的」
· -ity 名 表「性質；狀態」

It is the HR director's **responsibility** to maintain our workforce's effectiveness.
人力資源部主任的職責就是要保持勞力的有效運用。

| 應用 | 形 responsible 負責的
be responsible for N.
= be in charge of N. 為……負責 |

---

14 assessment
[əˋsɛsmənt]

名 評估

· assess 動 評估
· -ment 名 表「行為；結果；狀態」

Assessment of potential hires should be done according to our ranking system.
潛在求職者的聘任評估，應該照著我們的排名制度來決定。

---

15 recruit
[rɪˋkrut]

動 招收新成員

The president specifically stated we were not to **recruit** overseas workers for this position.
董事長特別說明這個職缺不會從國外招募人選。

---

16 seek
[sik]

動 尋找；探索

Headhunters typically **seek** talent among long-term middle managers.
獵人頭公司通常會在長期擔任中階經理的人當中找尋人才。

| 相似詞 | 片 look for 尋找
片 search for = in search of 搜索
片 in pursuit of 追尋 |

Job Hunting 求職

17 applicant
[ˋæpləkənt]

名 申請人；求職者

· apply 動 申請
· -ant 名 表「人」

Job **applicants** should always try to make the best first impression.
求職者應該要一直思考如何留下最好的第一印象。

18 apply

[ə`plaɪ]

動 申請；應徵

Before **applying** for this position, please confirm you have a graduate degree.

應徵這份工作之前，請確認您有碩士以上的學歷。

| 應用 | 1 apply for/to + N. 申請；應徵 |
| | 2 apply A to B 應用A於B上；塗抹A於B上 |

---

19 consider

[kən`sɪdɚ]

動 考慮；認為

People **considering** a career change should first decide whether the new position will help them achieve their career goals.

想要轉換跑道的人，應該先確定新工作是否有助於他們達成職業生涯的目標。

| 應用 | S. + consider + O. + (to be) Adj./N. |
| | （用consider不接as） |

---

20 suitable

[`sutəbl]

形 適當的；適合的

• suit 動 適合
• -able 形「可以……的，有……特性的」

To decide whether a job is **suitable** for you, you must first establish your career goals.

確定自己適不適合一份工作之前，你必須先設立自己的職涯目標。

應用	A be suitable for B
	= A match/fit/suit B
	= A go with B A適合B

Interview 面試

21 achievement

[ə`tʃivmənt]

名 成就；達成

• achieve 動 實現
• -ment 名 表「結果」

During a job interview, you should be able to list your **achievements** and explain their significance.

在面試當中，你應該要列出你的成就並解釋它們有多重要。

22 arrange
[ə`rendʒ]

動 安排；佈置

Candidates who are unable to take the written exam on the scheduled day may **arrange** a make-up test.

不能在預定時間參加筆試的求職者，可以安排補考。

---

23 background
[`bæk͵graʊnd]

名 背景；經歷

・back 後面的
・ground 地；基底

Questions regarding candidates' **backgrounds** should be limited to education and employment history.

有關求職者背景的問題，應該只限於學歷及工作經歷。

---

24 candidate
[`kændədet]

名 候選人；應試者；
  應徵者

There are 12 **candidates**, but only five positions are available.

這份工作來了十二名求職者，但僅提供五名職缺。

---

25 experience
[ɪk`spɪrɪəns]

名 經驗；經歷

How much **experience** do you have with maintaining large databases?

你有多少維護大型資料庫的經驗？

---

26 interview
[`ɪntə͵vju]

名 面談；面試

・inter- 在……之間
・view 動 看

There will be no group **interviews**. We will meet each candidate on a one-to-one basis.

我們不會有團體面試，我們將會一對一面試每一位應徵者。

---

27 prior to
[`praɪə]

片 在……之前

Did the candidate research the company's current activities **prior to** the interview?

面試之前，該求職者搜尋過公司目前的活動嗎？

> **應用**　prior to = before 在……之前

---

28 reference
['rɛfərəns]

名 推薦信

- refer 動 涉及
- -ence 名 表「行為；性質；狀態」

Three **references** are required to apply to this position.
應徵這份工作需要三封推薦信。

---

29 résumé
[rɛzjʊ`me]

名 履歷

We were very impressed with your **résumé** — especially your work history.
你的履歷讓我們印象深刻，尤其是你的工作經歷。

Self-Introduction 自我介紹

30 accomplishment
[ə`kɑmplɪʃmənt]

名 成就；實現

- accomplish 動 完成
- -ment 名 表「行為；產物；結果」

I consider the release of my home accounting software to be one of my greatest **accomplishments**.
我認為我發表的家庭會計軟體是我最大的成就之一。

應用	a sense of accomplishment/achievement 成就感

---

31 capability
[ˌkepə`bɪlətɪ]

名 能力；性能

- capable 形 有能力的
- -ity 名 表「特徵；狀態」

In my previous job, I had many opportunities to prove my **capability** in multitasking.
上一份工作中，我有很多機會證明我可以同時處理多項任務。

---

32 potential
[pə`tɛnʃəl]

名 潛力

- potency 名 潛力
- -al 形 表「具其特徵的」

I believe my full **potential** has yet to have been realized.
我相信我還沒發揮我所有的潛能。

33 prefer

[prɪ`fɝ]

動 更喜歡

I would **prefer** a position in IT, even though I have little experience or education in that field.

儘管我沒有甚麼相關的工作經驗或教育背景，我還是想要一份資訊科技業的工作。

應用
1 prefer N./V-ing to N./V-ing
喜歡……勝過……
2 prefer to V. (rather) than V.
寧願去做……也不願意做……

---

34 proficiency

[prə`fɪʃənsɪ]

名 語言能力；精通；熟練

· proficient **形** 精通的
· -ency **名** 表「性質；狀態」

I have documented **proficiency** in English, Japanese, and Chinese.

我擁有英語、日語和中文的語言能力證明。

---

35 profile

[`profaɪl]

名 人物簡介

I hope my **profile** clearly shows my dedication to the preservation and improvement of community.

希望我的自我介紹，能清楚呈現我在維護改善社區這方面的貢獻。

Personal Strength / Characteristic 強項／個性

36 degree

[dɪ`gri]

名 等級；度數

His résumé exhibits a high **degree** of mastery of social media marketing.

從他的履歷可看出他非常精通於社群媒體行銷。

應用
1 to some degree = to some extent
在某種程度上
2 bachelor's/master's/PhD degree
學士／碩士／博士學位
3 at . . . degrees Celsius/Fahrenheit
攝氏／華氏……度

37 ethic
[`ɛθɪk]

名 道德；倫理

• ethos 名 社會或民族等的精神特質
• -ic 名 表「有……特性」

He claims to have a strong work **ethic**, but he's had four jobs in the past two years.

他宣稱他有很高的職業道德，但是他過去兩年中做了四份不同的工作。

---

38 recommendation
[ˌrɛkəmɛn`deʃən]

名 推薦；推薦信；
　　勸告；優點

• re- 加強語氣
• commend 動 推薦
• -ation 名 表「行為」

If you have any **recommendations** regarding what personal qualities we should look for, please let me know.

如果您有推薦的人格特質，請告訴我。

應用	recommendation letter 推薦函

---

39 weakness
[`wiknɪs]

名 弱點；缺點

• weak 形 弱的
• -ness 名 表「性質；狀態」

Not looking for a better position is considered a **weakness** by many hiring managers.

許多招募經理認為「人不往高處爬」是一項缺點。

---

40 ability
[ə`bɪlətɪ]

名 能力；才能

• able 形 有能力的
• -ty 名 表「性質；狀態」

She has the proven **ability** to plan and implement large-scale, online marketing campaigns.

她規劃、執行大型網路促銷活動的能力獲得認可。

相似詞	名 skill 技能
	名 talent 天賦
	名 power 能力

學後小試 A **Multiple Choice Questions**
請選擇合適的單字填入空格

_____ ❶ We believe she will prove to be a valuable _____ to the company.

(A) position   (B) addition
(C) experience   (D) interview

_____ ❷ According to his _____, he speaks three languages.

(A) profile   (B) applicant
(C) assessment   (D) admission

_____ ❸ I will _____ employment elsewhere, because I'm not happy with how the company is treating me.

(A) recruit   (B) match
(C) hire   (D) seek

_____ ❹ She hasn't received her _____ yet, but she already knows more about the job than any of the other candidates.

(A) ability   (B) potential
(C) degree   (D) background

_____ ❺ We think he is the best _____ for the position. Just look at his experience.

(A) candidate   (B) résumé
(C) reference   (D) capability

正確答案請參考 408 頁

B | Match

請在空格填入合適的單字，動詞需依時態變化，名詞需填入正確之單複數。

| prefer | ethic | achievement | ideal | prior to | recommendation |

1. My proudest _____ is heading the marketing team that won the competition.

2. While he is not _____, he does know enough to get the job done.

3. To apply for this position, you need to provide three professional _____.

4. _____ working at Matsudo Holdings, did you have any other financial experience?

5. She _____ to work in accounting, but I think she'd be better in marketing.

6. We seek someone with a strong work _____ and lots of experience.

C | Listening Practice

請聆聽音檔，將單字填入空格 010

1. When choosing a candidate, we _____ both their experience and education.

2. As far as we can see, her lack of motivation might be her biggest _____.

3. She's just finished university; _____, she has little work experience.

4. We seek someone with _____ in both word processing and data entry.

5. We thought he was _____ for management, but it turned out he lacked leadership.

6. As hiring manager, it is my _____ to choose the most qualified candidate to fill positions.

正確答案請參考 408 頁

Unit 02

Salary & Benefits

薪資與福利

職場情境是多益測驗中最常出現的題型之一：

1. 瞭解各種精確的名詞使用，例如請假是 leave 不是 vacation，加薪是 raise 不是 salary increasing。

2. 升遷（promotion）、退休金（pension）或是其他嘉獎（bonus）是公司為了獎勵員工的貢獻而給予（entitle）的，故也必須熟悉改善（improve）、奉獻（devote/contribute）、領導（lead）等強調功勞的動詞用法。

學前暖身　請閱讀英文定義，並將正確單字與之配對

| wage | lead | complimentary | optional | contribute |

1. _____ : free of charge
2. _____ : to guide or direct progress; to be in charge of
3. _____ : not required
4. _____ : regular payment for work done or services provided
5. _____ : to give or help; to add value to a process

Benefit 福利

01 **benefit**
[ˋbɛnəfɪt]

名 利益；好處

• bene- 好的；有益的
• fit 做

Free gym membership, yearly professional development courses, and on-site daycare are some of the **benefits** the company offers.

這間公司提供員工一些福利，像是免費健身房會員、年度專業進修課程和當地的托育中心。

> 應用　A benefit from B　A從B中受益

02 **complimentary**
[ˌkɑmpləˋmɛntərɪ]

形 贈送的；免費的；讚美的

• compliment 名 讚美
• -ary 形 表「具有某性質」

I don't like early meetings, but I definitely do enjoy the **complimentary** breakfast we get!

我不喜歡一大早開會，但我倒是很享受我們的免費早餐。

03 **generous**
[ˋdʒɛnərəs]

形 慷慨的；大量的

The company doesn't offer much leave, but it is certainly **generous** with the salaries it offers.

這間公司提供的假不多，但是薪水真的很豐厚。

04 **leave**
[liv]

名 休假

I would gladly work for a lower salary if I could have more paid **leave**.

如果有更多天的給薪休假，薪水減少我也願意。

05 **practical**
[ˋpræktɪkl]

形 實際的；實用的

• practic 實行
• -al 形 表「關於……的」

The training is very nice in theory, but it has no **practical** application to my work.

這個訓練理論上很好，但不能實際應用在我的工作上。

06 satisfy
[ˋsætɪsˏfaɪ]
動 滿足

The benefits here really don't **satisfy** my needs—there is no dental care, no day care, and not much leave offered.

這裡的福利真的不能滿足我的需要，沒有牙齒保健、沒有托育中心，也沒有什麼休假福利。

應用
1 satisfy/meet one's needs/demands/desires 滿足需求
2 Sb. be satisfied with + N. 人對……感到滿意
3 N. is satisfactory to Sb. ……令人感到滿意

Bonus 獎金

07 acceptable
[əkˋsɛptəbl]
形 可接受的

・accept 動 接受
・-able 形 表「可……的」

Her work has not been **acceptable** so that she won't be getting a raise this year.

她的工作沒被接受，所以她今年沒有辦法加薪。

08 diligent
[ˋdɪlədʒənt]
形 勤勉的；勤奮的

She's got good ideas, but she's not particularly **diligent** when it comes to team work.

她是有好點子，但是要團隊合作的時候，她不是特別用心。

09 dividend
[ˋdɪvəˏdɛnd]
名 紅利；股息

・divide 動 分配
・-end 名 表「物」

Our company is paying **dividends** in the form of a year-end bonus.

我們公司的分紅方式是發放年終獎金。

應用
1 A company/corporation pays dividends to shareholders 公司配發股息給股東
2 cash/stock/property dividends 現金／股票／財產股息

同義字 名 share 股份；股票

31

10 eligible
[ˈɛlɪdʒəbl̩]

形 合適的

He's not **eligible** for the position, since he doesn't have a college degree.

他不適合這個職位，因為他沒有大學學歷。

---

11 entitle
[ɪnˈtaɪtl̩]

動 授權（或資格）

・en- 使
・title 名 標題

According to our company's policy, after a year, I'll be **entitled** to three weeks of vacation.

根據我們公司的規定，服務一年後我就享有三週的休假天數。

> **應用**
> 1 be entitled to + N. 有資格權利獲得⋯⋯
> 2 be entitled to V. = have the right to V.
> = be granted the right to V. 有權去做⋯⋯

---

12 grant
[grænt]

名 獎學金；補助金

I am really hoping to get a **grant** from that research company.

我真的很希望那個研究機構能給我補助。

---

13 maintain
[menˈten]

動 維持；保持

・main 手
・tain 握

If we can **maintain** these sales figures, we'll definitely win the title of Sales Team of the Year.

如果我們維持這樣的業績，一定會贏得年度最佳業務團隊。

---

14 optional
[ˈɑpʃənl̩]

形 隨意的；非必須的

・opt 動 選擇
・-ion 名 表「行為；結果；狀態」
・-al 形 表「具其特徵的」

I know bonuses are technically **optional**, but I think the managers know that we expect them each year.

年終不是年年都發，但我想經理知道我們每年都很期待領年終獎金。

15 productive
[prəˈdʌktɪv]

形 多產的

· product 名 產品
· -ive 形 表「有……特性」

After his performance review, he got a raise for being so **productive**.

評完考績以後，他因高生產力而獲得加薪。

---

16 representative
[ˌrɛprɪˈzɛntətɪv]

名 代表

· re- 再
· present 呈現
· -ive 名 表「人」

I'm going to speak to our human resources **representative** about getting some extra time off this year.

我要跟人事代表談一談，看今年能不能有更多假。

應用 動 represent
= 片 stand for = be on behalf of 代表

---

17 respectively
[rɪˈspɛktɪvlɪ]

副 分別地；各自地

· respect 動 尊敬
· -ive 形 表「與……
有關的；有……傾向的」
· -ly 副

Based on our seniority, we get three and four weeks paid leave, **respectively**.

根據我們的年資，我們分別有三週和四週的有薪假。

應用 動 名 respect 尊敬；問候
形 respected 受尊敬的
形 respectable 值得尊敬的
形 respectful 莊重的

---

18 tempt
[tɛmpt]

動 引誘；吸引；打動

I am very **tempted** to take their offer, because the benefits are so much better than my current position.

他們開的條件很吸引我，因為他們的福利比我現在的工作好太多了。

Incentive 獎勵

---

19 acknowledge
[əkˈnɑlɪdʒ]

動 承認

· ac- 前往；表示
· knowledge 名 知識；知道

He took the credit for the project's success and didn't **acknowledge** her contribution at all.

這個案子的功勞都被他搶走了，他完全不承認她也有貢獻。

33

20 contribute

[kən`trɪbjut]

動 貢獻

- con- 一起
- tribute 給予

I can't take all the credit for the plan. Everyone on the team **contributed** to it.

這個企劃不是我一個人的功勞，每個團隊成員都有貢獻。

| 應用 | contribute to 貢獻、捐獻；導致、造成 |

21 dedication

[,dɛdə`keʃən]

名 奉獻；獻身

- dedicate 動 獻身於
- -ion 名 表「行為；結果；狀態」

They're hoping to inspire **dedication** by offering stock in the company rather than cash bonuses.

他們希望可以用分股的方式來激勵員工奉獻，而不是用現金來分紅。

| 應用 | 1 show dedication + to + N./V-ing 顯示某人對……貢獻 |
| | 2 S. + be dedicated to + O. 貢獻於…… |

22 motivate

[`motə,vet]

動 刺激；激發

- motive 名 動機
- -ate 動 表「使成為」

The bigger bonuses are meant to **motivate** the employees to work harder.

更高的獎金是用來激勵員工更努力工作。

23 winner

[`wɪnɚ]

名 贏家；優勝者

- win 動 贏；獲勝
- -er 名 表「人」

After working on it night and day for a week, it looks like our proposal is going to be the **winner**!

日以繼夜工作一週之後，我們的提案應該會勝出！

Promotion 升遷

---

24 improve
[ɪmˋpruv]

動 增進；改善

She's volunteering for every work group because she's really eager to **improve** her chances for a promotion.
因為她很想要升職，所以她志願到每個工作小組去幫忙。

---

25 look forward to
[luk] [ˋfɔrwəd] [tu]

片 期待

I like my work, but I'm really **looking forward to** my vacation next week.
我很喜歡我的工作，但是我真的很期待下星期的假期。

> **應用** look forward to + N./V-ing 期待⋯⋯

---

26 loyal
[ˋlɔɪəl]

形 忠誠的；忠心的

I hope my **loyal** service to the company will be rewarded when they give out bonuses this year.
今年發年終獎金的時候，我希望我為公司忠心效勞會獲得回報。

---

27 merit
[ˋmɛrɪt]

名 績效；價值；優點

I'm tired of being passed over for promotions. I'm going to move to a company that values **merit** over seniority.
我受夠了升職的時候總是被跳過，我要換到重視績效過於年資的公司。

---

28 devote
[dɪˋvot]

動 奉獻

• de- 加強意義
• vote 發誓

In his new position, most of his time will be **devoted** to client relations.
換工作之後，他大部分的時間都將花在維護客戶關係上。

> **應用** Sb. devote/commit oneself to + N./V-ing
> = Sb. be + dedicated/devoted/committed + to + N./V-ing 將自己奉獻於⋯⋯

29 lead
[lid]

動 領導

I'm surprised that he was promoted, because I don't think he **leads** his work group very well.

我很驚訝他升職了，因為我不覺得他把他的工作小組帶得很好。

| 應用 | ① S. + lead + O. + to V. 某人領導……去做…… |
| | ② lead to + N. 導致某事發生 |

---

30 lifetime
['laɪf,taɪm]

名 終身

· life 一生
· time 時間

She rose from cashier to chief financial officer over her **lifetime**, which is a very impressive achievement.

她這一生，從收銀員一路做到財務長，真是了不起的成就。

Salary 薪水

31 adjustment
[ə`dʒʌstmənt]

名 調整

· adjust 動 調整
· -ment 名 表「行為」

With the cost of living rising so quickly, I believe we deserve a salary **adjustment**.

生活開銷漲得這麼快，我們的薪水也應該要作調整。

應用	adjust/adapt + oneself + to + N./V-ing
	= Sb. make adjustment to + N./V-ing
	調整使適應……

---

32 flexible
['flɛksəbl]

形 有彈性的

· flex 彎曲
· -ible 形「可……的」

My hours in the office are **flexible**, but I have to be on call from 9 a.m. to 5 p.m.

我進辦公室的時間很彈性，但是早上九點到下午五點必須隨傳隨到。

33 limit
[ˈlɪmɪt]
名 限制；界限

They're talking about creating a salary cap and setting separate **limits** for each level in the hierarchy.

他們在討論要不要設薪資上限，讓每個層級都有各自的薪資限制。

---

34 pension
[ˈpɛnʃən]
名 退休金；養老金

I'm very glad the company will start matching our **pension** contributions next year.

我很高興明年公司要開始採用退休金提撥制度。

---

35 raise
[rez]
名 加薪

If I don't get a **raise** soon, I'm going to look for another job.

如果最近再不調薪，我就要找別的工作了。

---

36 rise
[raɪz]
動 上升；增加

If the cost of living continues to **rise**, the company is going to have to increase people's salaries.

如果物價持續上漲，公司必須要提高員工的薪水。

應用	① rise 上升，不及物動詞，後面沒有受詞
	② arise = happen 發生
	③ A arise from B　A起因於B

---

37 salary
[ˈsælərɪ]
名 薪水

• sal 鹽
• -ary 名 表「與……有關之物」

The **salary** in my new position is terrible, but the work is so interesting that I don't mind.

這份新工作的薪水實在很差，但是工作非常有趣，所以我不介意。

38 **tenure**
['tɛnjʊr]

名（教授等的）終身職位

Once he's gotten **tenure** in the position, his salary won't change.

一旦轉為終身職，他的薪水永遠不會變。

文化 **補充**	美加地區的大學教授一旦通過考核，就可以獲得終身職位，沒有正當法律因素，校方不得無故解聘或調薪。這個制度是為了鼓勵學者能發表更多具原創性的著作，不受外界壓力影響。

---

39 **value**
['vælju]

名 價值

I don't think my salary reflects the **value** I bring to the company.

我不認為我的薪水能反應出我為公司創造的價值。

---

40 **wage**
[wedʒ]

名 薪水

I work such long hours that I'm glad I get an hourly **wage** rather than a set salary.

我很高興我是領時薪，而不是固定薪水，因為我的工作時數很長。

比較	1 pay：泛指所有類型的工資，不可數名詞。 2 salary：專業勞動者的薪水，常按月／季／年計算。 3 wage：勞力工作者的薪資，常以小時／日／週／月計算。 4 income：和earnings相似，但強調總收入。 5 fee：指提供某服務收取的固定費用。

學後小試　A　**Multiple Choice Questions**
請選擇合適的單字填入空格

_____ ➊ I really hope my good performance this year will earn me a _____.

(A) merit　　　　　(B) winner
(C) raise　　　　　(D) dedication

_____ ➋ My work hours are usually _____, but this week I must be in office from 9 a.m. to 6 p.m.

(A) flexible　　　　(B) productive
(C) complimentary　(D) diligent

_____ ➌ If I'm still feeling ill next week, I'll have to take more sick _____.

(A) representatives　(B) leave
(C) grant　　　　　(D) wages

_____ ➍ I'm not _____ for another bonus until next year.

(A) optional　　　　(B) acceptable
(C) eligible　　　　(D) practical

_____ ➎ Anne does almost nothing on the team. I wish she would _____ more.

(A) tempt　　　　　(B) entitle
(C) lead　　　　　(D) contribute

正確答案請參考 408 頁

B | Match

請在空格填入合適的單字，動詞需依時態變化，名詞需填入正確之單複數。

| improve | devote | look forward to | maintain | motivate | benefit |

1. I don't think my company understands how much we are _____ by bonuses.
2. If he doesn't _____ his performance, he may get fired.
3. I am really _____ the company trip to Hawaii!
4. To become a CEO, you have to _____ most of your time to work.
5. We won't be able to increase sales, but I hope we can _____ last year's levels.
6. A free gym membership is a great _____ the company offers.

C | Listening Practice

請聆聽音檔，將單字填入空格 🎧 020

1. She has put in a _____ of work at this company, so she deserves a good pension.
2. Albert isn't the brightest employee, but he's very _____.
3. I wish my boss would _____ my role in our team's success.
4. My supervisor keeps making changes to my proposal. It seems like nothing will _____ him.
5. Once I get _____ in my position, I'll finally feel secure.
6. The lack of benefits is balanced by the very _____ salary offered.

正確答案請參考 408 頁

Unit 03

Company Events

公司活動

多益測驗中一定會出到社交生活的相關考題：

1. 各式各樣的訓練課程（training）與宴會（party）必然會是重點。
2. 熟悉生日宴會（birthday party）、歡送會（farewell party）等不同的宴會主題（theme）。
3. 熟悉參加（attend/take part in/participate）與慶祝（celebrate/commemorate）的各種動詞用法。

學前暖身 請閱讀英文定義，並將正確單字與之配對

invite	theme	train	celebrate	bring together

1. _____: to instruct someone on how to complete a task
2. _____: to cause two or more people to meet
3. _____: a certain idea or style for an event
4. _____: to have a party for a specific purpose
5. _____: to ask someone to attend an event

021 **01** 美英 **02** 美加 **03** 澳美 **04** 加英

Orientation 開幕／始業式

---

01 attend
[ə`tɛnd]

動 出席；參加

The letter does not make it clear that new employees must **attend** orientation. Please clarify this.

這封信沒有說清楚新進員工必須參加教育訓練，請您重申一下。

---

02 introduce
[ˌɪntrə`djus]

動 介紹

- intro- 向內
- duce 帶領

The principal function of orientation is to **introduce** the company's culture and its methods of operation.

新進員工教育訓練的主要目的，就是介紹企業文化和組織運作方式。

---

03 regulation
[ˌrɛgjə`leʃən]

名 規章；條例；調節

- regulate 動 規範
- -ion 名 表「行為的結果」

Rules concerning the **regulation** of intellectual property rights will be introduced during orientation.

教育訓練課程中會介紹智慧財產權法規的規定。

相似詞	名 policy 政策；策略
	名 rule 規定；統治
	名 principle 原則；原理；主義
	名 directive 指示；命令

---

04 set up

動 片 豎立；架起

Mr. Rasheed has agreed to **set up** the audio system for this month's seminar.

拉席德先生已同意為這個月的研習安裝音響設備。

---

05 take part in
動 片 參加

Unlike last year, new programmers have to **take part in** the first stage of orientation this year.

和去年不同的是，今年新進的程式設計師必須參加第一階段的員工訓練。

> **相似詞** 片 participate in = 動 attend = join 參加

Training 培訓

06 leadership
[ˈlidɚʃɪp]

名 領導地位；領導才能；
領導層

· lead 動 領導
· -er 名 表「人」
· -ship 名 表「狀態；特質；能力」

This month's training excursion will focus on **leadership**, which the president feels is lacking in many managers.

這個月的實地考察將會著重於領導力，因為董事長認為許多經理缺乏這項特質。

07 required
[rɪˈkwaɪrd]

形 要求的；必須的

The **required** training will be handled by an outside contractor, but paid for by the company.

外部承包商會負責這次公司要求的訓練，費用則由公司負擔。

> **應用**
> 1 S. + require + O. + to V. 需要……去做……
> 2 S. + require + that + S. (should) + V.
> 某人要求某人去做……

08 train
[tren]

動 訓練；培訓

We need to find someone who can **train** the staff to use the new office software.

我們需要找人來訓練員工使用新的工作軟體。

09 annual
['ænjʊəl]

形 一年的;每年的

The **annual** training course is held every August.
年度訓練課程將於每年八月舉行。

---

10 bring together

動 片 招募;聚集

We hope to **bring together** the most motivated and competitive employees.
我們希望招募最積極進取、競爭力強的員工。

---

11 build up

動 片 建立

The purpose of this excursion is to **build up** a sense of teamwork.
這次出遊的目的是建立團隊合作的默契。

---

12 guide
[gaɪd]

動 引導

Five former participants will **guide** trainees through the course.
五位舊生會在課程中引導受訓學員。

---

13 instructor
[ɪn'strʌktɚ]

名 教練;指導者

· instruct 動 指示
· or 名 表「人」

She said she did not want to be an **instructor**, even though she will plan the training course.
她說雖然她會規劃訓練課程,但她不想親自指導。

44

14 mentor
[ˈmɛntɚ]
名 導師；良師益友

Each group of trainees will be assigned a **mentor**, who will assist them during the hands-on portion.
實作課時每組學員都有一個導師協助他們。

15 session
[ˈsɛʃən]
名（授課活動等的）時間；會議

Each **session** will run for two hours, followed by a 20-minute break.
每一堂課上課時間是兩小時，接著有二十分鐘休息時間。

16 site
[saɪt]
名 地點

The **site** for this year's training seminar will be in Frankfurt.
今年培訓研討會的地點將會在法蘭克福。

Party 宴會

17 entertainment
[ˌɛntɚˈtenmənt]
名 娛樂
· entertain 動 使娛樂
· -ment 名 表「行為；狀態」

Karaoke has become a popular form of **entertainment** at birthday parties.
卡拉OK在生日派對裡變得很受歡迎。

同義詞
名 recreation = amusement 消遣；娛樂
片 leisure activity = pastime 休閒活動

18 invite
[ɪnˈvaɪt]
動 邀請

Be sure to **invite** all the managers, even ones from other departments.
請記得邀請所有經理，連其他部門經理也一併邀請。

19 **present**

[`prɛzənt]

名 禮物

While bringing a **present** is not required, it is highly recommended.

雖然送禮並非必要，但非常建議你帶禮物來。

| 相似詞 | 名 gift 禮物 |
| | 名 offering 禮品；供品 |

---

20 **welcome**

[`wɛlkəm]

動 歡迎

• wel- 很好地
• come 動 來

I would like to **welcome** you all to Kathy and Steve's first baby shower.

我想歡迎各位來參加凱西和史提夫第一個寶寶的產前送禮會。

| 文化補充 | baby/bridal shower 是美加地區為懷孕的準媽媽和即將結婚的準新娘所舉辦的慶祝宴會，此類宴會中「送禮」是非常重要的習俗，通常會由準媽媽或準新娘列一張所想要的禮物清單，並由親朋好友「認領」要贈送的禮物。 |

---

21 **congratulate**

[kən`grætʃə͵let]

動 恭喜

• con- 一起
• gratul 高興
• -ate 動 表「使成為」

Let me be the first to **congratulate** you on your upcoming wedding and to wish you the very best.

讓我當第一個恭喜你們要結婚的人，並祝你們一切圓滿。

應用	congratulate Sb. on N./V-ing
	= congratulations to Sb. on N./V-ing
	恭喜某人某事

---

22 **due**

[dju]

形 到期的

We need to hurry up and plan the baby shower because the baby is **due** on November 1.

我們得趕快計畫產前送禮會，因為預產期是十一月一日。

23 **farewell**

[ˈfɛrˈwɛl]

形 送別的

• fare【古語】行走
• well 很好地

Is Mrs. Kerry retiring before or after her **farewell** party?

凱瑞太太是歡送會之前還是之後要退休呢？

---

24 **party**

[ˈpɑrtɪ]

名 宴會；派對；政黨

Do you think it would be better to hold Mr. Smith's farewell **party** at a restaurant or a bar?

你覺得史密斯先生的歡送會，是辦在餐廳還是酒吧比較好呢？

| 應用 | 1 throw/have/give a party 開派對 |
| | 2 a farewell party 送別會；歡送會 |

---

25 **theme**

[θim]

名 主題；題材

Has anyone decided if the party's **theme** will be a cruise voyage or an Italian getaway?

有誰決定好派對要辦郵輪式主題，還是義大利渡假式主題呢？

---

26 **attribute**

[əˈtrɪbjut]

動 歸因於

• at- 向
• tribute 給予

She **attributes** her successes to the support of her coworkers and staff.

她把成功歸因於同事和工作人員的支持。

| 應用 | attribute Sth. to Sth./Sb. |
| | 將……歸功／歸因於…… |

---

27 **awards ceremony**
[ə`wɔrdz] [`sɛrə‚monɪ]

名 片 頒獎典禮

The president will present the achievement awards during the **awards ceremony** following dinner.

董事長會在晚宴後的頒獎典禮頒發成就獎。

應用	1 award presenter 頒獎人
	2 award winner 獲獎人
	3 a thank-you speech 獲獎感言

---

28 **banquet**
[`bæŋkwɪt]

名 宴會；設宴款待

The organizers have arranged for the **banquet** to be held in the hotel's conference room.

負責人把宴會安排在飯店的會議廳舉行。

---

29 **celebrate**
[`sɛlə‚bret]

動 慶祝

• celebr 經常出沒、著名的
• -ate 動 表「成為」

Once the president has finished her speech, we will **celebrate** the entrance of new employees into the company.

等董事長致完詞，我們要歡迎新同仁的加入。

---

30 **commemorate**
[kə`mɛmə‚ret]

動 慶祝；紀念

• com- 一起
• memor 記得的
• -ate 動 表「成為」

This event will **commemorate** our organization's 20th year of operation.

這場活動是為了紀念這個機構成立了20年。

同義詞	動 remember 記得；想起
	動 memorialize = monumentalize 紀念
	片 pay tribute to ... 致敬；紀念

Holiday/Festival 節慶

31 activity
[æk`tɪvətɪ]

名 活動

- act 動 行動
- -ive 形 表「有……特性的」
- -ity 名 表「性質，狀態」

Which **activities** did you have in mind for this year's Christmas party?

今年的聖誕派對你想到什麼活動了嗎？

---

32 ancient
[`enʃənt]

形 古代的；古老的

Giving children gifts of money at Chinese New Year is an **ancient** tradition in China.

在中國，新年發紅包給小孩子是古老的傳統。

---

33 atmosphere
[`ætməs,fɪr]

名 氣氛

- atmo 氣
- sphere 名 球

Keeping the time limit to three hours will help us maintain a festive **atmosphere**; more than that, and people will tire.

就算是慶祝過節，三小時也就是極限了，超過大家會很累。

---

34 costume
[`kɑstjum]

名 服裝；戲服

We would like to remind employees that the wearing of **costumes** will not be permitted this Halloween.

我們想提醒員工，今年萬聖節不可以穿特殊服裝來上班。

應用
[1] costume ball 化妝舞會
[2] costume drama 時代劇（古裝劇）

---

35 gather
[`gæðɚ]

動 聚集

Employees should **gather** for the New Year's party by 7 p.m.

全體員工應於晚上七點前集合參加新年派對。

---

36 observe
[əb`zɝv]

動 慶祝(節日等);遵守;觀察

· ob- 朝向
· serve 動 貯存;看守

This year, we will be **observing** both the Western and Chinese New Years.

今年我們會慶祝跨年,也會過農曆新年。

---

37 anniversary
[͵ænə`vɝsərɪ]

名 週年紀念

· anni- 年
· vers 轉換
· -ary 名

Johnson's 25th wedding **anniversary** is this Friday, so let's have a small party for him at the office.

這個星期五是強森的25週年結婚紀念日,我們在辦公室幫他辦一個小的派對吧!

> 應用
> 1 anniversary/annual sale 百貨公司週年慶
> 2 wedding anniversary 結婚週年紀念

Retirement 退休

---

38 admire
[əd`maɪr]

動 欽佩;欣賞;誇獎

· ad- 至;向
· mire 對……感到驚訝

I think I speak for everyone here when I say how much I have **admired** your professionalism over the years.

當我說非常敬佩您過去以來的專業精神,我想在場的每一位都是這樣想的。

---

39 expect
[ɪk`spɛkt]

動 預期

· ex- 向外
· (s)pect 看

When planning for retirement, it is important to **expect** medical costs to increase.

規劃退休的時候,一定要預估醫療花費會增加。

> 應用 expect (O.) to V. 預期/期待(某人)去做

---

40 retire
[rɪ`taɪr]

動 退休

· re- 後面
· tire 拉

I can't believe Mrs. Yamada will be able to **retire** at 55.

我不敢相信山田太太55歲就可以退休了。

學後小試 A Multiple Choice Questions
請選擇合適的單字填入空格

____ ① Once you complete the training, you will be able to act as a ____ to next year's recruits.

    (A) mentor   (B) leadership
    (C) costume   (D) theme

____ ② He's saved enough money over the years to be able to ____ at the age 60.

    (A) due   (B) expect
    (C) retire   (D) train

____ ③ Everyone will be able to ____ the barbecue as long as they pay the fee.

    (A) build up   (B) set up
    (C) bring together   (D) take part in

____ ④ Please let us know by 5 p.m. on Friday if you plan to ____ the New Year's party.

    (A) attend   (B) admire
    (C) guide   (D) invite

____ ⑤ For the party, we're looking for a place that has a bright, welcoming ____.

    (A) instructor   (B) atmosphere
    (C) anniversary   (D) regulation

正確答案請參考 409 頁

B Match

請在空格填入合適的單字，動詞需依時態變化，名詞需填入正確之單複數。

farewell	awards ceremony	present	gather	required	annual

1. Mr. Cheever will host this year's _____ at the Ramada Inn.

2. An entrance fee is _____ for anyone wishing to attend this year's dance.

3. There will be a _____ party in honor of Mrs. Smith's transfer.

4. People attending the Christmas party can bring only one _____.

5. The _____ shareholders' meeting will be held in the Milton conference hall.

6. Before the New Year's party begins, everyone should _____ in the main lobby.

C Listening Practice

請聆聽音檔，將單字填入空格 030

1. As part of your training, you will _____ the workers on the production line and suggest possible changes.

2. Ms. Lee will be presented a certificate to _____ her achievements.

3. Everyone at the company _____ you on your promotion.

4. Darren and Sylvia will be in charge of _____, and that means they will have to organize the music.

5. We _____ the fault in the airbags to the manufacturer using cheaper parts.

6. There will be four training _____ this year, with one held each quarter.

正確答案請參考 409 頁

Personnel

人事組織

人事（personnel）情境除了招募任聘之外，多益測驗中也經常出現：

1. 職稱（title/position）與職責（responsibility/duty）的各種用法，以及任務（assignment）、輪班（work shift）等指稱工作狀態的名詞。

2. 管理（manage）、負責（be in charge）、指揮（direct）、指派（appoint）等強調上對下的動詞絕對是考試重點，必須要熟悉使用時機和差異。

學前暖身 請閱讀英文定義，並將正確單字與之配對

appoint	control	spare	transfer	direct

1 _____: to direct or have power over

2 _____: to lead, operate, or guide the progress of

3 _____: to assign someone a job or role

4 _____: to move from one place or area of control to another

5 _____: extra; in addition to requirements

031 **01** 美英 **02** 美加 **03** 澳美 **04** 加英 **05** 美加

Personnel 人事

---

01 apprentice
[ə`prɛntɪs]

名 學徒；見習生

My mechanic is looking for an **apprentice**.
我的技師正在找實習生。

---

02 assistant
[ə`sɪstənt]

名 助手；助理

- assist 動 幫助
- -ant 名 表示「進行……動作的人」，「……者（人或物）」

I can't keep up with this paperwork. I need an **assistant**.
我無法應付這些文書工作，我需要一個助理。

---

03 associate
[ə`soʃɪˏet]

名 夥伴；合夥人

This is George, my business **associate**.
這是喬治，我生意上的夥伴。

相似詞	名 colleague 同事；同僚
	名 coworker 同事；夥伴

---

04 in charge of
[tʃɑrdʒ]

片 負責

She is **in charge of** North American sales.
她是北美業務部的負責人。

應用	A be in charge of B = A be responsible for B A 管理／負責 B

---

05 beneath
[bɪ`niθ]

介 在……之下

There are at least 10 people **beneath** her in the department.
她所負責的部門裡至少有十名員工。

---

06 executive

[ɪgˋzɛkjʊtɪv]

形 行政上的；管理階層的

· execute 動 執行
· -ive 形 表「與……有關的；具有……性質的」

This is her first time in an **executive** position.

這是她第一次擔任管理職。

| 應用 | CEO: chief executive officer 執行長 |

---

07 fluctuation

[ˌflʌktʃʊˋeʃən]

名 變動；變化

· fluctuate 動 變動
· -ion 名 表「行為；結果」

The constant **fluctuations** in personnel mean I never know who my real boss is.

因為公司人員流動頻繁，我從不知道我真正的上司是誰。

---

08 level

[ˋlɛvl̩]

名 程度；等級

I thought my work was good, but his performance is really on another **level**.

我以為我的表現已經很好了，但他真的令我難以望其項背。

---

09 personnel

[ˌpɝsn̩ˋɛl]

名 (總稱) 員工；人事

If they don't hire some new people, they're going to face a serious **personnel** crisis.

如果他們不聘請新人，就會面臨嚴重的人力短缺。

---

10 select

[səˋlɛkt]

動 選擇

I'm hoping to be **selected** as the new team leader.

我希望能被選為新的小組領導者。

---

11 settle

[ˋsɛtl̩]

動 解決 (問題等)；結束 (爭端、糾紛等)

I really hope she can **settle** the conflict between Joe and Jane. It's starting to hurt the group's morale.

我真希望她可以化解喬與珍之間的衝突，那已經開始打擊到士氣了。

12
supervisor
[ˌsupəˈvaɪzə]

名 主管

· supervise 動 監督
· -or 名 表「人」

I really need my **supervisor** to clarify what she wants me to do.
我真希望我的上司可以說清楚她要我做什麼。

13
understaffed
[ˈʌndəˌstæft]

形 人手不足的

· under- 不夠的
· staff 名 全體員工
· -ed 形

We're so **understaffed**; I've ended up working until 10 p.m. every night this week.
我們人手嚴重不足，讓我這週必須每天工作到晚上十點。

14
respectful
[rɪˈspɛktfəl]

形 尊重人的

· respect 名 尊敬
· -ful 形 表「充滿……的」

He has to learn to be more **respectful** of his superiors if he wants to get ahead.
假如他真的想要獲得拔擢，就必須要學習更加尊重上級。

15
individual
[ˌɪndəˈvɪdʒul]

名 個人；個體

· in- 不
· divide 分開
· -al 形 表「關於……的」

They aren't laying off whole teams of people, but some **individuals** will be let go.
他們不會裁掉全組人馬，但會解聘一些人。

16
spare
[spɛr]

形 多餘的

It is just a small business corporation, so it may not have **spare** workforce for this project.
這只是一家小公司，沒有多餘的人手去負責這個專案。

相似詞	形 extra 額外的；特大的
	形 additional 附加的；額外的
	形 surplus 過剩的；多餘的

17 **resign**

[rɪˋzaɪn]

動 辭職

I don't want to **resign** until I've found a new position.

在找到新工作前我不會辭職。

應用	1 resign + from 公司單位 從……辭職
	2 resign as 頭銜 辭去……職務
	3 resign one's post/seat/position 辭職

Work shift 值班

18 **assignment**

[əˋsaɪnmənt]

名 任務；作業

• assign 動 指派
• -ment 名 表「行為」

Have you finished the **assignment** yet?

你完成任務了沒?

19 **busy**

[ˋbɪzɪ]

形 忙碌的

She asked me to pick up her shift on Saturday, but I'm just too **busy**.

她請我在週六幫她代班,但我實在太忙了。

應用	S. + be busy with + N./V-ing 忙著做……

20 **shift**

[ʃɪft]

名 輪班

I've got early **shifts** all week, so I can't stay up late.

我這週都上早班,所以我不能晚睡。

應用	1 do/work a (10/12/24-hour) shift
	值班……小時
	2 work night/day shift
	= be on night/day shift 值早╱晚班
	3 graveyard shift 大夜班

Department 部門

21
collaborate
[kəˈlæbəˌret]

動 合作

· col- 一起
· labor 工作
· -ate 動 表「動作」

They've decided that they want sales and marketing to **collaborate** on the new plan.
他們已經決定要讓業務部與行銷部攜手合作這項新計畫。

22
department
[dɪˈpɑrtmənt]

名 部門；科系

· de- 離開
· part 分開；部分
· -ment 名 表「行為；狀態」

We used to have lunch together, but now that she's moved to another **department**, I hardly see her anymore.
我們以前常一起吃午餐，但自從她調去別的部門，我就再也沒見過她。

23
integral
[ˈɪntəgrəl]

形 不可或缺的

He's an **integral** part of the design team. I don't know what I'd do without him.
他是設計組不可或缺的一分子，我真不知道少了他，我該怎麼辦。

Mergers and Acquisitions 併購

24
buyout
[ˈbaɪˌaʊt]

名 買斷；(產權)全部買下

· buy 買
· out 介 可得到的、出來(問世)的

The company promises that nothing will change for employees after the **buyout**.
公司承諾在收購之後，員工不會有任何變動。

25 **control**
[kən`trol]

動 控制

I **control** the acquisition process at the company.

是我管控公司的併購流程。

---

26 **takeover**
[`tek͵ovɚ]

名 收購；接管

・take 動 拿；取走
・over 副 在上方

There will definitely be layoffs after the **takeover**.

在併購之後肯定會裁員。

---

27 **transition**
[træn`zɪʃən]

名 過渡；交接

・transit 動 過渡
・-ion 名 表「行為；結果；狀態」

They've sent a team of human resources specialists to help make sure the **transition** is smooth.

他們派一組人資專家來確保交接過程順利。

> **應用**　a transition from N1 to N2 從N1移轉到N2

---

28 **acquisition**
[͵ækwə`zɪʃən]

名 收購

・acquire 動 獲得
・-ion 名 表「結果；行為；狀況」

They get rid of their competition through **acquisitions**.

他們用收購的方式來消除競爭者！

---

29 **corporate**
[`kɔrpərɪt]

形 公司的；企業的

In my opinion, only a **corporate** lawyer can answer those questions.

在我看來，只有通曉公司法的律師才能回答那些問題。

30 institute
['ɪnstətjut]

名（專科性的）學校，學院，大學；研究所

The merging of these two well-known **institutes** has shocked the academic circles.

這兩所知名學校的合併震驚了學術界。

> **應用**
> 名 institute 學院；協會（範圍小、具體且明確）
> 名 institution 制度；機構

---

31 manage
['mænɪdʒ]

動 管理；處理

I don't know how she'll **manage** a team that has suddenly doubled in size.

我不知道她要怎麼管理一個人數突然倍增的小組。

> **應用** S. + manage to V. 設法去做……

> **相似詞**
> 動 control 掌管；控制
> 動 run 負責；執行；管理
> 片 be in charge of 管理；負責

---

32 merger
['mɝdʒɚ]

名（公司等的）合併

What will the company's name be after the **merger**?

合併之後，這間公司的名字會變成什麼呢？

> **比較** merger 用於兩個公司合併成為一個新公司，通常這個新公司會有一個新的名字；acquisition 則是指一家公司收購另外一家公司，而新公司的名字和制度通常沿用收購公司的舊制。Mergers and Acquisitions (M&A) 即是一般所稱的公司併購案。

---

33 transfer
[træns`fɝ]

動 轉讓
・trans- 轉；越過
・fer 拿

We're going to **transfer** all our design work to them as part of the merger.

因為公司合併，我們將把所有的設計作品轉移給他們。

Board & Committee 董事會與委員會

34

appoint

[ə'pɔɪnt]

動 任命；委派職務

• ap- 向
• point 點；指

I can't believe the CEO **appointed** his daughter as chair of the research committee!

我不敢相信執行長竟然指派他女兒，作為研究委員會的主席！

35

be accounted for

[ə'kaʊntɪd]

片 出席；到齊

All the board members **are accounted for**, so I think we're ready to get started on the vote.

所有董事會成員都已經到齊，我想我們已經準備好可以開始投票了。

> 應用　Sth. be accounted for 要被納入考慮……
> （後面不接受詞）

36

board

[bord]

名 董事會；
（有特定用途的）板；
牌子

I think it's a great idea, but the **board** is so conservative that they might not approve it.

我覺得這主意非常好，但董事會很保守，可能不會同意。

> 應用
> 1 board of directors 董事會
> 2 go by the board 被丟棄；計畫落空
> 3 be on board with something 贊同；認可

37

boardroom

['bord,rum]

名 董事會會議室

All the executives are gathered in the **boardroom** right now. I wonder what's going on.

所有主管現在都聚集在會議室，到底發生了什麼事？

38 **direct**
[dəˋrɛkt]

動 指揮；主持；管理

Who's going to **direct** the research team?
誰將指揮研究小組？

---

39 **reliable**
[rɪˋlaɪəbl]

形 可靠的

・rely 動 依靠
・-able 形 表「可……的」

He's so **reliable**; he's never missed a deadline.
他真是可靠，總是在期限內完成工作。

相似詞　形 countable = dependable 可靠的

---

40 **title**
[ˋtaɪtl]

名 頭銜

The promotion is really just a change of **title**.
I don't have any new responsibilities.
這次升職其實只是職稱改變而已，我沒被指派新的職務。

應用　the title of the book is + 書名
= the book is entitled + 書名
這本書的書名是……

相似詞　名 position 職稱；職位
名 name 名字；頭銜

學後小試 A **Multiple Choice Questions**
請選擇合適的單字填入空格

_____ 1 I'm going to need a(n) _____ to help me handle all this extra work.

(A) assistant (B) institute
(C) merger (D) level

_____ 2 The huge market _____ mean my stock changes value drastically from day to day.

(A) fluctuations (B) personnel
(C) assignments (D) individuals

_____ 3 What will your new _____ be after your promotion?

(A) board (B) buyout
(C) transition (D) title

_____ 4 If the CEO and I continue to argue, I'm going to _____. I can't work like this.

(A) collaborate (B) resign
(C) select (D) direct

_____ 5 I'm sorry, I'm much too _____ to take on any new work right now.

(A) busy (B) respectful
(C) integral (D) executive

正確答案請參考 410 頁

B Match

請在空格填入合適的單字，動詞需依時態變化，名詞需填入正確之單複數。

beneath	apprentice	boardroom	accounted for	shift	settle

1 The project team has a meeting in the _____ at 9 a.m.

2 After my promotion, there will be an entire department _____ me.

3 We're going to have to get a manager to _____ this dispute.

4 My son wants to learn a trade, so he's going to be a carpenter's _____ for a year.

5 Once everyone is _____, we can begin the sales meeting.

6 My next _____ starts at 4 p.m.

C Listening Practice

請聆聽音檔，將單字填入空格 040

1 There's a job opening for a sales _____ at my company.

2 Honestly, I don't think our new _____ is going to bring in a lot of money.

3 He has never _____ a large team before.

4 I hope I get along with my new _____.

5 Who is _____ maintaining client address lists?

6 We're so _____; everyone on the team is working overtime.

正確答案請參考 410 頁

Unit 05

The Office

辦公室

多益測驗的工作環境並不僅指涉辦公室本身：

1. 工作空間的名詞必須掌握，像是入口（entrance）、隔間（compartment）、或是停車場（garage）、中庭（patio）等周圍環境。
2. 地產觀念也不能輕忽，像是辦公室大樓的租金（lease）、水電（utilities）；這些名詞常會以對話的形式出現，務必要特別留意。

學前暖身 請閱讀英文定義，並將正確單字與之配對

monitor	basic	suburb	mortgage	wing

1. _____ : either of two parts of a building
2. _____ : of the essential or simplest elements
3. _____ : a loan used for the purchase of a house, a building, or land
4. _____ : a video device connected to a camera, often used for security
5. _____ : a community just outside a town or city consisting mostly of houses and small stores

Office Building 辦公大樓

01 brick
[brɪk]

名 磚

The interior is wood paneling, but the exterior is red **brick**.

內部是木板裝潢，但外部是紅磚。

---

02 carpet
[ˋkɑrpɪt]

名 地毯

Putting down **carpet** would help reduce the noise levels.

鋪設地毯可以幫助降低音量。

---

03 closet
[ˋklɑzɪt]

名 衣櫥

Seeing as there are no **closets**, storage space will be a problem.

由於這裡沒有衣櫃，儲藏空間會成為問題。

---

04 compartment
[kəmˋpɑrtmənt]

名 包廂；隔間

• compart 動 分開
• -ment 名 表「行為；結果；狀態」

Each room is divided into three **compartments**, each of which is large enough to accommodate three cubicles.

每個房間都被分割成三個包廂，而每個包廂都足以容納三個小隔間。

> 應用
> 1 a first class compartment
> （飛機／火車）頭等艙廂
> 2 overhead compartment 飛機艙頂置物箱

---

05 entrance
[ˋɛntrəns]

名 入口

• enter 動 進入
• -ance 名 表「行為；過程，性質；狀態」

The south **entrance** needs a new passkey machine installed.

南邊的入口需要安裝新的門禁系統。

---

06 **furnished**
[ˈfɜnɪʃt]

形 配有家具的

・furnish 動 裝備;供應
・-ed 形

A temporary solution would be to rent a **furnished** office, but it will be expensive.

租一個附家具的辦公室可以暫時解決問題,只不過所費不貲。

應用	形 unfurnished 未附家具的
	名 furniture 家具（集合名詞,只能用單數形）
	→ a piece of furniture 一件家具

---

07 **garage**
[ɡəˈrɑʒ]

名 車庫

The **garage** has space for thirty cars and two trucks.

這個車庫可以容納30輛車子和兩輛卡車。

---

08 **lobby**
[ˈlɑbɪ]

名 大廳;門廊

Given the large windows, the **lobby** should be bright enough to make visitors feel comfortable.

有了大窗戶,大廳採光好會讓訪客感到舒適。

---

09 **shelf**
[ʃɛlf]

名 (書櫃等的) 架子

We will need to install **shelves** in each cubicle so that workers have some place to display personal items.

我們需要在每個小隔間裡設置書架,這樣員工可以有些地方陳放個人物品。

應用	片 shelf life 保存期限
	形 off-the-shelf 有現貨供應的
	remove Sth. from the shelves 將……下架

10 **staff lounge**
[stæf] [laʊndʒ]

名 片 員工休息室

Employees have asked for a refrigerator to be installed in the **staff lounge**.

員工們要求在員工休息室放一個冰箱。

---

11 **wing**
[wɪŋ]

名 側廳；廂房

The north **wing** will house the IT department and all its servers.

資訊部門及其所有伺服器將座落在北區。

---

12 **workplace**
[`wɝk͵ples]

名 工作場所

• work 動 工作
• place 名 地方；場所

Will we be able to maintain safety in a **workplace** this narrow? There's limited space between the walls and the robots.

我們有辦法在這麼狹窄的工作場所保持安全嗎？牆和機器人中間的距離很有限。

Surroundings/Environment 周圍環境

13 **adjacent**
[ə`dʒesənt]

形 鄰接的

• ad- 向
• jac 座落；位於
• -ent 形

The **adjacent** building blocks most of the afternoon sunlight.

這棟鄰近的建築擋住了大部分的西曬光線。

14 **broad**
[brɔd]

形 寬的

The service road is **broad** enough so that our trucks will have no problem driving down it.

這條輔助道路夠寬，我們的卡車在上面通行毫無問題。

| 應用 | 動 broaden 增廣 → broaden one's horizons 增廣見聞 |

| 相似詞 | 形 wide = roomy = spacious 寬敞的；廣闊的 |

15 **construction**
[kənˈstrʌkʃən]

名 建築物

• construct 動 建造
• -ion 形 表「行為；行為的結果」

There are no large **constructions** nearby, so we anticipate no difficulties receiving satellite signals.

這附近沒有大型建築，所以我們預期接收衛星訊號沒有問題。

| 應用 | 1 under construction 在興建中 2 construction site 建築工地 |

16 **district**
[ˈdɪstrɪkt]

名 區域

Our new office is in a residential **district**, so it is expected there will be a lot of houses and schools there.

我們的新辦公室位於住宅區，所以預計那裡會有很多住家跟學校。

17 **indoor**
[ˈɪnˌdor]

形 室內的

• in- 在內
• door 名 門

It's too dark; there's not enough **indoor** lighting in the warehouse.

倉庫裡的室內燈光不足，實在太暗了。

18 location

[loˋkeʃən]

名 位置；場所；所在地

· locate 動 座落於
· -ion 名 表「行為的結果」

Rail and highway access is a key consideration when selecting a **location** for our new factory.

在選擇新工廠地點時，鄰近鐵路與高速公路是重要的考慮因素。

---

19 neighborhood

[ˋnebɚˏhʊd]

名 鄰近地區

· neighbor 名 鄰居
· -hood 名 表「狀態」

The surrounding **neighborhood** is mostly apartments and convenience stores, with a couple of small parks.

附近的社區主要是公寓和便利商店，還有一些小公園。

---

20 on-site

[ansaɪt]

形 就地的；現場的

Dangerous materials cannot be stored in **on-site** containers. Instead, they must be transported to a remote location.

危險物品不能放在本地的貨櫃裡，它們必須被運到偏遠的地方。

---

21 patio

[ˋpɑtɪˏo]

名 中庭；院子

The **patio** is wide enough for three sets of tables and chairs.

這個院子夠寬，可以放三組桌椅。

---

22 railing

[relɪŋ]

名 欄杆，扶手；柵欄，圍欄

To comply with safety regulations, every second-floor landing must have a **railing**.

為了符合安全規範，每個二樓樓梯口都必須要有圍欄。

---

23 statue
[ˈstætʃʊ]

名 雕像

The mayor's office is considering putting up a **statue** of the town's founder at the corner.
市長的幕僚正考慮在街角豎立本市開創者的雕像。

---

24 suburb
[ˈsʌbɝb]

名 郊區

· sub- 較低；附近
· urb 城市

Most **suburbs** have a large amount of residential housing, some small businesses catering to residents, and little to no industry.
大多數的郊區裡有許多住宅，還有一些為了居民而設的小餐飲店，至於工廠則不一定會有。

應用	形 suburban 郊區的
	形 rural 農村的
	形 urban 都會的

---

25 surround
[səˈraʊnd]

動 圍繞

· sur- 在上
· round 環繞

The city has ruled that all factories must be **surrounded** by a green zone not less than 10 meters wide.
這城市有個規定，所有工廠周圍要有至少十公尺的植物環繞。

---

26 work on

片 從事

Our recent environmental impact evaluation makes it clear we must **work on** reducing our emissions.
根據最近的環境汙染報告，我們必須著手減少廢氣排放量。

應用	1 work on + N./V-ing 正在做……
	2 work out 解決…… （接受詞）;
	健身（不接受詞）

71

Utilities 公共設施

27 **amenities**

[ə`minətɪs]

名 福利設施

These company dormitories have all the standard **amenities** of a mid-priced hotel, including Wi-Fi and cable TV.

這些公司宿舍擁有所有中等價位旅館該有的標準設施，包括無線網路以及有線電視。

---

28 **basic**

[`besɪk]

形 基本的；基礎的

- base 名 基礎
- -ic 形 表「具有⋯⋯特徵；與⋯⋯有關的」

The **basic** utilities, water and electricity, are included in the rental fee.

基本的設施使用費，也就是水電費，都包含在租金裡。

---

29 **convenient**

[kən`vinjənt]

形 方便的

- convene 動 集合
- -ent 形 表「有⋯⋯性質的」

The location is **convenient** for anyone needing easy access to downtown.

這地點對想要迅速到市中心的人來說非常方便。

---

30 **electricity**

[ˌilɛk`trɪsətɪ]

名 電力

- electric 形 電的
- -ity 名 表「性質」

The power company has a buy-back scheme for local households with solar power systems generating excess **electricity**.

對於當地配有太陽能系統的家庭，這家電力公司有可以買進過剩電力的機制。

應用 electricity bill 電費

---

31 **energy**

[`ɛnədʒɪ]

名 能量

The president is considering installing a geothermal **energy** system to heat the building.

總裁正考慮設置地熱能源系統為大樓提供暖氣。

---

32 reduce
[rɪˋdjus]

動 減少；降低

• re- 回；向後
• duce 引導

Is there any way to **reduce** our gas bill? It has gone beyond our budget for the third month in a row now.

有沒有辦法減少我們的瓦斯費？它已經連續三個月超出預算了。

應用
[1] reduce Sth. + by + half/20%
減少某物一半／20%的量
[2] cut down on + N. 削減⋯⋯

---

33 stationery
[ˋsteʃənˏɛrɪ]

名 文具

• stationer 名 文具店
• -y 名 表「行為；性質；狀態」

Given how much paper our office uses, we need to find a cheap **stationery** supplier immediately.

鑒於我們辦公室用紙量大，我們需要立即找到便宜的文具供應商。

---

34 utilities
[juˋtɪlətɪs]

名 公用事業（通常指水、電、瓦斯等）

Among the **utilities** we will need to hook up first, electricity and gas are the highest priority.

在我們需要接通的基礎設備中，電和瓦斯是最重要的。

相似詞
名 facilities 設施；設備
名 infrastructure 基礎建設
名 public service 公共建設

---

35 monitor
[ˋmɑnətɚ]

名 監視器

• monit 智力；忠告
• -ʊɪ 動 表「人或物」

The building has **monitors** for both the front and rear entrances.

這棟大樓在前後門都設有監視器。

Real Estate 房地產

---

36 **lease**
[lis]

名 租金;租約

動 租借

The cost of the **lease** is too high; it would've been cheaper if we had bought a space for long-term use.

租金太貴了。我們若是想要長期使用這空間,買下它應該比較划算。

應用	[1] A lease Sth. to B A將某物租借給B
	[2] take out a lease on Sth. 租用某物
	[3] renew a lease 續約
	[4] a lease expires/runs out 租約過期/失效

---

37 **mortgage**
[ˈmɔrgɪdʒ]

名 抵押借款

• mort 死亡
• gage 擔保

Before we consider taking out a **mortgage**, let's look into renting an office space.

在考慮抵押借款之前,我們可以先來試試租個辦公室。

| 應用 | [1] take out a 30-year mortgage 承接30年房貸 |
| | [2] pay off the mortgage 繳清貸款 |

---

38 **stationary**
[ˈsteʃənˌɛrɪ]

形 不動的;固定的

• station 名 站立
• -ary 形 表「……的」

Actually, the interior walls are not **stationary**; they can be removed to create a larger space.

其實內牆不是固定的,可以把它們移走讓空間更大。

| 相似詞 | 形 unmoving = still = static 不變的;靜止的 |

---

39 **tenant**
[ˈtɛnənt]

形 房客;承租人;住戶

The previous **tenants** failed to do necessary maintenance, so the property needs lots of cleaning and repairs.

由於先前的房客沒做好日常保養,所以現在需要很多清潔與維修。

| 應用 | 名 landlord/landlady 房東 |

---

40 **trustee**
[trʌsˈti]

名 受託人

Since the original owner died, the property has been managed by a **trustee**.

因為原來的主人過世了,這份資產現已由受託人管理。

學後小試

A Multiple Choice Questions

請選擇合適的單字填入空格

_____ ❶ Contact the power company and get them to hook up the _____ as soon as possible.

(A) lobby   (B) construction
(C) electricity   (D) shelf

_____ ❷ The local _____ is full of small shops and apartments.

(A) carpet   (B) neighborhood
(C) stationery   (D) patio

_____ ❸ They're looking for a _____ who is willing to pay five months' rent in advance.

(A) district   (B) tenant
(C) lease   (D) garage

_____ ❹ Each office has a separate _____ for use as storage.

(A) compartment   (B) utilities
(C) statue   (D) energy

_____ ❺ The second-floor _____ was bent during the earthquake, and it needs to be replaced.

(A) location   (B) suburb
(C) mortgage   (D) railing

正確答案請參考 410 頁

B Match

請在空格填入合適的單字，動詞需依時態變化，名詞需填入正確之單複數。

| amenities | on-site | broad | workplace | adjacent | closet |

1. We need a(n) _____ inspector, who can react quickly.
2. The main walkway is _____ enough to move office equipment down.
3. The _____ are limited to a sink, a microwave, and a very small refrigerator.
4. The file cabinets are _____ to the bookshelves.
5. There's a _____ in the back where employees put their coats.
6. In order to ensure a safe _____, please follow the safety procedures.

C Listening Practice

請聆聽音檔，將單字填入空格 (050)

1. The building is so old that its exterior walls are made of _____ and wood.
2. We need a _____ office with chairs, tables, and desks.
3. The _____ has two microwaves and a refrigerator.
4. The _____ can rent the property out, but they cannot sell it.
5. The office has an _____ Japanese garden for a soothing effect.
6. Apartments _____ this supermarket, so they get lots of customers.

正確答案請參考 410 頁

Unit 06

Equipment & Repair

設備與維修

多益測驗非常側重辦公室情境，公司內部可能遇到的各式硬體設備（equipment）的狀況，都有可能成為考試的重點：

1. 辦公室設備的說法必須精準，例如 appliance/equipment/facility/device/property 的差異與使用時機。

2. 出借（borrow/lend）、分享（share）、佔用（occupy）、修理（repair）等與設備使用相搭配的動詞，一定要隨時掌握住用法。

學前暖身 請閱讀英文定義，並將正確單字與之配對

directory	facility	renovate	demolish	method

1 _____: to destroy

2 _____: a book or list of contact information

3 _____: a place for executing a certain task or procedure

4 _____: a specific process for doing something

5 _____: to restore or repair, usually a room or building

Lend & Borrow 出借

01　borrow
['bɑro]

動 借入

Can I **borrow** that book when you're finished?
你看完後書可以借我嗎？

02　extension
[ɪk'stɛnʃən]

名 延長時間；延期

- ex- 向外
- tens 伸展
- -ion 名 表「行為；結果；狀態」

We haven't finished using the conference room—can we have an **extension** until 3 p.m.?
我們還需要用會議室——是否可以讓我們延長到下午三點？

應用	動 extend 延長
	片 extension number 分機號碼
	片 by extension 廣義來説；進而言之

03　rent
[rɛnt]

動 租入；租出

I'm looking for an apartment to **rent**, but I hope to buy a house soon.
我正在找房子租，但我希望能趕快買房。

04　reserve
[rɪ'zɝv]

動 預約；保留

- re- 返回
- serve 保存

I'm going to **reserve** a van to take us to the company picnic.
我要預約一部廂型車，載大家去員工野餐。

應用	① reserve = book = make a reservation 預定；預約
	② keep N. in reserve 預留……以備用

05　belong
[bə'lɔŋ]

動 屬於

Who does this tablet **belong** to?
這個平板電腦是誰的？

應用	片 belong to 屬於

78

Repair & Occupancy 修理與使用

06 **demolish**
[dɪ`mɑlɪʃ]

動 拆除；破壞

It can't be fixed. There is no other way but to **demolish** it.

這沒辦法修，只能把它拆了。

---

07 **dispose**
[dɪ`spoz]

動 處理

• dis- 分開
• pose 放

Where should I **dispose** of dead batteries?

廢電池該丟在哪裡？

相似詞	片 get rid of = throw away 丟棄；除去 動 desert 遺棄

---

08 **renovate**
[`rɛnə,vet]

動 整修

• re- 再次
• nov 新的
• -ate 動 表「成為」

The apartment is shabby now, but imagine how it could be if we **renovate** it!

這間公寓現在看來很破舊，但想想把它翻新的話看起來會怎樣！

---

09 **repair**
[rɪ`pɛr]

動 修理

• re- 再次
• pair 準備

Do you know of a shop that **repairs** watches?

你知道哪裡有修錶的店嗎？

---

10 **occupy**
[`ɑkjə,paɪ]

動 佔用

I'm afraid we're going to **occupy** the only meeting room all day.

我們恐怕要整天佔用這唯一一間會議室了。

應用	be occupied with V-ing 忙著／全神貫注做…… 形 occupied 被佔用的；忙碌的

11 share
[ʃɛr]
動 分享

I **share** an office with Tom Smith.
我跟湯姆·史密斯共用一間辦公室。

---

12 as needed
片 需要的時候

We don't restock our stationery according to any schedule, just **as needed**.
我們並不會定期補充文具，只會在需要的時候才進貨。

| 應用 | ① if needed 若有需要的話 |
| | ② much needed 非常需要的 |

Instruction 操作說明

13 alternative
[ɔl`tɝnətɪv]
名 選擇；替代方案

· alternate 形 交替的
· -ive 形 表「與……有關的；
  具有……性質的」、名 表「物」

What you're suggesting isn't possible. Can you give me an **alternative**?
你的建議不可行，可否給我其他選擇？

應用	the alternative to + N./V-ing
	可取代……的替代方案
	形 alternative 替代的
	→an alternative method 替代的方法

---

14 detailed
[`di,teld]
形 詳細的

· detail 名 細節
· -ed 形

I've never done this before, so please be as **detailed** as possible in your instructions.
我從來沒做過這件事，所以請盡可能給我詳細的說明。

應用	動 detail 詳述
	名 detail 細節
	→in detail 詳細地

15 instruction
[ɪnˋstrʌkʃən]

名 用法說明；操作指南

• instruct 動 教授；指示
• -ion 名 表「行為；行為的結果」

Could you read that **instruction** again? I didn't hear you.

可否再把使用說明唸一遍？我沒聽清楚。

---

16 insufficient
[͵ɪnsəˋfɪʃənt]

形 不足的；不充分的

• in- 不
• sufficient 形 足夠的

I thought I'd be able to assemble this by myself, but the manual is completely **insufficient**.

我以為我可以獨自組裝這個，但這說明書實在太簡陋。

	足夠的、充足的←→不足夠的、缺乏的	
應用	sufficient	insufficient/deficient
	adequate	inadequate
	plenty (+ of + N.)	a lack (+ of + N.)

---

17 once
[wʌns]

副 一旦；只要

Once you've fitted the bolt, slowly turn the gear.

當你放好螺絲之後，緩慢地轉動齒輪。

---

18 periodically
[͵pɪrɪˋɑdɪkl̩ɪ]

副 週期性地

• period 名 時期
• -ical 形
• -ly 副

Shake the can **periodically** so the paint doesn't settle.

每隔一段時間要搖一搖罐子，以免油漆凝固。

---

19 procedure
[prə`sidʒɚ]

名 程序；手續；步驟

• pro- 先；前
• ced 走
• -ure 名 表「動作；行為」

It's such a simple **procedure**; I don't think I need to read the directions.

這步驟非常簡單，我不認為需要讀説明書。

| 應用 | 1 take + procedures/steps/actions/precautions 採取措施 |
| | 2 SOP = Standard Operating Procedure 標準作業流程 |

---

20 secure
[sɪ`kjʊr]

動 把……固定

Secure the handle; then turn on the machine.

先固定好把手，再啟動機器。

Office Equipment/Property 辦公室設備

---

21 appliance
[ə`plaɪəns]

名 設備；用具；裝置

• appli (apply) 動 使用
• -ance 名 表「器具」

Our office **appliances** are so out-of-date.

我們的辦公設備實在非常陳舊。

---

22 container
[kən`tenɚ]

名 容器

• contain 動 包含
• -er 名 表「物」

Where's the **container** for paper clips?

裝迴紋針的盒子在哪裡？

---

23 contractor
[`kɑntræktɚ]

名 包商；承包人

• contract 名 契約
• -or 名 表「人」

No one here knows how to do a repair that complex. We'll have to hire a **contractor**.

這裡沒人知道要怎麼做那麼複雜的維修工作，我們必須僱個承包商。

24

device

[dɪ'vaɪs]

名 裝置；器械；儀器

In an office with no pencils, a pencil sharpener is a useless **device**.

在不用鉛筆的辦公室裡，削鉛筆機這個設備毫無用處。

25

directory

[də'rɛktərɪ]

名 電話簿；通訊錄

Could you check the personnel **directory** and find out how to contact each team member?

可否請你查一下員工通訊錄，找出每位組員的聯絡方式？

26

equipment

[ɪ'kwɪpmənt]

名 設備；配備；器材

• equip 動 配備
• -ment 名 表「產物」

I hope they're going to order some new printing **equipment**.

我希望他們可以訂購一些新的列印設備。

應用 　動 equip 使有準備；使有能力；訓練
　　　 → be equipped with + N. 裝備有……

27

facility

[fə'sɪlətɪ]

名（尤指包含多個建築物，有特定用途的）場所；設施

• facile 形 易使用的；易做的
• -ity 名 表「狀態」

If we want to produce things on such a huge scale, we're going to need a much bigger **facility**.

如果我們要如此大規模地生產，就必須要有個更大的場所。

28

maintenance

['mentənəns]

名 維修；保養

• maintain 動 維持
• -ance 名 表「行為」

We need a **maintenance** crew to come take a look at this leak in the kitchen.

我們需要維修團隊來檢查一下廚房的漏水。

應用 　動 maintain 維持、保養；供養
　　　 形 high-maintenance 需要細心保養的

29 property

['prɑpətɪ]

名 財產;所有物

• proper 自己的
• -ty 名 表「性質」

We're not allowed to take company **property** home, not even pens.

我們不可以把公司財產帶回家,就算是筆也不行。

---

30 resource

[rɪ'sors]

名 資源

• re- 再次
• source 升起

You can't move the scanner into your office—it's a shared **resource**!

你不可以把掃描器搬到你辦公室裡 —— 那是公用資源!

---

31 software

['sɔft,wɛr]

名 電腦軟體

• soft 軟的
• ware 製品

We need to update our accounting **software**.

我們需要更新會計軟體。

---

32 supply

[sə'plaɪ]

名 供應品;用品

• sup- 從下面
• ply 充滿;裝滿

If you're ordering office **supplies**, please put me down for a box of paper clips and a box of letterhead.

如果你要訂購辦公用品,請幫我訂一盒迴紋針和一包公司信紙。

Usage Manual 使用手冊

33 **acquaint**

[əˋkwent]

動 使認識；使熟悉

You really should **acquaint** yourself with the machine before you need to use it urgently.

你真的應該在急需使用前好好認識這部機器。

---

34 **at all times**

片 任何時候

Please use caution **at all times** when operating the espresso machine.

操作濃縮咖啡機時，請隨時小心注意。

> 應用
> 1 at all times = always = constantly 隨時
> 2 at a time 一次
> → one at a time 一次一個
> 3 from time to time = sometimes
> = occasionally 有時候

---

35 **carefully**

[ˋkɛrfəlɪ]

副 小心地

• care 名 在意
• -ful 形 表「充滿、具有某種特點」
• -ly 副

You have to add the cartridge very **carefully** or it'll jam.

在裝墨水匣時必須十分小心，不然會卡住。

---

36 **follow**

[ˋfɑlo]

動 跟隨；聽從

If you don't **follow** the instructions, you might break something.

你如果不遵照說明，可能會把東西弄壞。

37 helpful
[ˈhɛlpfəl]

形 有幫助的

• help 名 幫助
• -ful 形 表「有……傾向的；有……性質的」

If you don't bother to read the manual, you'll find it's very **helpful**.

如果你願意讀一讀操作手冊，會發現它非常有幫助。

---

38 manual
[ˈmænjʊəl]

名 手冊；簡介

Didn't the box contain a user's **manual**?

盒子裡沒附使用手冊嗎？

同義詞 名 guidebook = handbook 操作手冊

---

39 method
[ˈmɛθəd]

名 方法

The manual says "break down the machine" but doesn't give us any **method** for doing that!

說明書只說「將機器拆解」，但沒告訴我們該怎麼做！

---

40 structure
[ˈstrʌktʃɚ]

名 結構；構造；建築物

• struct 堆疊；建造
• -ure 名 表「結果」

There's an office shelving **structure** in the instructions diagram that I can't identify.

說明圖示說辦公室有一個收納構造，但我無法辨認。

學後小試 A | **Multiple Choice Questions**
請選擇合適的單字填入空格

_____ ① Didn't the new printer come with a(n) _____?

(A) structure   (B) contractor
(C) alternative   (D) manual

_____ ② I _____ all the instructions to set it up, but the machine still doesn't work.

(A) repaired   (B) acquainted
(C) followed   (D) borrowed

_____ ③ I can't fix this faucet. We have to call the _____ crew.

(A) maintenance   (B) instruction
(C) device   (D) supply

_____ ④ My dad's smartphone can't be fixed. Do you know where I should _____ of it?

(A) rent   (B) dispose
(C) reserve   (D) renovate

_____ ⑤ Our accounting _____ is really slow and out-of-date. We should update it.

(A) resource   (B) extension
(C) property   (D) software

正確答案請參考 411 頁

B Match

請在空格填入合適的單字，動詞需依時態變化，名詞需填入正確之單複數。

| as needed | insufficient | share | belong | procedure | detailed |

1 The _____ instructions made it very easy to set up the program.

2 Everyone on this floor _____ the same kitchen.

3 That laptop _____ to John.

4 With _____ time to prepare, the training is bound to be a failure.

5 Here is the _____ for unlocking the door.

6 We meet not every week, but only _____.

C Listening Practice

請聆聽音檔，將單字填入空格 🎧 060

1 Please handle the equipment _____, as it's very fragile.

2 I'll tell you how to use the program _____ I figure it out myself!

3 Is the sales team going to _____ the conference room all day?

4 Please put my new pencils in the _____ with the rest of them.

5 Please wear safety goggles in the workroom _____.

6 Anna gave me very _____ feedback on my report.

正確答案請參考 411 頁

Unit 07

Documentation & Administration

文書與行政

辦公室情境另外一大必須留意的重點是文書作業（documentation）：

1. 日常作業會使用到的名詞，如檔案（document）、附件（attachment）等。
2. 透過情境一起記誦這些與名詞互相搭配的動詞，如表格要填寫（fill in）、資料需要彙整（compile），使用起來才能更加融會貫通。
3. 留心單字詞性變化，如 file 做名詞是文件，做動詞卻是歸檔。

學前暖身 請閱讀英文定義，並將正確單字與之配對

efficient	revise	draft	duplicate	author

1 _____ : to change something written in order to improve it

2 _____ : the person who writes a document

3 _____ : performing a task in the least wasteful way possible

4 _____ : to write the first version of a document

5 _____ : to make an exact copy of something

Form 表格形式

01 complete
[kəm`plit]

動 完成

- com- 完全；徹底
- plete 充滿

Several employees have complained that even though they **completed** the customer's data entry, the system didn't save it.

幾位員工抱怨他們輸入完客戶的資料，系統卻沒有存檔。

相似詞	動 finish 完成；結束
	動 perfect 完成；使完美
	片 carry out 貫徹；執行；完成

---

02 fill
[fɪl]

動 填滿；填寫

The clients **filled** the remaining space with their e-mail addresses.

客戶在剩下空白的地方填寫他們的電子郵件信箱。

應用	fill N1 with N2 用N2注滿N1

---

03 item
[`aɪtəm]

名 項目

Data entry forms should not have more than 10 **items**.

資料輸入表格不該填寫超過十筆資料。

---

04 signature
[`sɪɡnətʃɚ]

名 簽名

- sign 記號
- -ate 動 表「成為」
- -ure 名 表「動作；狀態；結果」

Every form must have space for three **signatures**.

每個表格應該要有容得下三個簽名的空位。

---

05 template
[`tɛmplɪt]

名 範本

Be sure to use the approved **template** whenever creating new expense reports.

做新的開支報告時，請記得一定要用經過核可的範本。

---

062 **06** 加澳 **07** 美加 **08** 英澳 **09** 澳美 **10** 英美

---

06 **approve**

[ə`pruv]

動 贊成；同意；批准

• ap- 向
• prove 動 證明；表明

Before your loan **application** can be approved, you need to provide proof of your assets.

貸款申請核准之前，你必須先提供資產證明。

應用	① approve of 批准；贊同
	② be approved for Sth. 獲得……的許可

---

07 **deadline**

[`dɛd,laɪn]

名 截止期限；截稿時間

• dead 死的
• line 界線

The **deadline** is January 20, so make sure you finish the report no later than the 19th.

截止日期是1月20日，所以請務必在19日以前完成報告。

---

08 **reject**

[rɪ`dʒɛkt]

動 拒絕；駁回

• re- 回；相反
• ject 投擲

The most common reason for **rejecting** an application is completing the paperwork incorrectly.

書面文件填寫不正確是申請被駁回最常見的原因。

---

09 **rush**

[rʌʃ]

動 催趕；匆忙行事

There is no way to **rush** the process without sacrificing quality.

要加速處理過程而不犧牲品質是不可能的。

應用	名 rush 匆忙；趕時間
	→ in a rush = in a hurry 急忙地

---

10 **submit**

[səb`mɪt]

動 送出；繳交

• sub- 下
• mit 送

Fifteen candidates **submitted** applications for the assistant manager position.

有15位求職者來應徵副理的職缺。

Documentation 文書

11 **appendix**
[ə`pɛndɪks]

名 附錄

• append 動 附加
• -ix 名

A user's manual without an **appendix** is not user-friendly.
使用説明手冊沒有附錄真的很不方便。

---

12 **article**
[`ɑrtɪkl]

名 文章

Stevenson's **article** on corporate responsibility has been reprinted in the local newspaper.
本地報紙轉刊了史帝文生那篇有關企業責任的文章。

---

13 **author**
[`ɔθɚ]

名 作者；作家

Most word processors automatically list the **author** of a document as the owner of the computer.
很多文書處理軟體會自動把電腦系統管理員列為檔案的作者。

---

14 **compile**
[kəm`paɪl]

動 匯編；編纂；收集（資料等）

• com- 一起
• pile 壓緊；壓實

Please **compile** a list of inactive customers with their home addresses and phone numbers.
請把非常客的地址和電話編成一張清單。

---

15 **divide**
[də`vaɪd]

動 分；分開

Divide the page into three columns to make it easier to read.
請把這一頁分成三欄，這樣比較方便閱讀。

應用	divide Sth. into = separate/split Sth. into 把……劃分成

92

16 document
[ˋdɑkjəmənt]

名 公文；文件

Bring me any **documents** containing information related to the merger project.
請幫我拿所有合併案的相關文件。

---

17 fold
[fold]

動 摺疊

Do not **fold** the answer sheet; this may make it impossible for the scanner to read it correctly.
請不要把答案紙摺起來，這樣掃描器會沒辦法讀取。

> 應用
> 1 fold something in half 將某物對折
> 2 fold one's arms 交叉雙臂
> 動 unfold = unveil = reveal 攤開；揭露

---

18 manuscript
[ˋmænjəˌskrɪpt]

名 手稿；原稿

- manu- 手
- script 抄；寫

The **manuscript** of her latest novel needs a lot of editing.
她最新的小說原稿還需要大量編修。

---

19 translation
[trænsˋleʃən]

名 翻譯；譯文

- translate 動 翻譯
- -ion 名 表「行為；行為的結果」

The president is furious because the **translation** of the text from Arabic turned out to be almost unreadable.
總統勃然大怒，因為阿拉伯語的譯文根本讀不通。

> 應用 translate A into B 將 A 翻譯成 B

File 檔案／卷宗／歸檔

20 access

[ˋæksɛs]

名 進入的權利；接近的機
會；進入；使用

Anyone wanting **access** to these files will
need to get the password from one of the
managers.

想要使用這些檔案的人需要向經理要密碼。

> 應用　obtain/gain/get/have + the access + to + N.
> 取得通往／使用……的途徑

21 always

[ˋɔlwez]

副 總是；一直

You should **always** sort sales reports
alphabetically by the customer's last name.

你應該每次都按客戶的姓氏字母順序整理銷售報告。

22 discard

[dɪsˋkɑrd]

動 摒棄；丟棄

• dis- 除去；分離
• card 名 紙牌

The system will **discard** any files not
matching the approved formats.

系統會自動淘汰不符合核可格式的檔案。

23 duplicate

[ˋdjupləket]

動 複製；拷貝；複印

• du- 雙；二
• plic- 折
• -ate 動 表「成為」

Employees must **duplicate** their daily reports
and save a copy on the company's server.

所有員工必須複製他們每天的報告，並在公司的伺服器
上備份。

24 file

[faɪl]

動 歸檔

File all reports according to their creation
date.

請依照建立日期將所有報告歸檔。

25 **search**
[sɝtʃ]

動 尋找

Data files can be **searched** by date, author, or department.

資料檔可以用日期、作者或部門來搜尋。

| 相似詞 | 片 search for = look for 搜尋 |
| | 動 seek 尋找；搜尋 |

Paperwork 文書作業

26 **administrative**
[ədˋmɪnəˏstretɪv]

形 管理的；行政的

• ad- 至；向
• minister 動 協助；服務
• -ate 動 表「使成為」
• -ive 形 表「與……有關的；具有……性質的」

Currently, we produce too much **administrative** paperwork comprising managers' daily reports.

最近我們做了太多行政的文書工作，包含經理每日的報告。

27 **analyze**
[ˋænlˏaɪz]

動 分析

You need to **analyze** the information before deciding which results to include in your report.

你需要先分析資料，再決定哪些結果要放進報告。

應用	analyze + data/statistics/results
	分析數據／統計資料／結果
	名 analysis 分析

28 **clerical**
[ˋklɛrɪkl]

形 辦事員的；文書工作的

Much of the **clerical** staff, including half the secretaries and all the receptionists, are temporary workers.

大部分辦事員同仁，包含半數的秘書和所有接待員都是臨時工。

29 draft

[dræft]

動 起草

I need you to **draft** the proposal by next Friday.

下週五前我需要你為那個提案擬個草稿。

30 finalize

[ˈfaɪnḷˌaɪz]

動 完成

· final 形 最終的
· -ize 動 表「使；做該動作」

Will your staff be able to **finalize** the report today? It's due tomorrow.

你的員工今天能不能完成報告？明天就是截止日了。

31 paperwork

[ˈpepɚˌwɝk]

名 日常文書工作；書面作業

· paper 名 紙張
· work 名 工作

You need to find some way to handle your **paperwork** more efficiently.

你要找個更有效率的方法來處理你的文書工作。

32 revise

[rɪˈvaɪz]

動 修訂；校訂

· re- 再
· vise 看

Revise this report immediately and get rid of all those typing mistakes.

立刻修改這份報告，並訂正所有錯字。

相似詞	動 alter 改變；修改
	動 modify 修改；緩和；修飾
	片 make over 修正；修飾

96

33 **tight**

[taɪt]

形 緊的

The deadline is too **tight**. Can you extend it by a few days?

截止日期太趕了，能不能延後幾天？

---

34 **timely**

['taɪmlɪ]

形 及時的

Timely completion of accounting reports helps ensure the smooth financial operations of our business.

及時完成會計報告可以確保公司財務運作順利。

Mail & E-mail & Fax & Phone 書信與電話傳真

35 **attachment**

[ə'tætʃmənt]

名 附件

• attach 動 附加
• -ment 名 表「產物」

Our server rejects any e-mail with an **attachment** of 4MB or more.

我們的伺服器會擋掉附件超過4MB的信件。

> 動 attach 附上；連結
> 應用 → attach A to B 將A附在B（信件）之後
> 形 attached = enclosed 附加（在信件內）的

---

36 **attentive**

[ə'tɛntɪv]

形 有禮貌的；全神貫注的

• attent 留意
• -ive 形 表「傾向於……的」

An **attentive** tone would guarantee people will read the entire message.

誠摯的語調保證能讓大家讀完整段訊息。

> 名 attentiveness = attention 專注
> 應用 pay attention to + N. = be attentive to + N.
> 專注於……

37 **concerning**

[kən`sɝnɪŋ]

介 關於

- con- 一起；共同
- cern 篩選
- -ing 表「與……有關的東西」

Find me that e-mail **concerning** the customer's complaint about the headrests.

請幫我找出那封客訴頭枕的電子郵件。

應用 concerning/regarding/about + N./V-ing = in regard to + N./V-ing 有關於……

38 **enclosed**

[ɪn`klozd]

形 隨函檢附的

- en- 使
- close 關閉
- -ed 形

The **enclosed** sketches should give you some idea regarding the design we are looking for.

隨函附上的草圖應該可以讓您稍微了解我們想要的設計。

39 **reschedule**

[ri`skɛdʒʊl]

動 改約

- re- 再
- schedule 動 安排

They sent a fax asking us to **reschedule** the meeting, as Monday no longer works for them.

因為週一不太方便，所以他們傳真問我們能不能改約其他時間開會。

40 **efficient**

[ɪ`fɪʃənt]

形 效率高的；有效的；有能力的

Personal calls are not an **efficient** use of office phones.

用公司電話打私人電話不是一件有效益的事。

相似詞
- 名 efficiency 效率
- 形 effective 有效果／成效的
- 名 effect 影響
- 動 affect 影響

A | Multiple Choice Questions

學後小試

請選擇合適的單字填入空格

_____ 1 You need to _____ the report by Monday at the latest.

(A) fold
(B) reschedule
(C) divide
(D) complete

_____ 2 Use one of the saved _____; don't try to create a new format on your own.

(A) templates
(B) signatures
(C) authors
(D) translation

_____ 3 Based on the number of errors in this report, I'd say they _____ it.

(A) approved
(B) analyzed
(C) rushed
(D) filled

_____ 4 Hard copies of reports must be _____ five years after their completion date.

(A) drafted
(B) searched
(C) submitted
(D) discarded

_____ 5 We're hoping the computerized reports will reduce the _____.

(A) item
(B) paperwork
(C) attachment
(D) article

正確答案請參考 411 頁

B | Match

請在空格填入合適的單字，動詞需依時態變化，名詞需填入正確之單複數。

| timely | reject | administrative | deadline | appendix | enclosed |

1. The sick leave reports are part of the _____ paperwork.

2. The IT people are not finishing their reports in a _____ manner.

3. You will find pictures of the site _____ with the terms of the lease.

4. The system will _____ any document that doesn't have a date stamp.

5. You didn't submit the application before the _____, so you're not eligible for consideration.

6. There's an _____ at the back in case you need to look up a machine part.

C | Listening Practice

請聆聽音檔，將單字填入空格 070

1. Henderson will _____ a list of employees and their assigned office equipment.

2. You need to be _____ to details, because you're making too many mistakes.

3. Fortunately, she'd printed a copy of the _____ before the computer crashed.

4. Using the standard forms will ensure the most _____ use of the database system.

5. Remember to _____ double check your data before entering it into the computer.

6. Timecards are _____ according to date and department.

正確答案請參考 411 頁

Unit 08

Announcement

公告訊息

公告的情境經常出現在多益的聽力測驗中：

① 留意 firstly, secondly 等時間副詞以抓住重點。

② 掌握動詞也對於了解內容有非常大的幫助，例如強調（emphasize）、解釋（explain）、告知（notify/inform）後面往往接著的是重要資訊；總結（summarize）也有助於再次確認對題目的了解是否有誤。

學前暖身 請閱讀英文定義，並將正確單字與之配對

circulate	overview	temporary	circumstances	mandatory

① _____ : a general summary or review of something

② _____ : a situation or set of conditions

③ _____ : to distribute something

④ _____ : required by a law or rule; not allowed to be skipped

⑤ _____ : short-term; not permanent

Announcement 公告

01 **address**
[ə`drɛs]

動 對……講話;
向……發表演說

She's going to **address** the department this afternoon and tell us about the restructuring plan.

今天下午她要跟整個部門講點話,告訴大家改組的計劃。

| 應用 | ① address = deal with 處理 |
| | ② address Sb. as + 頭銜 稱呼……為…… |

---

02 **announce**
[ə`naʊns]

動 宣布;聲稱

• an- 對;向
• nounce 說;講述;報告

I think they're going to **announce** the next round of layoffs any day now.

我覺得他們隨時都會宣布下一批裁員的事。

| 應用 | make an announcement 發佈通知 |

---

03 **in advance**
[əd`væns]

片 預先;事先;提前

I really hope they will let us know the date of the performance reviews **in advance**.

我真希望他們提前讓我們知道哪一天要打考績。

| 同義詞 | beforehand = prior to + N. 預先;提前 |

---

04 **post**
[post]

動 公告;張貼(資訊)

They're going to **post** information about the human resources policy changes to the company website tomorrow.

他們明天要在公司網站上公布修改後的人事規定。

05 **emphasize**

[ˋɛmfəˌsaɪz]

動 強調；著重；
使顯得突出

・emphasis 名 強調
・-ize 動 表「使成為」

I really want to **emphasize** the need for teamwork in my presentation.

我真的很想在我的報告中強調團隊合作的必要性。

---

06 **overview**

[ˋovɚˌvju]

名 概述；概括

・over- 在上面
・view 名 視野；觀看

I plan to give an **overview** first, and then go into detail.

我打算要先概述一下，然後再說明細節。

---

07 **summarize**

[ˋsʌməˌraɪz]

動 作總結；概述；概括

・summary 名 總結
・-ize 動 表「做該動作」

We don't have time for a long explanation of the topic, so I'll just **summarize** it.

我們沒有很多時間可以解釋，因此我只會做個概述。

應用 | 名 summary 摘要
→ in summary = to be short = in short
= in brief 簡要來說

Attachment/Reference 附件／參照

08 **about**

[əˋbaʊt]

介 關於；附近

I've got to send my boss an e-mail **about** the changes that the client wants to make.

我一定要寄信給老闆，告訴他客戶想要改什麼。

09 detail
[`ditel]

名 細節

For more **details**, please contact your HR representative.

欲知詳情，請與你的人資專員聯絡。

---

10 explain
[ɪk`splen]

動 解釋

• ex- 向外
• plain 平面

The brochure I've given you should **explain** everything.

我給你的小手冊應該解釋了所有事。

---

11 further
[`fɝðɚ]

形 進一步的

副 再者

In the meeting, he only gave an outline of the changes. **Further** information will be coming soon, he said.

會議中，他只大概說一下會有哪些改變，進一步的資訊很快就會發布。

Message 訊息

12 circulate
[`sɝkjə,let]

動 流傳；流通

• circul 圓；循環
• -ate 動 表「使成為」

They really need to **circulate** information about policy changes more efficiently.

他們需要更有效的方法傳達更改規定的消息。

---

13 forward
[`fɔrwɚd]

動 轉交；轉寄

• fore 前面
• -ward 形 副 表「向……的；向……地」

Please **forward** any message she sends you about the project to me.

她寄給你所有跟那個案子有關的信，請都轉寄給我。

---

14 respond

[rɪ`spɑnd]

動 回應；回覆

・re- 往回
・spond 言語；許諾

I've got 50 unread e-mails in my inbox and no time to **respond** to them!

我的收件匣裡有五十封未讀信件，但我沒時間一一回覆。

應用　S. + respond + to N. by V-ing
= S. + V. + in response + to N.
對⋯⋯做出回應

---

15 inform

[ɪn`fɔrm]

動 通知；告知；告發

・in- 形成
・form 形狀

This e-mail is intended to **inform** you about the coming changes to the company dress code.

這封信是要通知您，公司的服裝規定將要改變了。

應用　inform Sb. + { that 子句　告知某人⋯⋯
of/about + N.

---

16 mention

[`mɛnʃən]

動 提及；說起

・ment 心；精神
・-ion 名

I thought it was odd that the memo didn't **mention** the new CEO.

我覺得備忘錄沒提到新的執行長很奇怪。

應用　Don't mention it.
① 【回覆感謝】不客氣
② 【回覆敏感話題】別提了

---

17 reminder

[rɪ`maɪndɚ]

名 提醒；催函

・re- 再
・mind 動 注意；記住要
・-er 名 表「人；物」

Could you please send me a **reminder** the day before the meeting? I'm afraid I'll forget about it.

你可以在開會前一天發信提醒我嗎？我怕我會忘記。

18 state
[stet]

動 陳述

The memo was comforting, but it never actually **stated** that there wouldn't be any layoffs.

這張便條安慰人心，但其實它沒提到不裁員的事。

Notice 通知

19 attention
[əˋtɛnʃən]

名 注意；關注

· attent 留意的
· -ion 名 表「行為；狀態」

Well, the title stating "RAISES COMING" certainly got my **attention**.

這個「即將調薪」的標題的確引起我的注意。

應用	1 catch/draw/get/attract + one's attention 得到某人的注意 2 pay attention to + N. 注意……

---

20 notify
[ˋnotə͵faɪ]

動 通知；告知

· not 知道
· -ify 動 表「使」

If you're planning to take time off, please **notify** your supervisor.

如果你打算要休假，請通知你的主管。

---

21 regard
[rɪˋgɑrd]

動 關心；關注

· re- 加強語氣
· gard 注視

Don't pay any **regard** to the rumors about the merger.

請別把公司合併的傳聞放在心上。

---

22 short notice
片 臨時通知

I'm so sorry to assign you this report on such **short notice**. Are you sure you can do it in time?

抱歉臨時指派你這份報告，你確定能及時完成嗎？

應用	1 on short notice 臨時通知的狀況下 2 give (one's) notice 請辭

23

notice
['notɪs]

名 注意；通知

Have you seen the **notice** in the hall about the new rules for using the kitchen?

你看到大廳裡關於廚房使用新規定的通知了嗎？

24

beforehand
[bɪ'for,hænd]

副 預先；提前地；超前地

- before 介 在……之前
- hand 名 手

My boss wants me to clear my presentation with him **beforehand**.

老闆希望我提前把簡報變得有條有理。

25

pertinent
['pɝtnənt]

形 恰當的；相關的

Please include only **pertinent** information in your trip report.

你的出差報告裡面只要包含相關資訊即可。

Regulation 規範

26

activate
['æktə,vet]

動 開始運作；使活動起來

- active 形 活躍的
- -ate 動 表「使成為」

The new hiring policy will be **activated** next year.

明年就要執行新的聘僱規定了。

27

enact
[ɪn'ækt]

動 實行（法律）

- en- 使……成為
- act 動 起作用

The new rules that the government has **enacted** to limit foreign labor will really affect us.

政府新實施的限制外籍勞工的法規，對我們的影響真的很大。

28 obligate
['ɑblə,get]

動 使……有義務

• ob- 處於
• ligate 捆綁

You are **obligated** to report any instance of harassment in the office.
你們有通報職場性騷擾的義務。

應用
be obligated/obliged + to V.
= Sb. have the obligation + to V.
有義務去做……

---

29 since
[sɪns]

連 介 自……以來

I've had no social life **since** they banned office parties!
自從他們禁止在辦公室聚會，我都沒有社交生活了。

應用
1 ever since 從……以來
2 since then 從那時以來

---

30 temporary
['tɛmpə,rɛrɪ]

形 暫時的
名 臨時工

They've initiated a **temporary** hiring freeze while they assess the budget.
他們評估預算的時候，暫時停止人才招募。

---

31 command
[kə'mænd]

動 命令；指揮；控制

• com- 完全
• mand 命令

My boss can **command** me to stay late and there's nothing I can do about it.
我老闆可以命令我留到很晚，而我完全沒辦法拒絕。

應用
S1 + command + (that) S2 + (should) + V.
= S1 command + S2 + to V.
S1命令S2去做……

相似詞
動 require 命令；需要
動 request 命令；請求

32 frequently

['frikwəntlɪ]

副 頻繁地;屢次地

· frequ 經常
· -ent 形
· -ly 副

We are **frequently** asked about our new promotion policy, so we've put together a factsheet about it for all employees.

我們經常被問及新的促銷規定,因此我們為所有員工整理了一張表。

---

33 mandatory

['mændə,torɪ]

形 強制的;必須履行的

· mandate 動 命令
· -ory 形 表「具有......性質的」

Attendance at the final meeting is **mandatory**.

最後一次會議是強制參加的。

Warning 警告

34 affect

[ə'fɛkt]

動 影響;發生作用

· af- 向
· fect 做

This warning will not **affect** your chances of getting a promotion, but any future incidents could.

這次警告不會影響你的升遷機會,但是下次再犯就會了。

---

35 avoid

[ə'vɔɪd]

動 避開;避免

In the future, please **avoid** conducting lengthy discussions of your personal life at business events.

以後請避免在商業場合高談闊論你的私人生活。

> 應用　avoid + V-ing/O. 避免......

---

36 aware

[ə'wɛr]

形 知道的;察覺的

Now that you're **aware** of our dress code, we hope you'll abide by it.

現在你知道我們的服裝規定了,希望你遵守它。

> 應用　be aware + of N. / that 子句　了解/知道......

37 circumstances
['sɝkəm‚stænsɪs]

名 境況;境遇

· circum- 周圍
· stance 名 站

Under no **circumstances** are you to reveal confidential project information to individuals outside of the company.

無論如何都不能把企劃案的機密資訊告訴公司以外的人。

應用	Under no circumstances By no means On no account In no way	⎫ ⎬ + 倒裝句 ⎭

無論如何某人絕不會……

---

38 concern
[kən'sɝn]

名 疑慮;擔心的事

· con- 一起;共同
· cern 篩選

He hasn't done anything wrong yet, but his attitude is a matter of **concern** to his team leader.

他雖然沒出過包,但他的組長很在乎他的態度。

---

39 nearly
['nɪrlɪ]

副 幾乎;差不多

· near 形 近的
· -ly 副

We've had **nearly** 100 instances of sexual harassments since reporting began.

自從開放檢舉,我們收到一百件左右的性騷擾個案。

---

40 occur
[ə'kɝ]

動 發生

In my line of work, crises **occur** every day.

做我這一行,每一天都會發生危機。

學後小試 A Multiple Choice Questions

請選擇合適的單字填入空格

_____ 1 The new CEO is going to _____ the entire staff on Monday.

- (A) respond
- (B) forward
- (C) state
- (D) address

_____ 2 Please _____ me next time you're going to be late.

- (A) occur
- (B) notify
- (C) affect
- (D) command

_____ 3 I wish you had told me about the changes _____, so I could have been prepared in the meeting.

- (A) frequently
- (B) nearly
- (C) since
- (D) beforehand

_____ 4 I am not _____ to tell you why I went to the doctor yesterday.

- (A) regarded
- (B) obligated
- (C) enacted
- (D) activated

_____ 5 My supervisor and I had an argument, so I'm trying to _____ her for a little while.

- (A) avoid
- (B) announce
- (C) post
- (D) inform

正確答案請參考 412 頁

B Match

請在空格填入合適的單字，動詞需依時態變化，名詞需填入正確之單複數。

| aware | attention | in advance | details | mention | reminder |

1. I wasn't paying _____ in the meeting, and now I don't know what I've been assigned.

2. I wasn't _____ that we had an overtime policy.

3. Could you please send me a _____ about the presentation tomorrow so I don't forget?

4. If you want a customized design, you have to ask for it _____.

5. I need to see more _____ about the proposal before I can decide on it.

6. I'm going to _____ Sally's important idea to my boss the next time I see him.

C Listening Practice

請聆聽音檔，將單字填入空格 080

1. I don't see how my outfit is _____ to this discussion.

2. What was that announcement _____?

3. We have some _____ about your management style.

4. I'm sorry to call you in on such _____, but it's an emergency.

5. I can't make it to the meeting—could you _____ it for me later?

6. The manager said organizational changes would be coming, but she hasn't given us any _____ information.

正確答案請參考 412 頁

Unit 09

Finance & Accounting

財務與會計

財務會計的情境，在不管多益聽力或是閱讀測驗中都經常會出現：

① 搞清楚名詞的用法與差異，如個人的收入是income，公司企業的收入是revenue。

② 建議使用流程式記憶法加強印象和理解，例如：一個人去帳戶（account）存錢（deposit/save），為了繳帳單（bill）所以必須領錢（withdraw），因為如果不繳會拖欠（owe）。

學前暖身 請閱讀英文定義，並將正確單字與之配對

accountant	tax	appraisal	deduct	revenue

1 _____: an amount of money paid to the government each year

2 _____: to subtract from a total

3 _____: income earned; profit

4 _____: a person specializing in the counting of assets and liabilities

5 _____: the act of calculating the value of something

Accounting 會計

01 accountant

[ə'kaʊntənt]

名 會計師；會計人員

• account 動 報帳
• -ant 名 表「人」

According to the new rules, we have to contract an outside **accountant** to double check our cash statements.

根據新規定，我們必須聘請外面的會計師來確認現金流量表。

---

02 amount

[ə'maʊnt]

名 數量；總計

The total **amount** of expenditures is listed at the bottom of the second page.

總支出列在第二頁最下面。

應用	1 the amount of + 不可數名詞（+ 單數 V.） ……的數量（是……） 2 a huge/large/amount of + 不可數名詞 大量的…… 3 a small/tiny amount of + 不可數名詞 少量的……

---

03 appraisal

[ə'preɪzl]

名 評價；估價

• apprais(e) 動 評價；估量
• -al 名

Before we purchase the new building, we need an **appraisal** by a real estate agent.

在我們買這棟新建物之前，需要房屋仲介先來估價。

---

04 audit

['ɔdɪt]

動 審計；查帳

Every year, the accounting firm of Brooker and Stans do an **audit** of our balance sheet before tax time.

每年報稅前，布魯克史丹會計公司都會審核我們的損益表。

---

05 budget

['bʌdʒɪt]

图 預算;經費

The finance department said we need to seriously reduce our **budget** for executive cars.

財務部門說,我們必須大幅減少主管用車的預算。

應用
1 on a (tight) budget 拮据地;預算吃緊
2 on/within budget 在預算以內
3 over budget 超出預算

06 collateral

[kə'lætərəl]

图 擔保;抵押

The fundamental rule of getting a loan is having enough **collateral** to reduce the bank's risk.

貸款的基本原則是有足夠的抵押品來降低銀行的風險。

07 discretionary

[dɪ'skreʃənəri]

形 自行決定的;自主的

• discretion 图 決定權
• -ary 形

Discretionary spending is up, which means managers need to have more control over their departments.

可自由支配的開支增加了,這意味管理者需要加以控管自己的部門。

08 figure

['fɪgjɚ]

图 數字

Any **figure** in red is a sign of going over budget.

任何紅色的數字都代表超出預算。

應用 unemployment/sales/trade + figures
失業/銷售/貿易量

09 income

['ɪn,kʌm]

图 收入

All sources of **income** must be reported on the revenue sheet.

各項收入來源都必須登記在收益表中。

10 revenue
[ˈrɛvəˌnju]

名 收入；收益

Our **revenue** from rental properties is large enough to cover this quarter's investment in marketing.

我們出租物業的收入足以支付本季的市場投資。

應用	tax revenue 政府稅收
相似詞	名 income = earnings 收入
	名 profits 收入；獲利

---

11 surplus
[ˈsɝpləs]

名 資金餘額；盈餘；結餘

• sur- 超過
• plus 更多的

This year, the HR department managed to save enough on its expenses to generate a **surplus**.

今年人資部門成功降低支出，產生了盈餘。

---

12 total
[ˈtot!]

形 總共的

The **total** cost of doing business includes both variable and fixed expenses.

經營事業的總成本包括了變動支出與固定支出。

應用	1 in total 總計
	2 subtotal 小計
	3 grand total 總計

Banking 銀行

13 account
[əˈkaunt]

名 (銀行) 帳戶

You should open a savings **account** if you want to earn more interest on your money.

如果你想要賺更多利息的話，你應該開一個存款帳戶。

文化補充	在西方國家銀行開戶和在臺灣不太一樣，西方國家的銀行有兩種帳戶：支票帳戶（a checking account）和存款帳戶（a savings account）。支票帳戶就像流動現金一樣，經常使用，而存款帳戶則是用來儲蓄管理。

14 accrue
[ə`kru]

動 積累；(逐漸) 增加，
增多

Funds left in an account will continue to **accrue** interest as long as they are not withdrawn.

只要不提領，帳戶裡剩餘的資金就會繼續生息。

---

15 balance
[`bæləns]

名 平衡；均衡；結餘

Your available **balance** does not include deposits made on the previous day.

您的帳戶目前的可用餘額未含幾天前的存款。

應用
1 bank balance 銀行結存
2 balance sheet 資產負債表

---

16 convert
[kən`vɝt]

動 轉變；變換

• con- 共同；一起
• vert 轉

What's the quickest way to **convert** gold certificates into stocks?

什麼是將黃金憑證轉成股票最快的方式？

應用　convert A to/into B 將A轉換成B

---

17 deposit
[dɪ`pɑzɪt]

動 存錢

• de- 向下
• posit 放

You need only your bank card to **deposit** funds into your account.

要存款到你的帳戶，你只需要你的銀行卡。

---

18 interest
[`ɪntrəst]

名 利息

The **interest** that your account has earned is reported on your monthly bank statement.

您帳戶內的利息會記錄在銀行每個月的帳單裡。

應用
1 charge interest on sth. 收取利息
2 repay with interest 連同利息償還

19 **loan**
[lon]

名 借出;貸款

Our bank offers a variety of **loans** for both individuals and businesses.

本銀行提供多種個人與企業貸款的方案。

應用	
	① take out a loan 借貸
	② repay / pay off / pay back a loan 償還貸款
	③ bank loan 銀行貸款
	④ home loan = mortgage 房貸

---

20 **remit**
[rɪ`mɪt]

動 匯款;匯寄

Payments **remitted** by check require an additional two days to clear.

用支票付款需要多兩天才能結清。

---

21 **save**
[sev]

動 儲蓄

A term deposit account is one of the surest ways to **save** money over the long term.

定期存款帳戶是最能確保長期儲蓄的方法之一。

---

22 **transaction**
[træn`zækʃən]

名 交易;業務

• transact 動 交易
• -ion 名 表「行為;結果;狀態」

All your account **transactions** can be checked online, as long as you have your password.

只要有密碼,您帳戶內所有的交易都可以透過網路查詢。

---

23 **withdrawal**
[wɪð`drɔəl]

名 提款

• with 向後
• draw 拖;拉
• -al 名

Withdrawals of more than $500 in one day require a signature and an ID.

若要在一天當中提款超過五百美金,就需要簽名與出示證件。

Bill 帳單

24

bill

[bɪl]

名 帳單

Many people now make arrangements with their banks to have their monthly **bills** withdrawn automatically from their accounts.

現在很多人都以每個月從銀行帳戶自動扣款的方式付帳。

> **應用** pay the bill 付帳單

25

delinquent

[dɪˋlɪŋkwənt]

形 到期未付的;拖欠的

• de- 完全
• linqu 離開
• -ent 形

Your job is to contact **delinquent** accounts and arrange payment.

你的工作就是聯絡欠款的客戶,並安排他們付款。

26

outstanding

[ˋaʊtˋstændɪŋ]

名 未支付的;未解決的;
未完成的

• out- 超過
• stand 站
• -ing 形 表「……的」

We've deducted your previous payment, so the amount shown is your total **outstanding** debt.

我們已經扣除你先前的付款,因此這裡顯示的金額是你所有未支付的債務。

27

overdue

[ˋovəˋdju]

形 過期的

• over- 超過
• due 形 到期的

Overdue payments are subject to a 5% administrative fee.

逾期付款要酌收5%的手續費。

28 owe

[o]

動 欠債

The GIM insurance group currently **owes** $100,000 in taxes, which they must pay by the end of the month.

GIM保險集團必須在月底前,繳清目前積欠的十萬美金的稅。

> 應用
> 1 owe Sth. to Sb. 欠某人錢;將……歸功某人
> 2 I owe you one. 我欠你一個人情。

---

29 payable

[ˈpeɪəbl]

形 應支付的;可支付的

• pay 動 付款
• -able 形 表「可……的」

The **payable** balance will vary depending on which day of the month the bill is generated.

隨著每月帳單列印日期變動,應付的金額也會變動。

---

30 bounce

[baʊns]

動 (因存款不足) 拒付;(支票) 退回

Your check will be **bounced** if you have insufficient funds to cover the promised amount.

當你的錢不夠支付所開出的金額,你的支票會被退。

Payment Details 付款明細

31 cash

[kæʃ]

名 現金

Clients can pay either by **cash** or by electronic payment, but we do not accept checks.

客戶可以付現或線上付款,但我們不接受支票。

> 應用
> 1 pay in cash 以現金支付
> 2 pay by credit card 用信用卡付款

088 **32** 美加 **33** 英加 **34** 美英 **35** 澳加

unit

09

Finance & Accounting

財務與會計

32 **commission**

[kə`mɪʃən]

名 報酬；佣金

· com- 共同；完全
· mission 名 任務

We charged a 2% **commission** fee because the payment was made in foreign currency.

我們會收取2%手續費，因為這筆錢是以外幣付款。

---

33 **payment**

[`pemənt]

名 付款

· pay 動 付款
· -ment 名 表「行為；結果；狀態」

According to our records, all of their **payments** have cleared except for the most recent one.

根據我們的紀錄，除了最近一筆費用之外，他們所有的款項都結清了。

---

34 **rate**

[ret]

名 利率

The rate on 10-year bonds is currently 5%, but it is expected to **rise** next year.

目前十年期債券利率為5%，但預計明年會升高。

> **應用**
> [1] birth/unemployment/crime/interest + rate
> 出生／失業／犯罪／利率
> [2] at the rate of . . . 以……的比率

---

35 **statement**

[`stetmənt]

名 (銀行) 對帳單

· state 動 陳述
· -ment 名 表「行為；結果；狀態」

Your monthly **statement** details all payments from your account, plus interest earned on your account.

您每月的對帳單詳細列出帳戶內所有的支出，以及所獲得的利息。

121

36 **sum**
[sʌm]

名 總數;總額

The total **sum** of payments is listed on the line above total deductions.

付款總額列在總扣除額的上一行。

> 應用　in sum = to sum up = in conclusion 總而言之

37 **wire**
[waɪr]

動 轉帳

Deposits **wired** to your account will arrive sooner, but are subject to a small fee.

您會更快收到轉帳給您的款項,但會被酌收小額手續費。

Tax 稅務

38 **deduct**
[dɪ'dʌkt]

動 扣款

The current tax rules state you can **deduct** $1000 for each child in your household.

現在的稅制規定,家中有孩子的人,每個孩子可抵稅一千美元。

39 **return**
[rɪ't3ʳn]

動 退回;歸還

• re- 回
• turn 動 旋轉

Any taxes paid in excess of what you owe will be **returned** to you after May 1.

多繳的稅款會在五月一日後退還。

40 **tax**
[tæks]

名 稅

The government is considering an 8% increase on property **taxes**.

政府正考慮財產稅要調漲8%。

學後小試 A **Multiple Choice Questions**
請選擇合適的單字填入空格

_____ 1 The _____ of your payments is too much, so we will return the extra to you.

(A) budget   (B) cash
(C) sum   (D) income

_____ 2 The government will perform an _____ next year, so let's make sure the numbers are clear.

(A) account   (B) audit
(C) amount   (D) interest

_____ 3 The interest _____ on savings will increase next year.

(A) statement   (B) rate
(C) accountant   (D) revenue

_____ 4 I'm sorry, but for this type of loan, you cannot use your car as _____.

(A) collateral   (B) tax
(C) balance   (D) figure

_____ 5 The bank will charge a 5% _____ on all foreign currency exchanges.

(A) appraisal   (B) surplus
(C) commission   (D) loan

正確答案請參考 413 頁

B | Match

請在空格填入合適的單字，動詞需依時態變化，名詞需填入正確之單複數。

| transaction | deposit | total | overdue | accrue | bill |

1. According to our records, your account is two months _____.

2. For as long as you have money in your account, your savings will continue to _____ interest.

3. There's a $2 fee for every _____ conducted on an ATM.

4. We always pay our gas _____ the last week of the month.

5. You can _____ money into your account either electronically or in person.

6. _____ profits equal the amount you earned minus the amount you spent.

C | Listening Practice

請聆聽音檔，將單字填入空格 090

1. They _____ the payment, so it should have cleared by now.

2. We stop your account if it ever becomes _____.

3. All fees are _____ on the 15th of the month.

4. Payments cannot be _____ after the deadline, so send the money as soon as possible.

5. The bank automatically _____ credit payments made in a foreign currency.

6. If we want to _____ money, we will have to reduce our expenses first.

正確答案請參考 413 頁

Unit 10

Investments

投資理財

投資也是多益測驗中的重要情境，是必須要拿分的關鍵：

① 跟著子單元的分類，一起學習投資的重點單字，例如：資產（asset）、
   信用（credit）、基金（fund）、股市（stock market）、債務（debt）。

② 務必掌握如上升（increase）、成長（grow）、降低（lower）、暴跌
   （plummet）等用以描述投資情況的動詞。

學前暖身 請閱讀英文定義，並將正確單字與之配對

accumulate	debt	wise	stagnant	permanent

1 _____: long-lasting; intended to remain

2 _____: unmoving or unchanging; sluggish

3 _____: to amass or build up; to gradually acquire

4 _____: showing good knowledge and experience

5 _____: an amount of money that is owed to someone or
   something

Economics 經濟狀況

01
approximately
[ə`prɑksəmɪtlɪ]

副 大概;近乎

• ap- 向
• proximate 形 近的
• -ly 副

Next month, I'll be earning **approximately** the same amount for much less work.

下個月,我的工作量會比現在少一點,但賺的錢差不多。

02
debt
[dɛt]

名 債務

I have to use most of my paycheck to pay off my student loan **debt**.

我大部分的薪水都用來還學生貸款。

應用	[1] be in debt to Sb. 欠某人錢(債務) [2] pay (off)/repay/clear/settle a debt 清償債務

03
economy
[ɪ`kɑnəmɪ]

名 經濟

They say the **economy** is going to contract next year.

他們説明年會經濟不景氣。

04
financial
[faɪ`nænʃəl]

形 財政的;金融界的

• finance 財政
• -ial 形 表「具有……特性」

I've been working late for the last few nights, putting together the last **financial** statement for the year.

前幾個晚上,我都為彙整年度財務報表工作到很晚。

應用	[1] financial aid 獎助學金 [2] financial difficulties/problems/crisis 金融困境／問題／危機

---

05 **fiscal**
[ˋfɪsk!]

⊞ 財政的

We're planning the budget for the next **fiscal** year.

我們正在編下一個會計年度的預算。

應用	片 fiscal year 會計年度 補充：與year合用，指會計年度，不一定是1月到12月這樣的算法，隨各國不同。

---

06 **lose business**
[luz] [ˋbɪznɪs]

動片 丟掉生意

If we keep **losing business**, we may have to think about closing some branches.

如果繼續丟生意，我們就得考慮關掉一些分公司。

應用	1 lose + money/business/profits = be in the red 虧損 2 make/earn + money/profits = be in the black 獲利

---

07 **lower**
[ˋloɚ]

動 降低；減少

・low 形 低的
・-er 用來形成形容詞比較級

Given the economic downturn, we need to **lower** our expectations for growth.

要是景氣下滑，我們需要降低對成長的期望。

應用	lower one's standards 降低標準

相似詞	動 reduce = decrease 減小；減少

---

08 **market**
[ˋmɑrkɪt]

名 市場

The stock **market** is expected to go up after a week of losses.

股市下跌一週之後，預計將止跌回升。

應用	stock market 股市

09 **overall**

[ˋovɚˏɔl]

形 從頭到尾的；總的；
全面的

• over- 加強意義
• all 形 全部的

The scarf shop has had a bad month, but their **overall** sales for the quarter looks good.

這家圍巾店這個月的生意很差，但他們這一季的總銷量看起來不錯。

---

10 **policy**

[ˋpɑləsɪ]

名 政策；策略

| 應用 | [1] foreign/economic/public + policy
外交／經濟／公共政策
[2] insurance policy 保單 |

I just don't agree with this government's economic **policy**.

我就是不同意政府這次的經濟政策。

---

11 **stagnant**

[ˋstægnənt]

形 不景氣的；停滯的

It's hard to get excited about the future with the economy so **stagnant**.

在經濟如此蕭條的情形下，很難對未來感到興奮。

---

12 **trade**

[tred]

動 賣；交易

Apple's stock has just started **trading** at a really high value.

蘋果的股票才剛開始交易，股價就很高。

Fund 基金

13 **fund**
[fʌnd]

名 資金；基金；專款

We have a small office **fund** for birthdays and other celebrations.

我們辦公室有一筆慶祝生日和其他活動的小型基金。

14 **permanent**
[ˋpɝmənənt]

形 永久的；永遠的；固定性的

・per- 完全地
・man 停留
・-ent 形 表「在……狀態的」

Share prices have fallen, but my broker assures me it's not **permanent**.

我的經紀人向我保證股價不會一直下跌。

15 **yield**
[jild]

名 收益；出產；收成

The yearly **yield** from the Travelwell Luggage Company isn't as high as some other funds.

佳旅行李箱公司的年產量沒有其他公司高。

16 **insurance**
[ɪnˋʃʊrəns]

名 保險；保險業

・insure 動 投保
・-ance 名 表「行為；狀況」

It's important to have renter's **insurance** to protect your belongings in rented accommodation.

有承租人的保險來保護您在出租建物內的物品是很重要的。

應用
[1] insurance policy 保單
[2] beneficiary 受益人

Investment 投資

17
accumulate
[ə`kjumjə,let]

動 堆積；累積

• ac- 向
• cumul 堆積；大量
• -ate 動 表「使成為」

I don't want to **accumulate** too much debt before I start working full time.

我不想在全職就業前就積累太多債務。

18
approach
[ə`protʃ]

名 方法

• ap- 到；至
• proach 近

My **approach** to investing is that it's always better to be safe than sorry.

我的投資方法是：安全總比後悔好。

應用	an approach + to + N./V-ing 處理……的方法
相似詞	名 method 方法；方式 名 way 方式；道路

19
asset
[`æsɛt]

名 資產；財物

The company has lots of **assets**, but no ready cash.

該公司擁有大量資產，但沒有現金。

應用	asset 資產←→liabilities 負債 （常用複數形） （複數名詞）

20
conservative
[kən`sɝvətɪv]

形 保守的；守舊的；傳統的

• con- 共同
• serv 保存
• -ive 形 表「有……特性的」

Even a very **conservative** estimate shows this stock will be soaring next year.

就連一項非常保守的預估都顯示，這支股票明年價格會飆漲。

21
credit
[`krɛdɪt]

名 信用

She has built up excellent **credit** by accumulating debt and paying it off on time.

按時償還累積的債務讓她建立良好的信用。

---

22 **exceed**
[ɪk`sid]

動 超過;勝過;超出

• ex- 向外
• ceed 走;去

The performance of this stock is **exceeding** my expectations.

這支股票的表現出乎我意料之外。

---

23 **expense**
[ɪk`spɛns]

名 費用;開銷

• ex- 出
• pense 秤量;支付

I don't mind taking risks, as long as they don't involve major **expenses**.

只要不會牽涉到主要開銷,我不介意冒險。

---

24 **fairly**
[`fɛrlɪ]

副 公平地;公正地

• fair 形 公正的
• -ly 副 「……地」

I don't think our dividends are distributed **fairly**.

我不認為我們的股息公平分配了。

---

25 **invest**
[ɪn`vɛst]

動 投資;投入

• in- 向內
• vest 使穿上

I'm never sure which stocks to **invest** in.

我從來不確定要投資哪一支股票。

| 應用 | invest in + N. 投資……
名 investment 投資 |

---

26 **option**
[`ɑpʃən]

名 選擇;選擇權;選項

• opt 動 選擇
• -ion 名 表「行為;結果;狀態」

I have several **options** for paying off my debt, including having payments taken from my salary each month.

我有幾個選擇可以還債,包括每個月從薪水裡扣錢。

---

27 primary
[`praɪˌmɛrɪ]

形 主要的；原始的

• prime 最初
• -ary 形 表「與……有關的」

My **primary** investment is bonds, but I am exploring other stock options..

我主要投資債券，但也在找股票的投資方案。

---

28 profit
[`prɑfɪt]

名 利潤；利益

It always seems like the only way to get big **profits** is to take big risks.

看起來「高風險，高報酬」是不變的真理。

> 應用　get/make/earn/turn + a profit 獲利

---

29 toss
[tɔs]

動 拋；投

I decided to **toss** aside my usual prudence and take a big risk.

我決定拋開我一貫行事謹慎的作風，來個大冒險。

> 應用　leave behind/aside
> = put behind/aside + N. 屏棄

---

30 waste
[west]

動 浪費

My mother says not to **waste** my time researching the stock market and just keep my money under my mattress!

我媽說不要浪費時間去研究股票市場，只要把錢存在我的床墊下就好！

> 應用　waste/spend + time/money + on N./V-ing
> 浪費／花費時間／金錢在……

---

31 wise
[waɪz]

形 有智慧的；明智的

A stock with solid past performance seems like a **wise** investment.

投資過去表現穩健的股票似乎是明智的。

Stock Market 股市

32 **plummet**
['plʌmɪt]

動 暴跌;急遽下降

The market will **plummet** after they announce the currency devaluation.

他們宣布貨幣貶值後,股市將會暴跌。

---

33 **assess**
[ə'sɛs]

動 評估;估價

A basic rule for **assessing** risk is that if you can't afford to lose what you're about to invest, it's a bad risk.

評估風險的一個基本原則是,如果你不能失去你所要投資的東西,那就是負面的風險。

---

34 **bid**
[bɪd]

動 出價;投標

I will **bid** on the security—I hope it's accepted.

我想投標買證券,希望不會被拒絕。

---

35 **growth**
[groθ]

名 成長;增長

• grow 動 生長
• -th 名 表「行為」

Experts are predicting greater market **growth** this year.

專家預測今年市場會成長得更多。

---

36 **predict**
[prɪ'dɪkt]

動 預言;預料;預報

• pre- 預先
• dict 說;言

My supervisor has been **predicting** a stock market crash for weeks.

好多週以來,我的上司一直預言股市將會崩盤。

37 **steadily**

[ˈstɛdəlɪ]

副 穩定地

· stead 固定的
· -ily 副

Toyota stock has been rising **steadily** since last year.

自去年以來豐田的股價一直穩定上升。

---

38 **stock**

[stɑk]

名 股份；股票

I've got **stocks** in lots of different companies.

我持有許多不同公司的股票。

---

39 **turnover**

[ˈtɜnˌovɚ]

名 營業額；成交量

Unless you keep **turnovers** low, you're going to pay a lot in commissions.

除非你的成交量維持得很低，不然的話你要付很多回扣。

---

40 **immensely**

[ɪˈmɛnslɪ]

副 非常；極其

· im- 無
· mens 度量
· -ly 副

This new social media stock is going to increase **immensely** in value.

這支新的社群媒體股票將大大增值。

學後小試 A **Multiple Choice Questions**
請選擇合適的單字填入空格

_____ 1 Last year I invested half my savings in this _____ and today it has doubled in value!

(A) expense (B) growth
(C) stock (D) turnover

_____ 2 We follow a very aggressive investment _____.

(A) economy (B) credit
(C) policy (D) profit

_____ 3 I can't _____ what's going to happen with my stock tomorrow.

(A) yield (B) toss
(C) plummet (D) predict

_____ 4 Are you going to _____ on that security when it goes on sale?

(A) bid (B) waste
(C) exceed (D) lower

_____ 5 I have saved up a small _____ that I use for investing.

(A) approach (B) fund
(C) insurance (D) market

正確答案請參考 413 頁

B | Match
請在空格填入合適的單字，動詞需依時態變化，名詞需填入正確之單複數。

| options | steadily | financial | conservative | invest | approximately |

1. I don't like to take risks, so I am very _____ when it comes to the stock market.
2. I have to sell it; I have no other _____.
3. A good _____ adviser can help you plan for retirement.
4. My new salary will be _____ twice the amount I used to make!
5. Our stock values didn't increase dramatically at first, but they have grown _____.
6. Would you _____ in your own company?

C | Listening Practice
請聆聽音檔，將單字填入空格 🎧 100

1. If we close our shop for repairs, we will _____.
2. Buying the right stock at the right time can change your life _____.
3. This is our budget for the next _____ year.
4. My Sony stock just started _____ at a low price.
5. I don't know how to _____ whether prices are going to rise or fall.
6. I don't think I am being treated _____ by my broker.

正確答案請參考 413 頁

Unit 11

Business Operation

企業營運

企業營運的情境會經常性地出現在多益測驗中，其重點在於：

1. 形容發展狀況的形容詞，如要如何形容企業形象（image）、或是品牌（brand）經營的狀況。
2. 動詞也是重點，必須掌握經營（run/operate）的不同種說法，以及強調發展的擴大（expand/enlarge）、生產（generate）、成功（succeed）等常見詞彙。

學前暖身 請閱讀英文定義，並將正確單字與之配對

accountable	leading	publicity	compliance	workforce

1 _____: to be among the best in a certain field or competition

2 _____: to be considered responsible for some problem

3 _____: any action which results in consumers, becoming aware of a product

4 _____: people employed in a business operation

5 _____: to follow certain rules or regulations

Branch Office 分店

---

01 commensurate

[kə`mɛnʃərɪt]

形 同量的；相稱的

- com- 互相
- mensure [古英文] 測量
- -ate 形

Salaries are **commensurate** with work experience; so the more years you've worked in this industry, the higher your pay will be.

薪水跟經驗成正比，所以你在這行越久，薪水越好。

相似詞	形 comparable 可比較的；比得上的
	形 proportional 相稱的；合比例的
	形 equal = equivalent 相等的；相同的

---

02 run

[rʌn]

動 經營

She has been **running** the Tacoma office for three years without incident.

她管理塔科馬辦事處已有三年，從來沒有出過錯誤。

相似詞	動 operate = execute 實施；執行
	動 manage = administrate 處理；管理
	動 direct 指導；從事

---

03 workforce

[`wɜk,fors]

名 勞動力；工人；勞動人口

- work 名 工作
- force 名 力量

Our **workforce** has gone through extensive training.

我們的勞工都經過大規模的訓練。

---

04 chain

[tʃen]

名 連鎖

One of the benefits of operating a **chain** store is an established brand name combined with developed marketing campaigns.

經營連鎖店的好處是品牌已經打響知名度，且有完善的市場行銷策略。

| 應用 | a chain of 一系列；一連串 |

05 enlarge

[ɪn`lɑrdʒ]

動 擴大;放大

• en- 變為;使
• large 大的

We are seeking to **enlarge** our customer base by opening branches overseas.

我們想透過海外設點來增加顧客人數。

---

06 expand

[ɪk`spænd]

動 展開;擴大

• ex- 向外
• pand 展開

To **expand** our operations, we must increase our number of suppliers.

為了擴大營業,我們必須增加供應商的數量。

| 相似詞 | 動 spread 擴大;擴散 |
| | 動 extend 展開;延伸 |

---

07 ownership

[`onɚ͵ʃɪp]

名 所有權

• own 動 擁有
• -er 名 表「人」
• -ship 名 表「狀態」

The **ownership** of a chain store is usually in the hands of a single individual.

分店的所有權通常在個人手裡。

Consultation 諮詢

08 consult

[kən`sʌlt]

動 諮詢

All persons seeking a loan must **consult** one of our financial advisors first.

欲貸款者必須先諮詢我們的理財顧問。

| 應用 | consult Sb. about Sth. 向某人請教/諮詢某人 |

---

09 count on

動 片 指望;信賴

Customers can **count on** our experienced staff to provide the best possible financial planning.

客戶可以信任我們的資深同仁,他們會提供最好的理財規劃。

| 相似詞 | 片 depend on = rely on 依仗;信任 |

Image 形象

10 compliance

[kəm`plaɪəns]

名 服從；遵守；
　依從；屈從

- comply 動 依從；遵守
- -ance 名 表「行為」

The clarity of the new rules should resolve the **compliance** issues.

解釋清楚新規定之後，應該可以解決遵守上的問題了。

| 應用 | 1 in compliance with 依照；順從 |
| | 2 compliance cost 依從成本 |

---

11 concentrate

[`kɑnsɛn͵tret]

動 集中力量

- con- 一起
- center 中心
- -ate 動 表「使成為」

The PR campaign will **concentrate** on creating a green image for our firm after that problem with the chemical spill.

公關活動將致力於美化我們化學原料外漏之後的形象。

| 相似詞 | concentrate on = focus on 專注於…… |

---

12 daring

[`dɛrɪŋ]

形 大膽的

- dare 動 敢
- -ing 形

We're looking for a public figure known for his or her **daring** feats to give our company a youthful, energetic image.

我們在尋找一個敢做敢言的公眾人物，以助我們營造年輕有活力的形象。

---

13 dependable

[dɪ`pɛndəbl]

形 可靠的

- depend 動 依靠
- -able 形 「可……的」

After 100 years in operation, we have become the most **dependable** insurance firm in the nation.

經過百年的經營，我們已成為全國最可靠的保險公司。

| 相似詞 | 形 reliable = countable 可靠的 |

14 distinctive

[dɪˋstɪŋktɪv]

形 有特色的；特殊的

· distinct 形 有區別的
· -ive 形 「具有……性質的」

The key to setting us apart from our competitors is finding a **distinctive** marketing approach.

讓我們領先競爭對手的關鍵，是找到一個獨特的行銷手法。

---

15 established

[əˋstæblɪʃt]

形 已建立的

· establish 動 建立
· -ed 形

This is an **established** brand, with a long history and wide recognition.

這個建立已久的品牌，具有悠久歷史和廣泛知名度。

---

16 favorable

[ˋfevərəbl]

形 贊同的；討人喜歡的

· favor 贊成；有利於
· -able 形 表「有……
  特性的」

Our product is viewed as overpriced and too exclusive, so we wish to create a more **favorable** image for it.

大眾認定我們的產品高價獨特，所以我們希望創造一個更親民、更有吸引力的形象。

相似詞	形 flattering 奉承的；討人喜歡的
	形 attractive 吸引人的；有魅力的
	形 complimentary 恭維的；讚賞的

---

17 leading

[ˋlidɪŋ]

形 頂尖的

· lead 動 領導
· -ing 形

The **leading** cosmetic company invested millions of dollars in its newest ad campaign.

這家首屈一指的化妝品公司，在最新的廣告宣傳上投資了數百萬美元。

---

18 restore

[rɪˋstor]

動 恢復

· re- 再；重新
· store 設立

Novex wishes to **restore** its image as a community centered business by setting up a scholarship fund.

諾維斯希望透過創立獎學金，來恢復它以社會大眾為中心的企業形象。

19 retrieve
[rɪ`triv]

動 找回

• re- 再
• trieve 找到；得到

We need to **retrieve** the marketing data first before we can analyze its significance.

我們需要先回收行銷數據，以分析其顯著性。

---

20 vulnerable
[`vʌlnərəbl]

形 脆弱的；有弱點的

• vulner 傷害
• -able 形 表「可……的」

Our image is **vulnerable** because our product is seen as trendy and likely to lose popularity soon.

我們的形象不夠鮮明強烈，因為很多人認為我們的產品只會跟流行，有可能很快失去人氣。

| 相似詞 | 形 fragile 脆弱的；易損壞的 |
| | 形 delicate 脆弱的；嬌嫩的 |

---

21 brand
[brænd]

名 品牌

Our **brand** is not very recognizable in North America, but it enjoys wide popularity in Asia.

我們的品牌在北美知名度不高，但在亞洲卻大受歡迎。

Operation 營運

22 confidence
[`kɑnfədəns]

名 信心；信任

• confide 動 信任
• -ence 名 表「狀態」

Management had such little **confidence** in the proposed project that they refused to allocate funds to it.

管理階層對這個提案沒什麼信心，所以他們拒絕分配資金給這個專案。

---

23 discontinue
[dɪskən`tɪnju]

動 停止；中止

• dis- 不；否定
• continue 動 繼續

Given its poor sales record, we are going to **discontinue** the line.

因為銷售業績不佳，我們將停止生產該商品。

---

24 anticipate

[ænˋtɪsəˌpet]

動 預期；預先考慮到

・anti- 在……之前
・cip 拿取
・-ate 動

Previous management failed to **anticipate** the economic downturn, which led to serious problems in our operations.

前任管理階層沒預料到景氣會下滑，導致營運出現了嚴重的問題。

相似詞	動 expect 期待；預期
	動 await 等待；預期
	動 hope for 期待；希望
	動 watch for 留神；密切注意

---

25 compare

[kəmˋpɛr]

動 比較

・com- 互相；共同
・par 不相上下

Typical consumers **compare** clothing brands in terms of price and image.

一般消費者會比較衣服的價格和形象。

應用	compare A to/with B 比較A和B

---

26 current

[ˋkɝənt]

形 當前的

・curr 跑
・-ent 形 表「處於某種狀態或動作」

Our **current** business model does not allow for outsourcing.

我們目前的經營模式不允許外包。

---

27 declare

[dɪˋklɛr]

動 宣布；聲明

・de 加強語氣
・clare 清楚的

Businesses wishing to sell insurance must **declare** their intent to do so at the local government office.

欲銷售保險的公司必須向當地政府單位報備。

143

28 **enterprise**
[ˈɛntɚˌpraɪz]

名 事業；企業；公司

· enter 之間
· prise 抓；獲得

This **enterprise** is only a small part of our total operations, but it requires a lot of capital.

這個公司只占我們總業務的一小部分，但卻需要大量資金。

---

29 **operation**
[ˌɑpəˈreʃən]

名 企業；經營

· operate 動 操作
· -ion 名 表「行為」

As a multinational corporation, we have **operations** in Australia, the Americas, and Western Europe.

作為跨國企業，我們在澳洲、美洲和西歐都有公司。

---

30 **priority**
[praɪˈɔrɪtɪ]

名 優先事項

· prior 形 在先的
· -ity 名 表「特徵；狀態；行為」

Upgrading the server in order to speed up Web traffic is our top **priority**.

我們的首要任務是升級伺服器，以加快網路流量。

---

31 **succeed**
[səkˈsid]

動 成功

In order for this project to **succeed**, we're going to need the right staff and location.

為了使這個專案成功，我們需要適合的工作人員和地點。

> **應用** succeed in 在……成功

Publicity 宣傳活動

32

accomplished

[ə`kɑmplɪʃt]

形 有造詣的；有才藝的

• accomplish 動 完成
• -ed 形

She is an **accomplished** publicist, with several awards to her name.

她是個傑出的公關，得過許多獎項。

33

accountable

[ə`kaʊntəbl]

形 有責任的

• account 動 對……負責
• -able 形 表「有……
特性的」

As the **accountable** party, we would first like to offer our sincerest apologies.

作為責任方，我們首先要致上最誠摯的歉意。

34

adjust

[ə`dʒʌst]

動 調整；校正

• ad- 向
• just 適當；正當

They will need to **adjust** their estimate downward, given the weak market data.

因為市場數據疲軟，他們需要降低自己的期望。

35

claim

[klem]

動 說；聲稱

The customer **claims** the commercial sends the wrong message.

顧客說這則廣告散播錯誤的訊息。

36

generate

[`dʒɛnə,ret]

動 產生；引起

• gener 生
• -ate 動 表「使……」

An online viral campaign might **generate** buzz better than an ad campaign.

網路病毒式行銷所產生的效果，可能比廣告行銷來得大。

37 publicity
[pʌbˋlɪsətɪ]

名（公眾的）注意；
名聲；宣傳

- public 形 公眾的
- -ity 名 表「性質；狀態」

The key to generating **publicity** is to get the young adult demographic interested in it.

打造知名度的關鍵，在於讓年輕族群感興趣。

38 risk
[rɪsk]

名 風險

The **risk** in using a musician as a spokesperson is that their popularity can suddenly plummet.

請音樂家擔任代言人的風險是，他們的人氣可能突然暴跌。

應用
1 at the risk of 冒著……的危險
2 take a risk 冒險；承擔風險

39 withhold
[wɪðˋhold]

動 拒絕給與；扣留

- with- 反抗；向後
- hold 動 抓住

The network said they will **withhold** airtime until the payment issue is resolved.

新聞網說，他們將暫緩播放直到解決付款問題。

40 withstand
[wɪðˋstænd]

動 抵擋；反抗；禁得起

- with- 反抗；向後
- stand 動 站立

The brand can **withstand** the negative publicity, as long as it doesn't continue more than a few weeks.

只要負面消息不要流傳超過幾個星期，這個品牌就不會受其影響。

146

學後小試 A Multiple Choice Questions
請選擇合適的單字填入空格

_____ 1 Once a _____ becomes popular, customers become less concerned with the prices of its products.

(A) brand　　　　　(B) workforce
(C) claim　　　　　(D) confidence

_____ 2 Mr. Hanson is the most _____ marketing consultant in North America; there simply is no one better.

(A) established　　　(B) commensurate
(C) current　　　　　(D) accomplished

_____ 3 We need to _____ key parts of the design plans from our subsidiary so they cannot copy our ideas.

(A) run　　　　　　(B) declare
(C) withhold　　　　(D) expand

_____ 4 The boss wants us to _____ with the accountants about the new project.

(A) consult　　　　(B) generate
(C) succeed　　　　(D) adjust

_____ 5 Jennings will be in charge of the _____, so direct your questions to her.

(A) ownership　　　(B) enterprise
(C) priority　　　　(D) risk

正確答案請參考 414 頁

B | Match

請在空格填入合適的單字，動詞需依時態變化，名詞需填入正確之單複數。

retrieve	vulnerable	concentrate	withstand	chain	enlarge

1. I warned them that the new website is _____ to hacking.
2. It'll take about an hour to _____ the data from the old hard drive.
3. We've enough surplus in storage to _____ a long strike at the factory.
4. It's going to cost a lot more than the amount you proposed to _____ the factory.
5. The new shopping mall contains nothing but _____ stores.
6. We should _____ all our R&D efforts on gene therapy.

C | Listening Practice

請聆聽音檔，將單字填入空格 110

1. Given our weak sales performance, I recommend we _____ operations in South America.
2. We must be able to _____ our suppliers to deliver on time, every time.
3. When _____ suppliers, it's important to consider shopping costs and time.
4. It's going to cost a lot more than the amount you proposed to _____ the factory.
5. They are known for their _____ advertising featuring a family of dogs and cats.
6. The only way to _____ consumer confidence in our product is to show the safety test results.

正確答案請參考 414 頁

Unit 12

Contract & Warranty

合約與保固

在多益的對話與閱讀題型中，合約保固的情境時常會出現：

1. 與顧客利益相關的名詞必然是重點，如合約條款（terms）的修改（alteration）與限制（restriction），或是保固的試用期（trial）和是否需要收費（charge）。

2. 動詞非常重要，例如必須要遵守（abide by / adhere to）合約，而合約何時會生效（take effect）或失效（terminate）。

學前暖身 請閱讀英文定義，並將正確單字與之配對

valid	depend	logical	confidential	adhere to

1. _____: sensible; relating to the thinking or reasoning process

2. _____: to rely on or to trust; to be determined by

3. _____: legally or officially acceptable

4. _____: to follow the practice of; stick to, as a set of rules

5. _____: secret or private

111 **01** 美英 **02** 美加 **03** 澳美 **04** 加英

Patent 專利

01 authorize
['ɔθə‚raɪz]

動 授權；批准

- author 名 作者
- -ize 動 表「使」

Will you **authorize** us to use your software?
你能授權我們使用你的軟體嗎？

| 應用 | authorize/permit + Sb. to do Sth.
授權某人去做……
名 the authorities 政府當局 |

---

02 code
[kod]

名 密碼

The only way to unlock the program is to enter the correct user **code**.
開啟程式的唯一辦法是輸入正確的用戶密碼。

---

03 confidential
[‚kɑnfə'dɛnʃəl]

形 機密的

- confide 動 信任
- -ence 名 「性質；狀態」
- -al 形 表「具其特徵的」

This document about our new product is completely **confidential**, so please don't share it with anyone.
有關我們新產品的文件完全是機密，因此請勿告訴任何人。

| 應用 | keep + O. + confidential 保密…… |

---

04 patent
['pætnt]

名 專利；專利權

She hasn't received a **patent** for the new process she invented yet.
她還沒收到她所研發的新製程的專利。

| 應用 | apply for a patent on/for + N. 申請……的專利 |

(112) **05** 美加 **06** 加澳 **07** 美加 **08** 英澳

unit

12

Contract & Warranty 合約與保固

---

05 penalty

[ˋpɛnḷtɪ]

名 處罰；罰款；罰球

・penal 形 刑罰的；應受刑的
・-ty 名 表「狀態」

The **penalties** for violating patent law in this country are quite strict.

在這個國家違反專利法的罰責很重。

---

06 security

[sɪˋkjʊrətɪ]

名 安全；防禦

・secure 形 安全的
・-ity 名 表「狀態」

The inventor wants us to give him some kind of **security** before he'll let us use his new technique.

發明人希望我們先提供他一些保障，才能使用他的新技術。

> **應用**　片 security guard 警衛

---

07 valid

[ˋvælɪd]

形 有效的；有根據的；
　合法的

This patent will only be **valid** for 50 years.

這項專利有效期僅有五十年。

> **應用**　be valid for 有效期為……

> **反義字**　形 invalid 無效的

Contract 合約

08 abide by

[əˋbaɪd]

動 片 遵守

Let's make sure we can **abide by** the rules of the contract before we sign it.

簽約之前，讓我們確認雙方會遵守合約的規定。

> **相似詞**　conform to = keep to = comply with
> 遵照；達到

151

09 **accommodate**
[ə`kɑmə͵det]

動 滿足；使適應

· ac- 向
· com- 共同
· mod 方法
· -ate 動 表「致使」

I'm afraid there is nothing in this contract that **accommodates** our needs.

我想這個合約完全不符合我們的需求。

> **相似詞** 動 gratify = content = please 滿足；使開心

---

10 **adhere to**
[əd`hɪr]

動 片 堅持；遵守；忠於

The architects are not **adhering to** the rules we agreed to!

建築師們沒有遵守我們協議的規定！

---

11 **alteration**
[͵ɔltə`reʃən]

名 (通常指輕微地)
改動，修改；改變

· alter 動 變動
· -tion 名 表「行為；結果」

The contract looks good, but we'd like to make a few small **alterations**.

合約看起來不錯，但我們想做一些小更動。

---

12 **amendment**
[ə`mɛndmənt]

名 修訂；修正案

· amend 動 修訂
· -ment 名 表「行動；狀態」

We can change the contract in the future by adding **amendments** and signing them.

未來我們可以透過增補協議和簽名來變更合約。

---

13 **at the latest**
[`letɪst]

片 最晚；最遲

We have to return the signed forms by Friday, **at the latest**.

我們最晚要在週五之前歸還簽好的表格。

152

14 **ban**

[bæn]

動 禁止；取締

We are **banned** from discussing the terms of the contract with anyone outside the company.

我們禁止與非公司人員談論合約條款。

> 應用
> 1 ban/prohibit/forbid + S. from V-ing
>   禁止某人去做……
> 2 lift/impose + a ban + on + N./V-ing
>   解除/實施對……的禁令

---

15 **consensus**

[kənˋsɛnsəs]

名 一致；共識；輿論

・con- 共同
・sense 名 知覺；感覺

We finally reached a **consensus** on the terms of our agreement.

我們終於在合約條款上達成了共識。

> 應用
> reach a consensus on/about + N.
> 對於……達成共識

---

16 **constraint**

[kənˋstrent]

名 約束；限制

・con- 一起
・strain 拉緊
・-t 名

I'm not happy with the number of labor force **constraints** in this contract.

我不滿意這份合約裡對於勞動人力的限制。

---

17 **determine**

[dɪˋtɝmɪn]

動 決定

・de- 去除
・termin 限制

Before we sit down to draft the agreement, we need to **determine** what both sides' needs are.

在我們坐下來擬草約之前，需要先確定雙方的需求。

> 應用
> determine/resolve/decide + to V.
> 下定決心去做……

> 相似詞
> 動 decide 決定；決心
> 動 resolve 決定；解決

153

18 duty
[ˋdjutɪ]

名 責任；義務；(複) 職責

After signing, the contractor has the **duty** to uphold the terms of the agreement.

簽定合約以後，維護合約條款是承包商的責任。

> **應用** be on/off duty 執勤中／勤務結束

19 logical
[ˋlɑdʒɪk!]

形 合理的

• logic 名 邏輯
• -al 形 表「關於……的」

It is only **logical** that they want a signed contract before beginning work.

開始工作前，他們希望先簽約是很合理的。

20 premises
[ˋprɛmɪsɪz]

名 (尤指公司或機構的) 生產場所；廠區

The contract is valid only on company **premises**.

本合約僅在公司範圍內有效。

21 retain
[rɪˋten]

動 保留；記住

• re- 往回
• tain 握

We must **retain** our right to sell this idea to third parties.

我們必須保留將此想法賣給第三方的權力。

22 subject to
[ˋsʌbdʒɪkt]

動 片 受……管制

If Mercedes violates the terms of this contract, they'll be **subject to** legal action.

如果賓士汽車違反合約條款，他們將會受法律制裁。

23 subsequent to
['sʌbsɪˌkwɛnt]

動 片 隨後；接著

· sub- 下方
· sequ 跟隨
· -ent 形

Subsequent to signing, Hyundai will be liable for any damages.

簽約之後，現代汽車將負擔所有損害賠償。

---

24 substantial
[səb'stænʃəl]

形 大的；可觀的；重大的

· sub- 下面
· stant 站立
· -ial 形

They want to make **substantial** changes to the design we sent them.

他們想要大幅調整我們傳給他們的設計。

---

25 suggest
[sə'dʒɛst]

動 建議；暗示

· sug- 下
· gest 攜帶

I **suggest** we meet again and try to reach an agreement on the contract.

我建議再開一次會，達成合約的共識。

---

26 take effect
[ɪ'fɛkt]

動 片 生效

The new conditions of the contract won't **take effect** until next year.

這個合約的新增條款明年才生效。

> 應用
> 1 have an effect on 對⋯⋯產生影響
> 2 side effect 副作用

---

27 tedious
['tidɪəs]

形 沉長乏味的

· tedium 名 無聊
· -ous 形 表「充滿⋯⋯的；有⋯⋯性質的」

Going through all the fine print on these contracts is **tedious** work.

要審查這些所有合約的附屬細則，真是件苦差事。

---

28 **terminate**
['tɝmə,net]

動 使停止；使結束；終結

• termin 界限
• -ate 動

We can **terminate** the contract by submitting a written notification.

我們可以透過提交書面通知終止合約。

---

29 **term**
[tɝm]

名 條款；項目；

任期；術語

The new **terms** they want to add are really not beneficial to us.

他們想追加的新條款對我們真的很不利。

Warranty 保固

30 **adequate**
['ædəkwɪt]

形 足夠的；適當的；

勝任的

• ad- 往；向
• equ(al) 使水平；使相等
• -ate 形

I wouldn't buy a new piece of equipment without an **adequate** warranty.

如果沒有合理的保固，我才不買新的設備。

---

31 **allow**
[ə'laʊ]

動 允許；容許

We're not **allowed** to get our money back if the machine broke due to negligence.

如果機器是因為人為疏失壞掉，我們就不能退錢。

---

32 **cautious**
['kɔʃəs]

形 很小心的；謹慎的

• caution 名 當心
• -ous 形 表「擁有……的；
有……性質的」

I'd be really **cautious** about buying that car without some kind of insurance.

如果要在沒保險的狀況下買那輛車，我會非常謹慎。

| 應用 | be cautious about = be careful with/about = be alert to 對……謹慎小心 |

156

33

certain

[`sɝtən]

形 無疑的；確定的

・cert 確定
・-ain 形

It is **certain** that we will get our money back, since the computer arrived broken!

我們一定可以拿回我們的錢，因為電腦送來的時候就壞了！

34

charge

[tʃɑrdʒ]

名 收費

There will be no **charge** for the repair.

維修不會收費。

> **應用**　at no charge = free of charge
> = at no cost = for free 免費

35

depend

[dɪ`pɛnd]

動 依賴；信賴

・de- 向下
・pend 懸掛

You can always **depend** on our company to offer a fair warranty.

你可以永遠信賴我們公司提供的優良保固。

36

due to

[dju]

片 由於

Due to circumstances beyond our control, the equipment was left out in the rain and is now unusable.

由於不可抗力因素，那套設備一路淋雨，現在已經無法使用。

> **應用**　due to = because of
> = owing to = as a result of 因為

37 guarantee
[ˌgærənˋti]

動 保證；品質保證；擔保

· guarant 保證
· -ee 動

I **guarantee** that if this program doesn't work the way you need it to, you can have a refund.
我向你保證，如果這個程式不能照你需要的方式運作，你可以退費。

---

38 trial
[ˋtraɪəl]

名 試用期

The warranty only covers the initial **trial**.
僅在試用期階段有保固。

---

39 warranty
[ˋwɔrəntɪ]

名 保證書；擔保；保固

· warrant 名 保證
· -y 名 表「物」

The **warranty** says that if the server stops working within one year, the company will replace it.
保證書說，如果伺服器在一年內故障，該公司會送一個全新的伺服器來更換。

---

40 offer
[ˋɔfɚ]

名 提議；主動幫忙

A very thorough warranty was part of their **offer**.
非常完整的保固是他們提供的服務之一。

學後小試 A **Multiple Choice Questions**
請選擇合適的單字填入空格

_____ ① I can't log into the system without the correct user _____.

    (A) amendment   (B) penalty
    (C) code   (D) consensus

_____ ② Are you _____ we'll get our money back if the machine doesn't work?

    (A) tedious   (B) adequate
    (C) cautious   (D) certain

_____ ③ I'm going to apply for a _____ for my new invention tomorrow.

    (A) term   (B) duty
    (C) constraint   (D) patent

_____ ④ I need you to _____ that this machine will work under the conditions I've described.

    (A) guarantee   (B) authorize
    (C) accommodate   (D) ban

_____ ⑤ They're going to _____ us for fixing the clock, which I think is unfair, since it was broken when we bought it.

    (A) suggest   (B) retain
    (C) charge   (D) determine

正確答案請參考 415 頁

B Match

請在空格填入合適的單字，動詞需依時態變化，名詞需填入正確之單複數。

allow	trial	subsequent to	abide by	due to	premises

1. _____ the bad weather, the shipment will not arrive on time.

2. _____ signing the contract, our partners will be legally responsible for a number of tasks.

3. Will you _____ us to use this software without a license?

4. I'll decide if I want to buy the equipment after the initial _____.

5. Let me give you a tour of the _____.

6. As long as we _____ the terms of the contract, we won't have any problems.

C Listening Practice

請聆聽音檔，將單字填入空格 120

1. How can we _____ the contract if we need to?

2. The new rules will _____ at the beginning of next month.

3. I can't make _____ changes without discussing them with my supervisor.

4. I'll be back by 5 p.m. _____.

5. What were the details of their _____?

6. I would never buy a computer without a _____.

正確答案請參考 415 頁

Unit 13

Research & Development

研究與開發

研究與開發經常被縮寫為R&D，此情境經常會結合科技發展的時事，一起進入考題：

1. 留心專業知識的詞彙，例如：人體工學的（ergonomic）、尖端科技的（state-of-the-art）。

2. 閱讀測驗的簡短對話也時常論及產品開發（invent），所以基礎的單字也不可不留意，例如：實驗（experiment）、專家（expert）、研究（research）。

學前暖身 請閱讀英文定義，並將正確單字與之配對

research	follow up	state-of-the-art	laboratory	experiment

1 _____: the examination or study of something repeatedly to reach new conclusions

2 _____: a systematic testing of an idea or theory

3 _____: something that has the newest features

4 _____: to check on a task, project, or product, after it has finished

5 _____: a place where controlled testing can be performed in safety

Computer 電腦

01 computerized

[kəm'pjutə,raɪzd]

形 電腦化的

• computer 名 電腦
• -ize 動 表「……化」
• -d 形

The disadvantage of a **computerized** clock is we can't verify dates and times if there's a computer error.

數位時鐘的缺點是如果電腦出現錯誤，我們無法驗證日期和時間。

---

02 delete

[dɪ'lit]

動 刪除

To free up hard disk space, all employees must **delete** files more than five years old.

為了清出硬碟空間，所有員工必須刪除五年以上的檔案。

---

03 digit

['dɪdʒɪt]

名 (零到九中的任一) 數字

The accounting software allows entry of amounts up to nine **digits** in length.

會計軟體可以輸入高達九位數的長度。

應用	double-digit/three-digit/four-digit number 雙／三／四位數

---

04 system

['sɪstəm]

名 系統

Before we install the new **system**, we should back up all data to a remote server.

在安裝新系統之前，我們應該把所有資料都備份到遠端伺服器。

Digital Equipment 數位設備

05 **automated**

[`ɔtəmetɪd]

形 自動化的

• auto 自己
• mat 思考
• -ed 形

The **automated** call logging software should enable us to identify branch offices with the most complaints.

自動記錄來電軟體可以讓我們得知，哪些分公司接獲最多投訴。

---

06 **calculate**

[`kælkjə,let]

動 計算；估計

All managers are instructed to use the approved spreadsheet to **calculate** their office's supply expenses.

所有經理都受指示要使用規定的試算表，來計算他們辦公用品的花費。

---

07 **electronically**

[ɪ,lɛk`trɑnɪklɪ]

副（尤指設備）電地；
　　電子地

• electron 名 電子
• -ical 形 表「具有特徵的；
　與……有關的」
• -ly 副

Documents stored **electronically** will, of course, be easier to locate once employees are familiar with the search engine.

等員工熟悉搜尋引擎之後，要找電子檔一定更容易。

---

08 **flaw**

[flɔ]

名 錯誤

One tiny **flaw** in the fiber optic cable caused all those e-mails to be directed to the wrong branch office.

一個光纖電纜的小錯誤，就造成了所有電子郵件被誤送到別的分部。

	名 defect 缺點；缺陷
相似詞	名 fault 缺點；錯誤
	名 glitch 錯誤；故障

09 increase

[ɪnˈkris]

動 增加

• in- 向內
• crease 生長

We need to **increase** our number of servers to handle the larger number of work stations.

我們需要增加伺服器的數量來應付這麼多工作站。

> **應用** on the increase/decrease 增加中／減少中

---

10 fit

[fɪt]

動 符合

Can they create a database that **fits** the demands of our R&D department?

他們可以建一個符合我們研發部門需求的資料庫嗎？

> **應用** Fit like a glove. 非常合適，恰到好處。

---

11 state-of-the-art

[ˈstetəvðiˈɑrt]

形 (科技、機電等產品)
最先進的，最高級的

The proposed 3D printer is **state-of-the-art** and therefore extremely expensive.

計畫要研發的3D印表機是最先進的，因此非常昂貴。

Lab 實驗室

12 examine

[ɪgˈzæmɪn]

動 檢查；檢驗

Our researchers **examined** five samples from the supplier and found no problems.

我們的研究人員檢驗了五個供應商的樣品，沒發現問題。

---

13 experiment

[ɪkˈspɛrəmənt]

名 實驗；試驗

• ex- 向外
• peri 試驗
• -ment 名 表「行動；
狀態」

We need to notify security that the staff are running an **experiment** and will need to stay overnight to monitor its progress.

我們需要通知保全人員，同仁正在進行一項實驗，需要通宵監看實驗過程。

unit
13

Research & Development 研究與開發

14 **expert**
[`ɛkspɚt]

名 專家

Dr. Li is a recognized **expert** in organic chemistry.
李博士是赫赫有名的有機化學專家。

> 應用
> ① an expert in/on . . . 在……方面的專家
> ② an expert at . . . 專精於……；擅長於……

15 **fail**
[fel]

動 失敗；不及格

Since the experiment **failed** to produce any useful data, it will not be repeated.
該實驗並未得到可用的資料，因此不會再重複進行。

> 應用 fail miserably 慘敗

16 **flammable**
[`flæməbl]

形 可燃的

· flame 動 點燃
· -able 形 表「可……的」

All **flammable** materials must be clearly marked and kept in sealed containers.
所有易燃物質必須有清楚的標示，並保存在密封的容器中。

17 **laboratory**
[`læbrə,torɪ]

名 實驗室；研究室

· labor 名 勞力
· -tory 地方；場所

We have three **laboratories**, each used for the study of a different type of plastics production.
我們有三個實驗室，分別研究不同類型的塑膠製品。

Product Development 產品開發

18 constitute

[ˈkɑnstə.tjut]

動 構成

• con- 共同
• stitute 站立

The process they are developing **constitutes** a new method of mass production.

在開發的過程中,他們建構了一種大量生產的新方法。

---

19 consume

[kənˈsjum]

動 消耗;吃完;毀滅

• con- 完全
• sume 取

The proposed experiment would **consume** too many resources and man-hours.

這項實驗計畫會消耗太多的資源和工時。

相似詞	動 devour 狼吞虎嚥地吃;吞沒
	動 exhaust 使精疲力盡;耗盡
	片 use up 用光;耗盡

---

20 create

[krɪˈet]

動 創造;創作

Our competitor hopes to **create** a cheaper alternative to our pain killers.

我們的競爭對手希望能製造出更便宜的替代品,來取代我們的止痛藥。

---

21 develop

[dɪˈvɛləp]

動 發展;開發

They announced at last month's conference that they had **developed** a new type of silicon chip.

在上個月的會議上,他們宣布已開發出一種新型的矽晶片。

---

22 follow up

[ˈfaloʊ]

動 片 追蹤;跟進;跟上

We need to **follow up** on the marketing campaign to see if it has made progress establishing our brand.

我們需要追蹤行銷活動的成果,看看品牌建立有沒有進展。

---

23 following
[ˋfɑləwɪŋ]

形 接著的；下述的

Report all development expenses in the **following** fiscal period, not in the current one.

所有的開發費用請在下個會計年度申報，而不要在這年度。

> **應用**
> 1 the following + N. 以下的……
> ←→ the above + N. 以上的……
> 2 as follows 如下
> ←→ as mentioned above 如上述

24 give up
[gɪv]

動 片 放棄

They said it might be more efficient to just **give up** on the current project and start over from the beginning.

他們說，放棄目前的案子，從頭再開始可能還比較有效率。

> **相似詞**
> 動 abandon = desert = discard 摒棄；丟棄
> 動 quit 放棄；停止

25 glimpse
[glɪmps]

名 瞥見；一瞥

Blint Manufacturers offered us a brief **glimpse** into their production facilities, and even that little bit was impressive.

儘管布林特製造公司只讓我們看了一眼他們的生產設施，還是讓人讚嘆不已。

> **應用**
> 1 catch a glimpse of 一閃而過地瞥見
> 2 have a glance at . . . 看了（某物）一眼

26 invent
[ɪnˋvɛnt]

動 發明；創造

Mr. Yasumura **invented** a new method of measuring the density of rock samples.

安村先生發明了一種測量岩石密度的新方法。

27 **keep**
[kip]

動 持有；保存

As a company, we try to **keep** patents in house, meaning that employees cannot apply for patents as individuals.

身為企業，我們希望公司能持有專利權，也就是員工不得申請個人專利。

> **補充** 動詞 keep 後面要接動名詞 (V-ing)，相同情形的動詞有：enjoy 享受, finish 完成, practice 練習

---

28 **research**
[rɪ`sɝtʃ]

名 研究；調查

• re- 再；加強語氣
• search 尋找

They have submitted a plan to begin **research** in battery production.

他們已經提出了一項研究電池製造的計畫。

---

29 **specialize**
[`spɛʃəl͵aɪz]

動 專攻；使專門化；使特殊化

• special 形 專門的
• -ize 動 表「使」

Only by devoting all of our R&D's budget can we **specialize** in the development of new pharmaceuticals.

只有投入我們所有研發經費，我們才能專攻新藥品的開發。

> **應用** S. specialize in + N. 某人專長於……
> 名 specialty 特色；特產

Technology 科技

30 **engineer**
[͵ɛndʒə`nɪr]

名 工程師；技師；機械工

• engine 名 引擎
• -eer 名 表「與……有關的人」

We need **engineers**: people who can take scientific data and design marketable, profitable devices.

我們需求數名工程師；他們必須能處理科學數據並設計暢銷的儀器。

unit

13

Research & Development 研究與開發

31 ergonomic

[ˌɝgəˈnɑmɪk]

形 人體工學的

- ergo- 工作
- -nomy 名 表「……學」
- -ic 形 表「具有特徵的；與……有關的」

All of our programmers have asked for **ergonomic** keyboards to reduce the possibility of injury from repetitious activity.

我們所有的程式設計師都要求用人體工學的鍵盤，以降低重複動作的潛在傷害。

---

32 fascinating

[ˈfæsṇˌetɪŋ]

形 極好的；迷人的

- fascinate 動 使神魂顛倒
- -ing 形

The most **fascinating** feature of this game system is its voice control.

這套遊戲最迷人的特點是可以語音控制。

相似詞　形 appealing = captivating 迷人的；吸引人的
　　　　形 compelling 扣人心弦的；有說服力的

---

33 fatigue

[fəˈtig]

名 疲乏；疲勞

Use composites in the car frame to lessen the chance of metal **fatigue**.

為了降低金屬疲乏的機會，汽車車架要用複合材料。

---

34 field

[fild]

名 領域

He's the top researcher in the **field** of genetics, so we need him.

他是遺傳學領域頂尖的研究人員，因此我們需要他。

---

35 floor

[flor]

名 地板；樓層

If we get in on the ground **floor** of this technology, we'll have the best chance of establishing a brand.

如果我們及早掌握這項科技的基礎，極有可能發展出自己的品牌。

應用　1 take the floor 起身演講
　　　2 walk the floor 焦躁不安；猶豫不決

169

36 foundation

[faʊnˋdeʃən]

名 基礎

· found 動 建立；創立
· -ation 名 表「動作；
　狀態；結果」

The **foundation** of this fuel will be hydrogen, not carbon.

這種燃料的基本元素是氫，而不是碳。

37 involve

[ɪnˋvɑlv]

動 牽涉；包含；使忙於

· in- 入
· volve 旋轉

Sorry, but your design **involves** too many patents held by other companies.

對不起，您的設計涉及太多項其他公司的專利了。

| 應用 | [1] involve + N./V-ing 包含、牽涉到 |
| | [2] involve + O. + in + N./V-ing 被……牽涉其中 |

38 resourceful

[rɪˋsorsfəl]

形 足智多謀的

· re- 加強語氣
· source 上升
· -ful 形 表「充滿的」

We need someone **resourceful**, who can make the most of what we give them, even if it's very little.

我們需要一個足智多謀的人，就算我們給他很少的資源，他還是能充分利用。

39 technical

[ˋtɛknɪkl̩]

形 科技的；技術的

· technic 名 技術
· -al 形 表「關於……的」

Avoid using **technical** language in the user manual, as most consumers won't understand it.

切勿在使用手冊中使用術語，因為大多數消費者根本看不懂。

40 trend

[trɛnd]

名 趨勢；時尚

The **trend** toward using touch panel continues, as more and more devices employ this technology.

隨著越來越多裝置採用觸控式面板這項技術，這個趨勢還會持續發燒。

學後小試

A Multiple Choice Questions

請選擇合適的單字填入空格

_____ 1 There is a definite upward _____ in the demand for online movies.

(A) foundation   (B) experiment
(C) trend   (D) engineer

_____ 2 You will need to _____ all the data, including the test results, so that no one can get them.

(A) constitute   (B) fit
(C) delete   (D) fail

_____ 3 I thought it was incredibly _____. They've used the waste to make packing materials.

(A) resourceful   (B) computerized
(C) state-of-the-art   (D) ergonomic

_____ 4 Our new tracking _____ allows us to monitor customer requests as well as complaints.

(A) floor   (B) research
(C) fatigue   (D) system

_____ 5 We need someone who has worked in the _____ of international finance.

(A) expert   (B) field
(C) laboratory   (D) digit

正確答案請參考 415 頁

B | Match

請在空格填入合適的單字，動詞需依時態變化，名詞需填入正確之單複數。

| flammable | involve | glimpse | electronically | consume | flaw |

1. Arrange a factory tour so they can get just a quick _____ of our new robots.
2. Its principal _____ is that the engine overheats too easily.
3. All of our raw materials were _____ in the fire.
4. You can send the money _____ by bank transfer.
5. We like to _____ our clients in the decision-making process.
6. _____ materials must be kept outside the factory at all times.

C | Listening Practice

請聆聽音檔，將單字填入空格 130

1. We prefer employees who _____ in a single field.
2. No staff are needed because the process is _____ .
3. _____ details of the system are available online.
4. Please consult the _____ list to confirm when each product will be released.
5. We will _____ the new samples in our laboratory.
6. Taking into account the increasing costs, I think we should _____ this product line.

正確答案請參考 415 頁

Unit 14

Production & Quality Control

生產與品管

生產和品管是多益測驗中的必考情境：

1. 首先必須熟悉的就是動詞，描述生產的最大化（maximize）、流線化（streamline）、增加（enhance），以及檢驗生產結果的detect/scrutinize/inspect之間的差異也必須留意。

2. 靈活使用形容詞以形容產品狀態（condition）、品質（quality）和功能（function）也是應試的重點。

學前暖身 請閱讀英文定義，並將正確單字與之配對

handcrafted	independent	acclaimed	strict	hectic

1 _____ : carefully following rules; precise and inflexible

2 _____ : made by a person, not by a machine

3 _____ : busy, chaotic

4 _____ : not subject to control; not relying on someone else

5 _____ : known and admired for something; praised

Assembly Line 生產線

01

assemble

[əˋsɛmbl]

動 裝配；組裝

- as- 向
- semble 相像；相關聯

Typically, we need three days to **assemble** this car.

我們一般需要三天組裝這部車。

相似詞　片 put together 組裝；拼湊
　　　　　 動 piece 組合；裝配

02

component

[kəmˋponənt]

名 (機器、設備等) 零件組成的

- com- 一起
- pon 擺放
- -ent 名 表「事物」

Some of the toy's **components** are made in this country, and some are outsourced.

這個玩具的零件有一些是在國內製造的，有一些則是外包製造。

03

consistency

[kənˋsɪstənsɪ]

名 一致性

- con- 共同
- sist 站立
- -ency 名

Maintaining quality **consistency** is the most crucial aspect of the assembly.

保持品質一致是裝配線最重要的事。

04

equip

[ɪˋkwɪp]

動 裝備；使……配有

We have **equipped** our assembly line completely—now we just need to hire staff.

我們已經組裝好裝配線了，現在只需招募人手。

應用　be equipped with + N. 裝備有……

05

halt

[hɔlt]

名 停止；終止

If an emergency occurs, press this button to bring all activities to a **halt**.

萬一發生緊急事故，按下這個按鈕會終止所有運作。

應用　grind to a halt (過程中) 逐漸停止

06

maximize
['mæksə,maɪz]

動 使……最大化

- maxim(um) 名 最大值
- -ize 動 表「……化」

We're trying to **maximize** our efficiency with this process.

我們試著用這個程序使效率最佳化。

07

streamline
['strim,laɪn]

動（常透過簡化辦事程序）
使（機構）效率更高；
簡化

- stream 名 流動
- line 名 線

We have **streamlined** the flow of the production line to assure efficiency and safety.

我們已簡化了生產線的流程，以確保高效率及安全性。

Factory 工廠

08

function
['fʌŋkʃən]

名 功能

- funct 執行
- -ion 名 表「動作；結果」

Can you tell me what **function** this lever has?

你可以告訴我這個控制桿有什麼功能嗎？

09

industry
['ɪndəstrɪ]

名 產業

My father has been working in the automotive **industry** for 20 years.

我父親已經在汽車工業服務了20年。

10

mechanical
[mə'kænɪkl]

形 機械的

- mechanic 機械工
- -al 形 表「關於……的」

I advise the car designers on **mechanical** processes.

我給汽車設計師一些機械加工方面的建議。

11 **rely**

[rɪˋlaɪ]

動 依賴；信賴

We **rely** on our workers to make quality products.

我們仰賴員工製造出優良產品。

| 應用 | rely on / count on / depend on + O. (+ to V.)
依賴……（去做……） |

---

12 **fuel-efficient**

[ˋfjʊəlɪˋfɪʃənt]

形 省油的

The car looks nice, but it isn't **fuel-efficient**.

這輛車看起來很棒，但是一點也不省油。

---

13 **hand over**

動 片 交出

I can't believe we're about to **hand over** all responsibility for security to a contractor.

我不敢相信我們將要外包所有的保全職責。

| 應用 | 1 hand on 轉交；傳遞
2 hand out 分發；發送 |

---

14 **license**

[ˋlaɪsn̩s]

名 許可；執照

Have we got a **license** to use this software?

我們有使用這個軟體的許可嗎？

| 比較 | 【美式拼法】license
【英式拼法】licence |

176

15 美英 16 加美 17 英澳 18 英美

unit
14

Production & Quality Control 生產與品管

15 chemical
[`kɛmɪkl̩]

形 化學的

・chemic 形 煉金術的；
化學的
・-al 形「具其特徵的」

We have to be sure we achieve the correct **chemical** reaction.

我們要確定得到正確的化學反應。

Monitoring/Overseeing 監控

16 closely
[`kloslɪ]

副 嚴密地；仔細地

All aspects of production are **closely** watched.

我們嚴密監督整個製造過程。

17 condition
[kən`dɪʃən]

名 情況；(健康等)狀態；
條件

・con- 一起
・dic 說
・-ion 名 表「行為；結果」

The first thing that the safety team does in the morning is check the **condition** of all our equipment.

安全小組每天早上做的第一件事，就是檢查所有設備的狀況。

應用

① in (a) good/poor condition 狀態良好／很差
② under . . . conditions 在……的情況下
③ on (one) condition that 子句
在滿足……的前提下

18 detect
[dɪ`tɛkt]

動 察覺；查出

・de- 離去
・tect 掩蓋

I have never **detected** any serious problem with this machine.

我從來沒有查出這部機器有什麼嚴重的問題。

相似詞
動 find = discover 找到；發現
動 spot 看見；注意到

177

19 scrutinize
[ˋskrutn̩ˏaɪz]

動 細看；仔細審查

• scrutiny 名 仔細檢查
• -ize 動 表「按某方式處理」

The safety monitors **scrutinize** every move we make.

監視器監視我們的一舉一動。

相似詞
動 inspect 檢查；審查；視察
動 examine 檢查；診察
動 dissect 解剖；仔細分析

Production 生產

20 capacity
[kəˋpæsətɪ]

名 容量；能力；生產力

• capaci 寬敞的
• -ty 名 表「性質」

We produce 200 units a day, but we have the **capacity** to make 300.

我們一天生產兩百台，但我們其實有三百台的生產力。

---

21 distinguish
[dɪˋstɪŋgwɪʃ]

動 區別

• dis- 分開
• sting 刺
• -ish 動 表「做」

At this step in production, we **distinguish** between top quality products and those with errors.

在生產過程的這個階段，我們會區分最優良的產品和瑕疵品。

應用
distinguish/differentiate between A and B
區分 A 和 B

---

22 element
[ˋɛləmənt]

名 元素；要素

There are so many **elements** to the production cycle, and no one could keep track of all of them.

沒有人可以追蹤所有製造過程裡用到的元素，因為它們實在太多了。

unit
14

Production & Quality Control 生產與品管

23 fulfill
[fʊlˋfɪl]
動 履行；達到；執行
・full 形 充分的
・fill 動 裝滿

Some factory workers will have to start working overtime if we want to **fulfill** our production schedule.
如果想達到我們訂的生產時程，有些工廠工人必須要開始加班。

相似詞
動 achieve 實現；到達
動 accomplish 完成；達到
動 realize 完成；實現
片 carry out 執行；進行

24 fully
[ˋfʊlɪ]
副 完全地；徹底地
・full 形 充滿的
・-ly 副

Once the line is **fully** operational, we'll produce thousands of units a week.
一旦生產線全面運作，我們一星期就可以生產幾千台。

相似詞
副 entirely 整個地；徹底地
副 totally 全部地；完整地
副 wholly 完全地；全部

25 handcrafted
[hændˋkræftɪd]
形 純手工製的
・hand 名 手
・craft 名 工藝
・-ed 形

I like to buy **handcrafted** products, but sometimes they're too expensive.
我喜歡買手工產品，但有時候它們太昂貴了。

26 hectic
[ˋhɛktɪk]
形 繁忙的；忙碌的

With all the equipment operating and people working, the factory can look quite **hectic**.
當所有設備都在運轉、所有人都在工作，工廠看起來相當繁忙。

反義詞
形 calm 冷靜的；鎮定的
形 peaceful 平靜的；和平的
形 quiet 安靜的；平靜的

179

27 independent
[ˌɪndɪˈpɛndənt]

形 獨立的；自主的

• in- 不
• depend 動 依賴
• -ent 形 表「有……性質的」

We maintain one **independent** source of power, in case the city grid goes down while we're on a deadline.

萬一我們趕著交貨，又停止供電，我們至少還有自主供電的來源。

---

28 manufacture
[ˌmænjəˈfæktʃɚ]

動 （大量）製造；加工

• manus 手
• fact 製造；做
• -ure 名 表「動作；動作的結果」

The factory **manufactures** high-quality camera lenses.

這家工廠生產品質優良的照相機鏡頭。

---

29 reduction
[rɪˈdʌkʃən]

名 減少；縮小；降低；簡化

• reduce 減少
• -ion 名 表「行為」

A **reduction** in the number of cars we produce is needed, because people aren't buying them.

我們必須減少生產汽車的數量，因為沒人要買我們的車。

Quality Control 品質管理

30 acclaimed
[əˈklemd]

形 備受推崇的

• ac- 向
• claim [古法文 clamer]
  呼喊
• -ed 形

Volvo products are **acclaimed** worldwide for their reliability. They should keep it that way.

富豪汽車以其安全可靠在國際間備受推崇，應該繼續保持下去。

---

31 **enhance**
[ɪn`hæns]

動 提高；增加

· en- 在裡面
· hance 高

We feel that having two independent overseers helps us **enhance** quality control.

我們覺得，兩位獨立的監督人員有助於我們提升品質管理。

---

32 **freshness**
[`frɛʃnəs]

名 新鮮

· fresh 形 新鮮的
· -ness 名 表「性質；狀態」

If Del Monte fruit is not of the utmost **freshness**, we don't sell it.

如果臺爾蒙的水果不是最新鮮的，我們就不賣。

---

33 **frozen**
[`frozn̩]

形 冰凍的；極冷的

Some **frozen** products are just as good as fresh.

有些冷凍產品和新鮮的一樣好。

---

34 **garment**
[`gɑrmənt]

名 衣服

At the end of the day, someone checks each **garment** for flaws.

每天下班前都有人檢查每件衣服有無瑕疵。

---

35 **inspect**
[ɪn`spɛkt]

動 檢查；審查；視察

· in- 內
· spect 看

I **inspect** each pair of shoes that we produce.

我檢查每雙我們生產的鞋子。

---

36 **loss**
[lɔs]

名 喪失；損失

We may suffer a **loss** in sales this year.

今年我們的業績會很慘淡。

| 應用 | 1 suffer a loss in/of + N. 蒙受……的損失 |
| | 2 at a loss (for words) 語塞 |

37 quality
['kwɑlətɪ]

名 品質

· qual 某性質的
· -ity 名

We would rather decrease our productivity than see **quality** suffer.

我們寧可降低產量也不願犧牲品質。

---

38 sample
['sæmpl]

名 樣品

Would it be possible to see a **sample** of your products?

我們可以看一下貴公司的樣品嗎？

---

39 standard
['stændəd]

名 標準；水準

· stand 立；安置
· -ard 名

We set very high **standards**, because our customers expect them.

為了回應顧客的期待，所以我們把標準定的很高。

應用	1 set a standard 訂定標準
	2 up to standard 達到標準
	3 below standard 不合格

---

40 strict
[strɪkt]

形 嚴格的

Management have set **strict** rules about what is and is not allowable in a final product.

管理階層在最終成品上立下嚴格的規定，關於何者可以接受、何者不能都有規定。

學後小試 **A** | **Multiple Choice Questions**
請選擇合適的單字填入空格

_____ ☐ I would like to see a _____ before I make my purchase.

(A) sample   (B) quality
(C) loss   (D) freshness

_____ ☐ We'll never _____ this order if we can't get our equipment to function correctly.

(A) distinguish   (B) rely
(C) fulfill   (D) scrutinize

_____ ☐ I think we should ask for a _____ in price before we sign the contract.

(A) function   (B) capacity
(C) garment   (D) reduction

_____ ☐ Do you want _____ strawberries or fresh ones?

(A) frozen   (B) mechanical
(C) chemical   (D) handcrafted

_____ ☐ This toy looks simple, but it has many different _____.

(A) industries   (B) components
(C) halts   (D) consistencies

正確答案請參考 416 頁

B Match

請在空格填入合適的單字，動詞需依時態變化，名詞需填入正確之單複數。

| fully | closely | inspect | streamline | condition | equip |

1. The equipment is brand new and in excellent _____.

2. Do you _____ every car you make before you sell it?

3. Please watch the process _____, so you can understand it.

4. We will _____ our workers with the best safety gear on the market.

5. If we _____ our assembly process, we'll be able to produce more.

6. Our staff are _____ committed to producing top quality tablets.

C Listening Practice

請聆聽音檔，將單字填入空格 140

1. This factory _____ breakfast cereals.

2. It takes 48 hours to _____ this type of car.

3. Once I get the right _____, I'll be able to operate this machine.

4. With the new, faster assembly mechanism, we'll _____ our production capabilities.

5. When will we _____ the cars to the transport team?

6. We need to call someone in to _____ the leak.

正確答案請參考 416 頁

Unit 15

Retail & Purchasing

零售與採購

不論是多益中的聽力測驗或是閱讀測驗，購物是最常見的情境之一：

1 建議使用角色扮演記憶法：作為客人（consumer）時，偶爾排隊（line up）購買；作為商人時，要會定價（price）或給予折扣（discount）。

2 掌握各式各樣商品周邊的說法，例如目錄（catalog）、折價券（voucher），並配合子單元的情境以應用這些詞彙。

學前暖身 請閱讀英文定義，並將正確單字與之配對

order	clearance sale	compatible	down payment	subscribe

1 _____ : a percentage of the total price paid in advance to insure supply

2 _____ : to pay a fee for a regular service or product

3 _____ : the ability of two different things to work together

4 _____ : a reduction in prices to clear storage or floor space

5 _____ : to request the delivery of a product or service in exchange for payment

Bargaining 買賣

01 **affordable**
[ə`fɔrdəbl]

形 買得起；可負擔的

• afford 動 買得起
• -able 形 表「可……的」

If we pay in cash, could you bring the price down to a more **affordable** level?

如果我們付現金，你能把價格降得更便宜嗎？

相似詞	形 reasonable 合理的
	形 acceptable 可接受的
	形 inexpensive 便宜的

02 **bargain**
[`bɑrgɪn]

名 買賣；便宜貨，廉價品

Considering the price is 50% of what it used to be, I definitely think it is a **bargain**.

價格是之前的一半，我認為這確實很便宜。

| 應用 | strike a bargain = strike a deal 達成協議 |

03 **quantity**
[`kwɑntətɪ]

名 數量

• quant 多少
• -ity 名

The **quantity** purchased will not affect the individual unit price.

購買的數量不會影響單價。

| 應用 | buy/purchase Sth. + in quantity / in large amounts / in bulk 大量購買某物 |

04 **worth**
[wɝθ]

名 值得

If you extend the payment period from 12 to 24 months, we will make it **worth** your time.

如果你把付款週期從一年改成兩年，我們會讓你覺得更划算。

| 應用 | 1 worth a fortune 價值連城 |
| | 2 worth a try 值得一試 |

---

05 demand
[dɪˈmænd]

名 要求;需要

- de- 加強意義
- mand 吩咐;命令

Unfortunately, just as we were able to increase production, **demand** dropped off.
不幸的是,正當我們能夠提高生產時,需求卻下降了。

應用 meet/satisfy the demand for + N.
滿足對……的需求

06 suited
[ˈsutɪd]

形 合適的;相稱的

- suit 動 適合
- -ed 形

Perhaps you could name a price more **suited** to your company's budget?
也許你能說出一個更符合你公司預算的價格?

應用 A be suited to B = A be suitable for B
A適合B

07 order
[ˈɔrdɚ]

動 訂購

Their representative called to warn us that they will **order** 60% of our production next quarter.
他們的承辦人打電話來提醒,他們要訂我們下一季六成的產品。

08 supplier
[səˈplaɪɚ]

名 供應商

- supply 動 供給
- -er 名 表「人」

We need to find a **supplier** closer to our factory, in order to reduce shipping costs.
我們需要找到離工廠更近的供應商,以降低運輸成本。

09 wrap
[ræp]

動 包裝

We **wrap** any purchase free of charge, so long as it is intended as a gift.
只要購買我們的商品是為了送禮,我們都提供免費包裝的服務。

應用 wrap up
1 包好;裹住
2 完成;結束

10 purchase
['pɝtʃəs]

動 購買

· pur- 向前
· chase 追

When you **purchase** 10 items or more, we'll include another at no additional cost.

當您購買超過十件物品，我們將免費贈送一件。

Customer 顧客

11 aisle
[aɪl]

名 (戲院、教堂、列車等坐席間的)通道；走道

Some supermarkets in the US have an entire **aisle** displaying nothing but breakfast cereals.

在美國，某些超市會陳列整整一列的早餐麥片。

12 avid
['ævɪd]

形 熱心的；勁頭十足的

She is an **avid** shopper, and she is always looking for discounts.

她熱衷於購物，總是在尋找折扣品。

13 line up

動 片 排隊

People have **lined up** in front of the store, waiting for it to open.

很多人在商店前面排隊等它開門。

應用
line one's pockets 中飽私囊
補充：line up 不做被動式使用

14 consumer
[kən'sjumɚ]

名 消費者

· consume 動 消耗；花費
· -er 名 表「人」

These days, electronics **consumers** are opting for repurchase rather than repair.

最近，電子產品的消費者傾向以重新購買替代修理。

188

Goods 商品

15

goods
[gʊdz]

名 商品；貨物

The **goods** will be in your store and available for sale before the weekend.

這批貨物將送到您的店裡，在週末之前即可出售。

> **應用** goods/merchandise：商品總稱，集合名詞當單數

16

compatible
[kəm`pætəbḷ]

形 (電腦) 相容的

• com- 一起
• pat 容忍；忍受
• -ible 形 表「可……的」

We've just received word that our new smartphone is not **compatible** with chargers sold in that country.

我們剛收到消息，新的智慧型手機跟那個國家賣的充電器不相容。

> **應用** A be compatible with B　A和B可相容

17

inventory
[`ɪnvənˌtorɪ]

名 存貨清單；財產目錄

• invent 動 發明
• -ory 名 表「做……用的東西」

Because these items are perishable, we aim to keep as little **inventory** on hand as possible.

因為這些物品很容易變質，所以我們的目標是盡可能減少庫存。

18

merchandise
[`mɝtʃənˌdaɪz]

名 商品；貨物

• merchant 名 商人
• -ize 名 表「狀態」

Merchandise on display can be purchased at a discount if it shows signs of use or damage.

如果展示品有使用過或損壞的跡象，購買時可享折扣。

19 stack
[stæk]

名 乾草堆；(整齊)
　　一堆

There's a **stack** of cookbooks in the back that needs sorting before we can put them out for sale.

需要先整理過，才能出售後面那一堆食譜。

常見 **量詞**	a piece of paper 一張紙 a flock of birds 一群鳥 a loaf of bread 一條麵包 a flight of stairs 一段階梯

---

20 superb
[su`pɝb]

形 堂皇的；宏偉的；
　　上乘的；一流的

We've received several compliments regarding the **superb** quality of our massage chairs.

我們已經收到許多迴響，讚美按摩椅的品質優良。

---

21 variety
[və`raɪətɪ]

名 變化；種類

・vari 變化
・-ety 名 表「性質；狀態」

Biztek offers a **variety** of workstations, so customers can select those that match their needs.

比茲提克提供很多工作站，顧客可以選擇哪些符合自己的需求。

應用	a variety of N. = various + N. = all kinds/sorts of N. 琳瑯滿目的……

---

22 place an order

動 片 下訂單

We would like to **place an order** for a dozen electronic pianos, and we need them delivered by Monday.

我們想訂十二架電子琴，並且需要它們在星期　前送達。

Pricing 定價

23
cost
[kɔst]

動 花……費用

How much will it **cost** to change the color of these vehicles?

這些車子換顏色要花多少錢？

> **應用**　cost a fortune = cost a lot of money
> 花了一大筆錢

24
discount
[ˋdɪskaʊnt]

名 折扣

・dis- 不
・count 數；計算

Discounts can only be given to customers who already have a store membership card.

只有擁有本店會員卡的顧客才可享折扣。

25
expensive
[ɪkˋspɛnsɪv]

形 貴的

・expense 名 費用
・-ive 形 表「與……有關的；具有……性質的；有……傾向的」

The more **expensive** an item is, the fewer we should put on display to preserve an image of exclusivity.

商品越貴，就應越少展示，以保持物以稀為貴的形象。

26
quote
[kwot]

名 報價

They said they'd be willing to go below their **quote** if we'd extend the deadline.

他們說如果我們能延長期限的話，他們願意降低報價。

27 retail
[`ritel]

名 零售

• re- 再
• tail 裁切

To excel in **retail**, you have to convince people their lives would be better with your product.

要在零售業中出類拔萃，你得讓大家相信，他們的生活會因你的產品而更好。

應用
[1] retail price 零售價
[2] retail sales 零售額

Sales 銷售

28 assorted
[ə`sɔrtɪd]

形 各式各樣的

• as- 向
• sort 種類
• -ed 形

There are three boxes of **assorted** Christmas ornaments that need to be cleaned and individually wrapped.

這裡有三箱各式各樣的聖誕飾品，需要清理和個別包裝。

29 business hours

名 片 營業時間

The advantage of online retail is that **business hours** are 24/7.

線上零售的優勢，在於營業時間全年無休。

30 clearance sale
[`klɪrəns]

名 片 清倉大拍賣

At the end of every summer, the clothing stores have a **clearance sale** to make space for their fall wardrobes.

每個夏天結束時，服飾店會有清倉大拍賣，為秋裝清出空間。

31 down payment
[`pemənt]

名 片 頭期款

An installment plan is available, but it requires a **down payment** of 10% of the total price.

這個分期付款計畫需要先付總價10％的頭期款。

32 **overcharge**
[ˌovɚˈtʃɑrdʒ]

動 索價過高

• over- 超越;越過
• charge 動 要價

This receipt shows that your clerk **overcharged** me for the warranty I was told was on discount.

這張收據上寫了你的店員多收了我保固費用的錢,保固應該有打折。

> **文化**
> **補充**
> 在美國購買商品,有時是顧客另外付錢,選擇購買一年或兩年的保固,看起來不方便,但是美國退換貨的標準相當寬鬆,因此有時自己造成的損壞,還可以換全新商品。

33 **subscribe**
[səbˈskraɪb]

動 認捐;捐助;
  訂閱;訂購

• sub- 在下方
• scribe 寫

Customers who **subscribe** to our monthly newsletter will receive valuable store coupons not usable by other customers.

訂閱我們月訊的顧客將獲得豐厚的商店折價券,是其他顧客所沒有的。

> **應用**
> [1] subscribe to 訂閱
> [2] subscribe for 認購

34 **voucher**
[ˈvaʊtʃɚ]

名 優惠券

Because she couldn't exchange the item for a new one, we gave her a **voucher** for a later purchase.

因為這件商品她不能換新的,我們給她一張優惠券,下次消費時可以用。

Size/Shape 尺寸

35 **attire**
[əˈtaɪr]

名 服裝

Men's **attire** is on the third floor, just past the luggage.

男裝是三樓,就在行李區之後。

36 bulk
[bʌlk]

形 大量的

By selling candy in **bulk**, we limit the cost of packaging.

透過大量販售糖果，我們控制了包裝的成本。

37 catalog
[`kætəlɔg]

名 目錄；型錄

• cata- 完全
• logue 說

We're going to phase out our print **catalog** and instead put all our product descriptions online.

我們將逐步淘汰印刷產品目錄，並把所有的產品說明放在網站上。

| 比較 | 【美式拼法】catalog |
| | 【英式拼法】catalogue |

38 choose
[tʃuz]

動 選擇

Notice how their retail site lets browsers **choose** between different colors by using an avatar?

他們的零售網站讓閱覽者透過虛擬人物來選顏色，你注意到了嗎？

39 diverse
[daɪ`vɝs]

形 不同的；多樣的；多變化的

Our clients are extremely **diverse** in age and income, so we have to be flexible to tailor our presentation.

我們客戶的年齡和收入迥異，所以我們必須靈活地調整我們的介紹。

40 wrinkle
[`rɪŋkl]

名 皺紋；皺摺

Because they were stored improperly, these dresses are now full of **wrinkles**.

你這些洋裝沒有收好，所以起了很多皺摺。

學後小試 A **Multiple Choice Questions**
請選擇合適的單字填入空格

_____ 1 Our new supplier offers a(n) _____ and low-cost range of styles.

(A) diverse   (B) expensive
(C) avid   (D) suited

_____ 2 We've included our most recent _____ so you can browse our inventory.

(A) wrinkle   (B) business hours
(C) catalog   (D) supplier

_____ 3 These _____ T-shirts come in various color that I like, but their prices are over my budget.

(A) compatible   (B) bulk
(C) affordable   (D) assorted

_____ 4 White Dog is excellent at transporting retail _____ quickly and without incident.

(A) merchandise   (B) bargain
(C) stack   (D) voucher

_____ 5 Your order failed to state the exact _____ of tires you wished to purchase.

(A) goods   (B) quantity
(C) aisle   (D) consumer

正確答案請參考 416 頁

B Match
請在空格填入合適的單字，動詞需依時態變化，名詞需填入正確之單複數。

| variety | attire | purchase | retail | quote | wrap |

▢ You can _____ the item with either a credit card or cash.

▢ In the United States, demand for children's _____ usually goes up just before the start of the school year.

▢ If you want to work in _____, you need to excel at customer service.

▢ I think we should choose them, because their _____ is below the market average.

▢ There is a _____ of online sites that allow consumers to compare prices.

▢ Our shops _____ all Christmas purchases free of charge.

C Listening Practice
請聆聽音檔，將單字填入空格 150

▢ The new displays will _____ a lot more than the previous ones.

▢ We _____ our clients by about 4%, so we need to contact them as soon as possible.

▢ The merchandise is _____ too much to let it sit in storage for long.

▢ Customers who bring in stores coupons are eligible for _____.

▢ I'm afraid there is very little _____ for video tape players these days.

▢ The only way we're going to get rid of our _____ is to reduce prices.

Unit 16

Sales & Services

販售與服務

銷售與服務的情境在聽力測驗與閱讀測驗中都相當常見：

1. 連結會使用到的單字，如回應（response）顧客需求、評估
   （evaluate）退貨條件、寄送貨物（deliver shipment）。

2. 客訴、退換貨、貨運是為此單元的重點，故必須加強留意；如熟悉退費
   的不同說法：refund（動名詞同型）/reimburse（須接受詞）/rebate
   （部分退款）。

學前暖身 請閱讀英文定義，並將正確單字與之配對

defect	response	customized	evaluate	dispatch

1 _____: to assess the validity or value of an object or situation

2 _____: to send or ship

3 _____: an answer or reply to a question or complaint

4 _____: made to a particular set of specifications

5 _____: a flaw or problem

Complaint 客訴

01 **complaint**

[kəm`plent]

图 抱怨；抗議

• com- 完全
• plaint 訴苦

People with **complaints** are immediately brought to speak with a manager.

投訴者立刻被帶去見經理。

應用
[1] make/file a complaint against
對⋯⋯提出控訴；抱怨⋯⋯
[2] complaint letter 抱怨信

02 **defect**

[`dɪfɛkt]

图 缺點；缺陷

• de- 相反的效果
• fect 做

We're so sorry that the product you bought had a **defect**.

我們很抱歉你買的產品有缺陷。

應用   genetic defects 基因缺陷

03 **even if**

片 即使

Even if you were to offer me a working product, I wouldn't want it. I only want my money back.

即使你給我一個可用的產品，我也不想要了，我只想要拿回我的錢。

04 **incur**

[ɪn`kɝ]

動 招致；帶來

• in- 向內
• cur 跑

We don't want to **incur** any loss of business because of this incident.

我們不想因這件事造成任何業務損失。

應用
[1] incur someone's wrath 惹某人發火
[2] incur a debt 身陷債務

05 lately

['letlɪ]

副 近來；最近

· late 形 最近的
· -ly 副 表「……地」

The boutique has had a lot of returns **lately**. I wonder if there's a problem in production.

這家精品店最近收到很多退貨，不知道是不是生產出了什麼問題。

---

06 reason

['rizṇ]

名 理性；理由

Could you please tell me the **reason** you're returning this item?

你能告訴我退貨的原因嗎？

---

07 reasonable

['rizṇəbḷ]

形 通情達理的；合理的；明智的

· reason 名 理性
· -able 形「有……特性的」

I try to be polite with customers at all times, but sometimes they are not **reasonable**.

我一直試著對顧客保持禮貌，但有時候他們真的很不可理喻。

---

08 regret

[rɪ'grɛt]

動 遺憾

· re- 再
· gret 哭；呼喊

We deeply **regret** the inconvenience caused by the mistake.

對於這項錯誤造成的不便，我們深感遺憾。

應用

1 regret to V. (對接下來要說／做的)
很抱歉要……

2 regret V-ing/N. 對已造成的問題感到遺憾

199

09 **response**
[rɪˋspɑns]

名 回應；回覆

• re- 回
• spons 保證；許諾

You may expect a **response** from our customer service department within 24 hours.
我們的客服部門將在一天內回覆您。

| 應用 | response + to N. 對⋯⋯的回應 |

Customer 顧客

---

10 **assure**
[əˋʃʊr]

動 保證；確保

• as- 向
• sure 確定；安全

We would like to **assure** you that we are working on the problem right now.
我們向你保證，我們現在正努力解決這個問題。

| 應用 | assure someone + that子句 向某人保證⋯⋯ |

---

11 **client**
[ˋklaɪənt]

名 客戶

You are a valuable **client** and we want you to leave the store happy.
您是非常重要的客戶，我們希望您高高興興地離開本店。

---

12 **customized**
[ˋkʌstəmˏaɪzd]

形 客製化的

• custom 名 習慣；習俗
• -ize 動 表「⋯⋯化」
• -ed 形

I want a **customized** design, not something everyone is wearing.
我想要量身訂做的設計，不想到處撞衫。

| 相似詞 | 形 custom-made = tailor-made = tailored = made-to-order 客製化的；訂做的 |

13 support

[sə`port]

名 支持；支撐

• sup- 向上
• port 運送

I didn't get any **support** from the company when I was figuring out why I had been overcharged.

在我想要了解為何被多收費的時候，這家公司完全派不上用場。

Exchange 換貨

14 excluding

[ɪk`skludɪŋ]

介 不包括；除去

• ex- 外
• clude 關閉
• -ing 介

We are happy to exchange products under most circumstances, **excluding** cases where the product has been damaged through use.

在大多數情況下我們很樂意提供換貨，但不包括在使用中損壞的產品。

反義字 介 including 包含；包括

15 mail

[mel]

動 郵寄；寄送

Could you please **mail** me a refund?

你能將退款寄過來給我嗎？

16 rather than

[`ræðɚ]

片 而不是……

Rather than issue a refund, could you just send me a new printer?

我不要退款，你可以寄一台新的印表機給我嗎？

應用
I'd like to drink coffee rather than drink tea.
= I'd prefer coffee to tea.
我比較喜歡喝咖啡而不是茶。

17 restriction
[rɪˋstrɪkʃən]

名 限制；限制規定

• restrict 動 限制
• -ion 名 表「行為；行為的結果」

It's impossible to get your money back from that store—there are too many **restrictions** on returns.
那家商店根本不可能退你錢，有太多的退貨限制了。

---

18 storage
[ˋstorɪdʒ]

名 貯藏；保管；倉庫；庫存量

• store 動 貯藏
• -age 名 表「行為；狀態；結果」

Do you have **storage** facilities here at the conference center?
你們的會議中心有儲藏設施嗎？

---

19 breakable
[ˋbrekəbl]

形 會碎的；易碎的

• break 動 打破；弄壞
• -able 形 表「可……的」

Please be careful with that; it's easily **breakable**.
請小心，它很易碎的。

---

20 damage
[ˋdæmɪdʒ]

動 損害

You'll **damage** the spine if you keep bending your book like that.
如果你一直這樣摺你的書，你會把書背弄壞。

應用
[1] irreparably damage 無法挽回的傷害
[2] permanent damage 永久性的傷害

Refund 退款

21

compensate

[ˈkɑmpənˌset]

動 補償；賠償

· com- 一起
· pens 衡量
· -ate 動 表「成為」

I wish I could be **compensated** for the amount of time I spent on trying to fix that printer.

花在修復這台印表機的時間，我希望可以得到補償。

應用	compensate Sb. for Sth. 補償某人某物的損失

22

evaluate

[ɪˈvæljuˌet]

動 評估

· e- 出
· valu 價
· -ate 動 表「使……」

Our customer service department will have to **evaluate** your claim before we can process your refund.

在處理您的退款前，我們的客服部門必須先評估您的申請。

23

except

[ɪkˈsɛpt]

介 除……之外

All items are eligible for return **except** for undergarments.

除了貼身衣物，所有產品都可以退貨。

24

express

[ɪkˈsprɛs]

形 快遞的

· ex- 向外
· press 動 壓

Our warehouse team will send your items by **express** delivery.

我們的物流團隊將用快遞寄送您的物品。

25

rebate

[ˈribet]

名 部分退款

Because of the misunderstanding, we are going to offer you a **rebate**, applicable on your next purchase.

由於這次的誤會，我們將退部分款項給您，下次購物時可使用。

26 refund
['rɪ,fʌnd]

名 退還；退款

• re- 回
• fund 傾注

I would rather have a **refund** than an exchange, if that's possible.

如果可以的話，我寧願要退款也不願意換貨。

---

27 invoice
['ɪnvɔɪs]

名 帳單

I received the products I ordered, but there was no **invoice** included.

我收到我訂購的產品了，但是沒有附帳單。

---

28 receipt
[rɪ'sit]

名 收據

I don't know if I can return these shoes without a **receipt**.

不知道我能不能在沒有收據的情況下退掉這雙鞋子。

---

29 reimburse
[,riɪm'bɝs]

動 退還；退款；賠償

• re- 返回
• im 入
• burse 錢包

I'm afraid we can't **reimburse** you without a receipt.

沒有收據的話，恐怕不能退款給您。

Questionnaire 問卷調查

30 comment
['kɑmɛnt]

名 評論；意見

Please write down your **comments** on our questionnaire.

請在我們的問卷上寫下您的意見。

> 應用　make/leave one's comments/
> remarks on + N. 對……做評論

204

31 **excellence**
[ˈɛksləns]

名 優秀;傑出

・excel 優於
・-ence 名 表「性質;狀態」

Our maintenance team strives for **excellence** in their service.

我們的維修團隊在服務上精益求精。

---

32 **random**
[ˈrændəm]

形 隨機的

There will be a **random** drawing to decide who goes first.

誰先去將由抽籤決定。

---

33 **range**
[rendʒ]

名 範圍

Which product from our **range** would you like to comment on?

您想評論我們系列產品的哪一項?

> **應用** a range of + N. 一系列的;某一類的

Shipping 運送

34 **carrier**
[ˈkærɪə]

名 運輸公司

・carry 動 運載
・-er 名 表「人;物」

We use a very reliable **carrier** for our deliveries, so we are confident that they will always arrive on time.

我們和一家非常可靠的運輸公司合作,因此我們有信心貨物會準時送達。

---

35 **courier**
[ˈkʊrɪə]

名 快遞信差

To ensure a timely delivery, we will send your items by **courier**.

為確保及時交貨,我們將以快遞寄送您的物品。

36 deliver

[dɪˋlɪvɚ]

動 投遞

I'm so sad: my favorite pizza place doesn't **deliver** to my new neighborhood.

我很傷心，我最喜歡的披薩店不能外送到我現在住的這一帶。

---

37 dispatch

[dɪˋspætʃ]

動 派遣

• dis- 離開
• patch 腳步

We are so sorry we sent you the wrong item, and we will **dispatch** the correct item tonight.

我們很抱歉寄錯商品給您，今晚將寄送正確的商品給您。

---

38 reach

[ritʃ]

動 抵達，到達

A normal shipment usually takes three weeks to **reach** that location.

正常運送通常需要三週才能到達那個地點。

---

39 ready

[ˋrɛdɪ]

形 準備好的

The bouquet I ordered is intended to be a birthday surprise, so it's very important that it be **ready** on time.

我訂的那束花是要當作生日驚喜的，因此準時送到很重要。

---

40 shipment

[ˋʃɪpmənt]

名 運送的貨物

• ship 動 運送
• -ment 名 表「行動；狀態」

Can you tell me when the **shipment** was received?

你能告訴我這批貨是什麼時候收到的嗎？

學後小試

A Multiple Choice Questions

請選擇合適的單字填入空格

_____ 1 Please write your _____ in the space below.

    (A) excellence   (B) comments
    (C) storage   (D) couriers

_____ 2 How long will it take my order to _____ its destination?

    (A) assure   (B) compensate
    (C) reach   (D) reimburse

_____ 3 The shop will give me a _____ when I return these shoes.

    (A) complaint   (B) refund
    (C) carrier   (D) regret

_____ 4 We sell a(n) _____ of electronic products, from computers to smartphones.

    (A) rebate   (B) range
    (C) invoice   (D) receipt

_____ 5 I've been waiting for a long time, so I really hope my order is _____ today.

    (A) random   (B) breakable
    (C) ready   (D) reasonable

正確答案請參考 417 頁

B Match
請在空格填入合適的單字，動詞需依時態變化，名詞需填入正確之單複數。

| except | rather than | mail | even if | damage | deliver |

1. _____ repay me, you can just buy me lunch next time.

2. We always offer our customers refunds _____ they bring back products without a receipt.

3. We take all forms of payment,_____ for personal checks.

4. I'll meet you after I stop by the post office to _____ this letter.

5. Please don't _____ that book—it's very important to me.

6. I'm not sure if your company _____ to Taiwan.

C Listening Practice
請聆聽音檔，將單字填入空格 160

1. We always want our _____ to enjoy our services.

2. Please list the _____ for your complaint here.

3. I'm calling to figure out if there are any _____ to your return policy.

4. Winter hats have been selling really well _____!

5. Do you offer any technical _____ for this product?

6. We ship products all over the world, _____ Antarctica.

正確答案請參考 417 頁

Unit 17

Marketing & Business Planning

行銷與策劃

行銷與策畫常會與第八單元的公告一起出現在閱讀測驗當中，重點在於：

1. 加強描述性的動詞與名詞的結合，如執行計畫（implement a plan）、舉行會議（hold a meeting）。

2. 熟悉描述策略（strategy/tactic）的相關名詞，例如優點（advantage），以及形容詞，如有效的（effective）。

學前暖身 請閱讀英文定義，並將正確單字與之配對

competitor	strategy	attain	unrivaled	implement

1 _____ : a state of being the best or without competitor

2 _____ : to do or start a plan of action

3 _____ : to get something, usually after some effort

4 _____ : in business, a person or persons trying to attract the same consumers

5 _____ : a plan or course of action

Business Competitor 商業對手

01 **adversely**

[æd`vɝslɪ]

副 相反地;不利地

• ad- 向
• verse 旋轉
• -ly 副

We hope that by expanding our operations, the coming recession will not **adversely** affect our profit margin.

我們希望透過擴大營運,即將來臨的經濟衰退不會影響到我們的利潤。

---

02 **ambitious**

[æm`bɪʃəs]

形 費勁的;有抱負的

• ambition 名 雄心
• -ous 形 表「有……特質的;多……的」

To date, this is their most **ambitious** ad campaign, and it costs more than ours by almost 50%.

目前為止,這是他們最大費周章的一次廣告宣傳,花費幾乎超過我們50%。

---

03 **coincide**

[ˌkoɪn`saɪd]

動 同時發生;相符

• co- 一起
• incide 降臨

It is essential that the launch **coincide** with the start of the holidays.

上市日必須和假期開始同一天。

| 應用 | A coincide with B A和B撞期 |

---

04 **competitive**

[kəm`pɛtətɪv]

形 具競爭力的

• compete 動 競爭;比賽
• -ive 形 表「有……特性的」

Samrich's new tablet will sell at a **competitive** price, even though they are made domestically.

即使山姆里奇公司的新平板在國內生產製造,定價仍具有競爭力。

| 應用 | competitive edge/advantage 競爭優勢 |

---

05 **competitor**

[kəm`pɛtətɚ]

名 競爭者

• com- 一起
• petit 尋求
• -or 名 表「人」

They've been **competitors** for so long that their joint venture sent shockwaves through the markets.

他們是老對手了,所以他們聯手合作的消息震驚了整個市場。

06 unrivaled

[ʌn`raɪv|d]

形 無可匹敵的

· un- 不
· rival 動 競爭
· -ed 形

Henderson Medical has an **unrivaled** dominance in the field of home health-care products.

居家醫療保健產品之中,韓德森醫療公司獨佔鰲頭。

---

07 complicated

[`kɑmplə,ketɪd]

形 複雜的

· complicate 動 使複雜
· -ed 形

Thurston has proposed a rather **complicated** solution to our dilemma, but I think it can be done.

關於我們的難題,德思頓提出了一個複雜的解決辦法,但我認為是可行的。

---

08 implement

[`ɪmpləmənt]

動 執行;實施

· im- 在⋯⋯之中
· ple 充滿
· -ment 動 名
  表「行為;方法」

You need to **implement** the backup plan just as soon as you receive word from Head Office.

收到總公司的消息之後,你得立刻執行備案計畫。

應用	implement a plan/law/policy/regulation/measure 實施計畫/法規/政策/規定/方法
相似詞	片 take effect 產生效果;起作用 片 carry out 啟用;執行 動 realize 實現;執行

Investigation 調查

09 apparent

[ə`pærənt]

形 顯而易見的;
   表面上的;外觀的

· ap- 向
· par 出現
· -ent 形

According to our on-site workers, the fire was started in an **apparent** arson attempt.

據我們現場的工作人員説,這場火災明顯是有人故意縱火。

10 ascertain
[ˌæsəˈten]

動 查明；確定；弄清

- as- 向
- certain 形 確定的

Only by questioning the management can we hope to **ascertain** where or when the harassment began.

只有質問管理階層，我們才能弄清楚騷擾是何時何地開始的。

---

11 consist
[kənˈsɪst]

動 組成；在於

- con- 共同
- sist 站立

The investigating team will **consist** of five experts in IT and data management.

調查小組由五位資訊科技和數據管理的專家組成。

> 應用　A consist of B　A由B組成

---

12 dig
[dɪg]

動 挖掘；發掘

The Board fired the new president after he **dug** up a long-term concealment of huge losses.

新任總裁揭發公司長期隱瞞重大虧損之後，董事會開除了他。

---

13 eliminate
[ɪˈlɪməˌnet]

動 消除；淘汰

- e- 出
- limin 門檻
- -ate 動 表「使成為」

We need you to **eliminate** the least likely motives before we can choose which leads to pursue.

在我們決定要追查哪幾條線索之前，需要你先排除最不可能的動機。

---

14 investigate
[ɪnˈvɛstəˌget]

動 調查；研究

- in- 向內
- vestige 痕跡；足跡
- -ate 動 表「使成為」

SamElk Tractors will be **investigated** for tax fraud, so we should distance ourselves from them as soon as possible.

山姆艾爾克牽引機公司將因逃漏稅接受調查，因此我們應該盡快與他們保持距離。

15 **statistics**

[stə'tɪstɪks]

图 統計資料;統計學

· status 图 身分;階級
· -istics 图 表「學説;科學」

The **statistics** are not promising: 65% of corporate espionage cases go unresolved.

統計資料並不樂觀:65%的商業間諜案件無法破案。

應用	the statistics 總體數據,集合名詞當複數

---

16 **survey**

['sɝ,ve]

图 調查;測量

· sur- 到……上面
· vey 看

Our first step is to conduct a **survey** of employees to gauge their attitudes towards power harassment.

我們首先要調查員工,評斷他們對濫用職權的態度。

---

17 **thorough**

['θɝo]

形 徹底的;完全的;
  十足的;徹頭徹尾的

The investigators promised they will be discrete yet **thorough**, interviewing everyone from top management down to junior staff.

調查人員答應他們,會各別且全面地面談全公司上下。

相似詞	形 careful 小心的;謹慎的 形 complete 完整的;徹底的 形 detailed 詳細的;仔細的

---

18 **trace**

[tres]

图 痕跡;記錄

The hackers left no **trace** of their IP address, so we have no idea in which country to begin our search.

駭客沒有留下網路位址的記錄,所以我們也不知道該到哪一個國家搜索。

應用	disappear/vanish without (a) trace 沒留下任何線索地失蹤

相似詞	图 sign 跡象;徵兆 图 clue 線索;痕跡 图 signal 訊號;紀錄

Marketing 行銷

19 aim
[em]

動 瞄準

By using a desert location, our ad **aims** to create a sense of solitude and strength.

透過乾燥沙漠的地點，我們的廣告旨在創造孤獨感和力量。

> **應用** aim at 瞄準；旨在

---

20 associated
[əˋsoʃɪ͵etd]

形 相關的

• associate 動 聯想
• -ed 形

I'm sure you'll agree we should avoid any mention of "risk" or its **associated** images, such as skydiving.

我相信你們都會同意我們必須刪減任何有「風險」意涵的字眼，以及相關的圖片，例如跳傘。

> **應用** A be associated with B　A和B有關聯

---

21 attain
[əˋten]

動 達到

• at- 向
• tain 接觸

Only after we **attain** market dominance in chewing gum should we focus on advertising our mints.

只有等我們在口香糖的市場擁有主導的地位之後，我們才可以轉而行銷我們的薄荷糖。

---

22 cut
[kʌt]

名 刪減

The president has ordered a 30% **cut** in our advertising budget, so I propose we abandon our print ad campaign.

總裁已經下令削減我們30%的廣告預算，所以我提議放棄我們的文書宣傳。

---

23 lead role
[lid] [rol]

名 領導者

Murphy is taking the **lead role** in the design, so you'll need to run your ideas past her.

墨菲主導這次的設計，所以你需要告訴她你的想法。

24
markedly
[ˋmɑrkədlɪ]

副 明顯地；顯著地

- mark 名 記號
- -ed 形
- -ly 副

While our mountain bikes are not **markedly** different from our competitors', they are perceived as being of better quality.

雖然我們的登山車並沒有明顯不同於我們的競爭對手，但我們的品質更受肯定。

25
overwhelming
[ˏovɚˋhwɛlmɪŋ]

形 巨大的；極大的

- over- 過度；在上面
- whelm 動 蓋；壓倒
- -ing 形

Their new ad campaign has helped them gain an **overwhelming** majority of the under-20 market.

他們新的廣告活動幫助他們，獲得了壓倒性的多數青年市場。

應用	be overwhelmed with/by + Sth. 被壓力／負荷擊倒

Strategy 策略

26
advantage
[ədˋvæntɪdʒ]

名 利益；優點

- advant 先；在前面
- -age 名

Creative Solution's clear **advantage** is that its offices are located in the same office buildings as those of its clients.

創意解決之道公司明顯的優勢在於，我們和客戶的辦公室都在同一棟辦公大樓。

應用	① take advantage of + N./V-ing = make use of 利用 ② have an advantage of 擁有……的優勢

27
advisor
[ədˋvaɪzɚ]

名 顧問

- advise 動 建議
- -or 名 表「人」

Mrs. Gonzalez will act as our strategy **advisor**, but she will be in no way responsible for determining policy.

岡薩雷斯太太將擔任我們的策略顧問，但不負責做決定。

相似詞	名 consultant 顧問；諮詢者 名 counselor 輔導員；律師

28
characteristic
[ˌkærəktəˈrɪstɪk]

名 特色；特徵

· character 名 特性
· -istic 名 表「性質」

Our spokesperson's most identifiable **characteristic** is her strength of will.

我們發言人的特點是她的意志力很強。

	名 feature 特徵；特色；特別報導
相似詞	名 quality 品質；特徵
	名 trait 特徵；特性

29
duplication
[ˌdjuplɪˈkeʃən]

名 複製；拷貝

· duplicate 動 複製
· -ion 名 表「行為；結果」

For the most part, their business model has depended on the **duplication** of competitors' products.

他們做生意的方法主要是靠仿造競爭對手的產品。

30
effective
[ɪˈfɛktɪv]

形 有效的；生效的

· effect 效果
· -ive 形 表「與……有關的；具有……性質的；有……傾向的」

The current strategy of headhunting managers is no longer **effective** and should be abandoned.

人事經理目前的策略失效了，應該放棄它。

31
hold
[hold]

動 舉行

We need to **hold** our next meeting three months before the product launch.

我們需要在產品上市前三個月舉行下一次的會議。

	1 hold office 擔任公職；執政
應用	2 hold off 延期
	3 hold that thought 先保留那個想法

32 imply
[ɪm`plaɪ]

動 暗指；意味著

· im- 在……之中
· ply 摺疊

The president didn't say it, but I think she **implied** she wasn't happy with Marketing's decision.

總裁雖然沒有明說，但我認為她在暗示她不太滿意行銷部的決定。

相似詞　動 suggest 建議；暗示
　　　　動 infer 推論；猜想；意味著

33 link
[lɪŋk]

動 聯結

In the press release, please **link** our community outreach programs to our corporate identity.

在新聞稿中，請把我們的社區服務計畫跟企業形象聯結在一起。

34 mastermind
[`mæstɚ,maɪnd]

名 策劃者；主謀

· master 名 控制；統治
· mind 名 心；想法

You may want to talk to Stevenson about that. He is the **mastermind** behind the plan.

也許你想和史蒂文生談談，他是計畫的策劃者。

35 realistic
[,rɪə`lɪstɪk]

形 現實的；實際的

· real 形 真的
· -ist 名「……主義的人」
· -ic 形 表「……的」

The proposal was scrapped because it lacked a **realistic** time frame.

這個提案被取消了，因為它的作業時間不切實際。

217

36 revision

[rɪˈvɪʒən]

名 修訂

- revise 動 修正
- -ion 名 表「行為；結果」

This will be the third **revision** of the press release, so it should be much clearer.

這新聞稿修訂了三次，應該更清楚了。

---

37 revolution

[ˌrɛvəˈluʃən]

名 革命

- revolute 動 參加革命
- -ion 名 表「行為」

Kenan's decision to use silent commercials might have sparked a **revolution** in advertising.

肯南決定用沒有對白的廣告，這可能在廣告圈中掀起改革。

---

38 strategy

[ˈstrætədʒɪ]

名 戰略；策略

We need a **strategy** planning session to decide how we're going to deal with the new limits on campaign contributions.

我們需要開會討論因應競選捐款新限制的策略。

---

39 tactic

[ˈtæktɪk]

名 戰術；策略；手法

He's not good at long-term strategy, but in terms of short-term **tactics**, he's the best in the business.

長期策畫不是他的強項，但在短期策畫方面，他是業界首屈一指的。

---

40 traditional

[trəˈdɪʃən!]

形 傳統的；慣例的

- tradition 名 傳統
- -al 形 表「具其特徵的」

The **traditional** role of our president has been to conceive of business strategies.

傳統上，總裁的角色是要構思公司策略。

218

學後小試 A **Multiple Choice Questions**
請選擇合適的單字填入空格

_____ ❶ They're requesting _____ on last month's sales, but we don't have the data yet.

   (A) statistics   (B) mastermind
   (C) lead role   (D) cut

_____ ❷ If possible, please _____ the database to our sales report generator.

   (A) imply   (B) link
   (C) aim   (D) consist

_____ ❸ Our biggest _____ is our brand name, which is already famous.

   (A) characteristic   (B) competitor
   (C) revolution   (D) advantage

_____ ❹ Our launch date _____ with the beginning of summer vacation, so we're anticipating a lot of customers.

   (A) digs   (B) eliminates
   (C) coincides   (D) attains

_____ ❺ Their sales goals were not _____ and had to be reduced by almost 40%.

   (A) effective   (B) realistic
   (C) associated   (D) thorough

正確答案請參考 418 頁

B Match

請在空格填入合適的單字，動詞需依時態變化，名詞需填入正確之單複數。

| traditional | overwhelming | investigate | survey | adversely | advisor |

1 The CEO wants you to _____ the error in the accounting reports.

2 According to a _____ of our customers, we're not providing good enough after-sales service.

3 A clearance sale at the end of the year is _____ for most of the department stores here.

4 I told the president they have an _____ advantage, but she insists on competing.

5 We'd like you to serve as an executive _____ and leave the decisions to actual managers.

6 Finance predicts the economic downturn will _____ affect our sales for up to five months.

C Listening Practice

請聆聽音檔，將單字填入空格 🎧 170

1 Their marketing campaign was too _____, and drained the company of funds.

2 One of our _____ is to place displays in key convenience stores throughout the region.

3 _____ of the master copy won't be a problem once we get the new printer installed.

4 The accountants were able to _____ where the funds have been disappearing.

5 This is the third _____ she has done of the report.

6 They stopped being _____ once they cut their advertising budget.

Advertisement & Media

廣告與媒體

媒體廣告的情境是多益測驗中的必考題型：

1 必須精確地使用名詞，以表達不同的媒體種類（category），例如 commercial 是 電視廣告，broadcast 是廣播，social media 是社群媒體。

2 新聞報導經常出現在閱讀題型，故也須熟悉像是影響（impact）、消息來源 （source）等基礎單字。

學前暖身 請閱讀英文定義，並將正確單字與之配對

distraction	combine	highlight	mark	dominate

1 _____: to emphasize or make stand out

2 _____: to make a visible symbol, word, or stain on something

3 _____: something that draws attention away from a more important task or idea

4 _____: to bring together; to unite

5 _____: to control; to be the most powerful or successful at something

Ad 廣告

01
appeal
[ə`pil]

動 吸引

• ap- 對；向
• peal 推動；驅使

Our new product is intended to **appeal** to an older audience than we have traditionally aimed for.

我們的新產品要吸引的目標，比我們現在主要顧客的年齡更大一點。

相似詞 動 attract = charm = allure = interest
吸引；引起……興趣

02
beyond
[bɪ`jɑnd]

介 越過

We need to go **beyond** our usual print advertisements to reach a younger audience.

我們要跳脫慣用的平面廣告框架，去接觸更年輕的觀眾群。

應用
1 go beyond + N. 超越……的框架
2 beyond description/recognition
無法描述／辨識

03
category
[`kætə,gorɪ]

名 種類

• cat- 向下
• gory 集合

Our company doesn't really fall into any existing **category**, making it hard for us to advertise effectively.

我們公司無法被歸類於現有的產業類別，讓我們很難有效地進行廣告宣傳。

應用
fall into / belong in / fit into + a . . . category
= be in the category of . . .
被歸類於……的範疇

04
distraction
[dɪ`strækʃən]

名 分心；注意力分散

• distract 動 使分心
• -ion 名 表「行為；結果；狀態」

A new commercial will be a **distraction** from last year's scandal.

新廣告會讓大家不再注意去年的醜聞。

05 **exceptional**
[ɪkˋsɛpʃənl]

形 例外的;特殊的;
卓越的

・except 動 把……除外
・-ion 名 表「行為;
結果;狀態」
・-al 形 表「具其特徵的」

This is an **exceptional** offer and we need to make our clients understand that.
我們得讓客戶明白這是特殊待遇。

相似詞	形 extraordinary = outstanding = remarkable 特別的;傑出的

06 **flyer**
[ˋflaɪɚ]

名 傳單

Don't forget to put our address on the **flyer**!
別忘了在傳單上留地址!

相似詞	名 catalog 目錄;型錄 名 brochure 簡介手冊 名 booklet 小冊子

07 **highlight**
[ˋhaɪˌlaɪt]

動 強調;使突出

・high 形 高的
・light 名 光

We really want to **highlight** our exclusivity in this ad.
我們很想要在這支廣告裡強調我們是獨一無二的。

相似詞	動 emphasize 強調;著重 動 point (up) 強調;指出

08 **perfectly**
[ˋpɝfɪktlɪ]

副 完美地

・per- 完全
・fect 做
・-ly 副

These promotional videos capture the Saks 5th Avenue image **perfectly**.
這些宣傳影片完美地捕捉了薩克斯第五大道的面貌。

09 renew
[rɪ`nju]

動 更新

• re- 再
• new 恢復

We should **renew** our newspaper ad monthly next year.

我們明年應該要一個月更新一次報紙廣告。

---

10 run an ad
動片 刊登（廣告）

We need to **run an ad** in the *New York Times*.

我們需要在《紐約時報》上登廣告。

---

11 sequence
[`sikwəns]

名 影片中的片段；
順序；一系列

• sequ 跟隨
• -ence 名 表「行為；
性質；狀態」

In this **sequence**, the young woman goes looking for new shoes, but finds love instead.

在這一段裡面，年輕女子只是要去買新鞋，愛情卻找上門來。

應用	[1] a sequence of = a series of + N. 一系列的…… [2] in sequence = in order 按照順序地

---

12 target
[`tɑrgɪt]

名 目標

The new game's **target** is men from the ages of 18 to 35 who already have gaming systems.

這個新遊戲的目標是針對18歲到35歲，已有遊戲機的男性族群。

應用	target for/of + N. = aim for N. = set a goal for N. 以……為目標

---

13 testimonial
[ˌtɛstə`monɪəl]

形 見證的；介紹的

• testimony 名 證詞
• -ial 形

I'm not sure a **testimonial** statement will really catch people's interest.

我不確定推薦文能不能引起大家的注意。

unit

18

Advertisement & Media 廣告與媒體

14

upcoming
[ˋʌp͵kʌmɪŋ]

形 即將來臨的

The **upcoming** television commercials should bring in a lot of new business.

即將播出的電視廣告應該會讓我們大賺一筆。

Media 媒體

15

attract
[əˋtrækt]

動 吸引

• at- 向
• tract 拉；引

The new marketing consultant has suggested using YouTube and social media sites to **attract** more attention.

新的行銷顧問建議我們,用YouTube和社群網站來吸引更多人注意。

16

commercial
[kəˋmɝʃəl]

名 電視廣播的商業廣告

• commerce 名 商業
• -ial 名

I don't know why the marketing team keeps suggesting we make another TV **commercial**, since the last one had no impact.

我不懂為什麼明明上一支廣告沒什麼效果,行銷小組卻不斷建議我們再拍一支。

17

discreetly
[dɪˋskritlɪ]

副 審慎地;謹慎地;
小心地

• dis- 分開
• creet 辨別
• -ly 副

The ad **discreetly** suggests that women like to come to the shop when their husbands are away.

這支廣告隱約透露了女人喜歡趁丈夫不在時到這家店來。

18

discrepancy
[dɪˋskrɛpənsɪ]

名 不一致;出入;差異

• dis- 分開
• crep 裂開
• -ancy 名

There's a **discrepancy** between how the ad portrays our repair service and what people find when they walk through our doors.

廣告描述的維修服務,和我們實際上所提供的服務有點出入。

225

19

engage
[ɪnˋgedʒ]

動 吸引；處理；應付

• en- 使
• gage 擔保品

We're trying to **engage** more with younger clients.

我們試著引起年輕顧客的興趣。

| 應用 | ① be engaged in + N. 忙於某事 |
| | ② be engaged to Sb. 和某人訂婚 |

20

impact
[ˋɪmpækt]

名 影響；作用

• im- 進入
• pact 打；壓緊

The commercial was intended to be humorous, but the unintended **impact** was to brand the technology company as cheap and frivolous.

本來這支廣告希望達到詼諧的效果，卻沒想到讓這家科技公司蒙上廉價又低級的形象。

| 應用 | A have a(n) . . . impact/influence on B |
| | A 對 B 有⋯⋯的衝擊／影響 |

21

infectious
[ɪnˋfɛkʃəs]

形 會傳染的；有感染力的；
有影響力的

• infect 動 傳染
• -ious 形 表「具有⋯⋯
性質的；充滿⋯⋯的」

This kind of rumor is **infectious**—we really have to stop it.

這種謠言三人成虎，我們必須阻止。

相似詞	形 contagious 接觸傳染性的；(感情等)感染性的
	形 communicable 可溝通的；可傳達的；傳染性的
	形 transmittable 有傳染力的；有影響力的

22

media
[ˋmidɪə]

名 媒體 (medium 的複數)

We need to get the **media** on our side if we want to tell our version of the story.

如果想要照我們的版本說故事，就得讓媒體與我們同一陣線。

23 **press release**

[prɛs] [rɪˋlis]

名 片 (向媒體發布的)
新聞稿

Let's issue a **press release** about the incident and get ahead of the rumors.

我們要趕在謠言散播前發布此事的新聞稿。

應用	1 the press = the media 媒體總稱，集合名詞複數 2 press conference 記者會

News 新聞

24 **aspect**

[ˋæspɛkt]

名 方面

• a- 向
• spect 看；觀

The report was missing a key **aspect** of the story: why no one noticed the fire until it was too late.

新聞報導漏了事件的重要細節：為什麼直到為時已晚才有人發現這場大火。

25 **broadcast**

[ˋbrɔdˏkæst]

動 廣播；散佈

• broad 形 寬闊的
• cast 動 撒；播

Our piece will be **broadcast** tonight at 9 p.m.

我們的新聞今晚九點會播出。

應用	名 broadcast 廣播
補充	過去式和過去分詞皆為 broadcast

26 **constant**

[ˋkɑnstənt]

形 連續發生的；
連續不斷的

• con- 一起
• stant 站立

I get so tired of the **constant** stream of information coming from the TV!

我厭倦電視整天都在播報新聞！

27 **dimension**
[dɪˋmɛnʃən]

名 方面；範圍

• di- 分開
• mens 量度
• -ion 名 表「行為；狀態」

This channel offers only one **dimension** of what's happening in the world.

這個頻道只從一個角度去報導這世界上發生的所有事情。

---

28 **dominate**
[ˋdɑməˏnet]

動 支配；控制

• domin- 統治
• -ate 動 表「使成為」

Right now, our competitor is **dominating** the airwaves.

我們的競爭對手現在正在每一台節目播出。

---

29 **editor**
[ˋɛdɪtə]

名 編輯

• edit 動 編輯
• -or 名 表「人」

These stories are really sloppy. We need a better **editor**.

這些故事真的寫得很差，我們需要厲害點的編輯。

---

30 **source**
[sors]

名 來源；源頭

I know you can't tell me the name of your **source**, but can you at least say where he or she works?

我知道你不能告訴我你的消息來源，但能不能至少透露他在哪裡工作？

---

31 **tune in**
[tjun]

動 片 收看；收聽

I **tune in** to that informative program on politics every night.

我每個晚上準時收看那個資訊豐富的政論節目。

228

Social Media 社群媒體

32 **application**
[ˌæpləˈkeʃən]

名 應用程式

• apply 動 申請
• -ation 名 表「動作；結果」

There's a new **application** that helps you track your spending!

有一個新的應用程式可以記錄你的開銷。

應用　① application縮寫為app
　　　 ② an app/application for N./V-ing
　　　　 用來……的應用程式

33 **boost**
[bust]

動 增加

We want to **boost** our profile with the new online campaign.

我們希望透過新的網路宣傳活動提高我們的知名度。

34 **collective**
[kəˈlɛktɪv]

形 集體的；共同的

• collect 動 收集
• -ive 形 表「與……
　有關的；具有……性質的」

We're trying to understand the **collective** mind of Japanese teenagers.

我們想要了解日本青少年的集體心理。

35 **combine**
[kəmˈbaɪn]

動 結合

• com- 一起
• bine 兩個

The team is looking for a way to **combine** our print and online campaigns.

小組正在想辦法結合平面和網路宣傳。

應用　combine A and B 結合A和B

229

36 entire

[ɪn`taɪr]

形 整個的

We can't finish the **entire** ad today, I'm afraid, so we'll just have to meet again tomorrow.

今天恐怕不能做完這個廣告,我們明天再見次面吧。

---

37 identify

[aɪ`dɛntəˌfaɪ]

動 確認;識別;鑑定

· identity 身分
· -fy 動 表「形成;使……化」

Management needs to **identify** the person behind this new user profile in order to stop the harassment.

管理階層必須找出這個新用戶,才可以阻止他騷擾別人。

應用

1 identify Sb. (+ as . . .)
辨識某人身分(為……)

2 identify with N. 認同;將自己視為同一事物;感同身受

---

38 mark

[mɑrk]

動 做記號;注意

Let's **mark** this page to look at later.

我們把這個網頁加入書籤,以後再看。

---

39 power

[`paʊɚ]

名 能力

Online shoppers have a lot of spending **power** these days.

近來網路買家的消費能力驚人。

---

40 via

[`vaɪə]

介 經由;憑藉

Online retailers are hoping to reach young people **via** social media

網路零售商希望透過社群媒體來接觸年輕族群。

230

學後小試 A **Multiple Choice Questions**
請選擇合適的單字填入空格

_____ 1 You need a better _____ to help you, because this text is really sloppy.

(A) dimension (B) source
(C) editor (D) sequence

_____ 2 This _____ advertises a great deal on new computers.

(A) aspect (B) impact
(C) flyer (D) distraction

_____ 3 Women have much more _____ in the business world these days.

(A) commercial (B) power
(C) application (D) discrepancy

_____ 4 We need to _____ the right audience for this new product.

(A) boost (B) renew
(C) dominate (D) identify

_____ 5 I can't believe you read that _____ book in three days!

(A) upcoming (B) collective
(C) entire (D) constant

正確答案請參考 418 頁

B | Match

請在空格填入合適的單字，動詞需依時態變化，名詞需填入正確之單複數。

| attract | run an ad | perfectly | broadcast | tune in | via |

1. _____ to Channel 5 tonight to watch our new advertisement!

2. When will the new TV episode be _____?

3. We are hoping to reach young buyers _____ YouTube and Instagram.

4. The marketing head wants to _____ in the newspaper, but it seems so old-fashioned.

5. We're hoping our celebrity spokesperson will _____ attention to our new car design.

6. The new logo represents our company _____.

C | Listening Practice

請聆聽音檔，將單字填入空格 180

1. We need to put out a _____ about our new project.

2. We try to go _____ what our clients expect.

3. The marketing team wants to cast someone really famous in our next _____.

4. What can we do to _____ more to young women?

5. This week's most-played song is _____.

6. We hope the colorful cartoons in the campaign will _____ children.

Unit 19

Conferences & Exhibitions

Conferences & Exhibitions

會議與展覽

研討會和展覽的情境是常見的多益考題：

① 要非常留意動詞與名詞的意思變化，如 project 作為名詞是「專案；企劃」，但作動詞就變成「預計；推算」。

② 這裡也要加強留意相似詞的交互使用，如展示（display）、展示（exhibit）和示範（demonstrate），分配（distribute）與分派（allocate）。

學前暖身 請閱讀英文定義，並將正確單字與之配對

coordinate	reputation	participate	exhibit	demonstration

1 _____: what is commonly known about a person or organization

2 _____: the act of showing others how something works

3 _____: to organize two or more activities so that they happen smoothly at the same time

4 _____: to put something on display for others to see

5 _____: to join in an activity or event

Conference 會議

01 ready for
動 片 準備好

Make sure your presentation is **ready for** the conference by next week so I can look it over.

請在下星期前準備好你開會用的簡報，我才能幫你檢查。

---

02 beverage
[ˈbɛvərɪdʒ]

名 飲料

Beverages will be provided, so don't worry about bringing any drinks.

我們會提供飲料，請不須自備任何飲品。

---

03 coordinate
[koˈɔrdn̩et]

動 使相配合

• co- 一起
• ordinate 排列；安排

She will **coordinate** the ending of her speech with the beginning of your demonstration, so timing is crucial.

她的演講結尾會與你的示範開頭配合，因此時間至關重要。

---

04 designate
[ˈdɛzɪɡˌnet]

動 指派

• de- 分離；降下
• sign 名 符號
• -ate 動 表「使……成為；有……性質或狀態的」

I was surprised when they **designated** me as the keynote speaker. I had no idea they were even considering it.

我很驚訝他們指定我擔任主講人，我完全沒聽説他們考慮過這件事。

應用	designated driver/hitter 指定駕駛／指定打擊者

---

05 enrollment
[ɪnˈrolmənt]

名 登記

• en- 使；進入
• roll 名 名冊
• -ment 名 表「行為；結果；狀態」

Enrollment in this year's conference has soared, so we're definitely going to need a larger venue.

今年會議的報名人數暴增，因此我們勢必需要更大的會場。

應用	動 enroll 註冊加入某課程

unit

19

Conferences & Exhibitions 會議與展覽

06 facilitate

[fəˈsɪləˌtet]

動 使容易；促進；幫助

· facile 形 容易的
· -ity 名 表「特徵；狀態；行為」
· -ate 動 「使成為」

You are in charge of hiring temporary staff to **facilitate** in the setup and demonstrations.

你負責招聘臨時工來協助安裝和展示的工作。

07 organize

[ˈɔrgəˌnaɪz]

動 組織；安排

· organ 名 器官；機構
· -ize 動 表「使成為；使形成」

Whoever **organized** the lunch forgot to arrange a vegetarian option.

負責午餐的人忘了安排素食餐。

08 prepare

[prɪˈpɛr]

動 準備

· pre- 前
· pare 安排；準備

Smith **prepared** the slides and the audio files, but he didn't create them.

史密斯準備了投影片和影音檔，但那些都不是他做的。

09 project

[prəˈdʒɛkt]

動 預計；推算

· pro- 向前
· ject 拋

The cost of attending these conferences, **projected** over the next five years, is approximately $100,000.

參加未來五年會議的花費預計約為十萬美元。

10 register

[ˈrɛdʒɪstɚ]

名 登記簿；註冊表

· re- 回
· gister 承載；運送

Attendees need to sign the **register** and present their identification before entering.

參加者需在進入前登記並出示身分證明。

應用	Household Registration Office 戶政事務所

Exhibition 展覽

11 display

[dɪˋsple]

動 展出；顯示

• dis- 除去；分離
• play 折疊

Display the product name above the picture, not below it.

將產品名稱放在照片上面，不是放在下面。

---

12 exhibit

[ɪgˋzɪbɪt]

動 展示

• ex- 出
• hibit 有

Will we have enough time to **exhibit** all of this tablet's features and functions?

我們有時間可以展示這部平板電腦所有的特色和功能嗎？

相似詞	動 show 顯示；展示；表演 動 display 展出；顯示 動 present 呈現；演出

---

13 purpose

[ˋpɝpəs]

名 目的；用途

• pur- 向前
• pose 放

The **purpose** of the posters is to provide additional information the attendees might not have caught during the presentation.

如果參加者在簡報中沒跟上的話，這些海報的目的就是要提供補充資訊。

應用	on purpose = deliberately 刻意地 ←→ by accident/chance 巧合地

相似詞	名 intention 意圖；意向 名 aim = goal 目標；目的

---

14 volunteer

[ˌvɑlənˋtɪr]

動 自願參加者；志願者

• volunt 意願
• -eer 名 表「與……有關的人」

Two employees have **volunteered** to work the display booth this weekend, without mentioning overtime.

兩名員工自願週末負責展示攤位，甚至不需要加班費。

應用	volunteer + to V. / for N. 自願去做……

Inviting A Speaker 講者邀請

15 **arrive**

[əˋraɪv]

動 到達

• ar- 到
• rive 河邊

Please be sure to **arrive** by 10 a.m., because the opening speech will begin at 10:30 a.m.

請務必在早上十點前到達，因為開場演講十點半開始。

16 **confirm**

[kənˋfɝm]

動 證實；批准；確認

• con- 完全
• firm 堅固的

Either mail the enclosed, postage-paid postcard, or email us, to **confirm** your attendance.

你可以把隨函檢附、郵資已付的明信片寄回來給我們，也可以寄電子郵件來確認你是否出席。

17 **contact**

[ˋkɑntækt]

動 聯絡

• con- 共同
• tact 接觸

If you have any questions or concerns regarding the venue, please **contact** us at the number below.

如果你對會場有任何疑問，請撥下面這支電話聯繫我們。

應用	be/get/stay/keep in contact (with Sb.) (和某人)保持聯繫

18 **escort**

[ˋɛskɔrt]

動 護送；護航；陪同

Each speaker will be **escorted** by two security personnel in the event of protests.

在抗議活動中，每位講者將由兩位保全人員護送。

19 factor
[ˈfæktɚ]

名 因素;要素

Publications in trade magazines is the principal **factor** in selecting presenters.
挑選講者的主要因素是有沒有在商業雜誌上發表過文章。

---

20 presence
[ˈprɛzn̩s]

名 出席;面前

- present 形 出席的;在場的
- -ence 名 表「行為;性質;狀態」

Your **presence** at this year's conference is highly anticipated.
我們很期待您出席今年的會議。

---

21 unavailable
[ˌʌnəˈveləbl]

形 抽不開身的;沒空的

- un- 不
- avail 有用;有益
- -able 形 表「可……的」

If you are **unavailable** due to other engagements, please let us know.
如果您有約會不能來,請通知我們。

Participant 參與者

22 inquiry
[ɪnˈkwaɪrɪ]

名 詢問

- inquire 動 詢問
- -y 名 表「行為;性質;狀態」

Participants should hold their **inquiries** until all the panelists have finished.
與會者應該等到所有委員會成員發表結束後,才可以發問。

應用
[1] inquiry + about N. 詢問
[2] inquiry + into N. 調查

---

23 distribute
[dɪˈstrɪbjut]

動 分配;分發

- dis- 分開
- tribute 給予

Transcripts of each presentation will be **distributed** at the end of the day.
今天結束時會分發每場報告的文字稿。

unit

19

Conferences & Exhibitions 會議與展覽

24 draw

[drɔ]

動 吸引（注意）

Speakers must not **draw** attention to their exhibits by the use of shocking or offensive imagery.

講者不能用驚悚或另人反感的圖像來吸引人去看他們的作品。

應用
1. draw lots 抽籤
2. draw the line 設下界線

25 drowsiness

[`draʊzɪnɪs]

名 昏昏欲睡

• drowsy 形 睡意朦朧的
• -ness 名 表「性質；狀態」

Drowsiness should not be a problem, given that all attendees will be provided a variety of caffeinated beverages free of charge.

與會者有各種免費的提神飲料可以喝，應該不會有昏昏欲睡的問題。

26 participate

[pɑr`tɪsə,pet]

動 參加；分享；分擔

• part 部分
• cip 拿；取
• -ate 動

Anyone wishing to **participate** in the final panel should notify us as soon as possible.

想參加最後一場小組座談的人應該盡快告訴我們。

應用
participate in = take part in
= join/attend 參與……

27 relevant

[`rɛləvənt]

形 有關的

• re- 再
• lev 舉起；變輕
• -ant 形

Any **relevant** topic will be considered as a potential focus point for discussion.

任何相關主題都可能成為討論的焦點。

應用　A be relevant to B　A和B有關

Reception 招待

28 host
[host]

動 主辦;主持

The reception will be **hosted** by the CEO of Quickup, Thomas Gray.

快捷公司的執行長湯馬士 · 格雷會主持迎賓典禮。

---

29 extend
[ɪkˋstɛnd]

動 延長;擴展;伸出

· ex- 向外
· tend 伸展

In the event of scheduling conflicts, speakers may be asked to **extend** their speeches by up to ten minutes.

為了協調時間進程,講者可能會被要求演講多講十分鐘。

---

30 remark
[rɪˋmɑrk]

名 談論;議論;評論

· re- 再;加強意義
· mark 標記號

Remarks of an overtly political nature may result in their speaker's being excluded from subsequent conferences.

講者若公開談論政治傾向,可能將不得再參與接下來的會議。

---

31 require
[rɪˋkwaɪr]

動 需要

· re- 加強意義
· quire 尋;詢問

Attendance at the reception **requires** an invitation and a minimum donation of $250.

出席迎賓宴需要攜帶邀請函,並捐款超過250美元。

相似詞
動 need = demand 需要;需求
動 command 命令;應得;值得

Trade Show 商業展覽

32 **allocate**

[ˋæləˌket]

動 分配；分派

・al- 到
・loc 放置；地方
・-ate 動 表「使……」

The company should **allocate** no more than 5% of its total marketing budget to trade show demonstrations.

公司辦的商業展覽應該控制在宣傳總預算的5%以內。

33 **bring**

[brɪŋ]

動 帶來；導致

Attendees cannot **bring** any camera-enabled devices into the building.

出席者不能攜帶有照相功能的器材進入這棟大樓。

34 **cancel**

[ˋkænsḷ]

動 取消；刪除

Five of the twenty confirmed participants have **canceled** due to the expected snowstorms.

由於預報將有暴風雪的緣故，二十位與會者中有五人確定取消出席。

35 **cooperation**

[koˌɑpəˋreʃən]

名 合作

・cooperate 動 合作
・-ion 名 表「狀態；動作」

The organizers are asking for everyone's **cooperation** in setting up the public spaces outside the main building.

策展人請大家合力布置主要大樓外面的公共區域。

應用 　full cooperation 全力配合

36 demonstration

[ˌdɛmənˈstreʃən]

名 演示；示範

· demonstrate 動 示範
· -ion 名 表「行為」

No **demonstration** may extend beyond a participant's assigned area, and noise levels should be kept to an acceptable level.

與會者的示範不可以超過指定的範圍，並且必須要控制音量。

相似詞	名 display 展出；顯示
	名 feature 特徵；特色；專題
	名 presentation 報告；演講；簡報

---

37 exquisite

[ˈɛkskwɪzɪt]

形 精緻的；製作精良的

I've heard there will be an **exquisite** sample of man-made diamonds on display.

我聽說展覽品裡有一件精緻的人造鑽石樣品。

---

38 feature

[ˈfitʃɚ]

動 以……為特色；展示

· feat 功績
· -ure 名 表「動作；過程」

Manufacturers may not **feature** more than three vehicles in their display.

製造商不會展示超過三部車子。

---

39 reputation

[ˌrɛpjəˈteʃən]

名 名譽；名聲

· repute 名聲
· -ation 名 表「狀態」

Their company has a **reputation** for putting on extravagant displays at these shows.

他們公司在商展中以鋪張的展覽為名。

---

40 uniform

[ˈjunəˌfɔrm]

名 制服

· uni- 單；一
· form 名 形式

Any company **uniforms** must be approved by the organizers prior to the trade show.

商展之前，所有公司的制服都必須經過策展人同意。

學後小試 A **Multiple Choice Questions**
請選擇合適的單字填入空格

_____ 1 We need more money for this year's _____, because we're hiring more staff.

(A) drowsiness (B) inquiry
(C) presence (D) uniforms

_____ 2 Approximately 20% of the exhibition budget will be _____ to displays.

(A) canceled (B) allocated
(C) facilitated (D) required

_____ 3 Mr. Pane's _____ about the need for more oversight were not well received.

(A) remarks (B) beverages
(C) reputation (D) purposes

_____ 4 The staff will _____ pamphlets and brochures to attendees.

(A) extend (B) confirm
(C) distribute (D) contact

_____ 5 The host will _____ each speaker to the stage, and then sit on their left.

(A) organize (B) display
(C) escort (D) volunteer

正確答案請參考 419 頁

B | Match

請在空格填入合適的單字，動詞需依時態變化，名詞需填入正確之單複數。

| unavailable | designate | host | cooperation | exquisite | arrive |

1. As the attendees will _____ early in the morning, let's make sure there's plenty of hot coffee.

2. Of course the display sample was _____; just don't expect the sale items to be as good.

3. The keynote speaker just informed us she will be _____, so we need to find someone else fast.

4. Those persons in charge of demonstrations will _____ their own assistants.

5. Ms. Peterson is nervous because she just heard she will _____ this year's conference.

6. We'll need the full _____ of the conference center staff if we're going to make this exhibition work.

C | Listening Practice

請聆聽音檔，將單字填入空格 190

1. I couldn't see how his topic was _____ to the conference because it was so different.

2. She promised she would have the displays _____ the exhibition by Monday.

3. Participants need to _____ for the conference both in writing and on our website.

4. We don't have enough time to _____ the script for the demonstration.

5. Their exhibit _____ five different models of the same product.

6. Of course price is a _____, but we want you to prioritize style.

正確答案請參考 419 頁

Unit 20

Presentations & Charts

報告與圖表

報告的情境經常出現在多益測驗中，不只是簡短對話、簡短獨白，也有可能出現在照片描述中：

1. 必須要熟悉描述圖表與簡報的形容詞，例如精確的（accurate）、戲劇性的（dramatic）、下降的（down/descending）。

2. 建議藉由流程式記憶法：試著描述（describe）一個狀況，並指出（indicate）其代表的意義，最後做結論（conclude）。

學前暖身 請閱讀英文定義，並將正確單字與之配對

comprehensive	decade	bring up	minutes	take a break

1 _____: ten years

2 _____: to pause, usually briefly, during an activity

3 _____: complete, including all aspects

4 _____: to mention, especially as a topic for discussion

5 _____: a written record of a meeting; meeting notes

Chart and Graph 圖表

01 abundant

[ə`bʌndənt]

形 大量的；充足的；
豐富的

· abound 動 大量存在
· -ant 形 表「有……的；
顯示……的」

We have **abundant** data to back up our claims.

我們的資料充足，可以支持我們的說法。

> **相似詞** 形 ample = adequate = sufficient = enough 足夠的；充足的

---

02 accurate

[`ækjərɪt]

形 準確的；精確的

· ac- 向
· cur 注意；照料
· -ate 形

I don't think your presentation gives an **accurate** picture of the situation.

我不認為你的報告準確地呈現目前的情況。

> **相似詞** 形 precise 精確的；準確的；確切的

---

03 comprehensive

[ˌkɑmprɪ`hɛnsɪv]

形 詳盡的

· comprehend 動 理解
· -ive 形 表「具有……性質
的；有……傾向的」

Thank you very much for your **comprehensive** report on the past year.

謝謝你詳盡地報告我們過去這一年的情形。

> **相似詞** 形 complete 完整的；完全的
> 形 thorough 徹底的；完全的
> 形 detailed 完整的；詳盡的

---

04 contain

[kən`ten]

動 包含

· con- 一起
· tain 握持

The packets I've distributed **contain** our marketing plan for next year.

我剛發下去的袋子裡面有我們明年的行銷計劃。

> **相似詞** 動 include 包含；包括
> 動 hold 容納；包含

05

decade

['dɛked]

名 十年

• dec 十
• -ade 名 集合名詞

Over a **decade** in business, the My Tech Company has shown steady growth.

我技公司開業十年來穩定成長。

應用	over / in the past / last decade(s) 在過去這（數）十年來

06

descending

[dɪ'sɛndɪŋ]

形 下降的

• de- 向下
• scend 爬
• -ing 形

The **descending** green line, unfortunately, represents our sales trend.

很遺憾，那條往下走的綠色線代表我們的銷售趨勢。

07

down

[daʊn]

形 下降的

As you can see, sales have gone **down** this month.

如你所見，本月銷量一直下降。

08

dramatic

[drə'mætɪk]

形 驟然的；戲劇性的

• drama 名 戲劇
• -(t)ic 形 表「……的」

We attribute our **dramatic** growth to our great ideas and to the word of mouth of our clients.

我們戲劇性的成長歸功於好點子和好口碑。

09

evident

['ɛvədənt]

形 明顯的

• e- 完全；向外
• vid 看
• -ent 形

It is **evident** that Apple is experiencing some turbulence, but I still think it's a good investment.

蘋果公司很明顯正經歷一些動盪，但我想他們還是很值得投資。

應用	It is evident/obvious/apparent + that 子句 顯然地……

---

10 exact
[ɪgˈzækt]

形 準確的；精密的

We have not calculated the **exact** figures for the year yet, but it seems that labor costs have definitely increased.

我們還沒算出今年確切的數字，但看起來人力成本一定增加了。

---

11 exponentially
[ˌɛkspoˈnɛnʃəli]

副 指數型地；(增長率)越來越快地

· exponent 名 指數
· -ial 形
· -ly 副

The CEO is predicting that opening new branches will increase sales **exponentially**.

執行長預測開新的分店會讓業績增加得越來越快。

---

12 indicate
[ˈɪndəˌket]

動 指出；暗示

· in- 進入
· dic 說；指示
· -ate 動 表「使成為」

On the map, our branches are **indicated** by pink dots.

地圖上粉紅色的圓點就是我們的分店位置。

應用	S. + indicate + O. = S. be indicative of O. = S. have/give indication of O. 指出；顯示出

---

13 peak
[pik]

動 達到高峰

The bar graph shows that sales usually **peak** in December.

條狀圖顯示我們業績通常在12月達到頂峰。

---

14 radically
[ˈrædɪkli]

副 根本的；徹底的；完全的

· radic 根
· -al 形
· -ly 副

Six months ago, the marketing team decided to **radically** change its approach, and these are the results.

半年前，行銷團隊決定徹底改變方法，而這些就是成果。

15 sort

[sɔrt]

動 分類;區分

Our analysts are **sorting** the raw data right now.

我們的分析師正在整理原始資料。

> **相似詞** 動 classify = categorize 分類

16 stable

[ˋstebḷ]

形 穩定的;穩重的

- st 立
- -able 形 表「可……的」

The CEO promised us huge sales last year, but in this economy, we're happy just to have **stable** growth.

執行長去年承諾業績會大紅大紫,但這種景氣下,我們能穩定成長已經很開心了。

17 successive

[səkˋsɛsɪv]

形 連續的

- suc- 下面
- cess 行
- -ive 形

Each **successive** month has brought us new business.

每個月都有新的生意上門。

> **相似詞** 形 consecutive = continuing = continuous
> 不斷的;持續的;連續的

18 surpass

[sɚˋpæs]

動 勝過;大於;多於

- sur- 超過
- pass 動 通過

At this rate, we will **surpass** our monthly sales record with a week to spare!

以這種速度,我們不但會破以往月銷售量的紀錄,而且還多出一個星期的時間。

19 **view**
[vju]

動 觀看；視為

I want to **view** the results myself.
我想自己看結果。

Meeting Agenda 議程

20 **agenda**
[ə`dʒɛndə]

名 待議事項；議程

Unfortunately, the first item on today's **agenda** is layoffs.
很不幸地，今天第一個待議事項是遣散員工。

---

21 **available**
[ə`veləbl]

形 在手邊的；可得到的；
有空的

• avail 有用；有益
• -able 形 表「可……的」

Will you be **available** to talk in about ten minutes?
大約十分鐘後你有空跟我談談嗎？

---

22 **minutes**
[`mɪnɪts]

名（複數）會議紀錄

First, let's review the **minutes** from our last meeting.
首先讓我們回顧一下上次開會的會議紀錄。

> 應用　keep the minutes at the meeting/conference
> 作會議記錄
> 名 minute 分鐘

---

23 **take notes**
[nots]

動 片 做筆記

I wouldn't remember half of what was said in meetings if I didn't **take notes**.
如果我不寫筆記，我會忘掉一半開會的內容。

---

24 **tentative**
['tɛntətɪv]

形 試驗性的；暫時的

· tentat 試驗
· -ive 形

We have a **tentative** agreement with Sony, but nothing is definite yet.

我們跟索尼公司有個暫時的共識，但一切還未定。

Meeting 會議

25 **brainstorm**
['brenˌstɔrm]

動 自由討論；集思廣益；腦力激盪

· brain 名 大腦
· storm 名 風暴

The human resources department is meeting to **brainstorm** better ways to deliver benefits to employees.

人資部門正在開會，集思廣益怎樣造福員工。

---

26 **bring up**
動 片 開始談論；提出（話題）

I kept waiting for someone to **bring up** last month's sale's slump, but no one did.

我一直在等大家開始談上個月銷售額下滑的事，但是沒人提出來。

應用
1 bring up short 突然終止
2 bring up to scratch 令人滿意

---

27 **open to**
動 片 歡迎

Our CEO is **open to** new ideas, provided they are grounded in research.

只要有研究依據，執行長很歡迎新的想法。

28 update

[ʌpˋdet]

動 更新；使現代化

• up 副 在上；向上
• date 動 註明於日期

I'm waiting for my manager to **update** me on the latest project developments.

我在等經理告訴我計畫最新的進展。

---

29 weekly

[ˋwiklɪ]

副 每週

• week 名 星期
• -ly 形 副 表「每隔……時間的（地）」

Our public relations team holds **weekly** meetings to keep lines of communication open.

我們的公關組每週開會以保持良好溝通。

Presentation 簡報

30 aid

[ed]

名 幫助；支援

Without any visual **aids**, her presentation was quite boring.

沒有視覺輔助，她的簡報很無趣。

---

31 audience

[ˋɔdɪəns]

名 聽眾；觀眾；讀者群

• audi 聽
• -ence 名 表「人」

The **audience** at this conference is never very attentive.

這場會議的聽眾一點都不專心。

252

32 briefly
[`brifli`]

副 簡短地

・brief 形 簡短的
・-ly 副

I'd like to **briefly** touch on the updated design specifications.

我想簡短地談談最新的設計規格。

> 應用 to be brief/short = in brief/short
> = briefly speaking 簡短來說

33 conclude
[kən`klud]

動 結論；推斷出；結束

・con- 一起
・clude 結束；關閉

To **conclude**, I'd like to say that we all know it's been a tough year, but better times are coming.

最後我要說的是今年雖然很艱辛，但會好轉的。

> 應用 in conclusion = to sum up
> = in summary = in sum 結論上；最後

34 describe
[dɪ`skraɪb]

動 描述

・de- 向下
・scribe 書寫

I don't know how I can **describe** our new plan in only 30 seconds!

我不知道怎麼在三十秒之內講完新計畫！

> 相似詞 動 depict 描畫；描述；描寫
> 動 illustrate（用圖、實例等）說明；插圖；圖解
> 動 portray 描述；描寫

35 estimate
[`ɛstə,met`]

動 估計；評價

We **estimate** that 25% of potential sales are lost through a lack of follow-up.

我們預估若沒有後續追蹤，業績會少百分之25%。

36 general

[ˋdʒɛnərəl]

形 全體的；總的；普遍的

• gener 種類
• -al 形 表「與……有關」

I'm going to start with a **general** overview of our company history.

我會先從公司歷史綜覽開始介紹。

| 應用 | in general 大致來說 |

| 相似詞 | 形 common 普通的；共同的
形 ordinary 平常的；普通的 |

37 periodic

[ˌpɪrɪˋɑdɪk]

形 定期的

• peri- 周圍；接近
• -ode 路；像……的東西
• -ic 形 表「具有特徵的；與……有關的」

Microsoft makes **periodic** updates to its operating systems.

微軟會定期更新作業系統。

38 presentation

[ˌprɛznˋteʃən]

名 報告；演講

• present 動 提出
• -ation 名 表「動作，結果」

I hate giving **presentations**. They make me so nervous.

我很討厭報告，這會讓我很緊張。

39 simply

[ˋsɪmplɪ]

副 只是

• simple 形 簡單的
• -ly 副 表「方式；狀態」

We **simply** have to find a way to get the projector working.

我們只需要找個辦法讓投影機可以用。

40 take a break

動 片 休息一下

Let's **take a break** for 10 minutes and then return to our discussion.

我們休息十分鐘，然後再回來討論。

學後小試 　A | **Multiple Choice Questions**
請選擇合適的單字填入空格

_____ ① I don't know how to make the _____ pay attention to me when I speak.

(A) audience   (B) aid
(C) minutes   (D) decade

_____ ② I want to take a few minutes to _____ our new sales tactics.

(A) contain   (B) describe
(C) surpass   (D) peak

_____ ③ I don't have the _____ sales figures for this month, but I can assure you that they are positive.

(A) down   (B) descending
(C) evident   (D) exact

_____ ④ You don't need to take my word for it—there is _____ evidence that tastes are changing.

(A) periodic   (B) abundant
(C) tentative   (D) successive

_____ ⑤ My supervisor wants to get the team together to _____ new ways to attract clients.

(A) brainstorm   (B) conclude
(C) estimate   (D) indicate

正確答案請參考 420 頁

B | Match
請在空格填入合適的單字，動詞需依時態變化，名詞需填入正確之單複數。

take notes	accurate	open to	available	agenda	sort

1 I need the _____ for today's meeting as soon as possible.

2 I'm _____ new ideas, but my boss doesn't want to do anything that hasn't been done before.

3 She gave a great speech, but I'm not sure if her data was _____ .

4 Can I borrow a pen? I want to _____ on this meeting.

5 My supervisor is never _____ to talk about problems.

6 We have to _____ this data before we can understand what it means.

C | Listening Practice
請聆聽音檔，將單字填入空格 🎧 200

1 I've got to stay late all this week to work on my _____.

2 We need to _____ our software before next year.

3 These _____ meetings are really useful for keeping us all on track.

4 Our growth this year has been _____.

5 Sales have increased _____ over the past few months.

6 The CEO would rather see _____ growth than these huge gains and losses.

正確答案請參考 420 頁

Unit 21

Negotiations

協商

協商情境在多益的聽力測驗中經常出現：

1. 如何堅定卻不強硬的表達立場（stance）非常重要，所以必須留意同意／拒絕的不同種用法，例如：動詞的 consent/decline，以及片語的 consent to/turn down。

2. 協議（making deal）的時候必須正式，例如表達意見時用 assume 代替 think，拒絕的時候多加一個形容詞 afraid，使言詞不會太過尖銳。

學前暖身 請閱讀英文定義，並將正確單字與之配對

agreement	informative	judge	consequence	consent

1. _____ : the result of some actions or events

2. _____ : to make a decision about value or worthiness

3. _____ : to agree or give permission

4. _____ : an arrangement between two persons or parties, usually about some course of action

5. _____ : able to give useful information

Making An Apology 道歉

01

afraid

[ə`fred]

形（用來委婉地說出不好的
消息或者反對意見）
恐怕；很遺憾；對不
起；抱歉

I'm **afraid** that there has been an error in our
estimate.

我很遺憾我們的估價有錯。

| 應用 | ① be afraid to do Sth. 害怕做某事 |
| | ② be afraid of 害怕某物 |

02

apologize

[ə`pɑlə,dʒaɪz]

動 道歉

• apology 名 道歉
• -ize 動 表「按……方式
處理」

On behalf of everyone at Biztek, we
apologize for the delay.

謹代表比茲提克全體上下，為我們的延誤向您致上十二
萬分的歉意。

| 應用 | ① apologize to Sb. 向某人道歉 |
| | ② apologize for Sth. 為某事道歉 |

03

take back

動 片 收回

Of course, we cannot **take back** the damage
caused to your reputation, but we can return
all of your money.

我們不能改變對您聲譽造成的損害，但我們可以全額
退費。

Making A Deal 協議

04

anxious

[`æŋkʃəs]

形 焦慮的；渴望的

It will be an **anxious** meeting because both
sides fear they will not reach an agreement in
time.

因為雙方擔心他們無法及時達成協議，所以這場會議將
會開得很急切。

| 應用 | be anxious about N. / to V. 對……感到焦慮 |

202 **05** 美加 **06** 加澳 **07** 美加 **08** 英澳 **09** 美澳

unit

21

Negotiations 協商

05 **consent**

[kən`sɛnt]

動 同意；贊成；答應

· con- 在一起
· sent 想

CamRoders will **consent** to purchase suspension exclusively from you, if you can offer a 30% discount on shipping.

如果您願意運費打七折，開曼羅德同意只向您訂購懸吊系統。

應用	consent to V./N. 同意去做……；贊成某事

06 **consequence**

[`kɑnsə,kwɛns]

名 結果；後果

· con- 一起
· sequ 跟隨
· -ence 名 表「狀態」

The **consequences** of failure to uphold our end of the agreement will be severe.

無法堅守我們協議的後果是很嚴重的。

07 **continue**

[kən`tɪnju]

動 繼續

These talks will **continue** once your party has modified your proposal.

等你們修改好提案，我們才能繼續談。

08 **convince**

[kən`vɪns]

動 說服

· con- 加強語氣
· vince 征服

It might be difficult to **convince** them to change their mind, but I will try.

要說服他們改變心意恐怕很難，但我會試試。

應用	convince/persuade Sb. to V. = talk Sb. into V-ing 說服某人做……

09 **decline**

[dɪ`klaɪn]

動 拒絕；謝絕；下降

· de- 向下
· cline 傾斜；彎曲

Watson **declined**, saying the offer lacked three of his five requests.

華特森拒絕了這份工作，因為他提的五個要求對方只同意了兩個。

應用	decline a(n) invitation/offer 拒絕對方的邀約／工作機會或學校錄取

259

---

10 **deny**
[dɪˋnaɪ]

動 否認

They **deny** ever having proposed that price, and we have nothing in writing to prove it.

他們不承認提過那個價格，我們也沒有文字記錄可以證明。

> 應用　① deny + N. / V-ing / that子句　否認曾做過……
> 　　　② There is no denying that子句
> 　　　毫無疑問地……

---

11 **discourage**
[dɪsˋkɝɪdʒ]

動 阻擋；使洩氣；勸阻

・dis- 分離
・courage 勇氣

They've set the price high in order to **discourage** us from negotiating on other aspects of the proposal.

他們為了阻擋我們協商提案的其他地方，把價錢訂得很高。

> 應用　discourage Sb. from V-ing
> 　　　= talk Sb. out of V-ing 勸某人不要去做……

---

12 **entrust**
[ɪnˋtrʌst]

動 委託；交託；託付

・en- 使；進入
・trust 名 信任

The CEO **entrusted** the negotiations to Mrs. Hsieh and we will act as her support staff.

執行長把談判交給謝女士主導，我們則扮演支援她的角色。

---

13 **permit**
[ˋpɝmɪt]

名 允許；許可；准許

・per- 通過
・mit 送；放開

The deal includes construction **permits** for that area, so we don't need to arrange them ourselves.

這筆協議中包含那個區塊的施工許可，因此我們不用自己申請。

> 應用　動 permit N./V-ing 允許某事
> 　　　動 permit Sb. to V. 允許某人去做……

---

14 **seal**
[sil]

動 確認；正式批准
（協定）

I thought we had **sealed** the deal yesterday, so I don't understand why they are proposing changes.

我以為昨天就談定了，不曉得為什麼他們現在還想要改。

---

15 **setback**
[ˋsɛt͵bæk]

名 挫折；障礙

• set 動 放
• back 副 回

There's been a **setback** in the talks, so expect them to continue over the weekend.

會談遇到障礙，所以可能會持續到週末。

---

16 **shake**
[ʃek]

動 搖動

Shaking hands is a traditional sign of completing a deal.

雙方握手是談妥生意的傳統象徵。

---

17 **subjective**
[səbˋdʒɛktɪv]

形 主觀的

• subject 名 主觀
• -ive 形 表「具有……性質
的；有……傾向的」

We need a negotiator who excels at making **subjective** decisions rather than being tied down to facts and figures.

我們需要非常有主見的談判專家，而不是只會被事實和數據綁手綁腳的庸才。

---

18 **turn down**

動 片 拒絕

If they **turn down** your initial offer, we authorize you to increase our bid by 10%.

如果他們就拒絕你一開始的報價，我們授權你，出價可以再提高　成。

261

Negotiation & Reconciliation 協商與和解

19

agreement
[ə'grimənt]

名 合約；同意；協定

- agree 動 同意
- -ment 名「行為；結果；狀態」

The **agreement** clearly states your company is responsible for hiring and training the staff.

合約清楚載明貴公司負責招募及訓練員工。

20

burdensome
['bɝdn̩səm]

形 麻煩的；沉重的；繁重的

- burden 名 負擔
- -some 形 表「使人……的；有……傾向的」

They consider the legal process too **burdensome** and so are asking about alternatives.

他們認為法律程序太繁瑣，因此想問有沒替代方案。

21

congenial
[kən'dʒinjəl]

形 友善的；令人愉快的

- con- 一起
- geni 種族；出生
- -al 形 表「具其特徵的」

Despite the **congenial** atmosphere, the negotiations are close to collapse.

儘管氣氛融洽，但談判幾乎要破裂了。

22

consideration
[kən,sɪdə'reʃən]

名 考慮；需要考慮的事；體貼

- consider 動 考慮
- -ation 名 表「動作；狀態；結果」

Your offer is too low for **consideration**; please increase it if you are serious.

您開的條件太低不值得考慮，如果你是認真的，請加價。

23

even though

片 即使；儘管

We are prepared to offer you full price for this site, **even though** it was damaged in the fire.

儘管這個地點受火災損害，我們還是打算以全價購買。

24 **evenly**
['ivənlı]

副 平均；均等

Time for presentations has been divided **evenly** between the four competing firms.

四個互為競爭對手的公司平均分配了報告時間。

25 **final**
['faɪnl]

形 最後的

Yes, their **final** offer is below what we'd hoped, but it is the best offer we've received.

是的，他們最後的出價低於我們的期望，但是仍是我們目前最好的選擇。

26 **intensive**
[ɪn'tɛnsɪv]

形 加強的；密集的

• in- 向
• tens 伸展
• -ive 形 表「有……特性的；有……傾向的」

The **intensive** negotiations have exhausted everyone, so we're taking a break.

密集的談判讓大家累垮了，我們要休息一下。

| 應用 | 1 intensive course/program 密集課程 |
| | 2 knowledge/capital/labor-intensive 知識／資本／勞力密集的 |

27 **judge**
[dʒʌdʒ]

動 判斷

Don't **judge** too quickly: consider all aspects of the proposal first, and then tell me what you think.

不要太快下判斷：先考量提案的每個層面，然後告訴我你的想法。

28 **negotiate**
[nɪ'goʃɪ,et]

動 談判；協商

• neg- 沒有
• oti 閒暇；空閒時間
• -ate 動 表「成為」

Is your company prepared to **negotiate** on that, or is the price fixed?

貴公司打算談價碼，還是價格已定呢？

29 ongoing

[ˈɑnˌgoɪŋ]

形 進行中的

No one outside that room has any idea what they are offering, because talks are **ongoing** and secret.

房間外的人都不知道他們開了什麼條件，因為會談仍在進行且非常保密。

30 skeptical

[ˈskɛptɪkl]

形 懷疑的；多疑的

• skeptic 名 懷疑論者
• -al 形 表「具其特徵的」

A **skeptical** approach to their offer is the best: assume they are hiding something, and dig for it.

最好對他們開的條件抱持懷疑態度：假設他們有所隱瞞，然後找出真相。

> 應用　be skeptical about/of + N. 對……存疑

31 unanimously

[juˈnænəməsli]

副 一致同意地；無異議地

• un- 一
• anim 心
• -ous 形 表「擁有……的；有……性質的」
• -ly 副

The shareholders voted **unanimously** to reverse the Board's decision and agree to the union's demand.

股東投票一致決定要推翻董事會的決定，並答應工會的要求。

32 verify

[ˈvɛrəˌfaɪ]

動 證明；證實

Would you please show us your account information so we can **verify** the number of clients?

可以請告訴我們您的帳戶資訊？這樣我們才能確認客戶編號。

unit

21

Negotiations

協商

33 **attempt**
[əˋtɛmpt]

動 試圖，企圖；嘗試

• at- 向
• tempt 嘗試

They did not even **attempt** reconciliation, but instead broke off all dealings indefinitely.

他們不但沒試著和解，反而不明究理地中斷所有交易。

應用	attempt + N. / to V. 企圖（去做……）
相似詞	動 intend 意圖；打算

34 **compromise**
[ˋkɑmprəˏmaɪz]

名 妥協；和解；讓步

• com- 一起
• promise 名 約定

It is the nature of **compromise** to leave neither party completely satisfied with the outcome.

和解本來就是雙方都不會完全滿意結果。

Stating Objective 意見表述

35 **assume**
[əˋsjum]

動 以為；假定；裝出

• as- 向
• sume 拿

We have **assumed** a 4% inflation rate as part of our earnings projection.

我們假定有4%的通貨膨脹率來預測盈利。

應用	assume the worst 做好最壞打算
相似詞	動 presume 假定；設想；意味著 動 suppose 猜想；認為應該

36 **informative**
[ɪnˋfɔrmətɪv]

形 情報的；見聞廣博的；教育性的；有益的

• inform 動 通知
• -ative 形 表「有……性質的」

We are aiming for an **informative** exchange of marketing data.

我們的目標在於交換行銷數據的情報。

37 stance
[stæns]

名 立場

Her **stance** on workers' compensation has not changed: she believes employees deserve full medical coverage.
她對員工福利的立場不變：她相信員工應享醫療全險。

38 stand
[stænd]

動 站在……的立場

Where do you **stand** on the issue of corporate responsibility to the environment?
關於企業對環境的責任，你支持哪一方？

> **應用** take/make/mount a stand (against/for N.)
> 對某事持反對／支持立場

39 strong
[strɔŋ]

形 強壯的；強大的

There will be **strong** opposition to the proposed cuts, but I think we can justify them.
對提出的預算刪減會有很強的反對聲浪，但我想我們可以提出合理的原因。

40 urge
[ɝdʒ]

動 催促；極力主張；驅策

The president **urged** him to take this offer, in case of a no-win situation.
總裁催促他接受這個條件，以免雙輸。

> **應用** urge Sb. to V. = call for Sb. to V. = call for N.
> 訴諸／呼籲懇求……

Multiple Choice Questions
請選擇合適的單字填入空格

_____ 1 We hope to keep the negotiations as positive and _____ as possible.

(A) afraid　　(B) congenial
(C) anxious　　(D) strong

_____ 2 I'm panicking because the president has _____ the contract negotiations to me.

(A) urged　　(B) assumed
(C) continued　　(D) entrusted

_____ 3 If Margate Holdings doesn't increase its bid, we should _____ their offer.

(A) decline　　(B) discourage
(C) judge　　(D) shake

_____ 4 I am _____ that they can fulfill their commitments.

(A) skeptical　　(B) intensive
(C) burdensome　　(D) subjective

_____ 5 Their _____ on worker's compensation hasn't changed at all.

(A) permit　　(B) setback
(C) consequence　　(D) stance

正確答案請參考 420 頁

B | Match

請在空格填入合適的單字，動詞需依時態變化，名詞需填入正確之單複數。

| unanimously | final | take back | convince | apologize | verify |

1. Before we sign the contract, we'd like to _____ the value of the building ourselves.

2. The Board of Directors has voted _____ to appoint a new CEO next year.

3. Their _____ word was a rejection of our proposal.

4. We would like to _____ for any inconvenience our accounting error may have caused you.

5. I think our proposal will _____ them to buy from us.

6. The deal has been signed; you can't _____ the discount.

C | Listening Practice

請聆聽音檔，將單字填入空格 210

1. The _____ wage negotiations are in their sixth month now.

2. Of course, we can _____ the price after we have decided delivery terms.

3. You cannot _____ the accident: it was in all the papers.

4. I'm sorry, but we're going to have to _____ your offer.

5. Employee benefits are divided _____ between retirement planning and medical coverage.

6. If they _____ to push for a salary increase, offer a higher contribution.

正確答案請參考 420 頁

Unit 22

Communication

溝通

需要表達個人意見（express opinions）的情境，尤其在聽力測驗中經常出現：

1 留意態度（attitude）、行為（conduct/behavior）等可反映一個人想法的名詞。

2 形容詞的使用都能代表立場，所以必須格外熟悉如擔憂的（apprehensive）、必要的（essential）等的出現，都有可能是關鍵。

學前暖身 請閱讀英文定義，並將正確單字與之配對

conduct	apprehensive	perceive	commend	encourage

1 _____: to be aware of or understand something

2 _____: behavior or the method and process of carrying something out

3 _____: to stimulate or to give support or hope to someone or something

4 _____: anxious or fearful about a coming event

5 _____: to formally or officially praise someone or something

Argument 爭執

01

bear

[bɛr]

動 忍受

I can't **bear** arguments in the workplace.

我受不了在工作場合吵架。

相似詞	動 tolerate = endure 忍受;容忍
	動 stand 忍受
	片 put up with 忍受;忍耐

02

conduct

[ˋkandʌkt]

名 行為;舉止;
表現;為人

• con- 徹底;共同
• duct 引導

His **conduct** in the office is simply unacceptable.

他在辦公室的行為真的讓人無法接受。

| 相似詞 | 名 behavior 行為;表現 |

03

defensive

[dɪˋfɛnsɪv]

形 急於為自己開脫的;
懷有戒心的

• defense 名 保衛
• -ive 形 表「有……特性的;
有……傾向的」

I've tried to speak to her about her attire, but she becomes so **defensive** that I can't communicate with her.

我試著提醒她衣著的事,但是她一直替自己辯解,我無法跟她溝通。

Communication 溝通

04

admit

[ədˋmɪt]

動 承認;准許進入

• ad- 向
• mIt 發送

My manager has finally **admitted** that she was wrong to take the credit for my idea.

我的經理終於承認她搶走了我的主意。

| 應用 | admit/deny + N. / V-ing / that 了句 |
| | 承認/否認…… |

05 **all the more**
片 更加；越發；格外

Working in such close quarters makes it **all the more** important that the team gets along.
大家在這麼狹窄的空間一起工作，團隊和睦相處更加重要了。

---

06 **anecdote**
[ˈænɪkˌdot]

名 軼事；趣聞

• an- 沒有
• ec 出版
• dote 給予

My boss is always telling us **anecdotes** from the early days of our company.
我老闆總是跟我們說公司早期的軼事。

---

07 **apprehensive**
[ˌæprɪˈhɛnsɪv]

形（對將要做的事情）
擔憂的；擔心的

• ap- 向
• prehend 抓住
• -ive 形 表「傾向於……的」

I'm very **apprehensive** about telling my supervisor about the team leader's behavior at the conference.
我很擔心，不知道怎麼跟我的主管說組長開會時的行為。

> **相似詞** 形 worried = concerned 擔心的；關心的

---

08 **attitude**
[ˈætətjud]

名 態度；看法；姿勢

• att 適合
• -itude 名 表「狀態」

John's **attitude** of superiority makes him very hard to work with.
約翰的優越感讓人很難與他共事。

> **應用** have/hold + a(n) . . . attitude to/toward + N./V-ing 對某事抱持……的態度

09 basis

[`besɪs]

名 基礎；根據；準則

On the **basis** of his racist remarks, his application was rejected.

基於他種族歧視的言論，他的申請被駁回了。

| 應用 | 1 on a/the . . . basis 以⋯⋯的方式 |
| | 2 on a/the basis of . . . 以⋯⋯為基準／根據 |

---

10 dialogue

[`daɪə‚lɑg]

名 對話；交談；對白

• dia- 穿過
• logue 說

Since the new manager came in, our **dialogue** has become a lot more open and relaxed.

新任經理來了之後，我們的對話變得更開放、自在。

---

11 essential

[ɪ`sɛnʃəl]

形 必要的

• essence 本質
• -al 形 表「具有⋯⋯特性的」

Please forward me any e-mails about **essential** project details.

請把所有與這個案子有關的重要細節轉寄給我。

| 相似詞 | 形 significant = important = crucial 重要的 |
| | 形 main = major 主要的 |

---

12 messenger

[`mɛsṇdʒɚ]

名 使者；送信人

• message 訊息
• -er 名 表「人」

I'm bringing bad news, so don't shoot the **messenger**.

我要跟大家說一個壞消息，請不要遷怒我這個傳訊人。

---

13 **perceive**

[pɚ`siv]

動 認為;看待;視為

· per- 通過
· ceive 拿

How do you **perceive** our chances of getting more sick leave next year?

你覺得我們明年有更多病假的機會有多大?

---

14 **remind**

[rɪ`maɪnd]

動 提醒

· re- 再
· mind 動 注意;記住要

My manager sent a memo to **remind** us all about the casual Friday dress code.

經理發了公告提醒大家,週五可以穿休閒服來上班。

應用　remind Sb. + of/about N. / that子句
　　　　提醒某人……

---

15 **temperately**

[`tɛmprɪtlɪ]

副 有節制地;適度地;
　溫和地

· temper 適度
· -ate 形 表「有……性質或
　狀態的」
· -ly 副

Don't respond to the e-mail while you're still angry. Wait until you can write **temperately**.

如果你還是很生氣,不要回那封信;等你可以平靜下來再回。

---

16 **mutually**

[`mjutʃʊəlɪ]

副 互相地

· mut 改變
· -ual 形
· -ly 副

After two weeks of discussion, we've arrived at a **mutually** beneficial agreement.

討論了兩個星期之後,我們達成互惠的協議。

Conflict 衝突

17 aggressive
[ə`grɛsɪv]

形 富於攻擊性的；挑釁的

• aggress 動 侵略
• -ive 形 表「有……特性的」

I believe Steve means well, but his tone is so **aggressive**.

我相信史提夫的本意是好的，但是他的語氣太有攻擊性。

---

18 conflict
[`kɑnflɪkt]

名 衝突

• con- 一起
• flict 打

I hate **conflict** and always try to avoid it.

我很討厭衝突，所以始終避免它發生。

---

19 confront
[kən`frʌnt]

動 迎面遇到；面臨；遭遇；
　正視；使面對

• con- 一起
• front 名 前面

I'm going to have to **confront** my supervisor about her preferential treatment of some team members.

我打算質問主管關於她對組員的差別待遇。

> 應用 confront Sb. about/with Sth. = be in conflict with Sb. for Sth. 和某人為……起衝突

---

20 sharp
[ʃɑrp]

形 尖的

There were some surprisingly **sharp** words exchanged in the meeting.

開會時有不少唇槍舌劍的場面。

---

21 uncomfortably
[ʌn`kʌmfətəblɪ]

副 不舒服地；令人難受地

• un- 不
• comfort 名 舒適
• -able 形 表「有……特性的」
• -ly 副

My boss stands **uncomfortably** close to me when we talk.

老闆跟我說話的時候站得很近，讓我很不舒服。

22 unease

[ʌnˋiz]

名 心神不安

He hasn't done anything specifically hostile, but I feel a sense of **unease** around him.

他沒特別有敵意，但我還是覺得跟他相處很不安。

---

23 verbal

[ˋvɝbl]

形 口頭的；非書面的

• verb 詞語
• -al 形 表「具其特徵的」

This time, I'm going to give you a **verbal** warning. If it happens again, a report will be filed in writing.

這次我只給你口頭警告。下次再發生，我就要給你書面警告了。

---

24 behavior

[bɪˋhevjɚ]

名 行為；舉止

• behave 動 表現
• -or 名 「性質或狀態」

I have given Sarah lots of private advice and constructive criticism, but her **behavior** just hasn't improved.

我已經給莎拉很多私下建議和有建設性的批評，但他的行為還是沒有改善。

> **應用**　be on one's best behavior = be well-behaved = behave oneself 行為表現良好

---

25 cold

[kold]

形 寒冷的；冷淡的

Ever since I complained to HR about our working conditions, my manager has been quite **cold** to me.

自從我跟人事部門抱怨我們的工作環境，經理就一直對我很冷淡。

---

26 word

[wɝd]

名 簡短的交談；談話

Could I please have a **word** with you after the meeting ends?

會議結束後，請問我可以跟你談一談嗎？

Discussion 討論

27
arguable
[ˈɑrgjʊəbl̩]

形 有疑問的；有商榷餘地
的；可爭辯的

· argue 動 爭論
· -able 形 表「有……特性的」

The CEO is convinced by the data, but I believe the case is **arguable**.

執行長很相信數據，但我認為這個案例還有待商榷。

相似詞	形 controversial 爭議性的
	形 debatable 可爭辯的
	形 disputed 有爭議的
	形 questionable 可疑的

28
casual
[ˈkæʒʊəl]

形 非正式的

We had a **casual** discussion about the incident over lunch, and everything was resolved.

我們午餐的時候閒聊了一下這事件，一切都沒事了。

29
cover
[ˈkʌvɚ]

動 覆蓋；涵蓋

The team leader's report really doesn't **cover** the scope of the work we did.

組長的報告真的沒有涵蓋我們已完成的工作進度。

Expressing Opinion 意見表達

30
personal
[ˈpɝsn̩l]

形 個人的

· person 名 人
· -al 形 表「具其特徵的」

This is my **personal** opinion, of course, and not the official position of the Dell Company.

這當然是我個人的看法，不是戴爾公司的官方立場。

31
appreciate
[əˈpriʃɪˌet]

動 感激

· ap- 向
· preci 價值
· -ate 動

I would **appreciate** it if you kept our conversation to yourself.

如果你不跟別人說我們的談話，我會很感謝你的。

---

32 **appropriate**

[ə`proprɪ,et]

形 適當的

· ap- 向
· propi 擁有；自己的
· -ate 形

I don't think a sales meeting is an **appropriate** situation for a discussion of my maternity leave.

我不認為銷售會議是討論我產假的好地方。

---

33 **clarity**

[`klærətɪ]

名 (思想、文體)清楚；
　　清澈

· clar 清楚的
· -ity 名 表「特徵；狀態」

I'm hoping today's meeting will bring some **clarity** to this confusing issue.

我希望今天的會議可以澄清這個令人困惑的議題。

---

34 **commend**

[kə`mɛnd]

動 稱讚

· com- 共同
· mend 委託

The supervisor **commended** us on how we handled the situation.

主管稱讚我們處理這件事的方式。

應用	commend Sb. on Sth. 讚揚某人做某事
相似詞	praise = compliment 讚美；稱讚

---

35 **confusion**

[kən`fjuʒən]

名 困惑；混亂；混淆

· confuse 動 使困惑
· -ion 名 表「行為；狀態」

Since the CEO was fired, there's been a lot of **confusion** about who is actually in charge.

自從執行長被開除以後，大家都搞不清楚到底是誰負責管理。

---

36 **courteous**

[`kɝ`tʃjɪəs]

形 謙恭的；有禮貌的

· court 名 法庭
· -(e)ous 形 表「有……
　　特質的」

I don't think everyone on the team needs to be friends, but we have to be **courteous** to each other!

我不覺得身為組員就一定要當朋友，但至少要以禮相待吧！

---

37 encourage

[ɪnˈkɝɪdʒ]

動 鼓勵

• en- 動 使
• courage 名 勇氣

The new supervisor **encouraged** everyone in the department to come to her with any problems or questions.

新任主管鼓勵部門成員有什麼問題儘管去找她。

---

38 grateful

[ˈgretfəl]

形 感激的

• grate 高興的
• -ful 形 表「充滿」

I'm very **grateful** for the extra sick leave I was given when I was so ill last year.

去年我病得很嚴重的時候,我很感激公司多給了我一點病假。

> **應用** be grateful to + N. = appreciate + N.
> 感謝某事

---

39 signal

[ˈsɪgnl]

名 信號;號誌

• sign 記號;符號
• -al 名 表「狀態」

Give me a **signal**, like raising your eyebrows or clearing your throat, if you start to feel uncomfortable in the situation.

如果你開始覺得不舒服,就做個暗號讓我知道,像是挑眉毛或清喉嚨。

---

40 suppose

[səˈpoz]

動 猜想;認為應該

• sup- 在……下
• pose 安置;放

I **suppose** we can continue to work on the project together until he is reassigned.

等他調單位以後,我想我們可以繼續合作那個案子。

> **應用**
> ① suppose + that子句　推論;認為
> ② be supposed to do Sth.　應該做……

學後小試 A **Multiple Choice Questions**
請選擇合適的單字填入空格

_____ ❶ John and Sara missed the most recent update, which caused some
_____ at the meeting.

(A) basis (B) words
(C) confusion (D) signals

_____ ❷ That's my _____ opinion, of course, and not the company's official
policy.

(A) cold (B) apprehensive
(C) personal (D) grateful

_____ ❸ I wish she would just _____ she forgot about the meeting, rather
than making up lame excuses.

(A) admit (B) cover
(C) bear (D) appreciate

_____ ❹ Let's invite the new hire to a(n) _____ lunch so she can get to know
us in a relaxed setting.

(A) defensive (B) essential
(C) arguable (D) casual

_____ ❺ Have you heard Joan's _____ about running into the CEO in a
rainstorm?

(A) anecdote (B) attitude
(C) behavior (D) clarity

正確答案請參考 421 頁

B Match

請在空格填入合適的單字，動詞需依時態變化，名詞需填入正確之單複數。

| suppose | verbal | appropriate | confront | mutually | unease |

1. Today, I'm going to _____ my boss about taking credit for my work.

2. What do you _____ they're talking about in the conference room?

3. I'll give you a _____ warning this time, but if it happens again I will put the violation in writing.

4. I am sure we can find some _____ agreeable solution.

5. Knowing that layoffs are coming is creating a sense of _____ in the office.

6. Sure, she's a beautiful woman, but the clothes she wears to work just aren't _____.

C Listening Practice

請聆聽音檔，將單字填入空格 220

1. She's a good boss, but she can use _____ language when being provoked.

2. I don't like him, but I can be _____ to him when we work together.

3. Using an _____ tone in the meeting won't get us anywhere.

4. The tight deadline makes it _____ important that we work efficiently.

5. It's _____ warm in the office today.

6. If you don't _____ me of the party a day beforehand, I'll probably forget about it.

正確答案請參考 421 頁

Unit 23

Emergencies

緊急狀況

職場看重危機處理（troubleshooting）能力，因此緊急狀況情境愈來愈重要：

① 留意問題處理的各種片語，如處理（deal with）、想出方案（figure out/come up with）、擺脫（get out of）。

② 描述危機或是緊急狀況也至關重要，所以務必熟悉形容詞，或者也可以說在……情況下（in a . . . situation）。

學前暖身 請閱讀英文定義，並將正確單字與之配對

ensure	critical	patient	demanding	get out of

① _____: able to experience problems without becoming angry or frustrated

② _____: needing a lot of effort or skill to complete

③ _____: very important and must be dealt with soon

④ _____: to make certain that something will happen

⑤ _____: to resolve or avoid a problem

Accident 意外

01 coverage

[ˈkʌvərɪdʒ]

名 新聞報導；覆蓋範圍

• cover 動 覆蓋
• -age 名 表「行為；狀態；結果」

Surprisingly, the train accident has received little media **coverage**.

意外地，火車意外事故竟然只有零星新聞有報導。

02 emission

[ɪˈmɪʃən]

名 散發；放射

• emit 動 發射；散發
• -ion 名 表「動作；狀態」

The fire caused toxic **emissions**, so we had to notify local authorities.

火災導致毒氣外洩，因此我們得通知本地主管機關。

| 應用 | [1] cut/reduce the emission of greenhouse gases 減少溫室氣體排放量 |
| | [2] carbon (dioxide) emissions/footprint （二氧化）碳排放／碳足跡 |

03 extensive

[ɪkˈstɛnsɪv]

形 廣大的；廣泛的；大量的

• ex- 向外
• tens 伸展
• -ive 形 表「具有……性質的」

Following the chemical spill, **extensive** safety precautions have been put in place.

化學物質外洩以後，大量的安全防範措施開始上路。

04 shortly

[ˈʃɔrtlɪ]

副 立刻；不久；簡短地

• short 形 短的
• -ly 副 表「……地」

Shortly before the alarms went off, we noticed several odd readings on the monitors.

在警報大作不久之前，我們注意到螢幕顯示了很多奇怪的數據。

05 **situation**
[ˌsɪtʃuˋeʃən]
名 情況；處境

• site 地點
• -ate 動 表「使成為」
• -ion 名 表「行為；狀態」

The insurance investigators were able to understand the **situation** after just one look.
只要一眼，保險調查員就能了解情況了。

> **應用** in a . . . situation 在……的情況下

---

06 **call in**
動 片 來電

We have had several customers **call in** looking for an explanation about how to install the update.
許多顧客來電詢問如何安裝更新程式。

Crisis 危機

07 **close**
[kloz]
動 關閉；結束

It is imperative they **close** their operations as soon as possible to avoid incurring further costs.
他們必須盡快停止運作，以免造成更多損失。

---

08 **deal with**
動 片 處理

We need to **deal with** the data leak immediately by notifying customers and urging them to cancel their credit cards.
我們必須馬上處理資訊外流的事，通知顧客，請他們盡快註銷信用卡。

> **應用** deal a blow to Sb./Sth. 使（計畫或希望）破滅；使失敗；對……造成重大衝擊

09 **disappointed**

[ˌdɪsəˈpɔɪntɪd]

形 失望的；沮喪的；(希望
等)落空的；受挫折的

· dis- 不；相反
· appoint 動 任命
· -ed 形

The president was **disappointed** to learn we didn't have an action plan already in place.

總裁對我們沒有準備好行動計畫很失望。

應用	be disappointed + at N. / to V. 對……很失望

相似詞	形 frustrated 氣餒的 形 unsatisfied 令人不滿的

10 **durable**

[ˈdjʊrəbl̩]

形 耐用的；持久的

· dur- 持久
· -able 形 表「可……的」

The manufacturer assured us the containers were **durable** in even the most extreme weather.

製造商向我們保證，這些容器就算在很惡劣的天氣下也很耐用。

11 **familiar**

[fəˈmɪljɚ]

形 熟悉的；通曉的；
親近的

· family 名 家；家人
· -ar 形 表「有……特性的」

The locals are going to need some **familiar** faces on site to assure them things are safe.

當地人需要在地的熟面孔來保證他們很安全。

應用	Sb. be familiar with N. = N. be familiar to Sb. 某人熟悉某事

12 **figure out**

[ˈfɪɡjɚ]

動 片 弄懂；弄明白；想出

Smith said he needs you to **figure out** what happened to all of the money in that account fast.

史密斯說他需要你迅速弄清楚，那個帳戶的錢到底發生了什麼事。

應用	figure out / sort out + N. / wh-子句 釐清

13 **get out of**

動 片 脫離

To **get out of** this crisis, we're going to have to close about 20% of our outlets.

欲脫離危機，我們必須要關掉大約20%的專賣店。

14 **rare**

[rɛr]

形 稀有的；少見的

Managers who can keep calm during an emergency like this are **rare**.

可以冷靜處理這種緊急狀況的經理很少見。

15 **result**

[rɪˋzʌlt]

名 結果

Our current financial crisis is the **result** of years of negligence regarding long-term strategy.

長年下來的計畫疏失造成我們現在的財務危機。

16 **shut down**

動 片 關閉

I know it's a drastic step, but we need to **shut down** the plant immediately before another accident happens.

我明白這是個激烈的做法，但在另一個意外發生前，我們必須立刻關閉工廠。

17 **specific**

[spɪˋsɪfɪk]

形 特定的；明確的；有特效的

• speci- 種類
• -fic 形 表「製造；形成」

The president's instructions for dealing with this situation are very **specific**, but unfortunately they can't be carried out.

總裁對處理這個情形的指示非常具體，但不幸的是行不通。

18 **unfavorable**

[ʌnˋfevərəbl]

形 不利的；有害的；令人不快的

Due to **unfavorable** market conditions, all of our investments lost value this year.

因為股市景氣不佳，今年我們所有的投資都失利了。

Emergency 緊急狀況

19 be exposed to

[ɪkˋspozd]

🔊 片 接觸到

We're not sure exactly how many residents **were exposed to** the fumes, but so far a hundred people have reported symptoms.

我們不確定多少住戶接觸到濃煙，但目前發現已有一百人有症狀。

| 應用 | be exposed to + N./V-ing 接觸到…… |

---

20 come up with

🔊 片 （針對問題等）想出

You need to **come up with** a plan soon before this turns into an emergency.

在情況變糟前，你得馬上想出解決辦法。

| 應用 | come up with a solution/way/idea 想出解決方法／辦法／點子 |

| 相似詞 | 片 think of 想到 |

---

21 demanding

[dɪˋmændɪŋ]

形 費力的；吃力的

• de- 加強意義
• mand 吩咐；命令
• -ing 形

The shutdown steps are **demanding** to perform correctly, and that's why we need to have a drill.

這要很費力才能正常關機，所以我們才需要一把鑽子。

---

22 disturb

[dɪsˋtɝb]

🔊 打擾；擾亂

• dis- 加強意義
• turb 亂；煩惱

If the evacuation procedures happen to **disturb** any ongoing experiments, notify security, and leave the building.

如果疏散程序干擾到正在進行的實驗，要通知保全人員並離開大樓。

| 應用 | Do not disturb.（旅館房門掛牌）請勿打擾。 |

| 相似詞 | 🔊 bother = intervene 打擾；干擾 |

23 **insulation**

[ˌɪnsəˈleʃən]

名 隔熱；隔音；
　　絕緣材料

・insulate 動 使絕緣
・-ion 名 表「動作；狀態」

The back-up call center will need to have **insulation** put in the walls in case it is used in winter.

後備電話服務中心的牆壁裡面需要有保溫結構，以免冬天不能使用。

---

24 **pass out**

動 片 昏倒

If any member of your staff **pass out** during an evacuation, call medical services right away.

如果任何員工在疏散時昏倒了，請立即向醫療機構求助。

相似詞	動 faint 昏倒
	片 lose consciousness 失去意識

---

25 **status**

[ˈstetəs]

名 狀況；狀態

In the event of a natural disaster, we will need hourly updates on the **status** of the back-up generators.

自然災害發生時，我們每小時都需要知道備用發電機運作的狀況。

---

26 **warn**

[wɔrn]

動 警告；告誡；提醒

All employees will receive a text message **warning** them of the nature and severity of the emergency.

所有員工都會收到簡訊，告誡他們緊急事故的性質和嚴重性。

應用	warn Sb. + of/about N. / that 子句
	警告某人注意……

287

Helping Others 幫助他人

27

drop
[drɑp]

動 丟下

If you notice a fellow employee having difficulty exiting the building, **drop** what you are doing and offer assistance.

如果你發現有同仁無法自行離開大樓，放下你手邊的事去幫助他。

28

ensure
[ɪnˋʃʊr]

動 保證；確保；使安全

• en- 使
• sure 形 確實的

We have made it our business to **ensure** the safety and security of our fellow factory workers.

確保工廠員工的安全是我們的責任。

29

interaction
[ˌɪntəˋrækʃən]

名 互動

• inter- 在之間
• action 名 行動

The problem with cubicles is they cut **interaction**, preventing employees from seeing how and when they can help each other.

小隔間的問題在於它們切斷人們的互動，員工看不到就不知該如何適時彼此幫助。

> **應用**　interact with N. 和……的互動

Troubleshooting 危機處理

30

action
[ˋækʃən]

名 行動；行為

• act 動 行動
• -ion 名 表「行為；結果；狀態」

Unless **action** is taken soon, this rumor is going to reach our most valuable clients.

如果不盡快採取行動，這個謠言就要傳到我們最重要的客戶那裡了。

> **應用**　take actions/measures + to V. 採取行動

---

31 critical

[ˋkrɪtɪkl̩]

形 關鍵性的;決定性的;
　至關重要的

• critic 名 評論家
• -al 形 表「關於……的」

It is of **critical** importance that we discover the weaknesses in our firewall and eliminate them.

找出並消除防火牆的漏洞,對我們來說至關重要。

---

32 enough

[ɪˋnʌf]

形 足夠的

Do we have **enough** staff manning the call center to deal with the Christmas rush?

我們的客服中心有足夠的人力,來應付忙碌的耶誕節嗎?

---

33 frustrated

[ˋfrʌstretɪd]

形 挫折的

• frustrate 動 使灰心
• -ed 形

Most of the complaints are from **frustrated** homeowners wondering why their mortgage payments have suddenly increased.

大部分的抱怨都來自很挫敗的屋主,他們都不懂自己的貸款怎麼會突然變多了。

---

34 patient

[ˋpeʃənt]

形 耐心的

Finding the mistake is going to take a lot of **patient** research.

要找出錯誤需要耐心研究。

---

35 resolve

[rɪˋzɑlv]

動 解決;解答;決心

• re- 加強語氣
• solve 鬆開

In order to **resolve** the complaint, we need to find exactly what our staff promised.

為了解決客訴,我們必須找出我們的員工到底答應客戶什麼。

應用	S. resolve / be resolved + to V. 下決心去做
相似詞	動 solve 解決;解答;溶解
	動 fix 解決;補救
	片 work out 解決;處理

36 smooth

[smuð]

形 平滑的；平穩的；
順利的

We need a **smooth** transition to the new system, with the fewest possible number of conflicts.

我們需要順利轉換到新的系統，盡可能越少狀況越好。

---

37 solve

[sɑlv]

動 解決；解答；溶解

The IT department is trying to **solve** the compatibility issues, but it's taking longer than expected.

資訊部門正試著解決相容的問題，但是比想像中還要花時間。

---

38 substitute

[ˋsʌbstəˏtjut]

動 代替

・sub- 在下面
・stitut 站

Let's **substitute** our licensed software with some alternatives.

我們把合法授權軟體換成替代的軟體吧！

| 應用 | ① substitute teacher 代課老師 |
| | ② substitute A for B = replace B with A 用A取代B |

---

39 understandable

[ˏʌndɚˋstændəbḷ]

形 可理解的

・under- 在……之下
・stand 動 站
・-able 形 表「可……的」

We need you to explain the problem in a way that is **understandable** to all of the shareholders.

我們需要你用易懂的方式跟所有股東解釋現在的問題。

---

40 utilize

[ˋjutɪˏlaɪz]

動 利用

・utile 形 有用的
・-ize 動 表「使」

Utilize every resource available until you have fixed this problem.

請利用各種現有資源，直到你把問題解決了。

學後小試 A

Multiple Choice Questions
請選擇合適的單字填入空格

_____ 1 These fire doors are so _____ that they should last longer than the building.

   (A) durable   (B) understandable
   (C) rare   (D) familiar

_____ 2 There needs to be more _____ between the managers and the employees.

   (A) emission   (B) interaction
   (C) insulation   (D) result

_____ 3 Are you sure Mr. Phillips can _____ the issue in time?

   (A) warn   (B) resolve
   (C) utilize   (D) disturb

_____ 4 If anyone should _____, notify the emergency workers immediately.

   (A) pass out   (B) come up with
   (C) be exposed to   (D) deal with

_____ 5 The cost of medical insurance _____ keeps increasing and will soon put us in the red.

   (A) action   (B) situation
   (C) coverage   (D) status

正確答案請參考 422 頁

B | Match
請在空格填入合適的單字，動詞需依時態變化，名詞需填入正確之單複數。

| substitute | smooth | drop | solve | enough | unfavorable |

1. Our plan should enable a _____ evacuation of employees from the plant.

2. Due to _____ weather conditions resulting from the typhoon, our parts haven't arrived.

3. R&D found a better material we can _____ our plastics for.

4. The fire department said we do not have _____ fire extinguishers in the building.

5. The president told us to _____ the database problems this week.

6. Do not simply _____ tools at the construction site; return them to their proper locations.

C | Listening Practice
請聆聽音檔，將單字填入空格 230

1. There has been an _____ remodeling of the factory to limit potential accidents.

2. Several _____ customers have complained the user manual is incorrect.

3. In the event of a fire, _____ all the doors on your way out.

4. The earthquake caused us to _____ the plant for two days.

5. The plan is very _____ about what employees should do in case of emergencies.

6. I've spent five hours trying to _____ the problem with the server.

正確答案請參考 422 頁

Unit 24

Dining & Accommodations

用餐與住宿

此情境出現在多益測驗中的機率相當高：

① 建議使用模擬情境，例如點餐對話、訂房確認信、飲食偏好等交談，以熟悉字彙，像是預定（book）、服務（serve）、停留（stay）。

② 必須能應用不同的形容詞，以描述料理（cuisine）、餐廳（restaurant）或住宿（accommodation）環境，如有名的（prestigious/renowned）。

學前暖身 請閱讀英文定義，並將正確單字與之配對

dine	thirsty	spacious	overcrowded	culinary

1 _____: to eat, especially dinner

2 _____: having too many people in a space

3 _____: feeling a need to drink something

4 _____: relating to food or cooking

5 _____: large and airy; having a lot of room

Banquet 宴會

01 elegant
['ɛləgənt]
形 優美的；優雅的

The food was delicious, and the setting was **elegant**.
食物很美味，環境很優雅。

---

02 impress
[ɪm`prɛs]
動 使印象深刻；使感動；使銘記
• im- 向……內
• press 按；壓

If you want to **impress** a client, take him to The Ivy.
如果你想讓客戶印象深刻，帶他到常春藤餐廳。

應用	B impress A with + N. = B leave a . . . impression on A = A be impressed with/by + B B的表現讓A留下深刻印象

---

03 socialize
['soʃə,laɪz]
動 參與社交活動；交際
• social 形 社會的
• -ize 動 表「使」

I work so much, and my only chance to **socialize** comes at client dinners and working banquets!
我工作很多，我唯一跟人打交道的場合是與客戶共進晚餐和出席商業晚宴。

---

04 dine
[daɪn]
動 進餐；用餐；宴請

Don't you think the clients would prefer to **dine** somewhere that serves interesting local food?
你不覺得客戶比較喜歡在具當地特色的餐廳裡用餐嗎？

比較	[1] dining room：飯廳，家裡用餐的場所。 [2] restaurant：餐廳，可以泛稱所有賣食物的店家。 [3] diner：餐館，平價路線，供應三餐。 [4] café：咖啡廳，通常會有簡單的餐點和點心。

05 **influence**

[ˈɪnfluəns]

動 影響

· in- 向內
· flu 流
· -ence 名

I'm hoping the martinis we'll have at lunch will **influence** my boss's decision.

我希望我們午餐要喝的馬丁尼會讓老闆改變心意。

> 應用　A influence B = A have a . . . influence on B
> A 影響 B

Diet 飲食

06 **preserve**

[prɪˈzɝv]

動 維護；保護；
　 保存；保養

· pre- 前
· serve 貯存；看守

She's ignoring the cake—she must be trying to **preserve** her figure.

她刻意避開蛋糕，我想她一定是為了保持身材。

07 **recipe**

[ˈrɛsəpɪ]

名 處方；食譜；訣竅

I must ask Beth for her cranberry cookie **recipe**.

我一定要問貝絲蔓越莓餅乾的食譜。

> 應用　① a recipe for + N. 做出某道菜的食譜
> ② a recipe for disaster 會導致災難的事物

08 **spicy**

[ˈspaɪsɪ]

形 辛辣的

I grew up in Thailand, so I love **spicy** food.

我在泰國長大，所以我愛吃辣的食物。

09 **taste**

[test]

動 嚐

Please **taste** the curry and tell me if you think it's too salty.

請嚐一下咖喱，看看會不會太鹹。

> 應用　① taste + Adj. 某物嚐起來……
> ② S. taste like N. 某物嚐起來像……

10 thirsty

[ˈθɝstɪ]

形 渴的;渴望的;飢渴的

· thirst 名 口渴
· -y 形 表「具有……特性的」

All these salty snacks are making me **thirsty**!

這些鹹鹹的小點心讓我很渴!

應用	be thirsty for N. 渴望得到……

---

11 tray

[tre]

名 盤;托盤;碟

Should we order a cheese **tray** instead of dessert for the conference?

我們的會議要不要改訂起司拼盤來代替甜點呢?

---

12 vegetable

[ˈvɛdʒətəbl]

名 蔬菜

· veget 充滿活力的
· -able 形容詞轉為名詞

I'm going to stay here by the raw **vegetables** and avoid the temptation of seafood.

我要待在生菜這裡,避免海鮮的誘惑。

Hotel 飯店

13 accommodation

[ə͵kɑməˈdeʃən]

名 住處

· accommodate 動 提供住宿
· -ion 名 表「行為;狀態」

I don't think there are many inexpensive **accommodation** options in Singapore.

我不認為新加坡有很多便宜的住宿選擇。

應用	① flights and accommodations 機票及住宿
	② student accommodation 學生住宿

14 **check in**
[`tʃɛk`ɪn]

動 片 (在飯店) 辦理入住
手續;登記;報到

The receptionist told me to **check in** after 3 p.m.

接待人員告訴我下午三點後才能辦入住手續。

---

15 **checkout**
[`tʃɛk‚aʊt]

名 (在飯店) 辦理退房手
續,結帳離開

Checkout is at noon, but we can leave our bags with the receptionist until the evening.

中午要退房,但我們晚上之前都可以把包包寄放在接待人員那裡。

---

16 **concierge**
[‚kɑnsɪ`ɛrʒ]

名 飯店服務員;門房

I'm going to ask the **concierge** for a restaurant recommendation.

我要請飯店服務員幫我推薦餐廳。

> **補充** concierge是飯店服務員,通常負責幫客人訂票、餐廳等事宜。

---

17 **deluxe**
[dɪ`lʌks]

形 豪華的;高檔的

I'm going to splurge and go for the **deluxe** room on my holiday weekend.

我要揮霍一下,週末假期去住豪華套房。

---

18 **lock**
[lɑk]

動 鎖上

Don't forget to **lock** the door when we leave.

我們離開時,別忘了鎖門。

19 prestigious

[prɛsˋtɪdʒɪəs]

形 有名望的；受尊敬的

- prestige 名 聲望
- -ous 形 表「擁有……的；有……性質的」

The CEO always wants to stay at the most **prestigious** hotel in town, and I think it's a waste of money.

執行長總是要住鎮上最有名望的酒店，我認為這很浪費錢。

相似詞 形 renowned = celebrated = distinguished = famed 著名的

20 refreshing

[rɪˋfrɛʃɪŋ]

形 消除疲勞的；提神的

- refresh 動 使振作精神
- -ing 形

I was tired after my flight, but the spa was very **refreshing**.

我下飛機後很累，但水療讓我神清氣爽。

21 relaxed

[rɪˋlækst]

形 放鬆的；悠閒的

- relax 動 使放鬆
- -ed 形

This hotel has a very **relaxed** atmosphere.

這家飯店的氛圍讓人非常放鬆。

22 renovation

[͵rɛnəˋveʃən]

名 裝修

- renovate 動 整修；裝修
- -ion 名 表「行為；狀態」

The hotel is under **renovation**, which means construction noises begin at 6 a.m.

飯店正在裝修，因此早上六點後會開始有施工噪音。

23 renowned

[rɪˋnaʊnd]

形 有名的；有聲譽的

- renown 名 名聲
- -ed 形

The hotel is **renowned** for its excellent restaurants.

這家飯店因為裡面一流的餐廳而聞名。

美加 英加 加澳 英澳

rest
[rɛst]

動 休息

Let's **rest** in our rooms for an hour and then go sightseeing.
我們先在房間休息一小時，然後再出去觀光。

satisfaction
[ˌsætɪsˋfækʃən]

名 滿意；滿足；
愉快；滿意度

· satis 充足；滿意
· fact 做
· -ion 名 表「行為；狀態」

There's a little card on my pillow asking me to rate my **satisfaction** with the hotel's service.
我的枕頭上有張小卡片，要調查我對飯店服務的滿意度。

| 應用 | to Sb.'s satisfaction 令人感到滿意地 |

spacious
[ˋspeʃəs]

形 寬敞的；廣闊的

· space 名 空間
· -ious 形 表「具有……
性質的；充滿……的」

I've never seen such a **spacious** bathroom—it's as big as my bedroom at home!
我從來沒見過這麼寬敞的浴室，它和我的臥室一樣大！

| 相似詞 | 形 roomy 寬敞的 |
| 反義詞 | 形 crowded 擁擠的
形 cramped 狹小的 |

star
[stɑr]

名 星級

The Four Seasons in Chiang Mai has been awarded five **stars**.
清邁的四季度假村被評定為五星旅店。

24
Dining & Accommodations 用餐與住宿

299

28 stay
[ste]
動 停留

We're planning to **stay** in Seoul for at least a week.
我們計畫在首爾最少待一個星期。

29 book
[bʊk]
動 預訂

I can't believe I forgot to **book** a room!
我不敢相信我忘了訂房間!

Restaurant 餐廳

30 cuisine
[kwɪ`zin]
名 菜餚

The hotel restaurant serves English and Indian **cuisine**.
飯店餐廳供應英國和印度料理。

> 應用　traditional/exotic cuisine 傳統／異國料理

31 culinary
[`kjulɪ,nɛrɪ]
形 烹飪的
• culin 廚房；食物
• -ary 形

The restaurant is fine, but it's not exactly a **culinary** paradise.
餐廳不錯,但稱不上是美食天堂。

> 相似詞　culinary school 廚藝學校

32 **cutting board**
[ˋkʌtɪŋ] [bord]

名 砧板

I have both wooden and plastic **cutting boards**.

我有木頭和塑膠的砧板。

---

33 **dish**
[dɪʃ]

名 菜餚;盤子

My favorite **dish** at this restaurant is the snails in butter.

這家餐館我最喜歡的菜是奶油蝸牛。

> 應用   do/wash the dishes 洗碗

---

34 **flavor**
[ˋflevɚ]

名 味道;風味

· fla 吹拂
· -or 名 表「狀態;屬性」

The **flavors** here are very bold, so be prepared.

這裡的菜口味很重,所以要有心理準備。

> 應用   add/give flavor (to Sth.) 為……增加風味

---

35 **overcrowded**
[͵ovɚˋkraʊdɪd]

形 擁擠的

· over- 超過
· crowd 動 擁擠;擠滿
· -ed 形

Let's go somewhere else—this place is **overcrowded** and unpleasant.

我們去別的地方,這裡太擠了,而且很不舒服。

36 patron
['petrən]
名 顧客；老主顧

The slow service tells me this restaurant doesn't value its **patrons**.
服務慢代表這家餐館不看重顧客。

37 pot
[pɑt]
名 鍋；壺

I love sitting near the kitchen and watching the chefs work their magic with **pots** and pans.
我喜歡坐在廚房附近，看大廚大顯身手。

38 saucepan
['sɔspæn]
名 深平底鍋
• sauce 名 醬汁
• pan 名 平底鍋

The chef brought the **saucepan** out and spooned the sauces onto our plates himself!
廚師把鍋子帶來了，親自舀了一匙醬汁淋在我們的盤子裡！

> **文化補充** saucepan在西方料理中是較深的平底鍋，有柄可以拿，常用來煮醬汁。

39 serve
[sɝv]
動 服務

It's very late; we will be lucky to find a restaurant that is still **serving** dinner.
已經很晚了，如果找得到還有賣晚餐的餐廳算是幸運了。

> **應用** serve a dish = a dish is served 上菜

40 utensil
[ju'tɛnsl]
名 餐具

Oh no, these **utensils** don't look very clean.
喔不，這些餐具看起來不太乾淨。

學後小試 A

Multiple Choice Questions
請選擇合適的單字填入空格

_____ 1 I followed the _____ exactly, but my cake still didn't come out right.

(A) tray   (B) vegetable
(C) satisfaction   (D) recipe

_____ 2 Let's _____ a table for four at the Aroma Restaurant for tomorrow.

(A) lock   (B) rest
(C) book   (D) stay

_____ 3 Have you got a _____ I can use to cut the fruit on?

(A) star   (B) cutting board
(C) saucepan   (D) pot

_____ 4 I've tried it many times, but I just don't like the _____ of stinky tofu.

(A) patron   (B) renovation
(C) accommodation   (D) flavor

_____ 5 He's trying to _____ the new client by talking about how many politicians he knows.

(A) impress   (B) serve
(C) taste   (D) preserve

正確答案請參考 422 頁

B Match

請在空格填入合適的單字，動詞需依時態變化，名詞需填入正確之單複數。

utensils	socialize	concierge	check in	influence	refreshing

1. I was tired when I arrived, but then I went for a _____ swim.

2. They've brought our meals, but they haven't given us _____ to eat them with.

3. The _____ at the hotel was very helpful in recommending restaurants and museums.

4. I don't really like to _____ with colleagues outside of work.

5. We have to _____ at the hotel before we can go sightseeing.

6. My supervisor's hard-working example _____ me to do my best, too.

C Listening Practice

請聆聽音檔，將單字填入空格 240

1. _____ is usually at noon, but it's later at this hotel.

2. The mushroom lasagna is my favorite _____ at this restaurant.

3. I love _____ food, but I know it isn't for everyone.

4. What's your favorite type of _____?

5. This city is _____ for its dumplings.

6. The decorations in this hotel are so _____.

正確答案請參考 422 頁

Unit 25

Travel & Transportation

旅遊與交通

此情境與前一單元在多益測驗中，經常相輔相成的出現：

1 交通的情境尤其可能出現在聽力測驗的圖片描述中，所以必須熟悉相關字彙，
   例如車站（station）、航班（flight）、費用（fee）、接（pick up）。
2 留意介係詞的搭配用法，如去……的旅行（a trip/tour to . . .）、在……的方
   向（in a . . . direction）。

學前暖身 請閱讀英文定義，並將正確單字與之配對

pick up	destination	accompany	schedule	commute

1 _____: the place to which someone or something is going

2 _____: to go with someone or something

3 _____: to travel between home and work on a regular basis

4 _____: a plan or list of events and times

5 _____: to collect or take into a vehicle

01 accompany
[əˈkʌmpənɪ]

動 伴隨；陪伴

• ac- 向
• company 動 陪伴

Despite what you may have heard, secretarial staff will not be **accompanying** managers on this trip.

儘管你有聽到一些傳聞，秘書部同仁還是不會陪同經理出差。

| 應用 | N1 be accompanied by N2　N1伴隨N2 |

02 away
[əˈwe]

副 離（現在的時間）

Time **away** from the conference will be treated as work time, so employees should behave accordingly.

會議之前都算是工作時間，因此員工應該也有相稱的表現。

03 coastal
[ˈkostl]

形 海岸的

• coast 名 海岸
• -al 形 表「關於……的」

We will be spending a weekend in the **coastal** community of Gold Surf, which is famous for its white sand beaches.

我們將在黃金衝浪濱海社區度過週末，那裡的白沙灘相當出名。

04 commute
[kəˈmjut]

動 通勤

Attendees will **commute** from their hotel to the conference center by train.

與會者將搭火車往返酒店與會議中心。

| 應用 | commute from A to B / between A and B
從A處通勤到B處
名 commuter 通勤族 |

306

unit

25

Travel & Transportation 旅遊與交通

05 **depart**

[dɪˋpɑrt]

動 出發;離開

· de- 表「離去」
· part 分開

Your plane **departs** at 9:35 a.m., so be at the airport by 7:30 a.m.

你的飛機早上九點三十五分起飛,請在七點半前抵達機場。

| 應用 | depart/departure + from A / for B 出發離開A處／出發前往B處 |

---

06 **destination**

[͵dɛstəˋneʃən]

名 目的地;終點;目標

· destine 動 命定
· -ation 名 表「狀態;結果」

Please send me a list of sightseeing spots and restaurants for our **destination**.

請寄給我目的地那邊,有哪些旅遊景點和餐廳。

| 應用 | holiday/tourist/scenic destination/attraction/resort 觀光勝地 |

---

07 **distant**

[ˋdɪstənt]

形 遠的

· di- 分開
· sta 站立
· -ant 形 表「有……性質的」

Individual visits to **distant** locations are not recommended due to time constraints.

因為時間限制,不建議單獨造訪遙遠的地點。

| 應用 | A be distant from B = A be far from B A和B之間距離遙遠 |

---

08 **remote**

[rɪˋmot]

形 遙遠的

· re- 往回
· mote 移動

Being in the mountains and far from town, the site might feel too **remote** for some participants.

這個地點位在山裡又離小鎮有段距離,對某些參加的人來說似乎太遙遠了。

---

09 **trip**

[trɪp]

名 旅行

Please submit expense reports within three days of returning from your business **trip**.

請在出差回來三天內繳交差旅費申請表。

| 應用 | take/go on + a trip to . . . 前往某地旅遊 |

Delay/Transfer/Cancellation 延遲／轉乘／取消

🔟 **punctual**
[ˈpʌŋktʃʊəl]

形 守時的；準時的

• punct 刺
• -al 形

The trains are usually **punctual**, but if yours does happen to be late, call the office as soon as possible.

火車通常很準時，但如果你的車誤點了，請儘快跟公司聯絡。

---

⑪ **stuck**
[stʌk]

形 卡住的；困住的

Employees who are **stuck** in the train station due to a cancellation need to arrange another method of reaching the office.

因為火車取消被困在車站的員工，要想別的辦法到公司。

| 應用 | stick to N. = hang on to N. 堅持不放棄某事 |

---

⑫ **block**
[blɑk]

動 阻礙

Fallen trees have **blocked** that section of the road, preventing our workers from reaching the factory.

倒下來的樹擋住了那段路，使得工人都到不了工廠。

| 相似詞 | 動 stop 停止；妨礙
動 prevent 妨礙；阻止 |

---

⑬ **delay**
[dɪˈle]

動 延遲；延誤

The shipment has been **delayed** due to the typhoon near Singapore.

貨運因為新加坡附近的颱風延誤了。

| 應用 | delay / put off / postpone + V-ing 延遲做某事 |

Incentive Travel 獎勵旅遊

14
agency
['edʒənsɪ]

名 代辦處;經銷處;代理

• ag 做;行動
• -ency 名 表「性質; 狀態;結果;行為」

Employees eligible for the vacation reward must use a travel **agency** approved by the company.

符合休假獎勵的同仁,一定要找公司核可的旅行社。

應用	advertising/employment/travel/ real estate agency 廣告公司／人力仲介公司／旅行社／房仲公司

15
break
[brek]

名 休息時間;假期

Anyone needing a **break** from the busy city will love our employee tour package to Greece.

想要離開這座繁忙的城市度個假的人,一定會愛死我們這個希臘員工旅行方案。

16
breathtaking
['brɛθ,tekɪŋ]

形 令人驚嘆的; 極其刺激的

• breath 名 呼吸
• take 動 拿;取
• -ing 形

I went on the company's trip to Mt. Rainier last year, and let me tell you, the view was **breathtaking**.

去年我參加了去雷尼爾山的公司旅遊,那裡的風景真是嘆為觀止啊!

17
courtyard
['kort,jɑrd]

名 庭院;天井

• court 名 庭院
• yard 名 院子

The resort has a huge central **courtyard** with dozens of tables for outdoor dining.

度假村有一個大中庭,有好幾十張戶外用餐的桌子。

---

18 itinerary
[aɪˈtɪnəˌrɛrɪ]

名 行程計畫

· itiner- 旅程
· -ary 名 表「與……
有關的人、物」

Mr. Johnson is expecting you to get him his **itinerary** complete with notes about each destination by tomorrow.

強森先生等你把他那包含所有目的地細節的行程計畫，在明天前送去給他。

---

19 join
[dʒɔɪn]

動 參加

Workers who'd like to **join** this year's excursion should notify HR before 5 p.m.

要參加今年旅遊的員工要在下午五點之前告知人資部門。

---

20 local
[ˈlokl]

形 當地的

The tour will feature many **local** foods and crafts, most of which cannot be obtained elsewhere.

這趟旅行的特色是許多別處沒有的當地美食和工藝。

---

21 pack
[pæk]

動 打包

Employees are urged to **pack** one set of winter clothes in case of sudden cold weather.

為了預防天氣突然變冷，呼籲員工要打包一套冬天衣服。

---

22 pedestrian
[pəˈdɛstrɪən]

名 行人

· ped 腳
· -ian 名 表「人」

You'll need to leave early because the roads will be full of slow-moving **pedestrians** at that time.

你要早點離開，因為那個時間路上充滿了漫步的行人。

unit

25

Travel & Transportation 旅遊與交通

23 **round-trip**

[ˈraʊndtrɪp]

形 來回的

The bus is one-way, not **round-trip**, so we'll need to take the train back.

這班公車只去不回，因此我們需要搭火車回去。

---

24 schedule

[ˈskɛdʒʊl]

名 日程表；時刻表；
　課程表

• sched 紙片
• -ule 名 表「小」

When will we get the **schedule** of events so I can start planning?

我們什麼時候才會收到活動行程表呢？這樣我才可以開始規劃。

| 應用 | ① ahead of/behind schedule
　比預訂時間提早／延後完成
② on schedule 按照表訂時間
③ a tight/busy schedule 行程排得很滿 |

---

25 splendor

[ˈsplɛndɚ]

名 光輝；壯麗

• splend 發光
• -or 名 表「狀態；屬性」

Hikers will be able to experience the **splendor** of the Grand Canyon at sunset.

登山者將有機會見識大峽谷日落時分的壯麗。

---

26 thrill

[θrɪl]

名 興奮；恐怖；顫抖

The New Zealand Adventure Holiday has been designed specifically for tourists seeking **thrills** and danger.

紐西蘭探險假期專為尋求刺激和危險的遊客所設計。

| 相似詞 | 名 buzz = excitement 興奮
名 kick 極度的快感（或刺激） |

311

27 tourist

['tʊrɪst]

名 觀光客

- tour 名 旅遊
- -ist 名 表「做……的人」

Not many **tourists** visit this area, and that's why the hotels are so cheap.

觀光客不常造訪這個區域,這就是為什麼這裡的飯店便宜多了。

28 valley

['vælɪ]

名 山谷;流域

There's a beautiful village located in that **valley**, bordered on both sides by densely forested hills.

山谷那裡有一座美麗的村莊,兩邊環繞著茂密的森林山丘。

Transportation 交通工具

29 pick up

動 片 接(機);接(某人)

The tour bus will **pick** us **up** at the hotel at 9 a.m.

觀光巴士早上九點會到飯店接我們。

30 conjunction

[kən'dʒʌŋkʃən]

名 結合;關聯;連接詞

- conjunct 形 結合的
- -ion 名 表「行為的結果」

The bus company operates in **conjunction** with the travel agency, picking tourists up and dropping them off at their hotels.

客運公司和旅行社合作,到飯店接送觀光客。

31 curb

[kɝb]

名(道路的)路緣

The taxi driver told us he would pick us up at the **curb** in front of the hotel.

計程車司機說他會在飯店前面的路邊接我們。

> **應用** 【美式拼法】curb
> 【英式拼法】kerb

312

32 **direction**

[dəˈrɛkʃən]

名 方向

・direct 動 給……指路；指示
・-ion 名 表「行為；結果；狀態」

If you head in a northwest **direction** from the hotel, you should see the stadium on your left.

如果你朝飯店的西北方前進，你應該會看到左邊的體育場。

應用

1 in the direction of . . . = toward(s) . . .
往……的方向／方位
2 in all directions 來自四面八方

---

33 **fare**

[fɛr]

名 交通費用；車資

Because some taxis are more expensive than others, make sure you ask the **fare** before getting in.

因為有些計程車收費比其他高，你上車前要先問一下車資多少。

應用

1 bus/train/air/cab fare 公車／火車／飛機／計程車車資
2 half-fare/full-fare（交通費）半價優惠／全票費用

---

34 **flight**

[flaɪt]

名 航班；飛行

It's a tiny airport, with only 10 **flights** coming in and out each day.

這是個小機場，一天出入的航班才十班。

---

35 **passenger**

[ˈpæsṇdʒɚ]

名 乘客

・pass 通過
・-er 名 表「人」

This bullet train carries 400 **passengers** and their luggage.

這輛子彈列車可以載四百名乘客和他們的行李。

36 rental
[ˈrɛntl̩]

形 供出租的

・rent 動 出租
・-al 形

Rental bikes are available at $15 per day, including helmet.

附安全帽的自行車一天租金十五美金。

---

37 shore
[ʃor]

名 岸

The ferry doesn't move far from **shore**, so tourists can enjoy the scenery.

渡輪不會離岸邊很遠，因此觀光客可以享受風景。

---

38 station
[ˈsteʃən]

名 車站；電臺；電視臺

・stat 站
・-ion 名 表「狀態」

The nearest train **station** is 10 minutes away on foot.

距離最近的火車站走路要十分鐘。

---

39 track
[træk]

名 賽道；跑道

For those interested in horse racing, there is a **track** just outside of town.

對賽馬有興趣的人，城外就有賽馬場。

> 應用
> ① keep track of 瞭解……的動態；紀錄
> ② back on track 回到正軌

---

40 transportation
[ˌtrænspəˈteʃən]

名 運輸；運輸工具

・transport 動 運輸
・-ation 名「動作的結果」

Transportation to and from the convention center is provided by your hotel.

飯店提供往返會議中心的交通工具。

314

學後小試 A **Multiple Choice Questions**
請選擇合適的單字填入空格

_____ 1 All attendees are urged to be _____ as the buses leave at exactly 9 a.m.

(A) local (B) remote
(C) punctual (D) distant

_____ 2 For anyone interested in getting some exercise, there is a jogging _____ surrounding the field.

(A) track (B) flight
(C) transportation (D) agency

_____ 3 The view of the mountains from the hotel was absolutely _____.

(A) rental (B) coastal
(C) round-trip (D) breathtaking

_____ 4 They will send your _____ as soon as you confirm your attendance.

(A) itinerary (B) courtyard
(C) passenger (D) valley

_____ 5 The standard taxi _____ from the station to downtown is about $20.

(A) pedestrian (B) shore
(C) fare (D) tourist

正確答案請參考 423 頁

B Match

請在空格填入合適的單字，動詞需依時態變化，名詞需填入正確之單複數。

| station | pack | away | direction | splendor | delay |

1. Any trips _____ from the conference center can be arranged at the hotel lobby.

2. The rain will _____ our departure by about two hours.

3. You should always _____ your suitcase the day before your departure.

4. Please take us to the train _____ after the conference finishes.

5. The map isn't clear about which _____ we should go after this turn.

6. The tour will make sure everyone sees the _____ of the surrounding mountains.

C Listening Practice

請聆聽音檔，將單字填入空格 🎧 250

1. There's a truck _____ the street, so let's turn around and go back.

2. Your flight will _____ at two in the afternoon.

3. The agent said we'll _____ in the airport for about five hours because of the snow.

4. We took a short _____ to a lake and went fishing with the client.

5. If you would like to _____ the tour, you'll have to pay the fee ahead of time.

6. There will be a two-hour _____ for lunch following the first group of speakers.

正確答案請參考 423 頁

Unit 26

Performances & Shows

表演與節目

表演與節目的情境也常有可能出現：

1. 在聽力測驗中的圖片描述時，最常會考的是描述作品、表演者與觀眾，所以必須熟悉相關的名詞，像是會場（venue）、門票（ticket）。

2. 在閱讀測驗時，可能會以演出訊息或活動邀請的方式呈現，所以必須把握形容詞，如具有啟發性的（enlightening）、多才多藝的（versatile）。

學前暖身 請閱讀英文定義，並將正確單字與之配對

| masterpiece | counterfeit | nightly | venue | obtain |

1 _____ : a fake copy, especially of money or art
2 _____ : every night, for a period of time
3 _____ : the place where an event or performance happens
4 _____ : an exceptional work of art
5 _____ : to get or acquire something

Art 藝術

01 artifact
[`ɑrtɪ,fækt]

图 人工製品；手工藝品；
加工品

My favorite exhibit in this museum is the reconstructed ancient home, with **artifacts** from daily life.

這間美術館裡我最喜歡的展示品是重建的古代家室，以及裡面日常用的手工藝品。

---

02 artificial
[,ɑrtə`fɪʃəl]

图 人工的；人造的；
不自然的

· art 图 藝術
· fic 製造
· -ial 图

The entrance to the gallery is lined with **artificial** flowers that appear to bloom all year long.

藝廊的入口放了一整排人造花，看起來整年都春意盎然。

應用	artificial coloring/flavors/additives 人工色素／調味料／添加物
相似詞	图 synthetic 綜合的；合成的；人造的

---

03 artist
[`ɑrtɪst]

图 藝術家；大師

· art 图 藝術
· -ist 图「從事……的人」

I love flowers, so my favorite **artist** is Georgia O'Keeffe.

我愛花，我最愛的藝術家是喬治亞·歐姬芙。

文化 補充	喬治亞·歐姬芙是美國20世紀的藝術家，她的作品以綻放的花朵聞名。

---

04 artwork
[`ɑrt,wɜk]

图 美術品；藝術品

The new **artwork** that the gallery is displaying is really ugly.

藝廊展示的新藝術品真的很醜。

---

05 counterfeit
[`kaʊntə,fɪt]

图 贗品；仿冒品

· counter- 反
· feit 做

Sometimes, a historical **counterfeit** can be almost as valuable as the original.

有時，年代久遠的贗品可以和原作一樣寶貴。

---

06 enlightening
[ɪnˋlaɪtṇɪŋ]

形 啟迪的;
使人增進知識的

• en- 使
• lighten 動 照明
• -ing 形

The catalog's explanation of the piece of music is very **enlightening**.

目錄中這首樂曲的解説真是發人深省。

> 文化
> 補充 Age of Enlightenment 啟蒙時代

---

07 enrich
[ɪnˋrɪtʃ]

動 使富裕;使豐富

• en- 使
• rich 形 豐富的

I go to the theater regularly because I believe the arts **enrich** our lives.

我經常去戲院,因為我相信藝術豐富我們的生活。

---

08 favorite
[ˋfevərɪt]

形 最喜愛的(人;事)

• favor 名 偏愛
• -ite 形 名

All dances inspire me, but ballet is my **favorite** form.

所有舞蹈都激勵我,但是芭蕾是我最喜歡的。

---

09 masterpiece
[ˋmæstɚˌpis]

名 名作;傑作

• master 名 大師
• piece 名 作品

When it was published, Ian McEwan's *Atonement* was called a **masterpiece** by many.

伊恩・麥克伊旺的小説《贖罪》出版之時,被許多人譽為傑作。

> 文化
> 補充 伊恩・麥克伊旺是二十世紀知名的英國小説家,2008年《泰晤士報》將伊恩・麥克伊旺列入「1945年以來最偉大的50位英國作家」名單。

---

10 sculpture
[ˋskʌlptʃɚ]

名 雕刻品;雕像

Rodin's *The Thinker* is a classic **sculpture** most people know.

羅丹的《沉思者》是眾人皆知的經典雕像。

Concert 音樂會

---

11 assembly

[ə`sɛmblɪ]

名 集合;聚集

- assemble 動 集合
- -y 名「行為」

The advertisers have gathered quite a large **assembly** of people for the concert!

廣告商為音樂會召集了一大群人。

> **應用**
> 1 a large assembly of people
> （為特定目的集合的）一群人
> 2 assembly line 裝配線

---

12 composer

[kəm`pozɚ]

名 作曲家

- com- 在一起
- pose 放置
- -er 名 表「人」

Works by this **composer** are rarely played outside his home country.

這個作曲家的作品很少在他的家鄉以外的地方演奏。

---

13 conductor

[kən`dʌktɚ]

名 指揮家

- conduce 導致
- -or 名 表「行為者」

It is a treat to see this **conductor**, as he doesn't often leave his home in Russia.

能見到這位指揮家真是奇遇,因為他不常離開自己的國家——俄國。

---

14 live

[laɪv]

形 現場的

Recordings are nice to have, but nothing beats **live** music.

音樂檔固然有其價值,但沒什麼能敵得過現場表演的音樂。

> **應用**
> live performance/show/streaming
> 現場表演／直播節目／網路直播

Movie 電影

15 **autograph**
['ɔtə,græf]

名 親筆簽名

• auto- 自己
• -graph 寫

I'm going to go to the premiere to see if I can get Angelina Jolie's **autograph**.

我要去首映會，看看是否能得到安潔麗娜·裘莉的親筆簽名。

應用	① autograph session 簽名會
	② ask for / get Sb's autograph 取得某人的簽名

16 **box office**
名 片 電影票房

The film is now an international hit, but it didn't do well at the American **box office** originally.

這部電影現在享譽國際，但是一開始在美國票房並不好。

應用	① a film/movie become/be a box office hit 票房賣座
	② box office bomb 票房毒藥

17 **celebrity**
[sə'lɛbɹtɪ]

名 名人；名流

• celebr 有名的
• -ity 名 表「狀態；性格」

I would hate to be a big **celebrity** and never have any privacy.

我會很討厭當名人，完全沒有自己的隱私。

18 **film**
[fɪlm]

名 軟片；電影

I have read the book; now I really want to see the **film**.

我讀過原著小說，現在真的很想看這部電影。

19 issue
[ˈɪʃʊ]

名 問題；議題

The film takes on big **issues** like homelessness, prejudice, and inequality.
這部電影探討一些重大議題，像是遊民問題、歧視和差別待遇。

應用
1 raise/address/resolve an issue
提出／處理／解決議題
2 avoid/dodge/duck/evade a sensitive issue
閃避某敏感議題

---

20 material
[məˈtɪrɪəl]

名 素材；資料；材料

· mater 物質
· -al 名

The government tried to ban the documentary because of the sensitive **material** it showed.
政府想要禁播這支內容敏感的紀錄片。

---

21 movie
[ˈmuvɪ]

名 電影

On rainy days, I like to stay in bed and watch **movies**.
下雨天的時候，我喜歡窩在床上看電影。

---

22 nominate
[ˈnɑməˌnet]

動 提名

· nomin 名
· -ate 動 表「使成為」

The movie was so good; it's sure to be **nominated** for an Oscar.
這部電影真是太棒了，一定會獲得奧斯卡提名。

應用
Sb. { be nominated for N. } 提名某人
{ receive the nomination for N. } 角逐某獎項
be the nominee of N. 成為……的入圍者

322

23 review

[rɪˋvju]

動 評論

· re- 再
· view 動 看

I've been asked to **review** movies for the local paper!

我受本地報紙邀請來評論電影。

應用	receive good reviews 獲得高度評價
相似詞	動 comment = remark 評論；談論

24 suspend

[səˋspɛnd]

動 停止；暫停

· sus- 向上
· pend 懸掛

I know we must **suspend** our disbelief in fantasy films, but the talking chair was just too silly for me.

我知道看奇幻電影時不應該質疑它的不合理，但會說話的椅子對我來說實在太荒謬了。

25 theatergoer

[ˋθɪətɚˏgoɚ]

名 戲迷；戲院常客

The other **theatergoers** seemed to be into the comedy, but I was bored.

其他戲院常客似乎對喜劇很感興趣，但是我覺得很無聊。

26 versatile

[ˋvɝsətl]

形 多才多藝的

· verse 名 詩
· -ate 形 表「有……性質」
· -ile 形 (= -il) 表「能；與……有關」

Jennifer Lawrence is proving herself to be a **versatile** actress.

珍妮佛・羅倫斯證明自己是一個多才多藝的女演員。

27 exclusively

[ɪkˋsklusɪvlɪ]

副 唯一地；排他地；專門地

· exclude 動 把……排除在外
· -ive 形 表「與……有關的」
· -ly 副

The premiere screening of this movie is **exclusively** for donors, but it will open for the public the following day.

這場電影首映會只有捐款人能參加，但隔天會開放給一般民眾。

Stage & Theater 舞台與劇場

28 production
[prə`dʌkʃən]

图 劇作；藝術作品

• produce 動 生產
• -ion 名「行為；行為的結果」

I've seen better **productions** of *Les Misérables*, but this one was OK.

我看過《悲慘世界》更精采的劇作，但這個版本的也不錯。

---

29 debut
[de`bju]

图 首演；初次登場

Lea Alison just made her stage **debut** in London.

麗‧艾莉森剛在倫敦演出舞台的處女秀。

> 應用　make Sb's stage/directing/acting debut
> 某人第一次上台演出／執導／演戲

---

30 nightly
[`naɪtlɪ]

副 每夜

The play will be performed **nightly** for the next two weeks.

接下來兩個星期，這齣劇會每晚演出。

---

31 obtain
[əb`ten]

動 得到；獲得

• ob- 向
• tain 拿；持有

It's impossible to **obtain** tickets for any Times Square musicals.

要得到時代廣場音樂劇的票根本難如登天。

---

32 perform
[pɚ`fɔrm]

動 演出；表演

• per- 完全
• form 形；模式

I hear they've hired Michael Fassbender to **perform** the part of Macbeth!

我聽說他們請麥克‧法斯賓達來演馬克白的角色。

324

33
script
[skrɪpt]
名 腳本；劇本

The company has hired good actors, but with such a bad **script**, I have doubts about the final result.

公司請了好演員，但這麼爛的劇本讓我很懷疑會有什麼好成績。

34
seat
[sit]
名 座位；席位

Let's pay a little more and get good **seats** this time.

我們這次多付一點錢，買好一點的座位。

> **應用** have/take a seat = be seated 坐下；就座

35
stage
[stedʒ]
名 舞臺

Just being on a **stage** makes my knees shake. I hate public speaking.

只要站上台我的腳就會發抖，真討厭公開演說。

> **應用**
> ① on stage 在舞台上
> ② go on the stage 成為演員

36
theatrical
[θɪˋætrɪk!]
形 劇場的；戲劇的

• theater 名 戲劇
• -ical 形 表「具有……
  特徵的」

If plays bore you, there are lots of other kinds of **theatrical** productions to try.

如果舞台劇很無聊，還可以試試其他的戲劇作品。

37 ticket

['tɪkɪt]

名 票券；罰單

I'm afraid if we wait too long to buy, the **tickets** will all have been sold.

我怕我們等太久，票早就賣完了。

> 應用
> 1 a return/round-trip ticket 來回票
>   a single/one-way ticket 單程票
> 2 parking/speeding ticket
>   停車繳費單／超速罰單

38 tier

[tɪr]

名（多層次中的）一層

I don't mind sitting on the second or third **tier**, but much higher than that you can't see anything.

我不介意坐第二層或第三層，但再高一點就什麼也看不到了。

39 venue

['vɛnju]

名 舉行地點；會場

The play is great, but the **venue** is terrible, with uncomfortable seats and a bad sound system.

這齣劇很棒，但是場地很糟──座椅不舒服，音響也很差。

40 witness

['wɪtnɪs]

名 目擊者；見證人

• wit 名 機智
• -ness 名「性質；狀態」

I can't believe she was a **witness** to Jody Chiang's last stage performance!

我不敢相信她親眼目睹江蕙最後一次的舞台表演！

> 應用　be a witness to + N. 某人目擊到某事發生

326

學後小試 A **Multiple Choice Questions**
請選擇合適的單字填入空格

_____ 1 I like paintings and photographs, but _____ is the art form that moves me the most.

(A) sculpture   (B) assembly
(C) material   (D) witness

_____ 2 I love this piece of music. Who is the _____?

(A) ticket   (B) artifact
(C) composer   (D) artwork

_____ 3 Please try to get good _____ for the show. There's no point in going if we can't see.

(A) seats   (B) stages
(C) scripts   (D) artists

_____ 4 I'd be terrible at _____ films, because I like everything.

(A) reviewing   (B) suspending
(C) enriching   (D) performing

_____ 5 Nicole Kidman made her film _____ when she was 16.

(A) debut   (B) theatergoer
(C) tier   (D) conductor

正確答案請參考 424 頁

B | Match

請在空格填入合適的單字，動詞需依時態變化，名詞需填入正確之單複數。

artificial	enlightening	nominate	box office	autograph	issue

1. I hope the film *Guardians of the Galaxy* is _____ for an award.

2. It doesn't matter how good the movie *The Hateful Eight* is if it doesn't do well at the _____.

3. If you want to know more about the painting, read the _____ brochure.

4. I have a collection of _____ of famous people.

5. _____ flowers last longer, but I prefer to see fresh ones.

6. The book is hard but important to read because it addresses really difficult _____.

C | Listening Practice

請聆聽音檔，將單字填入空格 260

1. I love going to see _____ music.

2. My _____ movie as a kid was *Roman Holiday*.

3. I didn't enjoy the _____, but my husband did.

4. This theater shows foreign films _____.

5. The play was good, but I've seen better _____.

6. He's a very _____ musician: he plays piano, guitar, and oboe.

正確答案請參考 424 頁

Unit 27

Life & Recreation

生活與消遣

生活情境中，從事興趣與運動經常出現在多益測驗中：

① 此種情境常出現在聽力測驗的圖片描述，所以必須要熟記相關的字彙，如繪畫
（drawing）、樂器（instrument）。

② 留意動詞片語的使用，如聯絡（get in touch）、過時（go out of fashion）、養
成……習慣（have a habit of V-ing）。

學前暖身 請閱讀英文定義，並將正確單字與之配對

spouse	vary	catch up	habit	quality time

① _____: to purposely avoid similar actions or objects

② _____: to learn about another person's life, especially
after a long absence

③ _____: time dedicated to improving oneself or improving
one's relationship with others

④ _____: some action performed repeatedly without
conscious decision

⑤ _____: one of the people in a marriage

Relationship 關係

01 single
['sɪŋgl]

形 單一的;單身的

Our next project is to set up an exclusive dating site for **single** professionals.

我們下個案子要為單身貴族設一個獨特的交友網站。

相似詞	形 married 已婚的
	形 divorced 離婚的
	形 separate 分居的

02 embrace
[ɪm'bres]

動 擁抱

• em- 在裡面
• brace 手臂

In more conservative societies such as ours, couples do not **embrace** in public.

在多數像我們一樣保守的社會,情侶是不會在公共場合擁抱的。

03 ever
['ɛvɚ]

副 從來

Most friends don't think they would **ever** need to ask each other for financial help.

大多數朋友認為他們不會需要對方幫自己解決財務困難。

04 excursion
[ɪk'skɝʒən]

名 短途旅行

• ex- 外面
• cur 跑
• -ion 名 表「動作;狀態」

The one-week **excursion** through the Grand Tetons was designed to bring families closer together.

大提頓山脈的一週旅遊方案是為了讓家人更親近。

應用	1 be/go on an excursion 短程出遊
	2 excursion to + 地方 前往某地遊覽

05 explore
[ɪk'splor]

動 探測;探索;探險

• ex- 出
• plor 喊

The winner of this year's Weekend Getaway will be able to take two friends and **explore** all the wonders of London.

今年《週末度假》的贏家,可以帶兩個朋友去探索倫敦的各大奇景。

06 **get in touch**

動 片 聯絡

Employees working overseas will be able to **get in touch** with family anytime they need.

海外的員工將可以隨時跟家人聯絡。

應用	keep/get/stay/be in touch/contact with Sb. = contact Sb. = hear from Sb. 和某人聯絡、聯繫

07 **opportunity**

[ˌɑpəˈtjunətɪ]

名 機會；良機

• opportune 形 適宜的
• -ity 名 表「狀態」

Staff should not miss the **opportunity** to spend Saturday with their families at our annual children's picnic.

同仁千萬不要錯失週六與家人一同參加年度兒童野餐的大好機會。

應用	[1] miss the opportunity/chance + to V. 錯失……的機會 [2] take/seize/make use of + the opportunity + to V. 掌握……的機會

08 **positive**

[ˈpɑzətɪv]

形 正向的；積極的；陽性的

• posit 放置
• -ive 形 表「具有……性質的；有……傾向的」

Families looking for a **positive** experience should consider our guided camping trips.

想要留下美好回憶的家庭，可以考慮我們有導遊的露營行程。

相似詞	形 constructive 建設性的 形 aggressive 有進取心的 形 optimistic 樂觀的

反義詞	形 negative = pessimistic 悲觀的；消極的

09 quality time
名 片 珍貴的時光

This year's company barbecue is an excellent chance to spend **quality time** with friends, family, and coworkers.
今年的公司烤肉是很好的機會，可以跟親朋好友、同事共度美好時光。

10 spouse
[spauz]
名 配偶

When submitting a résumé to an American company, avoid any mention of having a **spouse** or children.
寄履歷到美國公司時，要避免提到配偶和孩子。

11 throw out
動 片 趕出

Johnson's party was **thrown out** of the bar because they'd already drunk too much.
強森那一夥人被轟出酒吧，因為他們太醉了。

12 contestant
[kən`tɛstənt]
名 參加競賽者；角逐者

Contestants who finish in the top five will receive certificates in addition to prizes.
前五名完成的參賽者除了獎品之外還會得到證書。

• contest 動 比賽
• -ant 名 表「人」

Hanging Out 同樂

13 catch up
動 片 趕上（某人）

The after-ceremony party will give everyone a chance to **catch up** after the long holidays.
典禮結束後的派對讓大家在長假後聊聊彼此近況。

14 fad
[fæd]
名 一時的流行

According to our market research, a recent **fad** among college students is to play chess while hanging out at bars.
根據我們的市調，現在大學生流行在酒吧裡下西洋棋。

---

15 **fashion**

['fæʃən]

图 流行；時尚

Most of the mid-priced cafés provide a selection of **fashion** magazines for the young housewives who meet there.

大多數中價位的咖啡廳提供很多時尚雜誌，供在咖啡廳碰面的年輕家庭主婦閱讀。

應用	[1] go/be out of fashion = be old-fashioned 退流行；落伍 [2] be in fashion = be fashionable 成為風潮

---

16 **habit**

['hæbɪt]

图 習慣

People have a **habit** of using their smartphones even when hanging out with their friends.

大家就算跟朋友出去玩，也還是習慣滑手機。

應用	[1] have a/the habit of + V-ing = be in the habit of V-ing 有……的習慣 [2] get into the habit of V-ing = make it a rule/habit + to V. 養成……的習慣

---

17 **lean**

[lin]

動 靠

You won't need to provide chairs, because most of these men will just **lean** against the bar anyway.

你不需要提供椅子，因為這些男人大部分只會靠著吧台站著。

補充	lean的過去式和過去完成式同形，可以寫成 leaned或leant。

18 postpone
[post`pon]

動 延期；延遲

· post 後
· pone 放

Mr. Nakashima **postponed** the dinner until 7:30 p.m. to give everyone a chance to change clothes after work.

中島先生把晚餐延後到七點半，讓大家有機會下班換衣服後再來。

> **應用** postpone + N./V-ing = delay = put off
> 延期……

19 without
[wɪ`ðaʊt]

介 沒有

· with 和
· out 外

It is rare to find a group of children at the park **without** one or more portable game devices.

在公園普遍可見一群孩子，人手一台掌上型遊戲機。

Hobby 興趣

20 collection
[kə`lɛkʃən]

名 收集；收藏品

· collect 動 收集
· -ion 名 表「行為；行為的結果」

Several people from Accounting will be displaying their **collections** of rare coins this afternoon.

今天下午很多會計部的人要展示他們收藏的稀有硬幣。

21 delighted
[dɪ`laɪtɪd]

形 高興的

· de- 加強意義
· light 輕快
· -ed 形

We are **delighted** to greet our newest member to the flower arrangement club: Mr. Troxler.

我們很高興地歡迎我們的新會員加入插花俱樂部：卓思樂先生。

> **相似詞** 形 glad = happy = pleased 喜悅的；高興的

334

22

drawing

[ˋdrɔɪŋ]

名 繪畫;圖畫

- draw 動 繪畫
- -ing 名 表「與……
  有關的東西」

There will be a display of **drawings** done by employees on the fifteenth floor.

十五樓有同仁畫作的展覽。

23

expose

[ɪkˋspoz]

動 暴露;揭露

- ex- 外
- pose 放置

Parent's groups are concerned that our new game **exposes** children to too much violence at an early age.

家長團體擔心新遊戲讓孩子小小年紀就接觸太多暴力。

應用	expose A to B = A be exposed to B (使)A暴露於／接觸到B中

24

idle

[ˋaɪdl̩]

形 閒置的;不工作的;
  失業的

One of the biggest complaints from our retirees is they don't have enough to do to fill their **idle** time.

我們退休人士最大的抱怨,是他們閒暇時間沒有事可做。

25

instrument

[ˋɪnstrəmənt]

名 樂器

- instruct 動 教授;指示
- -ment 名 表「結果;狀態」

We encourage all our employees to learn a musical **instrument**; we will even purchase one for them if needed.

我們鼓勵員工學樂器,需要的話甚至會幫他們購買樂器。

應用	1 musical instrument 樂器 2 string(ed)/wind/percussion instrument 弦樂器／管樂器／打擊樂器

26 **list**
[lɪst]

名 表；名冊

The Human Resources department wants to make a **list** of everyone's pastimes and hobbies.

人資部門想要把員工的娛樂和興趣列成清單。

---

27 **mind**
[maɪnd]

名 頭腦；心靈

Learning a second language is good for your **mind**, so how about offering employees courses in Spanish and Chinese?

學第二種語言對頭腦有益，所以要不要提供員工上西班牙文課或中文課呢？

---

28 **preference**
[ˋprɛfərəns]

名 偏愛

• prefer 動 寧可
• -ence 名 「結果；性質；狀態」

Surprisingly, most of our lawyers have a **preference** for camping, while our cleaning staff likes reading books.

出乎意料的是，我們大部分的律師都喜歡露營，而清潔人員喜歡閱讀。

> 應用　by preference 因喜好而作選擇

---

29 **usual**
[ˋjuʒʊəl]

形 通常的；平常的；慣常的

• use 用途；使用
• -al 名 表「具其特徵的」

A **usual** evening for us is watching TV, taking a bath, and then playing a board game.

我們平時晚上就是看電視、洗澡和玩桌遊。

---

30 **vary**
[ˋvɛrɪ]

動 變化

Our president's interests seem to **vary** from painting to restoring classic cars.

我們總裁的興趣似乎變來變去，一下是繪畫，一下是整修中古車。

> 應用　vary from place to place / person to person . . . 因地／人而異

Housework 家事

31 errand
['ɛrənd]
名 差事；任務

A typical housewife has six **errands** to run per day before cooking dinner.
家庭主婦每天在做晚飯前通常有六件事要完成。

應用	① run errands 辦雜事；跑腿
	② send Sb. on errands 派某人跑腿打雜

32 fertilizer
['fɝtl͵aɪzɚ]
名 肥料

• fertile 形 肥沃的
• -ize 動 表「使」
• -er 名 表「物」

Rural households tend to use compost as a **fertilizer** for home gardens.
農村家庭常用堆肥作家裡花園的肥料。

33 rack
[ræk]
名 架子

Our new dish drying **rack** is coated with a mold resistant plastic.
我們新的瀝碗架上了一層防霉塑膠塗層。

34 take out
動 片 扔

These handles are designed to make it easier for elderly persons to **take out** the garbage.
這些手把是為了讓老人家可以方便扔垃圾而設計的。

35 turn off
動 片 關掉

Our new stove has a timer that automatically cuts the gas if someone forgets to **turn off** the burner.
如果有人忘了關瓦斯爐，我們新的爐有計時器，會自動切斷瓦斯。

36 water
[ˋwɔtɚ]

動 灑水

He designed a system that will **water** houseplants upon receiving a signal from a cell phone or computer.

他設計了一個自動澆花系統，可以接收手機或電腦訊號。

---

37 weed
[wid]

名 雜草；野草

The company lawn is full of **weeds**, which need to be pulled immediately.

公司草皮雜草叢生，應該儘快處理。

Sport 運動

38 cyclist
[ˋsaɪklɪst]

名 自行車運動員；騎腳踏車的人

• cycle 名 腳踏車
• -ist 名 表「人」

He's already a **cyclist**, so convincing him to train for the company triathlon shouldn't be too hard.

他已經是自行車手了，說服他參加公司鐵人三項的訓練應該不難。

---

39 particularly
[pɚˋtɪkjələlɪ]

副 特別地

• particle 名 微粒
• -ar 形 表「有……特性的」
• -ly 副

She's not **particularly** talented, but she's the best player on our basketball team.

她不是特別天賦異稟，但她是我們籃球隊最強的選手。

相似詞	副 especially 特別地
	副 exceptionally 傑出地；例外地
	副 notably 特別地；明顯地

---

40 tournament
[ˋtɝnəmənt]

名 比賽；錦標賽

• tourney 動 參加比賽
• -ment 名 表「行為；狀態」

Our company's rugby team has a good chance of winning this year's region-wide **tournament**.

我們公司的橄欖球隊很有機會贏得今年的區賽。

A

Multiple Choice Questions
請選擇合適的單字填入空格

_____ ❶ Compliments will help your employees stay _____ about their work.

    (A) idle   (B) usual
    (C) positive   (D) single

_____ ❷ Anytime you want to _____, just call me.

    (A) get in touch   (B) throw out
    (C) turn off   (D) take out

_____ ❸ Our agency arranges many popular adventure _____ into New Zealand.

    (A) excursions   (B) racks
    (C) contestants   (D) drawings

_____ ❹ You should give your son a musical _____ for Christmas.

    (A) errand   (B) opportunity
    (C) bicyclist   (D) instrument

_____ ❺ Of course, we plan to _____ Mexico City for a few days.

    (A) expose   (B) explore
    (C) postpone   (D) lean

正確答案請參考 424 頁

B Match

請在空格填入合適的單字，動詞需依時態變化，名詞需填入正確之單複數。

tournament	water	collection	fad	delighted	ever

1. The help desk staff is always forgetting to _____ their plants.

2. He has a huge _____ of video games at home, but no time to play them.

3. If you _____ have the time, you should read some Russian literature.

4. She loves pop music, and follows every music _____ that comes out of America.

5. We are organizing an employee chess _____ for next month.

6. He was _____ with the gift basket the manager sent his family.

C Listening Practice

請聆聽音檔，將單字填入空格 270

1. Human Resources has developed a _____ of all the employees' current hobbies.

2. Ms. Juris is _____ interested in Italian, but she likes Spanish as well.

3. He spends his lunch break looking through _____ magazines.

4. The yard is full of _____, which needs to be cleaned up.

5. It is pretty common for spouses to _____ in public here.

6. I have a _____ for 19th century classical music, especially Brahms.

正確答案請參考 424 頁

Unit 28

Politics & Society

政治與社會

多益的閱讀測驗中，必然會出現政治與社會相關的字彙，通常是為新聞報導：

1. 政治的情境經常與國家（nation）有關，所以必須熟悉國際關係相關單字，例如全世界的（worldwide）、國內的（domestic）。

2. 與民主相關的字彙也必須掌握，例如投票（vote）、多數（majority）、權威（authority）。

學前暖身 請閱讀英文定義，並將正確單字與之配對

| mental | exemplary | typical | be made of | coalition |

1. _____: usual; standard

2. _____: primarily composed of something

3. _____: outstanding; a positive model or example

4. _____: a group united for a joint action; an alliance

5. _____: relating to the mind

Identity 認同

01 **disparate**

[ˋdɪspərɪt]

形 截然不同的；異類的

I have heard from **disparate** sources that you tell off-color jokes at the office, and that's not appropriate.

我從不同的人那裡聽到你在工作時講黃色笑話,這是很不恰當的。

---

02 **disperse**

[dɪˋspɝs]

動（使）擴散；（使）散開；（使）分散

• dis- 離開
• sperse 散

We hope putting our video on YouTube will attract attention to our cause and help **disperse** our message.

我們希望把影片放到YouTube上,會吸引大家注意我們的理念,幫助我們傳播我們的想法。

---

03 **separate**

[ˋsɛpə͵ret]

形 分隔的；個別的

I would feel much more comfortable if the company would provide a **separate** bathroom for women.

如果公司提供女性專用的洗手間,我會覺得比較舒服。

---

04 **accustomed**

[əˋkʌstəmd]

形 習慣的；適應的

• ac- 向；去
• custom 習慣
• -ed 形

People living in North Korea are not **accustomed** to modern Western music.

居住在北韓的人不習慣聽西方現代音樂。

應用	be/get + accustomed/used + to N./V-ing 習慣於……

---

05 **conform**

[kənˋfɔrm]

動 遵照；適應；符合；使一致

• con- 共同；聯合
• form 動 形成

Some psychologists point out, teenagers feel strong pressure to **conform** with their peers.

心理學家指出,青少年適應同儕時承受很大的壓力。

應用	conform with/to + N. = abide by = comply with 遵守；順從

06 **mental**
[`mɛntl]

形 精神的；心理的

・ment 精神；心智
・-al 形 表「關於……的」

Many people suffer from some type of **mental** illness during the course of their lives.

在人生的道路上，大家都會為種種心理疾病所苦。

應用	① mental illness/health 心理疾病／健康
	② mentally ill/handicapped/challenged 精神障礙的

---

07 **sense**
[sɛns]

名 感受；理智

I get the strong **sense** that my ethnic joke made her uncomfortable.

我強烈感受到我的種族歧視笑話讓她不舒服。

Nation 國家

08 **coalition**
[͵koəˋlɪʃən]

名（政黨、國家等）臨時結成的聯盟

France can't address the problem alone— they need a **coalition** to back them.

法國不能獨自解決問題，需要盟友來支持他們。

---

09 **domestic**
[dəˋmɛstɪk]

形 國家的；國內的

・dom- 家
・-tic 形 表「具有某特性的」

The workers' strike is a **domestic** problem, not an international issue.

罷工是國內的問題，不是國際議題。

應用	① domestic market/economy/demand 國內市場／經濟／需求
	② domestic abuse 家庭暴力

---

10 **worldwide**
[ˋwɜ͏ld͵waɪd]

形 全球各地的；世界的

・world 名 世界
・wide 形 寬廣的

The government needs to put a stop to the epidemic before it becomes a **worldwide** concern.

政府須控制流行病疫情，以避免衍生全球問題。

11 **disrupt**
[dɪsˋrʌpt]

動 使混亂；使中斷

- dis- 離開
- rupt 斷裂

The president is afraid holding an election now will **disrupt** our economic recovery.
總統很擔心現在辦選舉會影響正在復甦的經濟。

---

12 **exemplary**
[ɪgˋzɛmplərɪ]

形 模範的

- exemplar 名 範本
- -y 形

She's led an **exemplary** life and will make a great leader.
她過著模範生活，這會讓她成為好的領導人。

---

13 **forecast**
[ˋforˌkæst]

動 預測；預報；預料

- fore- 預先
- cast 投

All the experts **forecast** a Democratic victory in the last election, and they were all wrong.
在上次選舉所有專家都預測民主黨會贏，結果全都錯了。

---

14 **foremost**
[ˋforˌmost]

形 最前的；最先的

- fore- 預先；前面
- most 最

First and **foremost**, he's a politician and he's never going to say something controversial.
首先，他是一個從不談論爭議議題的政治家。

> **應用**　first and foremost 首先；首要的是……

---

15 **found**
[faʊnd]

動 建立；創立；創辦

Sir Thomas Stamford Raffles **founded** modern Singapore in 1819.
湯瑪士·斯坦福·萊佛士爵士於 1819 年創建了現代的新加坡。

> **應用**　S. be founded/established/set up on . . .
> 某事被建立於……

344

16 heritage

['hɛrətɪdʒ]

图 傳統；遺產

• herit 遺傳；繼承
• -age 图

In post-Soviet Kazakhstan, the government works hard to support the national **heritage** that was previously suppressed.

後蘇聯時期，哈薩克政府大力支持先前被壓制的國家傳統。

---

17 landmark

['lænd,mɑrk]

图 地標；界標；
　重大事件；里程碑

• land 图 土地
• mark 图 記號

The Great Wall of China is one of the world's best known **landmarks**.

中國的長城是世界最知名的地標之一。

---

18 resident

['rɛzədənt]

图 居民

• reside 動 居住
• -ent 图 表「人」

I'm an American citizen, but I'm currently a **resident** of Thailand.

我是美國公民，但我現在住在泰國。

---

19 state-owned

['stetond]

形 國有的

In many countries, strategic utilities like electricity or railroads are **state-owned**.

在許多國家，戰略性的公共設施像是電力或鐵路都是國有的。

相似詞	形 state-run = public = government-owned/run 政府經營的
反義詞	形 private 私人的

20 unprecedented

[ʌn`prɛsə͵dɛntɪd]

形 無先例的；空前的

· un- 不
· precede 動 先於
· ent 名 表「物」
· -ed 形

If voting patterns continue as they began, the president will win this election by an **unprecedented** margin.

如果投票情形依然如此，總統會獲得空前絕後的壓倒性勝利。

Politics 政治

21 criticism

[`krɪtə͵sɪzəm]

名 批評；評論；挑剔

· critic 名 評論家
· -ism 名 表「行為」

Authoritarian governments tend to be very intolerant of **criticism**.

專制政府往往無法接受批評。

- - - - - - - - - -

22 crucial

[`kruʃəl]

形 決定性的；重要的

Free expression and freedom of the press are **crucial** to democracy.

言論自由和新聞自主對民主至關重要。

> **應用**　A be crucial to B　A對B來說很重要

- - - - - - - - - -

23 disseminate

[dɪ`sɛmə͵net]

動 散播；宣傳

· dis- 分開
· semin 種子
· -ate 動 表「使成為」

I don't appreciate the CEO using our meetings as a way to **disseminate** pamphlets supporting his favorite politicians.

我不喜歡執行長在開會的時候，散播他最愛的政治人物的宣傳小冊。

- - - - - - - - - -

24 former
['fɔrmə]

形 從前的；在前的

I find it suspicious that the **former** secretary of defense is now the CEO of a private security firm.

前任國防部部長現在擔任私人保全公司的執行長，我覺得這很詭異。

| 應用 | the former . . . , the latter . . .
前者……；後者…… |

25 long-term
['lɔŋ,tɝm]

形 長期的；長遠的

The **long-term** speaker of the House of Representatives is due to step down soon.

眾議院一直以來的發言人很快就要下臺了。

| 應用 | in the long/short-term 就長遠／短期來說 |

26 spokesperson
['spoks,pɝsṇ]

名 發言人

• spoke 動 說話（過去式）
• person 名 人

With all the scandals, Anthony Weiner's **spokesperson** must have had a difficult few years.

因為這些醜聞，安東尼‧偉納的發言人這幾年一定很難熬吧！

27 unlikely
[ʌn'laɪklɪ]

副 不太可能地

It is **unlikely** that the congresswoman will recover from that unfortunate comment and win reelection.

這位女議員要從這些負面評論中，死而復生並贏得連任的可能性不大。

| 反義詞 | 副 likely 很可能地
副 possibly 也許地；有機會地 |

28 vote
[vot]

動 投票

In some countries, like Australia, it is mandatory to **vote**.

在某些國家法律規定人民一定要投票，澳洲就是一例。

> **應用**　vote for Sb. 投票給某人

Society 社會

29 authority
[əˋθɔrətɪ]

名 權力；權威人士；
（複數）當局

• author 名 作者
• -ity 名

I don't know who has the **authority** to tell me what to wear, but it certainly isn't you.

我不知道哪個主管機關可以規定我的服裝儀容，但一定不是你。

---

30 common
[ˋkɑmən]

形 普通的；共同的

A respect for group harmony is part of our **common** heritage.

合群是我們共同的傳統文化之一。

> **應用**　1 A and B have something in common
> A和B有共同處
> 2 common sense 常識

---

31 community
[kəˋmjunətɪ]

名 社區；共同體

• commun 共同享有
• -ity 名

I like the **community** I live in because it encompasses people from so many different countries.

我喜歡我住的社區，因為它住了許多不同國家來的人。

32

equivalent

[ɪˈkwɪvələnt]

[形] 相等的；相同的

• equi- 相等的
• valent 有……的價值

Yelling "Free PlayStation 4" in a room full of boys is **equivalent** to yelling "fire" in a crowded theater!

在一間全部都是男孩的房間裡大喊「免費PS4」，跟在水洩不通的戲院大喊「失火了」是一樣的！

應用　A be the equivalent of/to B　A相當於B

33

for free

[片] 免費

You don't get anything in life **for free**—you always have to work for what you want.

天下沒有白吃的午餐——你要什麼，就要去努力。

34

frequent

[ˈfrikwənt]

[形] 時常發生的；
頻繁的；屢次的

The president makes **frequent** comments about how much he loves dogs, but I've never seen him pet one.

總統常常說他有多愛狗，但我從來沒見過他摸過半隻。

35

be made of

[動][片] 由……組成的

Our charity committee **is made of** members of the diplomatic corps and their spouses.

我們慈善委員會是由外交使節和他們的配偶組成的。

相似詞　consist of = be composed of
= be comprised of 由……組成

349

36 majority
[mə`dʒɔrətɪ]

名 多數；過半數；大多數

• major 形 主要的
• -ity 名 表「性質；狀態」

Even though I didn't vote for him, a **majority** of my countrymen did, so I have to respect their decision.

雖然我不支持他，但我的同鄉半數以上都投給他，因此我得尊重他們的決定。

應用	the majority of N. = most (of) N. = a large number of N.（複數名詞）多數的……

37 region
[`ridʒən]

名 地區

The northern **regions** of the country are cold, but weather in the south is usually mild.

國內北方很冷，南方天氣通常比較溫暖。

38 sign
[saɪn]

動 簽名

The leaders have finally agreed on the terms of the treaty. Now, they just have to **sign** it.

各國領袖終於同意協定的條款，現在他們只需要簽名了。

39 spectrum
[`spɛktrəm]

名（看法、感覺等的）範圍；各層次；光譜

I suppose I fall pretty far to the left on the political **spectrum**.

我認為我屬於政治派系的極左派。

40 typical
[`tɪpɪkl]

形 典型的；有代表性的

• type 類型
• -ic 形 表「有……特性的」
• -al 形 表「關於……的」

I come from a **typical** family with three kids, a dog, and a station wagon.

我來自傳統家庭，有三個孩子、一隻狗和旅行車。

350

A Multiple Choice Questions

請選擇合適的單字填入空格

_____ ❶ She made a(n) _____ point that we have to work together to succeed.

    (A) state-owned   (B) disparate
    (C) crucial   (D) equivalent

_____ ❷ Getting up to leave now would _____ the presentation.

    (A) conform   (B) forecast
    (C) disrupt   (D) found

_____ ❸ I think the _____ of people in our office support the new CEO.

    (A) region   (B) heritage
    (C) resident   (D) majority

_____ ❹ I've never been to this restaurant. Is it near any major _____?

    (A) spectrum   (B) sense
    (C) criticism   (D) landmark

_____ ❺ My supervisor makes _____ references to her prestigious university.

    (A) frequent   (B) worldwide
    (C) domestic   (D) foremost

正確答案請參考 425 頁

B | Match

請在空格填入合適的單字，動詞需依時態變化，名詞需填入正確之單複數。

| sign | long-term | spokesperson | for free | disperse | former |

1. Today, Ben and Jerry's is giving away ice cream _____!
2. When are they going to _____ the new contract?
3. Sam can use this desk for a little while, but we need to find a _____ office for him soon.
4. The company's _____ said they would be looking into the matter.
5. Let's use social media to _____ our new design concept.
6. The _____ CEO had some pretty harsh words for the current board.

C | Listening Practice

請聆聽音檔，將單字填入空格 🎧 280

1. To what _____ should I appeal for more leave time?
2. Staffing is a _____ issue from design, which we're discussing now.
3. Sales of the new model have reached _____ levels!
4. I've gotten _____ waking up at 6 a.m.
5. It's extremely _____ that we'll hear anything about the new office today.
6. If you don't _____, then you don't have any right to criticize national policy.

正確答案請參考 425 頁

Unit 29

Medication

醫療情境雖然經常出現在多益測驗當中，但僅於日常看醫生（see a doctor）或疾病治療（treatment）等詞彙：

① 必須熟悉與症狀（symptom）相關的用語，如過敏（be allergic to）、打噴嚏（sneeze）、發燒（fever）。

② 與療程相關的動詞也不可忽略，如診斷（diagnose）、開刀（operate）、服藥（take medicine）。

學前暖身 請閱讀英文定義，並將正確單字與之配對

fever	vaccinate	allergic	medicine	operate

① _____: caused by or relating to sensitivity to certain substances or chemicals

② _____: a condition in which the body's temperature is much higher than normal

③ _____: to cut open the body as part of a medical treatment

④ _____: a chemical compound used to treat illnesses or alleviate their symptoms

⑤ _____: to give medicine, usually by injection, in order to protect against diseases

353

Seeing A Doctor 看醫生

---

01 allergic
[ə`lɜdʒɪk]

形 過敏的；對……反應的

- allergy 名 過敏症
- -ic 形 表「具有……特徵的」；與……有關的」

Make sure you tell the doctor you had an **allergic** reaction to the cream.

記得跟你的醫生說你對乳液過敏。

> **應用**
> be allergic to + pollen/seafood/ . . .
> 某人對花粉／海鮮……等過敏

---

02 appointment
[ə`pɔɪntmənt]

名 約定；正式約會；預約

- appoint 動 任命
- -ment 名 表「行為」

You don't need to make an **appointment** at the clinic, but you might have to wait if they are busy.

在診所看病不用預約，但如果人很多，你可能就要等等。

> **應用**
> make an appointment with Sb.
> 與某人訂下約會時間

---

03 diagnose
[`daɪəgnoz]

動 診斷

- dia- 徹底的
- gnose 了解；認知

We are developing a system that can **diagnose** patients based on a series of questions.

我們在發展一套系統，可以根據一系列的問題來診斷病患。

> **應用**
> be diagnosed + with 疾病 被診斷罹患……

---

04 go ahead

片 開始做；著手做

You don't have to wait for permission from your insurance company; just **go ahead** and visit your doctor.

你不需要等保險公司同意，直接去看醫生就好了。

---

05 immediately
[ɪˋmidɪɪtlɪ]

副 立刻地

・im- 表「不」
・medi- 中間
・-ate 形 表「……狀態的」
・-ly 副

Anyone who has suffered an accident in the factory, no matter how small, must report it **immediately**.

在工廠發生意外的人，不論情節大小都要立即上報。

06 in regard to
動 片 關於；至於

In regard to your question, the clinic staff again apologizes, but your medicine is still not available.

關於您的問題，診所員工再度向您致歉，但您的藥還沒準備好。

> 應用　with/in regard to = regarding/concerning/ about = as for/to = in view of + N. 有關於……

07 physician
[fɪˋzɪʃən]

名 醫師；內科醫生

・physic 醫治
・-ician 名 表「專家」

Though she has not yet received her medical degree, she still works as a local **physician**.

雖然她還沒拿到醫學學位，她已經在本地當醫師了。

08 promptly
[ˋprɑmptlɪ]

副 迅速地；立即

Reporting a problem to your doctor **promptly** is the most important step in treating an illness.

有任何問題立即告訴您的醫生，是把病治好最重要的一步。

09 dental

[ˋdɛntḷ]

形 牙齒的；牙科的

• dent- 牙齒
• -al 形 表「……的」
  或「具其特徵的」

Our company's insurance covers **dental**, so you can visit the dentist as often as you like.

我們公司的保險包含牙齒，所以你想看幾次牙醫都可以。

| 應用 | 1 dental floss 牙線 |
| | 2 dental treatment/care 牙齒治療 |

---

10 routinely

[ruˋtinlɪ]

副 定期地

• route 名 路線；道路
• -ine 名 表「小」
• -ly 副

My dentist recommends **routinely** cleaning my toothbrush in boiling water twice a week.

我的牙醫建議我每週用滾水清洗我的牙刷兩次。

---

11 care

[kɛr]

動 照顧；關心；在乎

The local hospital does its best to **care** for all its patients, but it just doesn't have enough beds.

地方醫院已經盡最大的力量照顧病患，但床位就是不夠。

---

12 clinic

[ˋklɪnɪk]

名 診所

Most of our contracts are with small **clinics**, not hospitals.

我們大部分的合約都是和小診所簽的，不是大醫院。

Illness/Disease 疾病

13 ailing

[ˋelɪŋ]

形 生病的；不景氣的；
  處境困難的

• ail 動 (使)生病
• -ing 形

Employees are urged to take **ailing** family members to the doctor first, and worry about insurance paperwork later.

我們勸員工先帶生病的家人去看醫生，之後再為保險申請擔心。

14 **chronic**

[ˋkrɑnɪk]

形 慢性的；長期的

・chron 時間
・-ic 形

Those suffering from **chronic** allergy symptoms such as itchy eyes, runny nose, and sneezing can call in sick.

那些長期患有過敏症狀，如眼睛發癢、流鼻涕、打噴嚏的人，可以打電話來請病假。

> 應用　chronic/acute disease 慢性病／急性病

15 **complication**

[ˌkɑmpləˋkeʃən]

名 併發症

・con- 共同
・tag 接觸
・-ion 名 表「結果；狀態」

There were **complications** resulting from the operation, so she should stay in the hospital an additional week.

因為手術後的併發症，她應該在醫院多留一個星期。

16 **contagious**

[kənˋtedʒəs]

形（疾病）接觸傳染性的；（人）有傳染力的

・contagion 名 接觸傳染
・-ous 形 表「有……特質的」

This type of flu is highly **contagious**, so employees need to limit physical contact to an absolute minimum.

這種流感的傳染力很強，因此同仁盡可能避免不必要的肢體接觸。

> 相似詞
> 形 infectious 有感染力的
> 形 transmittable 可傳染的
> 形 communicable 可溝通的；會傳染的

17 **dehydrate**

[diˋhaɪˌdret]

動 脫水；使乾燥

・de- 離開
・hydr- 水
・-ate 動 表「使成為」

The flu will **dehydrate** the body, so remember to drink plenty of water if you are suffering from it.

流感會讓人脫水，所以記得要多喝水。

18 **duration**
[djʊˋreʃən]

名 持續;持續期間

· dur- 持久的
· -ation 名 表「行為;
狀態;結果」

Patients should stay at home for the **duration** of their illness.
生病期間病患應該待在家裡。

---

19 **fever**
[ˋfivɚ]

名 發燒

If you develop a **fever** with a temperature over 39 degrees, contact your doctor immediately.
如果你發燒超過三十九度,請立刻跟你的醫師聯絡。

---

20 **serious**
[ˋsɪrɪəs]

形 嚴重的;嚴肅的

Any **serious** illness needs to be reported to the company nurse right away.
一旦發現嚴重的疾病必須馬上通知公司護士。

---

21 **sneeze**
[sniz]

動 噴嚏(聲);打噴嚏

I sent Jenkins home because she couldn't stop **sneezing** and so couldn't talk on the phone.
我叫詹金斯回家了,因為她一直打噴嚏,根本沒辦法講電話。

---

22 **sore throat**
[sor] [θrot]

名 片 喉嚨痛

He called in sick with a **sore throat**, but I couldn't hear anything wrong with his voice.
他因為喉嚨痛打電話來請病假,但我聽不出來他聲音哪裡不對勁。

---

23 **symptom**

['sɪmptəm]

名 症狀;徵候;徵兆

• sym- 一起;共同
• ptom 落

The most common **symptoms** of the flu are a fever, coughing, and a loss of appetite.

流感最常見的症狀是發燒、咳嗽和食慾不振。

Medicine 藥物

24 **comfort**

['kʌmfət]

名 舒適;安慰

This medicine won't provide you much **comfort**, but it will reduce your coughing.

這種藥不會讓你更舒服,但會減輕咳嗽症狀。

---

25 **expire**

[ɪk'spaɪr]

動 滿期;過期;到期

• ex- 出
• pire 呼吸

You'd better take them now, because these pills **expire** next month, according to the date on the bottle.

你最好趕快吃藥,因為根據瓶身上的日期,這些藥丸下個月就過期了。

---

26 **medicine**

['mɛdəsn̩]

名 藥

• medical 形 醫學的;醫療的
• -ine 名 表示帶有「技術;處置;行為」等抽象意義

The company doctor provides low-cost, generic **medicine** to all employees.

公司的醫生會給員工便宜的學名藥。

應用	take medicine 服藥
文化補充	學名藥(generic medicine)是指原廠藥專利過期之後,其他廠商依照原廠配方自行生產的藥,同樣要經過政府相關單位的審查,才可販售。

---

27 **pharmacy**

['fɑrməsɪ]

名 藥房

• pharmaco- 藥
• -y 名 表「性質;狀態」

There's a **pharmacy** on the third floor. You can buy aspirin there.

三樓有間藥局,你可以在那裡買到阿斯匹靈。

---

28 regardless
[rɪ`gardlɪs]

副 無論如何；不管怎樣

• regard 名 注重
• -less 形 表「無；沒有」

We believe in providing quality medical treatment **regardless** of financial status.

我們相信不管財務狀況如何，都該提供有效的治療。

> **應用**
> regardless of + N. = without regard(s) to N.
> = despite + N. = in spite of + N.
> 不考慮……；不論……

29 remedy
[`rɛmədɪ]

名 治療；療法

I know of only one **remedy** for a cold: plenty of bed rest and lots of orange juice.

我只知道一種感冒的療法：就是多睡覺和多喝柳橙汁。

> **應用**
> remedy/cure/treatment + for + a disease
> 某疾病的療法

Treatment 治療

30 alleviate
[ə`livɪ‚et]

動 減輕；緩和

• al- 向
• levi(s) 輕的
• -ate 動 表「使成為」

Most treatments simply **alleviate** the symptoms without actually curing the illness.

大部分的治療只是減輕症狀，不是真的在治病。

31 goal
[gol]

名 目標

Our **goal** is to provide long-term care for our elderly employees.

我們的目標是要提供年長員工長期照護。

> **應用**
> reach/carry out/realize a goal + of N. / to V.
> 達到……的目標

360

32 operate
[ˈɑpəˌret]

動 開刀;動手術

• oper 工作;勞動
• -ate 動 表「使成為」

It's a minor procedure: they will **operate**, and you will be out of the hospital the same day.
這是個小手術:他們開完刀,你當天就可以出院了。

應用 operate on / perform an operation on Sb.
在某人身上動手術

---

33 remove
[rɪˈmuv]

動 移動;去掉

• re- 往回;離開
• move 移動

In the event the appendix needs to be **removed**, we will schedule an operation as soon as possible.
如果要切除盲腸,我們會儘快安排動刀。

相似詞 動 delete = eliminate 消除;刪除
片 get rid of 擺脫掉;處理掉;清除

---

34 skill
[ˈskɪl]

名 技術;技巧

Laser surgery is an essential **skill** for any surgeon.
雷射手術是外科醫生必備的技能。

---

35 sufficient
[səˈfɪʃənt]

形 足夠的

• suf- 下面
• fic 做
• -ent 形 表「有……性質的」

This hospital has **sufficient** medical staff for daily operation but not for emergencies caused by natural disasters.
醫院每日的手術都有足夠的醫療人員,但是無法應付自然災害造成的緊急狀況。

---

36 surgical
[ˈsɝdʒɪkl]

形 手術的

We manufacture high-quality **surgical** equipment such as scalpels and forceps.
我們製造優質外科用具,像是手術刀和鑷子。

361

37 take care of

動 片 照顧

Employees who need to **take care of** elderly family members at home may request a four-day work schedule.

需要在家照顧長輩的同仁可以要求一週工作四天。

> **相似詞** 片 care for = look after 照顧；看管

38 vaccinate

[ˋvæksn̩‚et]

動 接種疫苗

• vaccine 形 疫苗的
• -ate 動 表「使成為」

Every year, we have a drive to **vaccinate** employees against the flu.

每年我們都計劃讓員工接種流感疫苗。

> **應用** Sb. be vaccinated = Sb. be given a vaccine
> 已接種疫苗

39 wellness

[ˋwɛlnɪs]

名 健康

• well 副 好地；健康地
• -ness 名 表「性質；狀態」

Both the physical and mental **wellness** of our factory workers is our top priority.

我們認為工廠工人的身心健康很重要。

40 go through

動 片 經過；經歷；遭受

Cancer treatment can be a long and painful process, but our councilors will make sure you don't **go through** it alone.

癌症治療的過程又長又痛苦，但我們的顧問會確保您不是獨自面對一切。

學後小試 A

Multiple Choice Questions
請選擇合適的單字填入空格

_____ ◻ Notify your doctor of a(n) _____ cough that persists for more than a day.

(A) sufficient　　(B) ailing
(C) surgical　　(D) chronic

_____ ◻ Urge your employees to _____ a fever soon, or it will mean more sick days.

(A) go ahead　　(B) in regard to
(C) take care of　　(D) go through

_____ ◻ Notify your _____ immediately if you are injured during work.

(A) wellness　　(B) physician
(C) goal　　(D) remedy

_____ ◻ Coffee and tea will _____ you, so avoid drinking them when you have a cold.

(A) dehydrate　　(B) alleviate
(C) expire　　(D) sneeze

_____ ◻ You need to stay in the hospital because of _____ resulting from the treatment.

(A) complications　　(B) skills
(C) medicines　　(D) clinics

正確答案請參考 425 頁

B Match

請在空格填入合適的單字，動詞需依時態變化，名詞需填入正確之單複數。

| promptly | contagious | pharmacy | care | appointment | sore throat |

1. You'll get your prescription filled at the _____ next door to the doctor's office.

2. You need to make an _____ at least 24 hours ahead of time.

3. We lack the facilities to _____ for employees injured on the job.

4. The influenza is extremely _____, so expect employees to take a lot of sick leave.

5. She's had a _____ for a few days, so I sent her home.

6. Notify the company's medical center _____ if an employee is showing signs of the flu.

C Listening Practice

請聆聽音檔，將單字填入空格 290

1. This pain reliever will give _____ even during the worst headache.

2. Your _____ plan does not cover non-essential treatments such as teeth whitening.

3. Mr. Harrison had his appendix _____, so he'll be out of the office for several weeks.

4. My doctor _____ me as suffering from stress and overwork.

5. The company nurse _____ schedules employees for health checks.

6. It's not a _____ injury, but you should have your doctor check it just to be safe.

正確答案請參考 426 頁

Unit 30

Charity

公益

多益測驗中常會出現與慈善有關的募資（fundraising）或宣傳（campaign）文章或文宣：

1. 熟悉表達目的的用法，如意圖要（intend to）、規劃（plan）、實現（achieve）、代表（represent）、提供（provide）。

2. 環境保護（environment protection）為此情境中的子單元，非常重要，務必要牢記其中所有單字。

學前暖身 請閱讀英文定義，並將正確單字與之配對

awareness	fundraising	prerequisite	significant	embark

1 _____ : work done to raise money for a specific activity or cause

2 _____ : important or noteworthy; worthy of attention

3 _____ : a necessary step or accomplishment before moving on in a process

4 _____ : feeling or experiencing something; knowing something exists

5 _____ : to begin a journey or an important task or action

Campaign 宣傳活動

01

awareness
[ə'wεrnɪs]

名 察覺；意識

• aware 形 察覺的
• -ness 名 表「性質；狀態」

Raising **awareness** is helpful, but the most important thing is to turn it into action.
喚起民眾的意識很重要，但最重要的還是化為實際行動。

應用	raise/arouse public awareness of N.
	喚起大眾對……的關切

02

campaign
[kæm'pen]

名 宣傳活動

• camp 田野
• -aign 名

The AIDS Ride **campaign** is designed to generate donations for AIDS research.
AIDS Ride 這個愛滋病的宣導活動，目的是為研究愛滋病募資。

03

definitely
['dɛfənɪtlɪ]

副 明確地；清楚地；
毫無疑問地

• define 動 下定義
• -ite 形
• -ly 副

After contributing funds for three years, I **definitely** feel invested in the outcome of the vaccination project.
投資了這個疫苗的案子三年後看到成果，我真心覺得這是一筆好投資。

04

embark
[ɪm'bɑrk]

動 從事；著手

• em- 登上
• bark 名 小帆船

My organization is about to **embark** on a major new project.
我的機構即將執行一個新的大案子。

應用	embark on N. = set out on N.
	= engage in N /V-ing
	= start/begin + to V./V-ing 開始做……

---

05 美加 **06** 加澳 **07** 美加 **08** 英澳

30

Charity
公益

05 **inspiring**
[ɪnˈspaɪrɪŋ]

形 激勵人心的；
啟發靈感的

・in- 往裡面
・spir 呼吸
・-ing 形

PlayPump's advertisements were **inspiring**,
but the idea behind them didn't really work.
玩蹦的廣告真是激勵人心，但背後的想法其實不太實際。

---

06 **intend**
[ɪnˈtɛnd]

動 想要；打算

・in- 向
・tend 伸展

They didn't **intend** to insult local community
leaders, but that's what happened.
他們並不打算要侮辱本地領袖，但事情就是發生了。

> **應用**
> intend/attempt to V.
> = have the intention to V. 企圖做……

---

07 **plan**
[plæn]

名 計畫；規劃

Before we start to invest this money, we need
a **plan**.
我們開始投入資金之前，需要先有規劃。

---

08 **significant**
[sɪgˈnɪfəkənt]

形 有意義的；
重要的；重大的

・sign 表「符號」
・fic 製造；創造
・-ant 形 表「處於……
狀態的」

Is a three percent increase in school
attendance a **significant** change?
學校出席率提升百分之三是重大的改變嗎？

367

Charity 慈善

09 **affiliation**
[ə,fɪlɪˈeʃən]

名 隸屬；入會；
　聯合；聯繫

- affiliate 動 使隸屬於
- -ion 名 表「動作；狀態」

The legal department is very nervous about having an **affiliation** with a controversial charity.
法律部門對於要和有爭議的公益團體有聯繫很緊張。

---

10 **charity**
[ˈtʃærətɪ]

名 慈善；善舉；慈善團體

I believe we all end up in need of **charity** at some point in our lives.
我相信我們人生中總有個時間點，會需要別人的救濟。

| 應用 | 1 S. + V. for charity 某人出於善心而去做…… 2 charitable group/organization = charity 慈善團體 |

---

11 **desired**
[dɪˈzaɪrd]

形 想要的；預期的

- desire 動 渴望
- -ed 形

Sometimes you achieve your **desired** outcome, sometimes you don't.
有時候你得到你想要的成果，有時候你得不到。

| 相似詞 | 形 favored = anticipated = expected 想要的；預期的 |

---

12 **fortune**
[ˈfɔrtʃən]

名 財產；財富；
　幸運；命運

The creator of the TV show *The Simpsons* is giving away his **fortune** before he dies.
電視節目《辛普森家庭》的作者在死前捐出他的財產。

| 應用 | 1 give away / donate one's fortune 捐出財產 2 make a fortune = make money 賺錢 |

---

13 **optimistic**

[ˌɑptəˋmɪstɪk]

形 樂觀的

- optim 最好
- -ist 名 表「……主義的人」
- -ic 形 表「有……特性的」

Honestly, I think their predictions are far too **optimistic** to be possible.

老實説，我認為他們的預測太過樂觀了，不可能實現的。

反義詞 形 pessimistic 悲觀的

14 **over**

[ˋovɚ]

介 超過

We've been waiting for **over** three weeks for a receipt for our donation.

我們等捐款的收據，已經等了超過三個星期。

15 **philanthropic**

[ˌfɪlənˋθrɑpɪk]

形 慈善的；樂善好施的

- phil- 愛
- anthropo- 人
- -ic 形 表「有……特性的」

She is a great CEO, but what I admire most about her is her **philanthropic** work.

她是很棒的執行長，但我最欣賞的是她的樂善好施。

16 **represent**

[ˌrɛprɪˋzɛnt]

動 代表；提出；表達

- re- 再；加強意義
- present 呈現

The heads of the legal and HR departments will **represent** our company at the annual gala.

法律部及人資部的主管將代表我們公司出席年度盛會。

17 **resounding**

[rɪˋzaʊdɪŋ]

形 響亮的；大聲的

We are proud to announce the **resounding** success of our toilet-building project!

我們很榮幸宣布廁所的營造計畫大成功。

18 **sponsor**

[ˋspɑnsɚ]

動 贊助

I've been asked to **sponsor** a child in Belize, but I think the program might be a scam.

我曾受邀贊助一位貝里斯的小孩，但我認為這個計畫可能是詐騙。

Donation 捐款

19
conscious
['kɑnʃəs]

形 有意識到的；有知覺的

· con- 共同
· sci- 知道
· -ous 形 表「充滿……的」

When I made the donation, I wasn't **conscious** of the organization's questionable methods.

我捐錢的時候，並沒有意識到這個機構的作法很可疑。

應用	be conscious of N. 意識到

20
donate
['donet]

動 捐獻；捐贈

· don 給予
· -ate 動 表「使成為」

I **donate** to domestic charities because I think there is a lot of work to be done within our country.

我捐款給國內的慈善團體，因為我認為我國還有需要努力的地方。

應用	donate + N. + to Sb./charities = make a donation to Sb./charities 捐獻……給某人或慈善團體

21
persuade
[pɚ'swed]

動 說服；勸服

· per- 完全
· suade 勸說

I was **persuaded** to contribute when they told me how important the new hospital would be for children.

當他們跟我解釋新的醫院是為了兒童建的，非常重要；我就被說服去捐款了。

應用	persuade Sb. to V. = talk Sb. into V-ing 說服某人去做……

22
regular
['rɛgjəlɚ]

形 定期的；經常的；通常的

I make **regular** contributions to a number of charitable organizations.

我會定期捐款給一些慈善機構。

---

23 **relieve**

[rɪ'liv]

動 緩和;減輕;救援

• re- 再;加強意義
• lieve 舉起

The first food aid packages have arrived and will **relieve** the worst cases of malnutrition.

第一批的食物救援送到了,將先給營養不良最嚴重的患者。

> **反義詞**
> 1 relieve Sb. of N. = rid Sb. of N.
> 使某人免除……
> 2 relieve tension/pressure/stress
> 解除緊張/壓力

---

24 **useful**

['jusfəl]

形 有用的

• use 名 使用
• -ful 形 表「充滿……的;有……性質的」

Honestly, I think a lot of international aid just isn't **useful**.

老實說,我認為很多國際救援一點用都沒有。

Environmental Protection 環境保護

25 **conservation**

[ˌkɑnsə'veʃən]

名 保存;保護

• conserve 動 保護;管理
• -ation 名 表「行為;狀態;結果」

I give all I can to environmental **conservation**, because once plant and animal species become extinct, they're lost forever.

我致力於環境保育,因為一旦動植物絕種,他們就永遠消失了。

> **反義詞**
> 1 environmental conservation 環保
> 2 energy conservation 節約能源

---

26 **ecology**

[ɪ'kɑlədʒɪ]

名 生態

• eco 環境
• -logy 學科

Australia has one of the world's most unique **ecologies**, and we must protect it.

澳洲有世上最獨特的生態環境,我們一定要保護它。

27 endangered
[ɪnˈdendʒəd]

形 瀕臨絕種的

• en- 使處於……的狀態
• danger 名 危險
• -ed 形

It is depressing to realize how many animal species are **endangered** today.

了解到有多少動物物種瀕臨絕種，真令人憂心。

相似詞	形 threatened 受威脅的；有危險的
	片 at risk = in danger 受威脅的；有危險的
	片 on the verge of extinction 瀕臨絕種的

28 energy-efficient
[ˈɛnədʒɪˈfɪʃənt]

形 節能的

Installing **energy-efficient** lighting and heating systems will save the company huge amounts of money.

裝設節能的照明及暖氣系統會讓公司省下一大筆錢。

29 environment
[ɪnˈvaɪrənmənt]

名 環境；自然環境

• environ 動 包圍，圍繞
• -ment 名 表「結果；狀態」

Our children will have to live in the **environment** we create, so we must take care of it.

我們的孩子要住在我們打造的環境，因此我們必須維護好它。

30 prerequisite
[ˌpriˈrɛkwəzɪt]

形 不可缺的；事先需要的

• pre- 預先
• require 動 需要
• -ite 形

Basic health training is **prerequisite** for being a forest ranger.

要當森林保護員一定要接受基本健康訓練。

31 **protection**
[prə`tɛkʃən]

名 保護

• protect 動 保護
• -ion 名 表「行為」

The new anti-hunting laws will provide some **protection** for the animals living in the park.

新的反狩獵法多少會保護住在這個園區裡的動物。

---

32 **reservation**
[ˌrɛzə`veʃən]

名 禁獵區；自然保護區；
居留地

• re- 往回
• serve 保存
• -ation 名 表「動作；結果」

The government is considering making part of this forest a nature **reservation**.

政府在考慮把這座森林的一部分變成自然保護區。

---

33 **species**
[`spiʃiz]

名 種類；品種

There are almost a million **species** of insects in the world.

世界上約有一百萬種昆蟲。

Fundraising 募資

34 **possible**
[`pɑsəbl̩]

形 可能的

Let's do some research before we donate to any charity to avoid any **possible** embarrassment.

為了避免尷尬，捐款給公益團體之前，我們要先做好功課。

---

35 **provide**
[prə`vaɪd]

動 提供

• pro- 預先
• vide 看

This organization **provides** water filtration systems to villages that apply for them.

這個機構提供濾水系統給向他們提出申請的村莊。

應用	provide Sb. with Sth. = provide Sth. for Sb. 提供某物予某人

373

36 achieve

[ə`tʃiv]

動 實現；完成；到達

- a- 前往
- chief 頭

With just one more large donation, we'll **achieve** our financial goal.

只要再一次的大筆捐款，我們就達到財務目標了。

---

37 appear

[ə`pɪr]

動 看來好像；似乎

My job might **appear** to be just going to parties, but getting commitments from donors is hard work!

我的工作看起來像是去參加宴會，但是要從捐贈者身上得到承諾真的很辛苦。

---

38 endeavor

[ɪn`dɛvɚ]

名 嘗試；努力

- en- 在裡面
- deavor 職責

Our **endeavor** would not be possible without your generous contribution.

如果沒有您的慷慨解囊，我們再努力也不可能成功。

---

39 fundraising

[`fʌnd͵rezɪŋ]

名 募款；慈善捐款

- fund 名 資金
- raise 動 舉起
- -ing 名

Fundraising is a job that requires a lot of skills—writing, negotiating, mediating, and more.

募款是一樣需要很多技巧的工作——像是寫作、協商、調解等。

---

40 need

[nid]

名 需要

Our most pressing **need** right now is for cash donations.

現在我們最急需的是現金捐款。

A Multiple Choice Questions

請選擇合適的單字填入空格

_____ 1 The story of her rise from poverty to become her nation's leader is so _____.

(A) inspiring   (B) regular
(C) conscious   (D) endangered

_____ 2 My team _____ a charity that provides bicycles for poor children to ride to school.

(A) appears   (B) achieves
(C) sponsors   (D) intends

_____ 3 We have a detailed _____ for our three-day trip.

(A) species   (B) plan
(C) charity   (D) affiliation

_____ 4 Getting these donations to the disaster zone will be a major _____.

(A) ecology   (B) environment
(C) reservation   (D) endeavor

_____ 5 Do you _____ money to any major charities?

(A) relieve   (B) persuade
(C) donate   (D) represent

正確答案請參考 426 頁

B | Match

請在空格填入合適的單字，動詞需依時態變化，名詞需填入正確之單複數。

| provide | awareness | resounding | over | possible | energy-efficient |

1. There has been a _____ outcry to end contributions to the controversial charity.

2. We are hoping our ads will increase _____ of the issue.

3. So far, we have given _____ five million dollars to environmental causes.

4. It is _____ that we'll have to cancel our donation this year, but we don't know yet.

5. Our new _____ lighting will save us a lot of money.

6. Our money goes to _____ books, pens, and pencils for poor schools.

C | Listening Practice

請聆聽音檔，將單字填入空格 300

1. I volunteer at the soup kitchen because I like to feel _____.

2. Environmental _____ is something I feel very strongly about.

3. Ask the organization what its biggest _____ is and I will try to fill it.

4. I'm _____ going to give more next year, when I have a bigger salary.

5. She left her entire _____ to an animal rights organization.

6. It's hard to be _____ these days, with so much conflict in the world

正確答案請參考 426 頁

Appendix
附 錄

Confusing Words

易混淆字
大解密

01 **regular** vs. **normal**

regular
[ˋrɛgjələ]

形 定期的；規律的

At our company we have **regular** staff meetings—every Monday at 9:30 a.m.

我們公司每週一早上九點半定期召開員工會議。

---

normal
[ˋnɔrml]

形 普通的；正常的

It's perfectly **normal** to be nervous on your first sales call.

第一次打電話跟客戶談生意，緊張是很正常的。

➡ **regular** 用於動作有「固定的規律或頻率」。
➡ **normal** 指某現象是「普通的、常見的」。

_____ **1** Doctors recommend that elderly patients have _____ health checkups once a year.

    (A) regular   (B) normal

02 **worth** vs. **worthy**

worth
[wɝθ]

形 值……的
名 價值

This deal is **worth** a lot of money to our company. We have to close it.

這筆交易對公司來說是一大筆錢，我們一定要成交。

---

worthy
[ˋwɝðɪ]

形 適合……的；
  有價值的、可尊敬的；
  值……的

He is neither qualified nor experienced. He's not a **worthy** candidate for this job.

他資格不符又沒有經驗，不適合這份工作。

➡ **worth** 代表「與……(金錢)等值的；值得做(動作)的」，後面接 N. ／ V-ing 代表等值的金錢、值得去做的動作。
➡ **worthy** 則代表「有價值的；可尊敬的」，若要用 worthy 表達「與……(金錢)相稱的」，則要先接 of 再接受詞。

_____ **2** The company's CEO believes that extra vacation time is a _____ investment because it increases employee productivity.

    (A) worth   (B) worthy

03 **contribute** vs. **attribute**

302 **03** 澳美 **04** 加英

contribute
[kən`trɪbjut]

勔 貢獻;導致

Our thanks to Mr. Peters, who **contributed** many ideas to our new marketing strategy.
我們感謝皮特斯先生,他貢獻了很多行銷策略的構想。

attribute
[ə`trɪbjut]

勔 把……歸因為……

Our CEO **attributes** his success to hard work and dedication.
我們執行長將他的成功歸因於勤奮和奉獻。

➡ A **contribute** to B 意指「A為B做出貢獻」、或「A(原因)導致B(結果)」。
➡ **attribute** B to A 意指「將B(結果)歸因於A(原因)」。

_____ **3** The product's successful launch was _____ to all of the hard work put in by the sales team.

(A) contributed　　(B) attributed

04 **provide** vs. **offer**

provide
[prə`vaɪd]

勔 提供

His company has been **providing** ours with office supplies for many years.
他的公司多年以來提供辦公室用品給我們公司。

offer
[`ɔfɚ]

勔 給予

I can **offer** you a 10% discount on any purchase of $100 or higher.
若您購物的金額達到一百元以上,我將給您九折的優惠。

➡ **provide** 代表「準備充足的份量來提供」,句型可用 provide + 人 + with + 物,或 provide + 物 + for + 人。
➡ **offer** 是「主動給予」,表達「提供某物給某人」,句型可用 offer + 人 + 物。

_____ **4** This supermarket _____ fresh fruits and vegetables from local farmers.

(A) provides　　(B) offers

announce
[əˈnaʊns]

動 公開宣佈；通告

We are delighted to **announce** that our new range of electric scooters is now available.
我們很開心地宣佈全新系列的電動車即日上市。

---

declare
[dɪˈklɛr]

動 宣告；聲明；申報

We showed the contract to our lawyer, and he **declared** that it wasn't valid.
我們把這份合約給我們的律師看，而他聲明此合約不具效力。

➡ **announce** 指對公眾或特定的一群人宣佈事項，常是大家感興趣的事，如國家大事、商品資訊、婚喪喜慶、開會等消息。
➡ **declare** 較正式，指在莊嚴的場合，由官方權威人士公開鄭重宣佈，像是申報應納稅的貨物或收入。

_____ **5** The government _____ that it was accepting bids from construction companies to build a new city hall.

(A) announced　　(B) declared

06 **result in** vs. **result from**

result in
片 導致

The merger **resulted in** lots of employees losing their jobs.
這場併購導致很多員工失業。

---

result from
片 起因於

I'm very interested to see what **results from** your online marketing initiative.
我對於你網路行銷的新手法所帶來的成效很感興趣。

➡ A **result in** B 意指「A（原因）導致 B（結果）」。
➡ B **result from** A 意指「B（結果）起因於 A（原因）」。

_____ **6** Our presence at this year's university job fair _____ the hiring of 20 new employees.

(A) resulted in　　(B) resulted from

07 **means** vs. **instrument**

means

[minz]

图 方法；工具

Do we have any reliable **means** of identifying the problem with our current system?

我們有沒有任何可靠的方法，可以以現行系統找出問題？

---

instrument

['ɪnstrəmənt]

图 器具；工具

Social media is a valuable **instrument** for making connections with clients.

社群媒體是和客戶建立關係的一大利器。

➡ **means** 常指達成某目的使用的「方法、手段」，是單複數同形，近似 way、method。

➡ **instrument** 常指「實體或明確的工具」，近似 tool。

_____ 🄍 Our company is too small. It doesn't have the _____ to compete in foreign markets.

    (A) means   (B) instruments

08 **remark** vs. **acknowledge**

remark

[rɪ'mɑrk]

動 評論；指出

In today's budget review, Janet **remarked** that Advertising's allocation might be too low.

今天在做預算審核時，珍納認為廣告部門的配額也許太低了。

---

acknowledge

[ək'nɑlɪdʒ]

動 承認；肯定；認可

We've **acknowledged** last quarter's errors and, as a result, will do better this quarter.

我們承認上一季的疏失，因此我們這一季會加以改進。

➡ **remark** 意指對事實做出「主觀評論」，後面接 that 子句表個人意見。

➡ **acknowledge** 是「承認、主張某事實」。

_____ 🄋 After he _____ his mistakes, the boss decided to give him another chance.

    (A) remarked   (B) acknowledged

09 **limitation** vs. **capacity**

limitation
[ˌlɪmə`teʃən]

名 限制；侷限

The government has set a **limitation** on how much of that product we can import.
政府為那項商品的進口數量立下限制。

---

capacity
[kə`pæsətɪ]

名 容納量；能力

We don't have anywhere to store those goods. Our warehouse is at full **capacity**.
我們沒地方存放那些貨品，倉庫都已經滿了。

➡ **limitation** 指「數量的限制或能力的侷限」。
➡ **capacity** 指「容納量或能力的最大限度」。

_____ 9 Management has introduced a _____ on new hires until spring of next year.

    (A) limitation   (B) capacity

10 **usual** vs. **common**

usual
[`juʒʊəl]

形 通常的；平常的

Our **usual** working hours are ten to seven, but we sometimes do overtime.
我們平常上班時間為早上十點到傍晚七點，但有時會加班。

---

common
[`kɑmən]

形 常見的；共同的；
  普遍的

Employees arriving late for work is the most **common** problem we face here.
員工遲到是我們這裡最普遍的問題。

➡ **usual** 常指「經常出現或重複例行性的行為」。
➡ **common** 指「高頻率的動作」或「某些人共有的特性」。

_____ 10 These online sales events are _____. Don't worry if you miss this one.

    (A) usual   (B) common

11 **standard** vs. **degree**

306 11 美英 12 美加

standard [ˋstændəd] 名 標準；水準	Your sales numbers this quarter simply aren't up to **standard**. You must do better. 你們本季的業績沒達到標準，要再更努力。
degree [dɪˋgri] 名 程度；等級；學位	There's a high **degree** of uncertainty about who'll get chosen for the promotion. 誰會升職變數還很大。

➡ **standard** 是指某人要求應達到的「標準、水準」，up to one's standard 指「達到標準」。

➡ **degree** 指「等級或程度」。

_____ 11 Our department must proceed with a _____ of caution on any new product launches.

(A) standard　　(B) degree

12 **pollution** vs. **pollutant**

pollution [pəˋluʃən] 名 汙染	Our new hybrid-engine vehicles will greatly help reduce **pollution** in cities and towns. 我們最新的油電混合車能大幅減低城鎮區的汙染。
pollutant [pəˋlutənt] 名 汙染物質	Our new filter safely removes chemical **pollutants** from contaminated drinking water. 我們最新的濾水器能去除飲用水中的化學汙染物。

➡ **pollution** 泛指「不同形式的汙染狀態」。

➡ **pollutant** 指「特定的汙染物質」。

_____ 12 The factory produces a gas that has been classified as a dangerous _____ by the government.

(A) pollution　　(B) pollutant

307 · **13** 美澳 · **14** 英美

value
[ˋvælju]

名 價值

At $70 per share, the company has a **value** of nearly $170 billion.

該公司股價每股七十美金,總市值將近一千七百億美金。

---

price
[praɪs]

名 價格

The **price** of the new model will be set at $1,200.

這款新機型的價格將訂在一千兩百美元。

➡ **value** 是「抽象的價值」。
➡ **price** 指「實質金額的價錢」。

_____ **13** Derek didn't know the real _____ of an insurance policy until he got sick and couldn't work for months.

(A) value   (B) price

tentative
[ˋtɛntətɪv]

形 暫定的

We have a **tentative** contract for cooperation, but nothing is yet set in stone.

我們有暫定的合作協議,但一切尚未定案。

---

temporary
[ˋtɛmpəˏrɛrɪ]

形 暫時性的

These salary cuts are just **temporary**. Things should be back to normal next year.

這波減薪只是暫時的,明年薪資會調回正常水平。

➡ **tentative** 指「暫定的、未確認的,隨時會視情況而改變」,常和 plan、agreement 連用,通常做決定的時候很認真,但因為有某些事不確定,因此還可能會改變。
➡ **temporary** 指時間上「暫時性的,臨時的,非永久的」。

_____ **14** Ellen thought she would remain head of the department. She didn't realize the promotion was _____.

(A) tentative   (B) temporary

15 **trip** vs. **tour**

trip [trɪp] 名 旅行	I can't make the meeting next week. I'll be away on a business **trip**. 我下週要出差，所以不能參加會議。

tour [tʊr] 名 參觀；遊覽	Shortly after I arrived, they gave me a thorough **tour** of their factory. 我抵達後不久，他們就帶我仔細地參觀工廠。

➡ **trip** 指短期的旅行，例如 business trip 商務旅行、family trip 家庭旅遊，後面接 to 再接目的地。

➡ **tour** 指到某地參觀、遊覽，在參觀之時常會學習新知識，接 of 再接參訪地點。

_____ 📖 Our boss is nervous today because someone from the head office is coming for a _____ of our facility.

    (A) trip   (B) tour

16 **effective** vs. **efficient**

effective [ɪˈfɛktɪv] 形 有效（果）的	The company's attempt to appeal to younger consumers was not **effective**. 這間公司企圖吸引年輕客群的策略並未奏效。

efficient [ɪˈfɪʃənt] 形 有效率的	In this business, time is money, so we need our workers to be **efficient**. 在這一行，時間就是金錢，所以我們要求員工要有效率。

➡ **effective** 指某動作「有效（果），可達成目的」。

➡ **efficient** 指做事是「有效率、快速且正確的」。

_____ 📖 The doctor tried several different prescriptions to relieve the patient's pain, but none of them were _____.

    (A) effective   (B) efficient

Confusing words 易混淆字大解密

situation

[ˌsɪtʃʊˋeʃən]

名 立場；處境

Sales are going through the roof. Financially, we couldn't be in a better **situation**.

目前業績一飛衝天，我們的財務狀況正處於最佳狀態。

---

condition

[kənˋdɪʃən]

名 狀態；條件

The goods arrived on time, but they arrived in terrible **condition**.

貨物雖然準時送達，但狀況很糟。

➡ **situation** 或 circumstance 指「外在或周圍的環境」。

➡ **condition** 指人事物的「本身或內在的狀態」。

_____ ⑰ Although our company paid almost nothing for the factory, the machinery inside is very old and in bad _____.

(A) situation　　(B) condition

18 **raise** vs. **rise**

raise

[rez]

動 提升；撫養；募集

The company **raised** our salaries by 2% at the end of last year.

去年年底公司為我們調漲2%的薪資。

---

rise

[raɪz]

動 上升

Fuel costs keep **rising**, so we have to keep increasing our delivery prices.

油價持續攀升，所以我們只能跟著調漲運費。

➡ **raise** 為及物動詞，指「提升；撫養；募集」，可有被動語態。

➡ **rise** 是不及物動詞，表「上升」，不可有被動語態。

_____ ⑱ The cost of living in this city is _____, causing some young people to move away.

(A) raising　　(B) rising

19 **donate** vs. **contribute**

310 **19** 英加 **20** 英美

donate
[`donet]

動 捐贈

Each cookie costs a dollar, ten cents of which we will **donate** to charity.

每塊餅乾售價一美金，每賣出一塊，我們將捐出十分美金給慈善團體。

contribute
[kən`trɪbjut]

動 貢獻；導致

We're each **contributing** $10 so we can buy some potted plants for the office.

我們每個人出資十美元，一起買些盆栽放在辦公室。

➡ **donate** 指「捐贈金錢或物資做慈善用途」。

➡ **contribute** 指為某目的做出「實質或抽象的貢獻」，contribute to 還有「導致」之意。

_____ 19 Julia felt so bad for the victims of the earthquake that she went on the Internet and _____ $250 to a relief charity.

(A) donated   (B) contributed

20 **require** vs. **request**

require
[rɪ`kwaɪr]

動 需要

This job **requires** you to have at least five years of related experience.

這份職務要求至少五年相關工作經驗。

request
[rɪ`kwɛst]

動 (提出) 需求

The client has **requested** a fully itemized bill if possible.

該客戶要求我們盡可能在帳單上詳列出所有品項。

➡ **require** 指某工作或事物「需要符合……的資格、條件」，受詞為資格或條件。

➡ **request** 指某人「提出需求」，受詞為需求內容。

_____ 20 The government has _____ a new environmental impact study for the area surrounding the construction site.

(A) required   (B) requested

21 **vulnerable** vs. **delicate**

vulnerable
[ˈvʌlnərəb!]

形 脆弱的；易受影響、
攻擊的

The global oil market is **vulnerable** to supply-side shocks such as wars.

全球原油市場容易受到供應端的影響，例如戰爭。

---

delicate
[ˈdɛləkət]

形 脆弱的；需小心處理的

The negotiations are **delicate**, and they could walk away from the table.

此次談判需要很小心，對方有可能會拂袖而去。

➡ **vulnerable** 指「易被外物所影響／傷害」。
➡ **delicate** 指「體質敏感或材質細緻」，而容易受到外在刺激。

_____ **21** The government passed new environmental laws to protect areas which are _____ to industrial pollution.

(A) vulnerable   (B) delicate

22 **be used to** vs. **used to**

be used to

片 習慣於

It seemed small at first, but Bill **is used to** his office now.

比爾起初覺得他的辦公室很小，但他現在已經習慣了。

---

used to

片 過去常／曾做過

John **used to** buy his lunch, but now he makes it at home.

約翰以前午餐會買外食，但他現在自己做便當。

➡ **be used to** 的 to 是介系詞，後面需要接名詞或是動名詞，表「習慣該事物」。
➡ **used to** 後面直接接動詞，表「過去曾做過，但現在停止」的動作。

_____ **22** Robert _____ drive to work before the new subway line was built.

(A) was used to   (B) used to

23 **favorable** vs. **favorite**

favorable
[ˋfevərəbl]

形 贏得贊同的；
令人喜愛的

Our company will wait for **favorable** market conditions before making an investment.
我們公司會等到市場狀況好轉後再投資。

---

favorite
[ˋfevərɪt]

形 某人最喜愛的

Becky is my **favorite** assistant because she always does a thorough job.
貝琪是我最喜歡的助理，因為她做事很仔細。

➡ **favorable** 意指「能被贊同或受喜愛的」。
➡ 所有格形容詞 + **favorite** 代表「某人最喜歡的」。

_____ 23 With record low prices in the real estate market, now is a _____ time to buy a house.

    (A) favorable   (B) favorite

24 **utilities** vs. **utensils**

utilities
[juˋtɪlətɪz]

名 水電瓦斯費

Our company is paying more for **utilities** since electricity prices spiked.
因為電費飆漲，我們公司水電支出也持續增加中。

---

utensils
[juˋtɛnsl̩s]

名 餐具

There are some **utensils** in one of the drawers in the staff room.
員工專用室的某個抽屜裡有一些餐具。

➡ **utility** 意指水電鐵路等公共設施，延伸複數形 utilities 代表「水電瓦斯費」。
➡ **utensils** 指餐具。

_____ 24 Our department moved into a smaller office to save money on _____.

    (A) utilities   (B) utensils

entrust
[ɪnˈtrʌst]
動 委託；託付

Our boss has **entrusted** me with locking up the office every night.
我們老闆交代我每天晚上要鎖辦公室的門。

entitle
[ɪnˈtaɪtl]
動 給予（某人）……
的權利╱資格

Under the agreement, she is **entitled** to receive $10,000 in compensation.
根據合約，她有權拿到一萬元的賠償金。

➡ **entrust** 指出於信賴的「委託」，常用「（某人）be entrusted with（責任）」。
➡ **entitle** 指「給予（某人）……的權利╱資格」，常用被動語態「（某人）be entitled to（資格）」。

_____ 25 Every employee is _____ to two weeks of paid vacation per year.

(A) entrusted　　(B) entitled

26 consult vs. counsel

consult
[kənˈsʌlt]
動 向（某人）諮詢、
尋求意見

Rebecca was **consulted** three times before the contract was signed.
合約簽署前已諮詢過瑞貝卡三次了。

counsel
[ˈkaʊnsl]
動 給予（某人）
建議、忠告

She is still being **counseled** on how to work well as part of a team.
她目前仍在接受如何提升團隊合作能力的輔導。

➡ **consult** 指 ask for advice：「向某人討教」，受詞為「提供意見的專業人士」。
➡ **counsel** 指 give advice，「給予某人建議」，受詞為「尋求建議者」。

_____ 26 After weeks of being _____ on management techniques, Patricia started her new job as department head.

(A) consulted　　(B) counseled

Confusing words 易混淆字大解密

respectable
[rɪˋspɛktəbl]

形 受人尊敬的

Johnson & Smith is a **respectable** firm with over 100 years of history.

強森與史密斯有逾百年歷史，是間備受尊崇的公司。

respectful
[rɪˋspɛktfəl]

形 充滿敬意的

He should be more **respectful** when speaking to potential business partners.

他在和未來生意夥伴說話時，態度應要更尊敬些。

➡ **respectable** 意指「受到他人尊敬的」，形容人或物。
➡ **respectful** 意指「充滿敬意的」，形容做事的態度。

_____ 27 Royal Fabrics is one of the most _____ names in the garment industry.

　　(A) respectable　　(B) respectful

28 **substitute** vs. **replace**

substitute
[ˋsʌbstəˏtjut]

動 使用……取代它者

Mr. Davis **substituted** for Mrs. Jones class for the week she was sick.

戴維斯先生幫生病的瓊斯女士代課一週。

replace
[rɪˋples]

動 取代

The entire communications department was **replaced** with a call center in India.

整個通訊部門被設在印度的電話服務中心所取代。

➡ **substitute** A for B 代表「以 A 暫時替代 B」。
➡ **replace** B with A 指「以 A 永久取代 B」。

_____ 28 Many of our older car models have been _____ with new ones that are better for the environment.

　　(A) substituted　　(B) replaced

process [`prɑsɛs] 名 過程	That company is still in the **process** of restructuring its finances. 該公司還在財務重整的階段。
procedure [prə`sidʒɚ] 名 程序；手續；步驟	Jake did not follow standard **procedure** when working on the Harrison deal. 在和哈利森進行交易時，傑克並沒有遵照標準作業程序。

➡ **process** 指「從頭到尾一系列步驟所構成的過程」，常用 in the process of 代表「在某過程中」。

➡ **procedure** 指「特定的、一個接續一個的步驟」，類似 step、method。

_____ ㉙ It's standard _____ to check a customer's credit history before offering them a long-term contract.

(A) process   (B) procedure

30 in conjunction with vs. in coalition with

in conjunction with 片 連同；以及……	Hard work **in conjunction with** intelligence and perseverance will lead to success. 勤奮加上智慧和毅力將邁向成功。
in coalition with 片 和……聯手合作	The plan was voted down by Judy **in coalition with** Jeff and Todd. 這個計畫在茱蒂、傑夫和塔德聯手下被否決。

➡ **in conjunction with** 代表廣義的「以及」，近似 and 或 along with。

➡ **in coalition with** 代表「和某人聯手合作」，受詞為人。

_____ ㉚ The merger was voted down by the company's main shareholder _____ with a few minor ones.

(A) in conjunction with   (B) in coalition with

31 notice vs. note

316 31 英澳 32 美加

notice

[ˈnotɪs]

動 注意到

名 公告、通知

I've been working so hard that I didn't even **notice** that it's Friday.

我這陣子忙著工作，沒注意到今天已經星期五了。

note

[not]

動 注意

名 字條

Please **note** that all vacation time is canceled until the deal is finalized.

請注意在這筆交易完成前，相關職員禁止休假。

➡ **notice** 當動詞指某人「無意間注意到」。

➡ **note** 當動詞指正式地通知、公告，「請全員注意」。

_____ 31 Trevor _____ that his coworker looked exhausted, so he pulled her aside to ask if everything was OK.

(A) noticed　　(B) noted

32 command vs. commend

command

[kəˈmænd]

動 命令

I have been **commanded** to pack up my desk and leave the office.

我被命令打包走人。

commend

[kəˈmɛnd]

動 讚揚、表揚

I have been **commended** for always staying until my work is done.

我總是克盡職責，工作做完才下班，因此獲得表揚。

➡ **command** 指「命令某人去做……」。

➡ **commend** 指「讚揚某人」，接 for 再接表揚的內容。

_____ 32 She has been _____ by several of her coworkers for always being willing to help out.

(A) commanded　　(B) commended

sum
[sʌm]
名 金額;總額

Current assets is the **sum** of cash, accounts receivable, and inventory.
流動資產一詞指的是現金、應收帳款和存貨的金額。

---

total
[ˈtotl]
名 總計;總額

The **total** of our first quarter revenues is over one million dollars.
我們第一季收益總金額超過一百萬美金。

➡ **sum** 指「某個數量」的金額。
➡ **total** 指「總計後」的金額。

_____ **33** The _____ of the factory upgrades' cost is three million dollars.

　　(A) sum　　(B) total

34 **assure** vs. **ensure**

assure
[əˈʃur]
動 向人保證;使人放心

The chairman tried to **assure** stockholders that the company will be profitable soon.
董事長向股東保證公司很快就能獲利。

---

ensure
[ɪnˈʃur]
動 確保

Strong regulations **ensure** that no one feels bullied or helpless in the workplace.
透過嚴格的規範,以確保員工在職場不會受到霸凌或感到無助。

➡ **assure** 指「向人保證、使人放心」,受詞為人。
➡ **ensure** 指「確保某事會實現、確保某物的品質」,受詞為事物。

_____ **34** Investing in research and development _____ that the company will have new products to sell in the future.

　　(A) assures　　(B) ensures

35 **retain** vs. **remain**

retain

[rɪ`ten]

動 保有；持有

Our company **retains** all intellectual property rights under the terms of the agreement.

在合約保障下，我們公司保留所有智慧財產權。

---

remain

[rɪ`men]

動 留下；維持

The negotiations are complete, and all that **remains** is signing the contract.

協商過程已完成，剩下要做的就是簽約。

➡ **retain** 指「持續擁有某物或權利」。
➡ **remain** 指「剩下來的；維持……的狀態」。

_____ 35 It's hard for a company to _____ talent if it doesn't pay its workers a competitive salary.

(A) retain　　(B) remain

36 **regular** vs. **frequent**

regular

[`rɛgjələ]

形 規律的；定期的

Please be sure to check in with me at **regular** intervals on how the project is going.

請務必定期向我回報該計畫執行的狀況。

---

frequent

[`frikwənt]

形 頻繁的

His questions about the project were **frequent** enough to be annoying.

他老是為這個專案問我問題，頻繁到令人厭煩。

➡ **regular** 指某動作發生有「規律的、定期的」的頻率。
➡ **frequent** 指發生次數「頻繁的、相當多的」。

_____ 36 Our team must provide _____ updates every Monday on how the project is going.

(A) regular　　(B) frequent

37 **percent** vs. **percentage**

percent
[pɚ`sɛnt]

名 百分之……

Sales are up by thirty-five **percent** this past quarter.

上一季銷售成長達35%。

percentage
[pɚ`sɛntɪdʒ]

名 百分比；百分率

A **percentage** of your salary is automatically transferred to the corporate retirement fund.

你們薪資有一定比例，會被自動提撥到公司退休金專戶。

➡ **percent** 指「精確的百分之……的數字」，前面有具體數字。
➡ **percentage** 指「整體百分比」，前面接the／a small／a large。

_____ 37 The _____ of women in the workplace has increased over the past decade.

(A) percent   (B) percentage

38 **income** vs. **revenue**

income
[`ɪn,kʌm]

名 個人收入

John learned to live with his reduced **income** by budgeting more.

約翰學會在收入減少的情況下，控制預算過日子。

revenue
[`rɛvə,nju]

名 公司營收

Corporate **revenue** is down due to soft sales in Asia and South America.

公司營收下降，歸咎於亞洲和南美洲銷售疲軟。

➡ **income** 指「個人」的收入、薪水。
➡ **revenue** 指「公司、企業」的營收。

_____ 38 Banks will only lend money to people who have a stable _____.

(A) income   (B) revenue

39 compare vs. contrast

compare
[kəm`pɛr]
動 比較

Our company's annual growth **compares** favorably with our competitors'.

我們公司的年成長和其他競爭對手相比之下頗為亮眼。

contrast
[kən`træst]
動 對比

The Asia division's success **contrasts** starkly with the Africa division's failure.

該公司在亞洲區的成功和非洲區的失敗形成強烈的對比。

➡ **compare** A with B 指「拿 A 和 B 做比較」，特指兩者有具體的共通點和不同點。
➡ **contrast** A with B 指「A 和 B 形成對比、對照」，強調兩者有明顯差異。

_____ Sales growth in January _____ with the weak numbers from last December.

(A) compares (B) contrasts

40 economic vs. economical

economic
[ˌikə`nɑmɪk]
形 經濟的

The government's new **economic** policy will impact our company's operations.

政府新的經濟政策會對我們公司的營運帶來衝擊。

economical
[ˌikə`nɑmɪkl̩]
形 節約的；省錢的

It would be more **economical** to do all of our corporate accounting in-house.

聘僱內部會計師為公司作帳比較划算。

➡ **economic** 指「和經濟相關的」。
➡ **economical** 指某舉動是「節約的、省錢的」。

_____ The board of directors decided that it would be more _____ to move the call center to India.

(A) economic (B) economical

41 guarantee vs. warranty

guarantee
[ˌɡærənˋti]
名 保證;擔保

They gave us a **guarantee** that the new units would be here by today.
他們跟我們保證新的零件今天就會到了。

warranty
[ˋwɔrəntɪ]
名 (商品) 保固卡、保固期

We bought the computer less than a year ago, so it's still under **warranty**.
我們這臺電腦是這一年內買的,所以還在保固期內。

➡ **guarantee** 指「保證、擔保」。
➡ **warranty** 指「商品保固卡;保固期」,under warranty 指商品還在「保固期內」。

_____ 1 Our computer broke down just days after the _____ expired. What bad luck!

(A) guarantee　　(B) warranty

42 enhance vs. enforce

enhance
[ɪnˋhæns]
動 強化;加強

Judy's hard work greatly **enhances** this department's efficiency.
茱蒂賣力工作提升了整個部門的效率。

enforce
[ɪnˋfors]
動 執行;實行

The company rule against personal Internet use was never **enforced**, and therefore soon forgotten.
公司禁止員工上網處理私事的規定從未執行過,因此很快就被拋諸腦後了。

➡ **enhance** 指「強化、加強」某現象、動作。
➡ **enforce** 指「執行」某規定、法律。

_____ 2 The unit's productivity has been greatly _____ by shorter work days. Our workers were just too tired before.

(A) enhanced　　(B) enforced

dependable

[dɪˈpɛndəbl̩]

形 可被信賴的

Japanese cars have a reputation for being inexpensive and **dependable**.

日產車以價格實惠和性能可靠著名。

- -

dependent

[dɪˈpɛndənt]

形 有依賴性的

He doesn't like to make decisions; he's very **dependent** on his superiors.

他不喜歡做決定，十分倚賴他的上司。

➡ **dependable** 指「令人信賴的、可信賴的」。
➡ **dependent** 指「依賴他人的、無自主獨立性的」。

_____ 43 Ever since Jake lost his job, he has been totally _____ on his wife's income.

(A) dependable (B) dependent

44 **diversity** vs. **variety**

diversity

[daɪˈvɝsətɪ]

名 多樣性

Deforestation is greatly reducing the **diversity** of wildlife in many regions.

森林濫伐大幅減少了很多地區野生動物的多樣性。

- -

variety

[vəˈraɪətɪ]

名 多樣化；多種類

We'll be producing the smartphones in a wide **variety** of colors and designs.

我們即將要生產各種顏色和款式的智慧型手機。

➡ **diversity** 特指「物種、動植物」的多樣性。
➡ **variety** 泛指「商品」的多元樣貌和款式。

_____ 44 Our telecom company offers a _____ of different smartphone plans. There's one for every kind of budget.

(A) diversity (B) variety

Confusing words 易混淆字大解密

45 shipping vs. shipment

shipping

['ʃɪpɪŋ]

名 運送；運輸

There's no additional **shipping** charge on orders over $100.

訂單金額滿一百美金就不必額外付運費。

---

shipment

['ʃɪpmənt]

名 貨物

Your **shipment** will be sent off tomorrow morning.

您訂購的貨品會在明天一早就寄出。

➡ **shipping** 指「運輸」,（尤指）船運,海運,類似 delivery。

➡ **shipment** 指運輸的「貨物」,類似 goods。

_____ ⑮ Items that are not in-stock will be sent in a separate _____ at a later date.

(A) shipping　　(B) shipment

46 quality vs. quantity

quality

['kwɑlətɪ]

名 品質

The air **quality** in many Chinese cities is extremely poor.

中國很多城市的空氣品質都很糟。

---

quantity

['kwɑntətɪ]

名 數量

A large **quantity** of milk had to be recalled when it was found to contain pesticides.

有大批的牛奶必須下架回收,因為被發現牛奶裡有殺蟲劑殘留。

➡ **quality** 指某物的「品質」。

➡ **quantity** 指某物的「數量」,a large quantity of 指「大量的」。

_____ ⑯ The workshop only produces 100 pieces of furniture yearly, but these pieces are renowned for their excellent _____.

(A) quality　　(B) quantity

47 character VS. characteristic

character
[ˋkærɪktɚ]

名 性格；風格；角色

Brian is such a **character**; he's the life of any office party.

布萊恩很有個人風格，是我們公司聚會的靈魂人物。

---

characteristic
[͵kærəktəˋrɪstɪk]

名 特徵；特色

The ability to make friends quickly is an important **characteristic** of the successful salesperson.

善於交際交友的能力是成功的業務人員很重要的特質。

➡ **character** 泛指「人的性格、人品，或指人的獨特個性風格」。
➡ **characteristic** 指「人或事物所具有的、不同於其他的特色、要素」。

_____ 47 The most important _____ of a good manager is knowing how to motivate workers.

(A) character　　(B) characteristic

48 comprehensive VS. apprehensive

comprehensive
[͵kɑmprɪˋhɛnsɪv]

形 綜合的；全方位的

The report was **comprehensive**, dealing with all aspects of the issue.

這則報導十分全面，從各種層面探討該議題。

---

apprehensive
[æˋprɪˋhɛnsɪv]

形 擔憂的；擔心的

It's her first day on the job, so naturally she's a little **apprehensive**.

今天是她第一天就職，理所當然她會有點緊張。

➡ **comprehensive** 指「全方面、綜合的」。
➡ **apprehensive** 指「（對將要做的事情）感到擔憂、擔心」。

_____ 48 Dale has a _____ approach to management. He likes to get involved in every little detail of the project.

(A) comprehensive　　(B) apprehensive

Confusing words 易混淆字大解密

49 state VS. status

state [stet] 名 狀態	The company's finances were in such a bad **state** that it nearly went bankrupt. 這間公司的財務狀況很糟，幾近破產邊緣。
status [ˈstetəs] 名 地位；狀態	It's impolite to ask someone his or her marital **status** if you just met. 初次見面就問對方婚姻狀態是很不禮貌的。

➡ **state** 指「個人心理狀態」、「物理狀態」、或人事物「處於某階段」。
➡ **status** 指「某人的社會地位、身份」或「正式文件在法律或處理過程中的狀態」。

_____ 49 What's the current _____ of the logo redesign? Head office wants it to be finished by April.

(A) state   (B) status

50 element VS. component

element [ˈɛləmənt] 名 元素；要素	He's very capable, but I think timing is the crucial **element** in his success. 他很有能力，但我想掌握時機是他成功的關鍵因素。
component [kəmˈponənt] 名 組成部件；成分；零件	We had to replace several **components** of the engine, which cost us additional time. 這件引擎要換許多零件，這花了點時間。

➡ **element** 泛指「抽象的組成元素」。
➡ **component** 指「具體的組成成分」，尤其指電子機械的零件。

_____ 50 Strategy, timing, and luck were all important _____ in reaching the merger deal.

(A) elements   (B) components

51 **bargain** vs. **deal**

bargain
['bɑrgɪn]

名 划算的交易

動 討價還價

In a poor real estate market, a new home can be a great **bargain**.

房市不景氣，買新屋可能比較划算。

---

deal
[dil]

名 交易

動 處理；交易

The two banks spent over a year working out a **deal** for their merger.

這兩家銀行花了超過一年的時間，終於完成他們的併購案。

➡ **bargain** 當名詞指「用優惠價格成交的交易」，有划算撿到便宜之意。

➡ **deal** 泛指各種「商務交易」。

_____ **51** Jenny is away negotiating an important business _____.

(A) bargain　　(B) deal

52 **likely** vs. **possible**

likely
['laɪklɪ]

形 有可能的

Greece is **likely** to default on its debt payments to the European Union.

希臘有可能違約拖欠歐盟借款。

---

possible
['pɑsəbl]

形 有可能的

It's not **possible** to make the improvements we need and still turn a profit.

改革的同時要獲利似乎不大可能。

➡ **likely** 指「期望中某人會去做，或某事可能會發生」，主詞可以是人事物。

➡ **possible** 指「推測某事可能發生」，描述事物，不可以用人當主詞。

_____ **52** She's not _____ to turn up for work tomorrow.

(A) likely　　(B) possible

aware

[ə`wɛr]

形 知道的;明白的

The vice president has been made **aware** of the problem and will deal with it immediately.

副總統已得知這個問題,會立即處理。

---

conscious

[`kɑnʃəs]

形 有意識的;意識清醒的

Most of the survivors of the factory fire were barely **conscious** when rescued.

工廠大火的倖存者中,大多數在被搶救出來時都失去了意識。

➡ **aware** 指「知道、察覺到某事實」。

➡ **conscious** 指「(生理跡象)意識清醒的」。

_____ **53** The CEO claimed he was not _____ that some of the company's products broke safety laws.

(A) aware   (B) conscious

54 **be made of** vs. **consist of**

be made of

片 由……組成的

The laptop's housing **is made of** very lightweight plastic for maximum portability.

這台筆電外殼是由極輕的塑料做成的,便於攜帶。

---

consist of

片 由……組成

Our research team **consists of** nearly 30 highly qualified professionals.

我們的研究團隊是由近30位權威專家組成的。

兩組片語都指「A由B組成」,差別是語態:

➡ A **be made of** B 用被動語態。

➡ A **consist of** B 用主動語態。

_____ **54** Our marketing department _____ three branches: broadcast advertising, Internet advertising, and social media relations.

(A) is made of   (B) consists of

55 engage vs. embark

engage
[ɪnˋgedʒ]

動 參與;進攻;訂婚

I'm sorry to call you back so late; I was **engaged** in a conference all morning.

很抱歉那麼晚才回電給您,我整個早上都在開會。

embark
[ɪmˋbɑrk]

動 開始做;上船;上機

Jack **embarked** for Sydney this morning; I'm sure he'll do well there.

傑克今早出發前往雪梨,我相信他在那一切都會很順利。

➡ **engage** 指「參與某個活動」,句型為「人 + be engaged in + 活動」。

➡ **embark** 指「開始去執行一個新的計畫;上機或上船」,後面接 on 再接活動,或接 for 再接目的地。

_____ 55 Mr. Reynolds is _____ at the moment. Please leave a message and he will call you back.

(A) engaged   (B) embarked

56 cost vs. expense

cost
[kɔst]

名 支出;成本

The low **cost** of labor in China has persuaded many foreign companies to manufacture there.

中國大陸低廉的勞力成本吸引了很多外商公司在中國設廠。

expense
[ɪkˋspɛns]

名 開銷;花費

New drapes and carpeting for the office are **expenses** we simply cannot justify.

我們無法認同把錢花在買新窗簾和地毯布置辦公室。

➡ **cost** 指「生產某商品的成本費用」,可帶來資產和獲利,常指勞力、原料、購地等成本。

➡ **expense** 指「不帶來生產獲利的開銷、花費」。

_____ 56 Emergency maintenance is a(n) _____ that isn't included in the company's annual budget.

(A) cost   (B) expense

57 rather than vs. instead of

rather than

片 而不是

Rather than name a new chief of operations, he simply takes on both jobs.

他沒有找人擔任新的業務主管，而是自己同時做兩份職務。

instead of

片 而不是

Just for a change, let's have pizza for lunch today **instead of** sandwiches.

為了換個口味，今天我們午餐不吃三明治，改吃披薩吧。

兩者差別是詞性：

➡ **instead of** 是「介系詞片語」，後面接名詞或動名詞。

➡ **rather than** 可當「連接詞」，連接詞性和形態對等的字詞，也可當「介系詞」使用，後面接名詞或動名詞。

_____ 57 The board of directors voted to suspend the CEO for a month without pay _____ firing him immediately.

(A) rather than　　(B) instead of

58 source vs. resource

source

[sors]

名 來源

An anonymous **source** told the press about the bank's corrupt practices.

有匿名人士將這間銀行貪污的行徑透露給媒體知道。

resource

[rɪˋsors]

名 資源

More people should switch to solar energy; unlike oil, it's a truly infinite **resource**.

人們應該要改用太陽能；不像石油，太陽能是永續能源。

➡ **source** 指某事物的「來源」，例如消息來源。

➡ **resource** 指「自然界資源」，例如石油、煤、能源、礦產。

_____ 58 China is the _____ of most of the world's rare earth metals.

(A) source　　(B) resource

406

59 **enroll** vs. **register**

enroll

[ɪnˋrol]

動 報名；註冊

Diane **enrolled** in business school to please her parents, but her real interest is art.

黛安報名商學院只是為了取悅父母，她真正的興趣是藝術。

register

[ˋrɛdʒɪstɚ]

動 登記報到；註冊

US citizens can **register** to vote at the age of 18.

美國公民年滿18歲可以登記投票。

➡ **enroll**特指「報名修讀某學校、課程」，先接in再接學校／課程。

➡ **register**指「登錄、註冊身分」，不限用於學術課程，適用所有身分申報的註冊手續。

_____ 59 Any owner who doesn't _____ their pet with the government could face fines of up to $500.

(A) enroll   (B) register

60 **solve** vs. **resolve**

solve

[sɑlv]

動 解決（問題）

The new director **solved** the problem of the company's losses within six months.

新任經理上任六個月內就解決了公司虧損的問題。

resolve

[rɪˋzɑlv]

動 決定；解除（爭議）

Jack **resolved** to ask his boss for a raise as soon as he got to the office.

傑克下定決心，一進辦公室就去找老闆要求加薪。

➡ **solve**指「找出問題的答案」。

➡ **resolve**指「解決衝突／爭議／意見不同的妥協」，也可指「下定決心去做」，同decide。

_____ 60 Jeremy _____ to find a new job by the end of the year.

(A) solved   (B) resolved

解答

學前暖身

1. interview
2. position
3. recruit
4. fire
5. applicant

學後小試

(A)

1. B　　2. A　　3. D　　4. C　　5. A

(B)

1. achievement
2. ideal
3. recommendations
4. Prior to
5. prefers
6. ethic

(C)

1. consider
2. weakness
3. accordingly
4. proficiency
5. suitable
6. responsibility

翻譯參考

(A)

1. 即使她是公司的新人，她會證明她的價值。
2. 他的個人簡介說他會講三種語言。
3. 因為我不滿意現在這家公司的待遇，我決定另謀高就。
4. 她還沒有畢業，但已經比其他競爭者更了解這份工作。
5. 他是這份職位最佳的人選，看看他的工作經驗。

(B)

1. 我最驕傲的成就是帶領行銷團隊贏得了競賽。
2. 雖然他不是最棒的，但至少他做了他該做的。
3. 若要應徵這份職位，你需要三份專業的推薦信。
4. 在松戶控股公司工作之前，你有其他的財務經驗嗎？

5. 她偏好在會計部門工作，但我認為行銷才是她的天職。
6. 我們正在尋找有職業操守和豐富工作經驗的人才。

(C)

1. 在決定應徵者時，我們會同時考量工作經驗和教育背景。
2. 就目前來看，她最大的缺點就是她缺乏幹勁。
3. 才剛畢業的她當然沒有太多工作經驗。
4. 我們正在尋找文書處理的專業人才。
5. 本來我們以為他適合管理，後來卻發現他缺乏領導能力。
6. 身為人事主管，我有責任找尋最適合的人才。

學前暖身

1. complimentary
2. lead
3. optional
4. wage
5. contribute

學後小試

(A)

1. C　　2. A　　3. B　　4. C　　5. D

(B)

1. motivated
2. improve
3. looking forward to
4. devote
5. maintain
6. benefit

(C)

1. lifetime
2. loyal
3. acknowledge
4. satisfy
5. tenure
6. generous

翻譯參考

(A)

1. 我真心希望我可以因為今年的好表現加薪。
2. 我的工時通常很彈性，但這週我必須朝九晚六的待在辦公室裡。

3. 如果我下週還是不舒服，我再請病假。

4. 直到明年前我都不適用於獎金的條件。

5. 安幾乎對小組沒有任何貢獻，我真希望她改善。

(B)

1. 我不認為公司真的知道獎金給我們多少動力。

2. 他再不改進會被開除的。

3. 我真的很期待去夏威夷的員工旅行。

4. 若要當執行長，你必須奉獻你大多的時間在工作上。

5. 業績是沒有辦法增加了，但我希望我們可以維持在去年的水準。

6. 健身房的免費會員真的是很棒的公司福利。

(C)

1. 她的一生為公司盡心盡力，所以她值得獲得優渥的退休金。

2. 亞伯特不是最聰明的員工，但他忠心耿耿。

3. 我希望我的老闆會認同我對我們小組成功也有功勞。

4. 我的上司不停地修改我的提案，似乎他就是不滿意。

5. 只有拿到終身職，我才會覺得有保障。

6. 優渥的薪水和不怎麼樣的福利正好打平。

Unit 3

學前暖身

1. train
2. bring together
3. theme
4. celebrate
5. invite

學後小試

(A)

1. A   2. C   3. D   4. A   5. B

(B)

1. awards ceremony
2. required
3. farewell
4. present
5. annual
6. gather

(C)

1. observe
2. commemorate
3. congratulates
4. entertainment
5. attribute
6. sessions

翻譯參考

(A)

1. 完成這個訓練之後，你就能擔任明年度新人的導師。

2. 這些年他終於存夠了錢，讓他可以在六十歲的時候退休。

3. 只要繳錢，人人都可以參加烤肉大會。

4. 如果你要參加新年派對，請在禮拜五下午五點以前告訴我們。

5. 我們希望為派對找一個燈光美氣氛佳的地點。

(B)

1. 崔佛先生會在羅曼達飯店主持今年的頒獎典禮。

2. 任何想要參加今年舞會的人，都必須要繳交入場費。

3. 大家要為史密斯女士舉辦送別派對，因為她將要調職了。

4. 參加聖誕派對的人只能帶一件禮物。

5. 年度股東會議將會在米爾頓會議廳舉行。

6. 在新年派對開始之前，請大家在大廳集合。

(C)

1. 你要觀察生產線上的工人並給予一些改善的建議，這是你訓練的一部分。

2. 李小姐會被授予證書以紀念她的成就。

3. 公司的所有人都在恭喜你升官了。

4. 德倫和席爾瓦將負責娛樂，也就是說，他們將會準備音樂。

5. 我們將安全氣囊的故障歸咎於廠商使用較便宜的零件。

6. 今年將會有四個階段的訓練，一季舉辦一個。

Unit 4

1. control
2. direct
3. appoint
4. transfer
5. spare

學後小試

(A)

1. A   2. A   3. D   4. B   5. A

(B)

1. boardroom
2. beneath
3. settle
4. apprentice
5. accounted for
6. shift

(C)

1. associate
2. acquisition
3. managed
4. supervisor
5. in charge of
6. understaffed

翻譯參考

(A)

1. 我需要一個助理來幫我處理所有額外的工作。
2. 市場的巨大波動代表我的股價每天都跟著大幅變動。
3. 升官之後你的職稱變成甚麼呀?
4. 如果執行長和我再這樣爭辯下去,我就要離職;我沒辦法這樣工作。
5. 我很抱歉,但我真的太忙,現在沒有時間做新工作。

(B)

1. 專案小組在早上九點時要去董事會議室開會。
2. 升官之後,我將要管理一整個部門。
3. 我們必須找個經理來解決這個紛爭。
4. 我兒子想要學習一技之長,所以他要去當木匠的學徒一年。
5. 等大家都到了,業務會議就可以開始了。
6. 我下一班從下午四點開始。

(C)

1. 我的公司開出了一個業務合夥人的職缺。
2. 老實說,我不認為我們公司新的收購案能賺錢。
3. 他從來沒有管理過這樣大的組。
4. 我希望能和我的新長官好好相處。
5. 誰負責顧客地址資料的?
6. 我們人手不足,小組的每個人都在加班。

Unit 5

學前暖身

1. wing
2. basic
3. mortgage
4. monitor
5. suburb

學後小試

(A)

1. C   2. B   3. B   4. A   5. D

(B)

1. on-site
2. broad
3. amenities
4. adjacent
5. closet
6. workplace

(C)

1. brick
2. furnished
3. staff lounge
4. trustees
5. indoor
6. surround

翻譯參考

(A)

1. 連絡電力公司盡快接上電力。
2. 小商店和公寓充滿了整個區域。
3. 他們在尋找願意預付五個月房租的房客。
4. 每間辦公室都有個倉儲用的小隔間。
5. 二樓的扶手在地震時震彎了,必須更換它。

(B)

1. 我們需要一個在場的監督,他可以快速的做反應。

2. 主要的走道夠寬了，可以讓我們搬運辦公室設備。

3. 所謂的福利設施，就只是一個水槽、一個微波爐和一個小冰箱。

4. 請把那個檔案架放在書架旁邊。

5. 後面有一個供員工掛外套的櫥櫃。

6. 為了確保工作環境安全，請遵守安全程序。

(C)

1. 這棟老建築的外牆是由磚塊和木頭所建造。

2. 我們需要一間備有桌椅的辦公室。

3. 員工休息室有兩個微波爐和一個冰箱。

4. 財產受託人可以將資產出租，但不能賣掉它們。

5. 這間辦公室的日式室內花園非常療癒。

6. 這間超市的四周都是公寓，所以它客源充足。

Unit 6

1. demolish	2. directory
3. facility	4. method
5. renovate	

(A)

1. D 2. C 3. A 4. B 5. D

(B)

1. detailed	2. shares
3. belongs	4. insufficient
5. procedure	6. as needed

(C)

1. carefully	2. once
3. occupy	4. container
5. at all times	6. helpful

(A)

1. 這台新的印表機沒有附使用說明書嗎？

2. 我完全照它的指示設定的，但機器就是沒反應。

3. 我修不了水龍頭，打電話找維修小組來吧。

4. 我爸爸的智慧型手機修不好了，你知道哪裡可以扔了它嗎？

5. 我們的會計軟體真的很慢又過時了，應該更新它。

(B)

1. 詳細的說明讓程式設定變的好簡單。

2. 這一層樓的每一個人都共用這間廚房。

3. 那台筆電是約翰的。

4. 因為準備時間不足，訓練一定會失敗。

5. 這裡有一份解鎖門的程序。

6. 我們沒有每週見面，只有有需要的時候。

(C)

1. 拿著那件設備的時候請小心，它非常的脆弱。

2. 等我搞清楚狀況之後，我就會教你怎麼使用這個程式。

3. 業務小組的人難道要霸占會議室一整天嗎？

4. 把我的新鉛筆跟其他鉛筆一起放在容器裡。

5. 請在工作室的時候請一直帶著護目鏡。

6. 安娜對於我的報告，給予了非常有用的回饋。

Unit 7

1. revise	2. author
3. efficient	4. draft
5. duplicate	

(A)

1. D 2. A 3. C 4. D 5. B

(B)

1. administrative	2. timely
3. enclosed	4. reject
5. deadline	6. appendix

(C)

1. compile
2. attentive
3. manuscript
4. efficient
5. always
6. filed

(A)

1. 你最晚必須在禮拜一完成報告。

2. 請套用已經有的模板,不要自己創一個格式。

3. 從這份錯誤百出的報告看來,我敢說是他們趕製的。

4. 檔案的紙本報告在存放五年之後必須被銷毀。

5. 我們希望電子化的報告可以減少紙本作業。

(B)

1. 疾病報告是行政文書的一部分。

2. 資訊科技部門的人沒有及時完成報告。

3. 你會發現地點的照片就檢附在租約裡面。

4. 這個系統會拒絕任何沒有日期章的文件。

5. 你沒有在截止日期繳交申請,所以你的申請無效。

6. 如果你需要部分搜尋的話,後面有附錄供你參考。

(C)

1. 韓德森會整理一份員工的清單,上面會有他們所分配的辦公室設備。

2. 你必須要特別留意細節,因為你已經錯太多次了。

3. 幸好她在電腦當機前印出了原稿。

4. 最有效運用資料庫系統的作法就是使用標準格式。

5. 在輸入資料進電腦前請永遠記得再次檢查。

6. 工時卡依照日期和部門歸類。

Unit 8

學前暖身

1. overview
2. circumstances
3. circulate
4. mandatory
5. temporary

學後小試

(A)

1. D   2. B   3. D   4. B   5. A

(B)

1. attention
2. aware
3. reminder
4. in advance
5. details
6. mention

(C)

1. pertinent
2. about
3. concerns
4. short notice
5. summarize
6. further

翻譯參考

(A)

1. 新的執行長將在禮拜一時對所有員工演講。

2. 下次你會遲到時請告知我。

3. 我希望你可以在做變更前告訴我,這樣我才能在會議中有所準備。

4. 我沒有義務告訴你為什麼我昨天去看醫生。

5. 我和我的長官起了爭執,所以我想避開她一陣子。

(B)

1. 開會時我沒有專心聽,現在我不知道我被分配了甚麼任務。

2. 我沒有意識到我們有加班政策。

3. 你可以寄一封提醒信給我嗎?我怕我忘記明天的報告。

4. 如果你想要一份客製化的設計,你必須提前要求。

5. 在決定之前,我必須看到更多提案的細節。

6. 下次見到老闆時,我會提起莎莉的重要想法。

(C)

1. 我看不出來為什麼我的穿著會和這次討論有關。

2. 公告是在說甚麼?

3. 我們對你的管理風格有些疑慮。

4. 我很抱歉臨時打給你,但這很緊急。

5. 我沒辦法參加會議了,可以請你之後簡介一下嗎?

6. 經理說很快就會有組織性的變革，但不肯透漏更多資訊。

4. 我們都在每個月的最後一週繳交瓦斯費。

5. 你可以親自去銀行存錢或是在線上完成。

6. 總獲利就是你的總收入減去總支出。

(C)

1. 他們以轉帳的方式付款，所以費用應該已經結清了。

2. 如果你再不繳費，我們只好中止你的帳戶了。

3. 所有費用應於每月十五號繳納。

4. 一旦過截止期限就不能再匯款了，所以請盡快繳款。

5. 銀行會自動將款項轉換成外幣。

6. 如果我們要存錢，就必須先減少支出。

Unit 9

學前暖身

1. tax
2. deduct
3. revenue
4. accountant
5. appraisal

學後小試

(A)

1. C   2. B   3. B   4. A   5. C

(B)

1. overdue
2. accrue
3. transaction
4. bill
5. deposit
6. Total

(C)

1. wired
2. delinquent
3. payable
4. remitted
5. converts
6. save

翻譯參考

(A)

1. 你給太多錢了，所以我們會把多的退給你。

2. 政府明年將會做一次審計，所以我們必須把數字弄清楚。

3. 明年的儲蓄利率將會增加。

4. 我很抱歉，但是這種型態的貸款無法用你的車作擔保。

5. 兌換外幣時，銀行會收取5%的手續費。

(B)

1. 根據我們的紀錄，你的帳戶已經逾期未繳兩個月了。

2. 只要帳戶裡有錢，它們就會在裡面繼續生利息。

3. 每筆使用ATM的交易會收取兩美金的費用。

Unit 10

學前暖身

1. permanent
2. stagnant
3. accumulate
4. wise
5. debt

學後小試

(A)

1. C   2. C   3. D   4. A   5. B

(B)

1. conservative
2. options
3. financial
4. approximately
5. steadily
6. invest

(C)

1. lose business
2. immensely
3. fiscal
4. trading
5. assess
6. fairly

翻譯參考

(A)

1. 我去年投資了一半的積蓄給這支股票，今大他翻了兩倍價！

2. 我們的投資策略非常激進。

3. 我沒辦法預測我明天的股價會如何。

4. 如果那張債券降價，你會投標嗎？

5. 我為投資存了一筆小錢。

(B)

1. 我不喜歡冒險，所以在股票投資的時候我非常保守。

2. 我必須賣掉它，沒有其他選擇。

3. 一個好的財務顧問可以幫助你規劃退休生活。

4. 我新的薪資大約是以前的兩倍！

5. 我們的股價起初沒有巨幅的成長，但它一直穩定的
增加。

6. 你會投資你自己的公司嗎？

(C)

1. 如果我們為了整修而歇業，我們會丟掉生意。

2. 在對的時間投資對的股票，將會大大改變你的
人生。

3. 這是我們下一個會計年度的預算。

4. 我的索尼股價以一個低價開始交易。

5. 我不知道如何評估價格是會漲還是會跌。

6. 我不認為我的經紀人有公平待我。

Unit 11

學前暖身

1. leading
2. accountable
3. publicity
4. workforce
5. compliance

學後小試

(A)

1. A   2. D   3. C   4. A   5. B

(B)

1. vulnerable
2. retrieve
3. withstand
4. enlarge

5. chain
6. concentrate

(C)

1. discontinue
2. count on
3. comparing
4. anticipate
5. distinctive
6. restore

翻譯參考

(A)

1. 一旦品牌打起知名度，消費者就比較不在意價錢。

2. 韓森先生是北美最厲害的行銷顧問，沒有人比他更好了。

3. 我們必須暫時扣下設計案的關鍵部分，這樣子公司就不會抄襲我們的點子。

4. 老闆希望我們向會計師諮詢那個新專案。

5. 珍妮絲將會是企業的負責人，所以請直接反映問題給她。

(B)

1. 我警告過他們，駭入那個新網頁輕而易舉。

2. 從舊的硬碟回收資料約需要一個小時。

3. 我們的倉儲還有足夠的剩餘，可以抵抗這次工廠的長期罷工。

4. 這將會比擴大工廠經營還要更花錢。

5. 這間新的購物中心裡面都是連鎖店。

6. 我們應該將研發部門所有的努力專注投入於基因治療。

(C)

1. 有鑑於我們業務表現不佳，我建議我們停止在南美洲的經營。

2. 每一次，我們必須都能夠仰賴供應商及時到貨。

3. 比較供應商時，考量運輸成本和時間非常重要。

4. 我預測下一次的發行會有問題，所以我們應該盡快開始測試。

5. 他們以其與眾不同的狗貓家族的廣告聞名。

6. 贏回顧客對我們商品的信心的唯一辦法，就是展示安全評估結果。

Unit 12

學前暖身

1. logical
2. depend
3. valid
4. adhere to
5. confidential

學後小試

(A)

1. C 2. D 3. D 4. A 5. C

(B)

1. Due to
2. Subsequent to
3. allow
4. trial
5. premises
6. abide by

(C)

1. terminate
2. take effect
3. substantial
4. at the latest
5. offer
6. warranty

翻譯參考

(A)

1. 沒有正確的使用者密碼我就沒辦法登入系統。
2. 你確定如果機器無法運作，我們可以拿回我們的錢嗎？
3. 明天我將為我的新發明申請專利。
4. 我要你跟我保證，在我剛剛所描述的情況下，機器將會運作。
5. 我認為他們修理時鐘跟我們收費不合理，因為它一買來就是壞的。

(B)

1. 由於壞天氣的影響，貨運沒有辦法準時抵達。
2. 簽約之後，法律上來說，我們的夥伴將會負責許多任務。
3. 我們可以在沒有授權的情況下使用這個軟體嗎？
4. 試用期結束後，我會決定要不要買這項設備。
5. 讓我帶你參觀一下我們的廠區。
6. 只要我們遵守合約，我們就不會有任何問題。

(C)

1. 如果我們必須終止合約，我們該怎麼做？
2. 新規定下個月初開始生效。
3. 我不能不跟我的上司討論，就採用替代方案。
4. 我最晚下午五點會回來。
5. 他們提議的細節是甚麼？
6. 我決不會在沒有保固的情況下買電腦。

Unit 13

學前暖身

1. research
2. experiment
3. state-of-the-art
4. follow up
5. laboratory

學後小試

(A)

1. C 2. C 3. A 4. D 5. B

(B)

1. glimpse
2. flaw
3. consumed
4. electronically
5. involve
6. Flammable

(C)

1. specialize
2. automated
3. Technical
4. following
5. examine
6. give up

翻譯參考

(A)

1. 線上電影的需求明顯正在增加。
2. 你必須刪除包括測試結果在內的所有數據，這樣才不會有人得到它們。
3. 他們真是太有才了，將廢物回收利用來做包裝材質。
4. 新的追蹤系統讓我們可以監視所有的顧客意見，包括客訴。
5. 我們需要在國際金融領域工作的人才。

(B)

1. 我們可以安排一個工廠導覽，讓他們一窺我們的新機器人。
2. 它最大的缺點就是引擎太容易過熱。
3. 我們所有的原物料都在大火中付之一炬。
4. 你可以透過銀行轉帳匯錢。
5. 我們喜歡邀請顧客參與決策的過程。
6. 易燃物質必須一直放置在工廠之外。

(C)

1. 我們喜歡專職在一個領域的員工。
2. 這個過程全自動化，所以不需要任何人力。
3. 這個系統的技術細節會被放在網路上。
4. 請參考下列清單以確認各項產品的簽約日期。
5. 我們會在實驗室檢驗新樣本。
6. 考量到成本增加，我想我們必須放棄這條生產線。

Unit 14

學前暖身

1. strict	2. handcrafted
3. hectic	4. independent
5. acclaimed	

學後小試

(A)

1. A   2. C   3. D   4. A   5. B

(B)

1. condition	2. inspect
3. closely	4. equip
5. streamline	6. fully

(C)

1. manufactures	2. assemble
3. license	4. maximize
5. hand over	6. detect

翻譯參考

(A)

1. 在購買之前我想先看樣品。
2. 如果設備沒辦法好好運作，我們永遠完成不了這張訂單。
3. 在簽約之前，我想我們應該要求降價。
4. 你想要冷凍還是新鮮的草莓？
5. 這個玩具看似單純，其實由很多不同的部分組成。

(B)

1. 這個設備不但全新，而且狀況良好。
2. 你會在你賣出之前檢查每輛車嗎？
3. 請仔細看這過程，你才會了解它。
4. 我們的員工都配備市面上最安全的服裝。
5. 如果我們簡化裝配流程，就可以生產更多。
6. 我們的員工全力的投入生產最高品質的平板電腦。

(C)

1. 這是一間生產早餐麥片的工廠。
2. 組裝這種款式的車子需要 48 小時。
3. 只要我一拿到相關證照，我就可以使用這項機器。
4. 我們將以新的、更快速的組裝工法，最佳化我們的生產力。
5. 我們甚麼時候要將車子交給交通部門？
6. 我們應該打給甚麼人來檢查滲漏。

Unit 15

學前暖身

1. down payment	2. subscribe
3. compatible	4. clearance sale
5. order	

學後小試

(A)

1. A   2. C   3. D   4. A   5. B

(B)

1. purchase	2. attire
3. retail	4. quote
5. variety	6. wrap

(C)

1. cost	2. overcharged
3. worth	4. discounts
5. demand	6. inventory

翻譯參考

(A)

1. 我們新的供應商提供多樣化的顏色和風格。

2. 其中會包括我們最新的目錄，讓你可以瀏覽我們的存貨。

3. 這裡各種顏色的T恤我都很喜歡，只可惜它們都超出預算。

4. 白狗是非常棒的公司，運送零售商品快速又不容易出差錯。

5. 你的訂單上沒有說清楚你想要買幾個輪胎。

(B)

1. 購買時你可以選擇付現或刷卡。

2. 在美國，童裝的需求在學年開始前通常會增加。

3. 如果你想要在零售業工作，必須擅於客戶服務的技巧。

4. 我認為我們應該選擇他們，因為他們的報價低於行情。

5. 有非常多的網站供顧客比較價錢。

6. 我們的商店提供免費的聖誕禮品包裝服務。

(C)

1. 新的展示品會比舊的稍微昂貴一些。

2. 我們多收了顧客4%的價錢，所以必須盡快連絡上他。

3. 這項商品太有價值了，不應讓它待在倉庫太久。

4. 任何持有折價券的顧客都可以享有折扣。

5. 恐怕近年來對於錄影帶機的需求真的非常小了。

6. 如果我們想要減少庫存，唯一的辦法就是降價。

Unit 16

學前暖身

1. evaluate	2. dispatch
3. response	4. customized
5. defect	

學後小試

(A)

1. B	2. C	3. B	4. B	5. C

(B)

1. Rather than	2. even if
3. except	4. mail
5. damage	6. delivers

(C)

1. clients	2. reasons
3. restrictions	4. lately
5. support	6. excluding

翻譯參考

(A)

1. 請在底下的空間寫下你的評論。

2. 要花多久時間我的訂單才會送達？

3. 如果我退回這雙鞋子，這家商店將會退款給我。

4. 我們販售一系列的電子產品，從電腦到智慧型手機皆有。

5. 我已經等了太久了，所以真的很希望今天就能收到商品。

(B)

1. 比起還我錢，不如下次請我吃午餐。

2. 我們一向提供退款，即便沒有收據也一樣。

3. 我們接受所有形式的付款方式，除了支票以外。

4. 我會去郵局寄信，並會順路見你一面。

5. 請不要損害這本書──它對我來說非常重要。

6. 我不確定你公司的送貨服務是否有包括臺灣。

(C)

1. 我們永遠都希望客人對我們的服務滿意。

2. 請在這裡列出你客訴的理由。

3. 我打來是因為想要知道，你們的退貨規定是否有任何限制。

4. 冬天的帽子最近賣的非常好。

5. 對於這項產品，你們有任何提供任何技術性的支援嗎？

6. 我們有全球送貨服務，除了南極以外。

Unit 17

學前暖身

1. unrivaled	2. implement
3. attain	4. competitor
5. strategy	

學後小試

(A)

1. A	2. B	3. D	4. C	5. B

(B)

1. investigate	2. survey
3. traditional	4. overwhelming
5. advisor	6. adversely

(C)

1. ambitious	2. tactics
3. Duplication	4. ascertain
5. revision	6. competitive

翻譯參考

(A)

1. 他們想要上個月的銷售數據，但我們還沒有那份資料。

2. 如果可能的話，請連結我們的銷售報告產生器和數據資料庫。

3. 我們最大的優勢就是我們的品牌，它已經廣為人知。

4. 我們的發行日期正巧和暑假開始同一天，所以預計會有很多顧客。

5. 他們的銷售目標不切實際，要降低幾乎40%才對。

(B)

1. 執行長想要你調查在會計報告裡的錯誤。

2. 根據顧客調查，我們的售後服務做的不夠好。

3. 年底的清倉拍賣，是多數這種的百貨公司都會有的傳統。

4. 我告訴總裁他們已有顯著的優勢，但是她依然堅持競爭。

5. 我們希望你來擔任執行顧問，讓真正的經理去煩惱決策。

6. 財務部預估景氣衰退將會影響我們的銷售量達五個月之久。

(C)

1. 他們的行銷活動太過有野心，幾乎榨乾了公司資金。

2. 我們其中一個策略就是，將展示品擺設在這一整區的重點便利商店內。

3. 只要新的印表機裝好，複印原稿就不是問題。

4. 會計師能夠查明消失的資金去向。

5. 這是她這份報告的第三次修改了。

6. 一旦他們刪減廣告預算，將失去競爭力。

Unit 18

學前暖身

1. highlight	2. mark
3. distraction	4. combine
5. dominate	

學後小試

(A)

1. C	2. C	3. B	4. D	5. C

(B)

1. Tune in	2. broadcast

3. via   4. run an ad
5. attract   6. perfectly

(C)

1. press release   2. beyond
3. sequence   4. appeal
5. infectious   6. engage

翻譯參考

(A)

1. 你需要一個更好的編輯來幫助你，因為這篇文章亂無章法。

2. 根據這張傳單，新電腦的價格其實還不錯。

3. 女人在事業上的權力比起以往更大了。

4. 我們必須確定新產品的目標客群是誰。

5. 我不敢相信才三天，你就讀完了這本書。

(B)

1. 今晚收看第五頻道，你就會看到我們的新廣告！

2. 新的一集甚麼時候會播出？

3. 我們希望透過YouTube和Instagram接觸到年輕的消費族群。

4. 行銷組長希望可以在報紙上登廣告，但這似乎有點過時了。

5. 希望我們的明星代言，可以吸引大家注意我們的新車設計。

6. 新的商標完美的代表了我們公司。

(C)

1. 我們需要針對新專案發表新聞稿。

2. 我們希望可以做的比客戶期待的更多。

3. 行銷小組希望能在下一季中，徵選一位非常有名的人來演出。

4. 我們能做甚麼去吸引更多的年輕女性？

5. 本週播放最多次的歌曲真的很有感染力。

6. 我們希望活動中五顏六色的卡通可以吸引到小孩子。

Unit 19

學前暖身

1. reputation   2. demonstration
3. coordinate   4. exhibit
5. participate

學後小試

(A)

1. D   2. B   3. A   4. C   5. C

(B)

1. arrive   2. exquisite
3. unavailable   4. designate
5. host   6. cooperation

(C)

1. relevant   2. ready for
3. register   4. prepare
5. features   6. factor

翻譯參考

(A)

1. 因為今年有更多的員工，我們需要花更多錢在制服上了。

2. 約有20%的展覽預算會被花在展覽品上。

3. 潘恩先生要求更多監督的評論未受好評。

4. 員工將會發小冊子和簡介給與會者。

5. 主持人會陪同每一位講者上台，並坐在他們的左手邊。

(B)

1. 因為參加者早上會早到，所以我們一定要準備足夠的熱咖啡。

2. 展示樣品當然都是精美的，不要期待實體會跟它一樣好。

3. 主講人剛剛才告訴我們她沒有辦法來，所以必須盡快找到可以替代她的人。

4. 那些負責展示的人會自行指派他們的助手。

5. 皮特森女士非常緊張，因為她才剛聽說她將主持年度會議。

6. 如果我們想辦好這次展覽，需要所有會議中心員工的合作。

(C)

1. 我看不出來他的主題跟會議哪裡有關，因為真的差很多。

2. 她保證禮拜一之前會準備好展覽用的展覽品。

3. 與會者必須透過紙本和網路報名這場會議。

4. 我們沒有足夠的時間準備示範用的講稿。

5. 這項展覽會展示這項產品的五個不同的款式。

6. 價錢當然會是考量，但我們希望你將風格放第一考慮順位。

Unit 20

學前暖身

1. decade	2. take a break
3. comprehensive	4. bring up
5. minutes	

學後小試

(A)

1. A   2. B   3. D   4. B   5. A

(B)

1. agenda	2. open to
3. accurate	4. take notes
5. available	6. sort

(C)

1. presentation	2. update
3. weekly	4. dramatic
5. exponentially	6. stable

翻譯參考

(A)

1. 我不知道該怎麼樣讓觀眾在我說話的時候注意聽。

2. 我希望花幾個分鐘來描述新的行銷策略。

3. 我沒有這個月確切的銷售數據，但我可以保證情況樂觀。

4. 你不需要聽我的——這裡有一堆證據證明口味正在改變。

5. 我的上司希望把整個小組聚在一起，集思廣益吸引顧客的新手法。

(B)

1. 我需要盡快拿到今天會議的議程。

2. 我很歡迎新的想法，但是我的上司卻墨守成規。

3. 她的演講很精采，但我不確定她的數據是否精確。

4. 我可以借支筆嗎？我想在會議中記筆記。

5. 我的主管從來不願意討論問題。

6. 我們必須先整理數據，才能了解它代表的含意。

(C)

1. 這一整週我都必須熬夜準備我的報告。

2. 我們必須在明年之前更新我們的軟體。

3. 這些週報真的很有用，有助於我們跟上進度。

4. 我們今年的成長非常戲劇化。

5. 這幾個月以來，銷售量的成長非常顯著。

6. 執行長寧願看到穩定成長，也不願意大起大落。

Unit 21

學前暖身

1. consequence	2. judge
3. consent	4. agreement
5. informative	

學後小試

(A)

1. B   2. D   3. A   4. A   5. D

(B)

1. verify	2. unanimously
3. final	4. apologize
5. convince	6. take back

(C)

1. ongoing
2. negotiate
3. deny
4. turn down
5. evenly
6. attempt

翻譯參考

(A)

1. 希望我們可以盡可能正面又友善地進行協商。

2. 我非常惶恐,因為總裁將合約協商的重責大任交付予我。

3. 如果瑪格麗特控股公司不肯提高出價,我們應該拒絕他們的提議。

4. 我對他們是否能完成承諾有疑慮。

5. 對於勞工賠償金一事,他們始終沒有改變立場。

(B)

1. 簽約之前,我們想親自確認這棟建築物的價值。

2. 董事會投票一致通過,選出了明年的新任執行長。

3. 他們最後拒絕了我們的提案。

4. 很抱歉因為我們的會計疏失,給您造成任何的不便。

5. 我認為我們的提案可以說服他們向我們下訂單。

6. 約都簽了,你不能就這樣收回你所給的折扣。

(C)

1. 進行的薪資協商已來到第六個月。

2. 決定寄送條件之後,我們就可以來談論價錢了。

3. 你不能否認這項意外,文件上都寫的清清楚楚。

4. 我很遺憾,但我們必須拒絕你的提案。

5. 員工福利被平均分配於退休規畫和醫療給付。

6. 如果他們企圖推動加薪,他們必須貢獻更多。

Unit 22

學前暖身

1. perceive
2. conduct
3. encourage
4. apprehensive
5. commend

學後小試

(A)

1. C   2. C   3. A   4. D   5. A

(B)

1. confront
2. suppose
3. verbal
4. mutually
5. unease
6. appropriate

(C)

1. sharp
2. courteous
3. aggressive
4. all the more
5. uncomfortably
6. remind

翻譯參考

(A)

1. 約翰和莎拉沒有跟上近況,所以在會議上造成不少困擾。

2. 這當然是我的個人意見,跟公司政策毫無關係。

3. 我寧願她承認她就是忘記了會議,也不要她編一些爛藉口。

4. 讓我們邀請新人一起來吃午餐,她可以在比較輕鬆的情況下認識大家。

5. 你有聽過瓊在暴風雨中巧遇執行長的這個趣事嗎?

(B)

1. 今天我要質問我上司,為什麼他要搶我的功勞。

2. 你想他們在會議室裡講些甚麼?

3. 我現在只給你口頭警告,但如果還有下一次就是書面警告了。

4. 我確信可以找到雙方都同意的解決方法。

5. 裁員的時刻將近,辦公室的氣氛非常凝重。

6. 她是漂亮,但她穿來上班的服裝實在不得體。

(C)

1. 她是一個好老闆,但當她被激怒時她的言詞也很傷人。

2. 我不喜歡他,但工作上我可以和他相敬如賓。

3. 在會議上言詞激烈對我們一點幫助都沒有。

421

4. 截止日期將近，有效率的工作成為我們最重要的事。

5. 今天的辦公室太悶熱，讓人不舒服。

6. 如果你不在一天之前提醒我有派對，我大概不會記得。

Unit 23

學前暖身

1. patient
2. demanding
3. critical
4. ensure
5. get out of

學後小試

(A)

1. A   2. B   3. B   4. A   5. C

(B)

1. smooth
2. unfavorable
3. substitute
4. enough
5. solve
6. drop

(C)

1. extensive
2. frustrated
3. close
4. shut down
5. specific
6. figure out

翻譯參考

(A)

1. 這些防火牆非常耐用，甚至可以用得比建築本身還要久。

2. 經理和員工之間需要有更多的互動。

3. 你確定菲利浦先生可以及時解決問題嗎？

4. 如果任何人昏倒了，請馬上通知急救人員。

5. 醫療給付的成本一直增加，很快就會把我們逼向赤字。

(B)

1. 根據計畫，應該可以讓員工順利地從工廠撤離。

2. 由於惡劣的颱風天氣，我們的貨還是沒有送到。

3. 研發部門發現了一個較好的材質可以代替塑膠。

4. 消防部門說我們這棟大樓中沒有足夠的滅火器。

5. 總裁要我們在這週解決數據資料庫的問題。

6. 在工地時不要把工具隨便亂擺，要好好歸位。

(C)

1. 為了減少潛在的風險，必須要進行大規模的工廠翻修。

2. 許多心力交瘁的客人打來抱怨，我們的說明書不正確。

3. 發生火災時，請一邊逃跑一邊關門。

4. 地震讓我們必須關閉工廠兩天。

5. 這份計劃具體解釋了，緊急情況發生時員工該怎麼辦。

6. 我花了五個小時試圖搞清楚伺服器的問題。

Unit 24

學前暖身

1. dine
2. overcrowded
3. thirsty
4. culinary
5. spacious

學後小試

(A)

1. D   2. C   3. B   4. D   5. A

(B)

1. refreshing
2. utensils
3. concierge
4. socialize
5. check in
6. influences

(C)

1. Checkout
2. dish
3. spicy
4. cuisine
5. renowned
6. elegant

翻譯參考

(A)

1. 我完全照食譜做的，可是出來的蛋糕就是不對。

2. 我們來訂明天在歐羅馬餐廳，四個人的位。

3. 你有我可以切水果用的砧板嗎？

4. 我試過很多次了，但就是不喜歡臭豆腐的味道。

5. 他談論著他認識多少政治人物，希望可以讓新客戶印象深刻。

(B)

1. 我到的時候非常疲憊，但是透過游泳打起了精神。

2. 他們送上了餐點卻忘了餐具。

3. 飯店的服務員推薦了很多餐廳和博物館，他們幫了大忙。

4. 我不是很喜歡在工作以外的時間和同事聊天。

5. 我們得要去觀光前先去飯店辦理住宿。

6. 我的老闆非常認真工作，因此我也期許能做到最好。

(C)

1. 辦理退房的時間通常是中午，但這間飯店比較晚。

2. 這間餐廳我最喜歡的一道菜是磨菇千層麵。

3. 我愛辛辣的食物，儘管我也知道不是每個人都喜歡。

4. 你最喜歡的料理是哪一種？

5. 這座城市最有名的就是它的餃子。

6. 這間飯店的裝潢真是優雅。

Unit 25

學前暖身

1. destination
2. accompany
3. commute
4. schedule
5. pick up

學後小試

(A)

1. C 2. A 3. D 4. A 5. C

(B)

1. away
2. delay
3. pack
4. station
5. direction
6. splendor

(C)

1. blocking
2. depart
3. be stuck
4. trip
5. join
6. break

翻譯參考

(A)

1. 所有與會者必須要準時，因為巴士在早上九點就會啟程。

2. 喜歡運動的人注意，在運動場周圍有一條慢跑跑道。

3. 從飯店看出去的山脈美得令人屏息。

4. 一旦確認你的出席，馬上就會寄行程表給你。

5. 從車站到市中心的標準車資是大約二十元美金。

(B)

1. 任何從會議中心出發的旅行計畫都可以在飯店大廳辦理。

2. 這場雨會讓我們晚大約兩小時出發。

3. 你永遠都要在出發前一天先打包好行李。

4. 會議結束之後，請帶我們到火車站。

5. 從這張地圖上看不出來，轉彎之後該走哪裡。

6. 這趟旅行保證會讓大家看到四周山脈的絕美風光。

(C)

1. 有一輛卡車堵住了路，所以我們調頭吧。

2. 你的飛機下午兩點起飛。

3. 辦事人員說我們會因為大雪被困在機場五個小時左右。

4. 我和顧客去了一趟小旅行，一起去湖邊釣魚。

5. 如果你想參加這次導覽，你必須先付錢。

6. 第一組講者結束之後，會有兩個小時的午餐時間。

Unit 26

1. counterfeit
2. nightly
3. venue
4. masterpiece
5. obtain

學後小試

(A)

1. A   2. C   3. A   4. A   5. A

(B)

1. nominated
2. box office
3. enlightening
4. autographs
5. Artificial
6. issues

(C)

1. live
2. favorite
3. film
4. exclusively
5. productions
6. versatile

翻譯參考

(A)

1. 我喜歡繪畫和攝影，但是雕塑是最觸動我心的藝術。
2. 我喜歡這首曲子，作曲人是誰？
3. 請一定要選到好位子，如果看不到表演那就沒意義了。
4. 我不擅長評論電影，因為我什麼都覺得好看。
5. 妮可・基嫚初登大銀幕時才十六歲。

(B)

1. 我希望《星際異攻隊》可以被提名一個獎項。
2. 如果《八惡人》沒有好的票房，它再好看都沒有意義。
3. 如果你想知道更多這幅畫的事，可以讀這本有啟發性的手冊。
4. 我有名人簽名的收藏。
5. 人造花可以保存很久，但我還是偏好鮮花。
6. 這本書很難讀但也很重要，裡面有許多艱深的議題。

(C)

1. 我喜歡聽現場的音樂會。
2. 小時候我最喜歡的電影是《羅馬假期》。
3. 我不喜歡這部電影，但是我丈夫喜歡。
4. 這家電影院只播放外國電影。
5. 這齣劇很棒，但我看過更好的版本。
6. 他是一個多才多藝的音樂家；他會彈鋼琴、吉他和吹雙簧管。

Unit 27

學前暖身

1. vary
2. catch up
3. quality time
4. habit
5. spouse

學後小試

(A)

1. C   2. A   3. A   4. D   5. B

(B)

1. water
2. collection
3. ever
4. fad
5. tournament
6. delighted

(C)

1. list
2. particularly
3. fashion
4. weeds
5. embrace
6. preference

翻譯參考

(A)

1. 獎勵會讓你的員工在工作時保持正向樂觀的心情。
2. 只要你想要聯絡我，任何時候都可以打我手機。
3. 我們的旅行社安排了許多紐西蘭的熱門冒險行程。
4. 你應該送樂器給你兒子當作聖誕禮物。
5. 當然我們會去墨西哥城玩個幾天。

(B)

1. 服務櫃檯的員工老是忘記幫他們的植物澆水。

2. 他收集了非常多的電玩遊戲，但都沒有時間去玩。

3. 如果你有時間，你應該來唸俄羅斯文學。

4. 她喜歡流行樂，尤其熱衷於美洲的所有音樂潮流。

5. 我們打算在下個月舉辦一個員工的西洋棋錦標賽。

6. 他非常高興，因為他的經理贈送了禮物籃給他家人。

(C)

1. 人資部門整理了一份員工興趣的清單。

2. 傑若斯女士對義大利文特別有興趣，但她也喜歡西班牙文。

3. 他把他的午餐休息時間都花在看流行雜誌上。

4. 應該要來清清庭院了，都是雜草。

5. 在這裡，情侶在大庭廣眾擁抱是一件很常見的事。

6. 我偏好十九世紀的古典樂，尤其是布拉姆斯的音樂。

Unit 28

學前暖身

1. typical
2. be made of
3. exemplary
4. coalition
5. mental

學後小試

(A)

1. C   2. C   3. D   4. D   5. A

(B)

1. for free
2. sign
3. long-term
4. spokesperson
5. disperse
6. former

(C)

1. authority
2. separate
3. unprecedented
4. accustomed to
5. unlikely
6. vote

翻譯參考

(A)

1. 她說的很重要：團隊合作才能帶我們走向成功。

2. 現在起身離開會打斷簡報的進行。

3. 我想我們辦公室的大多數人都支持新執行長。

4. 我從來沒有去過這間餐廳，附近有任何地標嗎？

5. 我的主管經常提到她鼎鼎有名的大學。

(B)

1. 今天，班傑利的冰淇淋免費供應！

2. 他們甚麼時候要去簽新合約？

3. 山姆可以暫時使用這張桌子，但我們必須盡快給他一間可以長期使用的辦公室。

4. 公司的發言人說他們會去了解情況。

5. 讓我們使用社群媒體來傳播我們新的設計理念。

6. 前任執行長對現在的董事會講了許多難聽的話。

(C)

1. 我應該找哪個相關單位要求更多休假？

2. 人事和設計是完全不同的兩件事，而我們現在討論的是後者。

3. 新模型的銷量達到前所未有的境界！

4. 我已經習慣在早上六點時起床。

5. 今天根本不可能聽到新辦公室的消息。

6. 如果你不投票，我不認為你有資格批評任何國家政策。

Unit 29

學前暖身

1. allergic
2. fever
3. operate
4. medicine
5. vaccinate

學後小試

(A)

1. D   2. C   3. B   4. A   5. A

(B)

1. pharmacy
2. appointment
3. care
4. contagious
5. sore throat
6. promptly

(C)

1. comfort
2. dental
3. removed
4. diagnosed
5. routinely
6. serious

翻譯參考

(A)

1. 告知你的醫生，你的咳嗽已經持續了一天以上了。

2. 督促你的員工不要對發燒掉以輕心，不然會病得更嚴重。

3. 如果你在工作時受了傷，請馬上通知你的醫生。

4. 咖啡和茶都會讓你缺水，所以感冒時要避免飲用它們。

5. 由於治療造成的併發症，你還需要留院觀察。

(B)

1. 醫生辦公室的旁邊有藥局，你可以拿你的處方籤去那裡領藥。

2. 你需要在至少二十四小時前預約。

3. 我們缺乏照顧因公受傷員工的場所。

4. 這流感的傳染力真的很強，所以要做好一大堆員工請病假的心理準備。

5. 她喉嚨痛好多天了，所以我讓她回家休息。

6. 如果任何員工有感染流感的徵兆，馬上通知公司的醫療中心。

(C)

1. 這種止痛藥可以緩解你的痛苦，即使是最劇烈的頭痛也一樣。

2. 你的牙醫給付不包括非必要的療程，像是牙齒美白。

3. 哈里森先生剛剛做完盲腸移除手術，所以有幾個禮拜他都不會來辦公室。

4. 醫生診斷我的症狀是因為壓力和超時工作導致的。

5. 公司護士會定期幫員工安排健康檢查。

6. 這不是多嚴重的傷，但是以防萬一還是找你的醫生檢查一下。

Unit 30

學前暖身

1. fundraising
2. significant
3. prerequisite
4. awareness
5. embark

學後小試

(A)

1. A
2. C
3. B
4. D
5. C

(B)

1. resounding
2. awareness
3. over
4. possible
5. energy-efficient
6. provide

(C)

1. useful
2. conservation
3. need
4. definitely
5. fortune
6. optimistic

翻譯參考

(A)

1. 她出身貧寒卻當上國家領導人的故事太激勵人心了。

2. 我們小組贊助一個慈善團體，他們提供腳踏車，讓貧窮的孩子可以騎去上學。

3. 我們三天的旅行有詳盡的計畫。

4. 最重要的就是把這些捐款送到災區。

5. 你有捐錢給任何主要的慈善團體嗎？

(B)

1. 大家大聲疾呼不要捐款給這個爭議性的慈善機構。

2. 我希望我們的協助能夠增加大眾對這個議題的關注。

3. 到目前為止，我們已經為環境事業捐款超過五百萬美元。

4. 今年我們可能不會再捐款，但我們還不確定。

5. 新的節能照明會幫助我們省一大筆錢。

6. 我們的錢將會用於提供書、鉛筆和原子筆給貧窮的學校。

(C)

1. 我自願去幫忙廚房，這樣我才覺得我有些用處。

2. 環境保育對我來說至關重要。

3. 詢問那個團體最需要的是甚麼，而我會盡可能的實現它。

4. 明年等到我加薪的時候，我絕對會給的更多。

5. 她把所有的財產都留給一個動保團體。

6. 最近世界上的衝突屢見不鮮，實在太難保持樂觀。

易混淆字

01. (A) 醫生建議年長的病人一年要做一次定期健康檢查。

02. (B) 公司的執行長相信，給予員工額外的假是一份好的投資，因為這增加員工生產力。

解析 若要在這裡使用worth，則必須說：The company's CEO believes that it is worth offering employees extra vacation, because it increases employee productivity.

03. (B) 多虧有整個業務團隊的努力，產品才能成功上市。

解析 若要在這裡使用contribute，則必須說：The sales team's hard work contributed to the product's successful launch.

04. (A) 超市提供的新鮮蔬果，都來自當地的農夫。

解析 offer是「主動給予」，意義上有其特殊性，故此處用provide較佳。

05. (A) 政府宣佈正在接受建商投標新建一棟市政大樓。

06. (A) 因為我們出席了本年度的大學就業博覽會，讓本公司多招收了二十名新員工。

解析 若要在這裡使用result from，則必須說：The hiring of 20 new employees resulted from our presence at this year's university job fair.

07. (A) 我們公司規模太小，不夠讓我們進入外國市場競爭。

08. (B) 既然他已坦承犯錯，老闆願意再給他一次機會。

09. (A) 管理部門設下了招募新人的限制，直到明年春天都有效。

10. (B) 這樣的網路優惠非常常見，就算你錯過了也沒關係。

解析 usual指的是「例行性行為」，故通常具有時間的線性概念；但此處的網路優惠只是想要傳達其「常見、普通」的特性，故用common較為治當。

11. (B) 每當發行新產品時，我們部門都需要繃緊神經。

解析 a degree of + N. 一定程度的……

12. (B) 這座工廠排放的廢氣，是政府認定的高危險汙染物。

13. (A) 直到德瑞克病到好幾個月無法工作，他才終於了解保險的價值。

解析 語意上來說，此處選value以表達保險的「抽象價值」較為符合題意。

14. (B) 艾倫以為她這個部長會一直做下去，殊不知這只是暫時的。

解析 tentative是「暫定地、具試驗性質、沒有把握的」，然而此處的升職指「暫時的」，具有時間上的相對性，故選擇temporary。

15. (B) 我們的上司非常緊張，因為今天總公司會派人來參觀工廠。

解答與翻譯

16. **(A)** 醫生開了許多不同的處方來舒緩病人的疼痛，但成效都不彰。

17. **(B)** 這間工廠的內部機械陳舊狀況又不好——雖然當初買的時候沒花多少錢啦。

解析 in . . . condition 在……情況下

18. **(B)** 這座城市的生活費不停上升，使年輕人紛紛出走。

19. **(A)** 茉莉亞為地震的災情感到難過，於是她上網捐了兩百五十給生還者基金。

解析 此處是指為地震而「捐款」，故donate較為切合語意。

20. **(B)** 政府要求提供一份工地周圍的環評報告。

21. **(A)** 為保護飽受工業汙染影響的區域，政府通過了新的環境法。

22. **(B)** 在有這條新地鐵線之前，羅伯特開車上班。

解析 此處就題意來說，應選used to，若是想要選擇be used to以表達「過去習慣於開車上班」，則時態必須變化，應為：Robert has been used to driving to work before the new subway line was built.

23. **(A)** 現在房價來到歷史新低，正是買房子的好時機。

24. **(A)** 為節省水電支出，我們搬去一間比較小的辦公室。

25. **(B)** 每年每位員工都可以有兩週的有薪假。

26. **(B)** 派翠西亞在上任部長之前，花了好幾週諮詢管理的技巧。

解析 若要在這裡使用consult，則必須說：After weeks of consulting on management techniques, Patricia started her new job as department head.

27. **(A)** 皇家紡織是服飾界最備受尊崇的品牌。

28. **(B)** 我們現在的汽車模型都是新的、比較環保的，舊的都不再生產了。

29. **(B)** 這是標準程序：與顧客簽長期約之前必須先檢查他們的信用歷史。

30. **(B)** 公司的主要股東聯合其他少數小股東一起否決了合併案。

31. **(A)** 崔佛發現他的同事看起來累，所以將她拉到一旁關心她。

32. **(B)** 她的同事紛紛讚揚他總是熱心幫忙。

33. **(B)** 工廠升級的總成本是三百萬美元。

34. **(B)** 投資研發部門是為了確保公司會繼續生產新產品。

35. **(A)** 如果給的薪水不夠好，公司很難留住人才。

36. **(A)** 我們小組每週一都必須定期追蹤企畫進度。

37. **(B)** 比起十年前，投入職場的女性比例愈來愈高。

38. **(A)** 唯有擁有穩定收入的人，銀行才會借錢給他。

39. **(B)** 成績慘澹的十二月，與業績成長的一月形成強烈對比。

40. **(B)** 董事會作出了決定，將客服中心搬到印度會比較省錢。

41. **(B)** 運氣真不好，保固剛過電腦就壞了。

42. **(A)** 竟然在更短的時間有更好的產量，看來我們的工人以前太累了。

43. **(B)** 傑克失業之後，完全仰賴他妻子的薪水過活。

44. **(B)** 我們電信公司提供了非常多種的智慧型手機方案，不論您預算多少都有可以參考的方案。

45. **(B)** 沒有庫存的商品在之後會另外再寄給您。

46. **(A)** 這家工作坊一年只生產一百件家具，他們以好品質聞名。

47. **(B)** 一個好經理最重要的人格特質，就是要了解如何激勵人心。

解析 character是指「個性、性格」，而characteristic另有強調「能力、特質」之意，故語意上來說characteristic較為符合。

48. **(A)** 戴爾對管理有全面的了解，他喜歡參與到每一個專案的細節。

49. **(B)** 商標重設計的過程走到哪裡了？總公司希望四月可以看到結果。

50. **(A)** 策略、時間規劃與運氣，是達成合併案最

重要的三元素。

51. **(B)** 珍妮不在位子上,她有一個重要的商業案需要談。

52. **(A)** 明天她不太可能來工作。

53. **(A)** 執行長宣稱他並不知道有些產品已經違反安全法。

54. **(B)** 我們行銷部門由三個部分組成:廣播廣告、網路廣告和社群媒體公關。

> **解析** 其實這兩個答案都可以選,只是 consist of 的用法較 be made of 正式,故這裡建議答案為 (B)

55. **(A)** 雷諾茲先生現在正在忙,請留下電話而他會回電給你。

56. **(B)** 年度預算中不包含緊急維修的花費。

57. **(B)** 董事會投票決定讓執行長留職停薪一個月,而不是直接開除他。

58. **(A)** 世界上多數的稀有金屬都產自中國。

59. **(B)** 沒有向政府登記寵物的飼主,可處以五百美金以下的罰金。

60. **(B)** 傑瑞米決定年底前要找到新工作。

索引

金選
新多益
單字1200

1200 KEY WORDS FOR THE NEW TOEIC
MP3

作　　者	Curtis M. Revis-Seubert / Michelle Witte / Jennifer Chen
譯　　者	陳怡靜／王婷葦（學後小試）
編　　輯	王婷葦
審　　定	Helen Yeh
校　　對	丁宥榆
企　　劃	Gina Wang / Kelly Yeh
協力作者	Owain Mckimm / Richard Luhrs / Zachary Fillingham
內文排版	劉秋筑
封面設計	林書玉
製程管理	洪巧玲
出 版 者	寂天文化事業股份有限公司
電　　話	+886-(0)2-2365-9739
傳　　真	+886-(0)2-2365-9835
網　　址	www.icosmos.com.tw
讀者服務	onlinesevice@icosmos.com.tw
出版日期	2019 年 12 月初版五刷

郵撥帳號　1998-6200 寂天文化事業股份有限公司
• 劃撥金額 600 元（含）以上者，郵資免費。
• 訂購金額 600 元以下者，請外加郵資 65 元。
　〔若有破損，請寄回更換，謝謝。〕

國家圖書館出版品預行編目 (CIP) 資料

金選新多益單字 1200 / Curtis M. Revis-Seubert ,Michelle Witte, Jennifer Chen 著；
陳怡靜, 王婷葦譯 .-- 初版 . -- [臺北市] : 寂天文化, 2019.12
　　面；　公分
ISBN 978-986-318-454-6 (20K 平裝附光碟片)
ISBN 978-986-318-528-4 (32K 平裝附光碟片)
ISBN 978-986-318-610-6 (25K 精裝附光碟片)
ISBN 978-986-318-763-9 (25K 平裝附光碟片)
ISBN 978-986-318-868-1 (32K 精裝附光碟片)

1. 多益測驗　2. 詞彙

805.1895　　　　　　　　　　　　　　　　108020027